POISON IVY

A DARK HIGH SCHOOL BULLY ROMANCE

STEFFANIE HOLMES

POISON IVY

I'll do anything to get in. I'll even become theirs.

Victor. Torsten. Cassius – the jock, the artist, the stepbrother.
The Poison Ivy Club.
Ruthless.
Connected.
Violent.
Untouchable.

They rule Stonehurst Prep with an iron fist.
If you want Harvard, Princeton, or Yale, they'll get you in.
Guaranteed.
But they'll take their pound of flesh first.
A deal's a deal – you give them whatever they want, and they'll
make your dreams come true.

And they want *me*.
In their beds.
On their arms.
Part of their gang.

I'll do anything to get into an Ivy League school.
I'll lie. I'll cheat.
I'll get on my knees.
I'll *kill*.
But those three dark princes will never have my heart.

This is a new adult, dark contemporary romance with three poisonous guys and one fearless girl. It is intended for 18+ readers.

Victor, Cas, and Torsten think they know everything that goes on in Emerald Beach, but do they? Find out when you sign up to Steffanie Holmes' newsletter and get a bonus scene in your free copy of *Cabinet of Curiosities* – a Steffanie Holmes compendium of short stories and bonus scenes – when you sign up for updates with the Steffanie Holmes newsletter.

A NOTE ON DARK CONTENT

I'm writing this note because I want you a heads up about some of the content in this book. Reading should be fun, so I want to make sure you don't get any nasty surprises. If you're cool with anything and you don't want spoilers, then skip this note and dive in.

Keep reading if you like a bit of warning about what to expect in this series.

- There is some bullying in this first book, but our heroine holds her own. No heroes in this story threaten or are involved in physical or sexual assault of the heroine.

- Fergie experiences revenge porn - both in her past and present.

- Fergie is sexually assaulted by a teacher in this book.

- The Poison Ivy guys are part of a dark criminal underworld in Emerald Beach. There is some murder, violence, torture, and other crimes in this and subsequent books.

I'd definitely call this book 'dark', and it's for reader who like their heroes a little psychotic and their heroines badass. If that's not your jam, that's totally cool. I suggest you pick up my Nevermore Bookshop Mysteries series – all of the mystery without the gore and creepiness.

Enjoy, you beautiful depraved human, you :) Steff

To James
For being my lighthouse

"Nitimur in vetitum.
We strive for the forbidden."

– Ovid's 'Amores'

1

FERGIE

My first clue that we aren't in Kansas anymore is someone flinging open the car door and ripping my Kate Spade purse from my arms.

"Hey!" I yell, because no one touches my Kate and lives to tell the tale. I swing my fist to clobber the thief, but he's too fast. My blow glances off his arm.

"*I'll* take your things, ma'am," the thief says in a stern voice. At least he's a polite criminal. They really do breed 'em different in Emerald Beach.

"Thank you, Seymour. You'll have to excuse my daughter. She doesn't know how to act around humans." Dad sounds tired. He sounds like that a lot lately. We used to have the kind of Hallmark movie father/daughter relationship where we'd laugh about me trying to take out Seymour, whoever the fuck Seymour is. But that was before I imploded our lives. Now, everything I do is another nuisance for him to deal with, because it's *perfectly normal* for random people to shove their hands into my lap and take away my stuff.

But I guess this is our new normal now.

Our new life. With our bag carrier named Seymour.

I wish I'd paid more attention when Dad told me about our move to Emerald Beach. He probably mentioned Seymour. But I've been a little busy eating my body weight in Butterfingers and smashing everything and everyone within swinging distance.

"—leave the keys with me, sir," Seymour says to Dad. "I'll park the car for you and bring the rest of your things inside. *She* is waiting for you."

Seymour whispers *she* like it's a prayer, a supplication. Who is this woman who doesn't even have a title? Who isn't Madam or the Mistress or Mrs. Dio to her staff, but simply *she*?

I step out of the car. The sun hits me like a freight train made of fire. Yup, definitely not in Kansas anymore. And by Kansas, I mean Witchwood Falls, Massachusetts. Or Cedarwood Cove, Massachusetts – it depends on who's asking. I'm a long way from home.

Unlike Dorothy, I'm not tapping my magic slippers to whisk me back there. No matter how boiling hot or plastic or fatuous Emerald Beach is, it can't be as bad as what I'm running from.

We have no home to go back to, thanks to me.

My feet crunch on pebbles. The house looms over me – an enormous wall of marble and glass and terror. I do remember Dad describing it to me, so I don't have to see it to know it's gaudy as fuck, with bleached white pillars holding up a carved portico, oversized oak doors, and probably a poorly-carved knock-off of Michelangelo's David in the center of the tinkling fountain, and gold, gold glittering everywhere. The houses here are probably all the same, like Paris Hilton and a Greek temple had a fuck-baby.

My new home.

I feel naked without my purse, so I grip my cane a little harder than normal as I move toward the looming edifice of our new life. The doors creak open, and I'm surprised to hear a dark voice speak.

"John. You made it in good time, I see."

She sounds like hot cocoa and razor blades.

"Cali." Dad says her name with this note of awe in his voice. "I'd like you to meet my daughter."

"Hello, Fergus." My new stepmother says my name stiffly, testing its shape on her tongue.

"Fergie," I say. "Everyone calls me Fergie."

Yes, my name is Fergus, and I'm a girl. It's the most fucking ridiculous story. Centuries ago, when my ancestors were a bunch of sword-swinging clansmen in Scotland, a rich laird promised a large sum of money to the firstborn son of every generation who was named Fergus. And even though not a cent of this money ever materialized, my clan never passes up the opportunity for an easy buck, so the name's stuck around. I was supposed to be a boy right up until the moment I shot out of my mother, and so I became Fergie.

"Hey, Fergalicious." Dad uses his pet name for me as he prods me with that tired note in his voice. "I'm so happy you finally get to meet Cali, your new stepmother."

Whoopty doo.

I don't want a fucking stepmother, especially not *this* woman. But like everything since The Incident, I don't have any choice in the matter.

A hand grabs mine and shakes, the grip firm and curt – Cali makes it clear she can break my wrist if given the chance. She has some kind of high-powered job in the fitness industry – I never cared enough to ask Dad – and I imagine this is the hand-shake she has to use for all the roid bros.

Even though I want to play nice for Dad, even though this woman has pulled all kinds of strings for me despite never having met me, I can't help myself.

I squeeze back.

I'm not going to be the weakling.

I won't be walked all over or made a fool of.

Not this time.

Cali's knuckle cracks. She drops my hand.

"My two favorite women, together at last," Dad's voice squeaks with fake brightness. "I know you're going to get along brilliantly."

"Come inside." Cali's tone hardens into rigid formality. It's the voice of someone who has no intention of 'getting along brilliantly.' She holds open the door, and I follow Dad into a towering foyer. My cane sweeps the floor, the ball tip rolling over cold marble. The sound resonates through three stories, the echo a complete mindfuck. I've never stood inside such a void of space before. I mean, mall atriums and concert halls sure, but they're always full of heaving bodies and noise and excitement and bustle. This house drips with oppressive silence.

This is a house of secrets.

Good. Maybe it will keep mine locked tight within its walls.

Cali's heels clack on the marble. "We've already eaten, but I can have Milo reheat something for you. You must be hungry after that long drive."

"That would be amazing. You have no idea how much I've missed Milo's food. Fergie?" Dad asks me.

"I'm not hungry."

I bite my lip, feeling bad for the snap in my voice. Dad wants this to work so bad. I've put him through absolute shit over the last few months. I feel like I'm already on the wrong foot with Cali and we're barely through the front door. But this house, this *woman*, it's too fucking much. I try to keep my voice even. "Can I see my room?"

"Follow me," Cali barks. Her heels *click-clack* on the stairs. She doesn't wait for me or grab my arm, which warms me to her a little. My cane hits the bottom step, and I move along until I locate the handrail. I turn my cane in my hand so it will tell me the depth and number of steps, and I climb after her. Dad puffs along behind me. In this empty void of floor wax and bleach, I smell our Volvo's stale air conditioning and the snack crumbs that cling to us both.

We don't belong in a house like this, with a woman like Cali.

Maybe Dad will see that soon.

The stairs circle up and up and up, disorienting me. I'm lost in a labyrinth with a minotaur at its center. But that's not fair – the monster isn't my new stepmother.

I left the *real* monster back in Massachusetts.

Cali leads us down a wide, grand hallway. The heels of my boots sink into thick, soft carpet. "Your father and I have a room in the east wing," she snaps. "There's a maid, Luella, who lives offsite. Seymour and Milo live in the annex behind the pool. There's a call button beside your bed if you need them. You and Cassius have this wing. You share a bathroom."

That's right – I still have to meet Cassius. My new step-brother.

I don't know anything about him. I never asked. The last few weeks have been a daze, what with my life and future going up in an inferno of my own making. I've barely remembered to eat, let alone concern myself about the kid I'll be sharing the house with. He's like twelve years old or something, probably smells gross, talks only in grunts, and has obnoxious taste in music. There's another brother, too, I remember Dad saying – he's a few years older than me, but he doesn't live here anymore.

Cali throws open a door. "I trust this is sufficient."

"It's wonderful, thank you so much." Dad squeezes my hand. "Fergie, what do you think?"

I can't say a thing. My lips are glued shut. I freeze in the doorway, greeting the void of my new room with icy silence.

"It's all decorated in red and gold," Dad says. "Your step-mother has great taste."

"I don't give a fuck about paint samples and throw pillows," Cali scoffs. "Livvie did this."

I don't know who Livvie is, but Dad obviously does because he laughs like Cali said something utterly hilarious. I try to ignore the squirrel burrowing into my stomach.

Dad has this whole life in Emerald Beach already, with Cali and Livvie. He has this world that's completely apart from me.

Did they invite Livvie to their wedding? Because they didn't invite me.

I'm not supposed to be here. They don't want me here.

I manage to drag myself forward, and I walk the perimeter of the room, touching the edges of the furniture. There isn't much, which I prefer. A bed with a brass bedstead, a shaggy rug covering the vast expanse of floor, a tall dresser, a desk and an overstuffed armchair under the window. My feet scuff a couple of strange divots in the rug, places where something heavy crushed the fibers. I wonder what it was that used to stand in the middle of the floor.

My bags have already been stacked beside the door to the walk-in closet. Seymour's doing, I suppose. The entire room is bigger than our old house.

"We'll leave you to get your bearings." Dad kisses the top of my head. "Come down to the kitchen if you want food. It's the back right corner of the house, through the living and formal dining room."

They leave, closing the door behind them. The moment it clicks shut, I sink into the bed and allow myself a single tear – one salty droplet for the fucking mess I've made of my life.

It's all I deserve.

I run my fingers over the exquisite silken material of the

bedspread. This Livvie person may earn a derisive smirk from Cali, but she *does* have taste.

The room even smells nice, like fresh flowers. I bet Seymour left an arrangement somewhere.

I hate myself.

Two weeks ago I stood on a bridge, willing myself to jump off and rid my dad of the burden of my mistakes. Now I'm drowning in silk sheets and manservants in my fucking *mansion* and I can't even be grateful. When we left, I tossed most of my possessions, even my jiujitsu Gi, in the trash. I can't bear any reminders of what my life is *supposed* to be.

Dad says I'll shop for new clothes after we settle in. "Most of your stuff won't work in Emerald Beach, Fergie. They're different down there."

He's never been concerned about me fitting in before.

Everything's changed since The Incident.

You're lucky, I remind myself. *You got your mistake wiped out. You can start over. New name. New life. How many other people get this chance?*

But I don't *want* a new name or a new life or a new mother. I want my old life back. I want my 1540 SAT score and my championship belts and for the worst thing in my life to be the stress of writing my personal statement for Harvard—

The air shifts.

The hairs on the back of my neck stand on end.

I hear a creak as the door to the ensuite bathroom swings open.

Someone's in my room.

2

FERGIE

"Hello?" I call out. I don't get up, because it's a bit fucking rude to just wander into someone's room uninvited, especially when that someone can't see you, so I'm not giving the intruder a standing ovation.

"Hello there," a gravelly voice says back.

I scramble back onto the bed, forcing myself to remain calm. It's a guy's voice, around my age, maybe a little older, and definitely *not* Seymour or my preteen stepbrother. His words drip with danger.

He knows he's not supposed to be in here, and he doesn't give a fuck.

My skin hums with the awareness of just how large Cali's home is, how thick and soundproof the walls and floor are, of what might happen to me in a house of secrets while my dad and stepmother eat downstairs.

I can't hear the intruder move across the thick carpet, but I *feel* his presence loom closer. I slam my hand onto the bedside table, grabbing for anything I can use as a weapon. My fingers close around a ceramic vase – the source of the floral scent.

"Come any closer and you'll be eating daisies," I growl at the intruder.

I know I should feel afraid. Or angry. Or *something*. This guy could be about to shoot me in the head or slice my face off or worse.

But I feel exactly the same as I've felt since The Incident – numb. Like I'm watching my life unfold around me from a comfy seat up in space. Things happen, but I don't feel them. I'm detached, weightless. Nothing touches me. Not even this prick.

"They're irises, actually," he says. Ah, so he's a *smart-ass* prick. My favorite type. That stormy voice of his drips with warning. With something wild and dangerous that's caged right now but might break free at any moment. "What are you doing in this room?"

He's asking *me* what I'm doing here?

"I live here," I say.

"Do you?" I can *hear* the smirk in his words.

"I do. And what are *you* doing here? Were you casing the neighborhood and thought you'd sneak in an open window and help yourself to some jewel-encrusted candlesticks?"

Yes, that's it, Fergie. Antagonize the man who's come to hurt you. Why do you always have to be such a shit-stirrer?

Because maybe if he hurts me, I'll feel something again.

The man laughs as though I've said something funny. It's a savage laugh, addictive and edged with menace. It penetrates my skin and pools in my stomach with a hot, needy ache. What the fuck is that about?

"I don't climb in windows for candlesticks," he says in a tone that implies there are many things he would climb in a window for. "I have a key. I'm the pool boy."

The pool boy. I snort. "You're my stepmother's plaything. That's the cliche, isn't it? The bored rich housewife fucking the pool boy."

He laughs gently. "Cali Dio has never been bored a day in her life. But I dare you to call her a housewife to her face. She'll tear your skin off and use it to wax the floors."

He pads closer. I hold up my hand for him to stop. I don't expect him to be as close as he is. My palm slams against a warm wall of muscle. *He's not wearing a shirt.*

Despite myself, my fingers curl into the warmth of his skin, skimming the planes of his pecs, tracing the lattice of raised lines that scar his chest.

He has a lot of scars for a pool boy.

"I don't think you should be in here." My words come out in a croaky whisper. "This is my room."

"Isn't that interesting." He grabs my wrist, squeezing tight. "What if I don't care what you think?"

Danger pulses from every word. His finger trails over the underside of my wrist. Goosebumps rise along my arm. I'm trapped in his grip, hemmed in by his body and the knowledge that no matter how hard I scream, no one will hear me.

I wait for fear to grip me, for raw panic to take hold, but it doesn't happen.

I do feel something else, though.

A flicker of excitement.

Great. The first real emotion since The Incident, and it's completely fucked up.

I don't *want* to push him away. His nails scrape over my skin, and the distance between my body and his broad, taut chest feels like a void that I want to jump into and lose myself. His scent curls around me – plum and musk and carnations – dark and wanton and *intoxicating*.

Why do the bad boys have to smell so good?

Girls like me don't crave scarred, broken men who wander uninvited into their rooms. Girls like me are supposed to close our legs, shut our mouths, and write our Harvard essays.

But the good girl in me died the day of The Incident. From her ashes rose New Fergie, the one who is numb and lost and broken herself. And I get the vibe that the lump of coal where my heart used to be senses the same darkness inside him, and it draws me in like an Emerald Beach girl to a Louboutin sale.

I swallow. "Don't you have a pool to scrub?"

He kisses me.

The kiss burns through me like a forest fire. One moment I am an ancient oak, stoic and impenetrable, and the next I melt into him as his lips shoot sparks into my veins.

Fuck.

I've been in Emerald Beach all of fifteen minutes and I've broken the cardinal rule I set for myself.

Don't get involved.

And you know what?

Fuck it.

Fuck it all the way to Hades.

I've already messed up as much as a person can possibly mess up. I've lost everything I spent my entire life working for. I have nothing left.

Except for this moment.

Except his lips on mine.

Except his poison burning through my veins, lighting up places inside me I thought were dead and dark and buried forever.

So yeah, why not kiss the pool boy?

Why not taste plum and carnation and sweet, sweet sin?

Why not...

He grabs me behind the neck, strong and possessive, bringing me closer as if he's trying to crawl inside my skin. My legs go around him, dragging his crotch against mine. He's wearing jeans, designer by the feel of them. The buttons clank against the metal of my belt buckle. He growls low in his throat as he leans me back on the bed, shoving my top up to grab my tits.

He's rough with them, tugging at the nipples until I bite his lip. The pads of his fingers are coarse from manual labor. They feel fucking amazing, so different from...

No.

I shut off the part of my brain that wants to go back there, back to another boy in another life who no longer gets to take up real estate in my head. I'm not that girl anymore.

I'm the girl who fucks the pool boy in her stepmother's mansion. I'm the girl who soaks her panties when he twists her nipple so hard that tears spring in her eyes.

"You like that?" he growls. "You like it rough, you thirsty slut? Good, because I'm going to be *brutal*."

I should slap him for that insolence, but his words only stoke the fire hotter. I lean on my elbows as the pool boy paws at my belt, whipping it from the loops and tossing it across the room. It clangs against the dresser. My tight black jeans follow, and he hooks a finger in the elastic of my scarlet lace panties, the pad of his thumb sliding over the ribbon threaded through the corset eyelets.

"You wore *these* to meet your stepmother for the first time?" I can't decide if he sounds amused or disgusted.

"Maybe I wear them for me," I shoot back. The pool boy doesn't get to know what this scarlet underwear set means to me. I saw it online during one of my more lucid moments after The Incident. *Made of jacaranda satin, soft mesh, and gold corsetry clips, this set is made for single malt whisky and wild nights of debauchery*, the description read. *Perfect.*

They're the exact opposite of the practical cotton panties Old Fergie used to wear – the kind of wholesome underthings *he* expected of me.

He made me into the girl who wears scarlet lace and corset ribbons. He made me the thirsty slut who gets off on coarse words and rough hands.

I plan on being exactly what they think I am.

The pool boy tugs off the scrap of scarlet and flings it away. His hands stroke my thighs, and my legs fall open for him. I don't care that I'm being a thirsty bitch – he's here and his touch feels *amazing* and maybe I'll regret this tomorrow but right now his rough thumb circles my clit and I'm a mess of fizzing nerve endings and lightning strikes and wild fucking debauchery.

I feel *something* again, and I want more.

He presses his thumb into my clit, and the orgasm slams into me. I jerk off the bed as the pleasure courses through me in a wave that starts between my legs and rises through my limbs, cresting in the tips of my fingers and behind my eyes. A thousand butterflies flap their wings inside me and I never, ever want them to stop.

Hello, Pool Boy.

I've never come like *that* before.

He doesn't give me a chance to recover. He grabs my thighs and drags me to the edge of the bed as he thrusts forward and impales me on his thick, hard cock. I cry out as he stretches me, because it's painful, but the best kind of pain. The kind of pain that forces you back into your body. The kind of pain that obliterates.

And I have so very, very much I wish to obliterate.

When did he even take his pants off? Is he wearing a condom? All things I should know, but I don't, and I don't care because his dick is like a knife slicing away at the last three months of hell.

I bury my nose into his collarbone as I buck my hips against him. His skin smells of salt and pool chemicals and that fruity carnation scent tinged with musk that drives me wild. I drag my teeth across the artery in his neck. All of a sudden, I'm *starving*.

His thrusts become deeper, more urgent. He swells inside me, and it stirs the butterflies into a frenzy. His lips brush my earlobe, and I feel them curl back into a smirk. "Welcome to the family, *sis*."

3

CASSIUS

She screams as my revelation hits her, or maybe that's the cry of a second orgasm being torn from her body. Her hips jerk against mine, but I have her. She's not getting away.

I laugh as I thrust into her one final time, my balls tightening as I come inside my new stepsister.

Fuck. Fuck.

I didn't intend to go this far. I was in my room looking for the ledger when I heard her come upstairs with my mother, and I wanted to play chicken with my blind stepsister who dares to sleep in Gaius' old room. I wanted to see how long it took her to figure out who I was. But then I saw her laid out on her silken sheets, a halo of red hair streaming around her. Then I tasted those pouty, petulant lips of hers.

Then she wrapped those long legs of hers around me.

Then she tilted her head back, exposing that lovely long neck, and made this *purring* sound that makes me harder than I've ever been before.

I've been with hundreds of girls. It's always fun, especially when they scream. Especially when they *bleed*. But I've never fucked someone like her. She's so completely *in the moment*.

She doesn't care what she looks like beneath me. She isn't trying to angle her body to flatter her stomach or swing her glorious tits in my face. She isn't performing. She isn't thinking about what jumping on my dick can do for her reputation.

She simply *is*.

My stepsister drew me in, and for the few messed up minutes I've been inside her, her long legs clamped around me and her mind lost in raw, primal fucking, I lost myself, too.

That's never fucking happened before.

The moment fractures. Just as I spill my load, she plants both hands on my chest and *shoves*. I laugh, but to my shock, I go flying. She's stronger than she looks.

I sail across the room. My back slams into her dresser and I go down. A cord of jizz squirts out the tip of my cock and lands on the rug. I run my tongue across my lip and taste blood. More blood dribbles down her chin. She must've bit my lip when I revealed my surprise.

She licks my blood off her lips, and it's the hottest thing I've ever seen. "You bastard. Touch me again and I won't be so gentle."

Her chest heaves, but she doesn't make any move to grab her clothing. She stares back at me with those cracked emerald eyes, unseeing, unrelenting.

My lip starts to sting.

A red haze descends over my eyes, tinging the corners of the room with blood. How fucking *dare* she?

Her scam artist of a father has conned his way into my mother's panties, and she dares to look at me from my brother's bed as if she can see right through me?

She's *blind*, for fuck's sake.

"You wanted it." I crawl to my feet and stick my fingers in my mouth, sucking her juices off them. I hadn't even stuck one inside her and she was so wet. So wet and delicious, like fresh raspberries from Milo's garden. I smack my lips loudly so she knows exactly what I'm doing. "You practically *begged* me, and from the taste of you, you enjoyed what I did to you, sis. I'm hard again just thinking about that sweet little *noise* you make when you come."

It's true. My cock twitches, desperate to be inside her again. My stepsister's face reddens as I keep on talking. I'm searching for the button to push that will make her snap. I know it's there somewhere.

She's not special. She might have a magical cunt that tastes like raspberries, but she's just a girl, a gold-digger, a distraction. Nothing more.

"Want me to sneak back in when your daddy goes to bed?" I taunt her. "Want me to eat out that tight little cunt while you come all over my brother's sheets? Want me to bend you over his dresser and spank that hot little ass of yours until you beg for my cock? I hope you're on the pill, because I only fuck bareback. We're going to have so much fun, *sis*."

Found it.

"Get out get out get out," she screams. Her face twists with fury as sweet tears pool at the edges of her eyes.

I love it when they cry.

The red mist retreats as my cock grows rock hard at the sight of those tears. But they don't spill over. She holds them back.

She leans across the bed and grabs the vase of flowers. I duck as it sails across the room and smashes against the dresser, right where I'd been standing a moment ago. For a blind girl, she's got decent aim.

I grab my clothes, shove her red panties into my pocket, and stride into my bathroom, slamming the door so hard the wall rattles.

"You don't belong here," I yell through the wall. "You'll never be part of this family."

"Rot in hell, Cassius!"

A wild laugh escapes my throat.

What the fuck did I just do?

I just fucked my new stepsister.

That's messed up, even by my standards.

I lean over the sink and stare at my reflection. Her raspberry scent clings to my lips.

Welcome to the family, Fergie Munroe.

When Mom told me she was marrying some dude from Massachusetts, I figured it must have something to do with work – an alliance or a debt owed. Cali Dio never does anything unless it's for the good of the family, and she doesn't do emotions, so it can't be sentimental. But the guy in our kitchen looks like he can't even unblock a shower drain, let alone break a man's neck with his bare hands. He's not part of our world. He's a *dentist*, for fuck's sake. What could my mother possibly see in a dentist?

I know why *he's* here – because my mother is rich and hot, and weak men have a hard-on for her kind of power. But I don't understand what she gets out of the arrangement.

And the cherry on top of this shit sundae, Cali declares that Torsten has to move out of Gaius' room so my new stepsister can have it. My *blind* stepsister.

I've never met anyone blind before. I expected a damsel in distress with no idea about the real world. I didn't expect Fergus fucking Munroe in her punk boots and her hair like a waterfall of fire. I didn't expect the way she turns her head to me and *glares* like even though she can't see me, she can slice through my skin.

At least now she knows how things are going to be. I had to do something to restore control of the situation. I had to make it clear that she's in *my* house, and I don't need some little blind girl poking around in my shit.

I splash cold water on my face and take a moment to rearrange myself, then head through the door on the other end of the bathroom into my room. It's identical to Fergus', but a mirror image – the bed against the opposite wall, the window on the other side. Clothes and shit are strewn everywhere, the mess worse than usual because Torsten's clothing and art supplies are stacked in here, too. Luella refuses to touch this room, and I don't blame her.

I grab my backpack and draw out the leather-bound ledger. As I do, her panties slip out of my pocket and fall on top. Her heady, raspberry scent invades my nostrils. The urge to bury my nose in the soft fabric courses through my body.

I caress my leather belt, drawing myself back to the present before the red mist slips in again. I can't help but imagine drawing my belt over Fergie's skin, yanking it tight enough to leave welts, tying her treacherous little body to the bed so I can do whatever I like to her...

I'm getting hard again just thinking about her.

"Fuck. Get over it. She's just a chick." I tuck the ledger under my arm and head back down the hall.

I fucked my stepsister. It's out of my system now. I can go back to hating her.

Fergie Munroe may have wormed her way into our house, our lives, and onto my cock, but she is *not* going to get under my skin.

4

FERGIE

*P*lease let this be a horrible practical joke.

Please let me not have slept with my new stepbrother.

But nope, the universe isn't that kind to me. I hear Cassius in the bathroom between our rooms, cleaning up and chuckling maniacally to himself. I wait a long time after I hear his door slam before I dare to move.

I pick my way across the floor, sweeping my arms in wide circles until I find where he tossed my clothes. I can't find my panties. Cassius probably took them. *Pervert.*

Well, fuck him. I have more pairs.

The bathroom is huge, and thankfully empty of knobjockey stepbrothers. It takes me a while to get my bearings – a luxurious rain shower takes up one full wall, with a toilet in a separate alcove on the other end, and between them, a wall-mounted vanity with two deep stone basins. While hunting for the towel rail, I knock several of Cassius' products off the counter. I don't bother to pick them up. Fuck him.

How can I be so stupid? I assumed my stepbrother was some little kid, but Cassius is all fucking man. I should have listened when Dad

*told me about them. I should have pulled my head out of my ass so
this didn't happen—*

I've spent eighteen years of my life living on the straight and
narrow, working twice as hard as everyone around me to get
myself to Harvard, and all to have my future torn away from me
at the eleventh hour. So I try for *one day* to live in the moment,
not giving a fuck about the consequences, and I accidentally
screw my stepbrother.

Either way, I'm cursed.

I take a long, steaming hot shower and scrub my body until
my skin's raw. I use an entire bottle of something that smells
amazing, like honeycomb and orange zest. But when I turn the
water off and pat myself dry, the salt tang, plum and carnation
scent of my stepbrother clings to my skin.

I slam the bathroom door to my room and go to lock it, but
there's no lock. No way to keep my stepbrother out of my
private space. A flicker of panic settles across my chest – that
sensation when you're swimming in a lake and you want to put
your feet on the bottom and rest for a moment, but it's deeper
than you think and there's nothing beneath you but cold
oblivion.

Interesting.

I touch my hand to my chest, feeling my heart hammer
against my ribs. Fear is another emotion I thought I'd never get
back. Some deep, hidden part of me still craves self-preservation
enough that the idea of my stepbrother having unfettered access
to me while I sleep makes my heart race.

Fear...or *hunger*.

I'll need to fix the lock first thing tomorrow. For now, I drag
the desk chair across the room and jam it under the door. With
his strength, Cassius could probably break it if he wanted in bad
enough, but the sound of wood splintering would give me
enough warning.

At least the main door locks. I slide the bolt across, and my chest loosens. I suck in a mouthful of floral-scented air.

My room somewhat secure, I dump out the contents of my suitcase and pull on fresh clothing – another pair of black skinny jeans, fuzzy socks, and a baggy hoodie from this old school band, Octavia's Ruin, that I like. I don't want to go downstairs, but I'm suddenly starving. Food might wash the taste of Cassius Dio from my mouth. Plus, I owe my dad an attempt at playing happy families.

I unlock my door and step into the hall, pausing to listen for Cassius. But I don't hear a peep from his room so I dare to plunge back into the labyrinthine house. Maybe I'm safe for now—

SLAM.

I jump as a sound like a gunshot echoes through the house. I lean against the wall and press my hand to my heart.

No, not a gunshot. A door slamming somewhere. *Cassius.*

I take a wrong turn down another hallway. I hear the faint sound of video game music through a wall. I backtrack quickly, not wanting another run-in with Cassius, and locate the marble staircase.

My cane rolls across more marble as I navigate down the stairs, through a vast living room containing an L-shaped sofa, and a dining room with a table the size of an aircraft carrier, following my dad's laughter into the kitchen. Pale moonlight streams from windows along the back wall. My dad and Cali talk in low voices. The room smells like pizza, and my stomach rumbles again. I've barely eaten anything except salted peanuts all day. No wonder I lost my marbles when Cassius touched me. I've gone temporarily insane from hunger.

"Hey, Fergalicious," Dad calls, his voice betraying his excitement at seeing me. "We have pizza. I got your favorite, buffalo chicken."

He appears by my side, his elbow sliding under my hand as he guides me forward and directs me to one of the tall stools surrounding the island. I grab a slice of pizza and shove half of it in my mouth. Nothing like bastardizing an Italian classic with big, juicy chunks of buffalo chicken and blue cheese sauce to make me forget that I've just possibly fucked up our lives for a second time.

Maybe Cali doesn't give a shit what her son and I get up to, but if Dad finds out, it will break his heart all over again. And I might be numb, but I don't want to hurt him any more than I already have.

"This is good pizza," I say. "Nice and spicy."

"It's from a place in Tartarus Oaks we like," Dad says. "We'll take you there one day. I think you'd love it. This crazy Italian lady runs it – once we went there for a date and she chased a drunk guy out of the restaurant with a rolling pin."

I try to think of something to say, but the words get stuck in my throat. It's that wistful note in Dad's voice when he talks about this date he went on with Cali.

A date he never told me about.

Dad's hand covers mine, a gesture that might've once been comforting but now makes my skin crawl because I don't deserve it. "You're quiet today. Are you nervous about school tomorrow?"

No, Dad, I'm pissed at myself because I just had my stepbrother's cock inside me... and I liked it.

"A little."

"You know that you don't have to go if you don't want to," he says. "You can study online, or take the rest of the year off and do senior year over—"

"No, she can't. I've arranged everything with Stonehurst Prep," Cali says in a voice that implies she's not used to people disobeying her. "You start tomorrow, Fergie. Cassius will drive you. Your father and I have an early meeting with our tennis coach."

Tennis coach? Since when does Dad play tennis?

And do I really have to drive to school with the stepbrother who I just screwed? The one who's made it clear he's out to make my life miserable? Not fucking happening.

"Isn't there a bus or something?" I ask.

"Cassius will take you." It's not a statement. It's a command.

I take another big bite of pizza, but it tastes like cardboard. I don't exactly know what's going on, but it's obvious my new step-mother is stamping her authority, and I'm expected to step in line.

While her son's upstairs jerking off in my panties. Fat chance.

I push back my chair. "Thanks for the pizza, Cali. I'm not as hungry as I thought."

"You sure you're okay?" Dad sounds worried. That's why he's dragging out his old nickname for me.

I plaster my best impression of a smile. I've forgotten how to do the real thing. "I'm fine, just tired from the drive. I think I'll go to bed; need a good night's sleep before I meet my new classmates."

As I trudge through the dining room, I overhear Dad sigh. "Maybe I *should* make her stay home, take the rest of senior year online. I'm afraid I've pulled her out of the frying pan to throw her into the fire."

"She can't hang around here all day," Cali says, her tone hard. "I've got two big jobs that will demand my full attention, and you're setting up the clinic. We have too much work to do to be babysitting her. She's a grown woman who needs to stand on her own, and Cassius will make sure no one lays a finger on her at that school. Nothing will happen to her."

Too late. I curl my fingers into a fist. *Cassius fucking happened to me.*

I'm haunted by the memory of his unhinged laughter as he walked into the bathroom. My new stepbrother revels in chaos and carnage, and he isn't done with me yet.

5

CASSIUS

I swing open the library doors and stalk inside, my stepsister's panties burning a hole in my pocket.

My mother has no use for books. No, that's not entirely true. Once she staved in a Russian oligarch's skull with a first edition of *Dead Souls*. But as for reading books? That's not Cali Dio's idea of a good time.

So when she purchased the house ten years ago, she was going to gut the library and install a soundproof room – an essential piece of architecture in her line of work. But my older brother Gaius convinced her to give the library to him and kit out the basement instead.

I'm not exactly a reader myself, but I love the library because it's Gaius' space. He was always in here, chilling with his friends or reading some dense Russian text. And when he started at Stonehurst Prep, it became the official headquarters of the first iteration of the Poison Ivy Club. He let me hang around as long as I didn't get in his way or make too much noise. I like all the hidden corners and the secret compartments he had installed. I like that it still smells like him. I like that I can scream as much as I like, and the shelves of books muffle the sound.

Over the years, as the club became profitable, Gaius made a few changes. He installed state-of-the-art security including 24/7 surveillance cameras, booby-trapped the secret compartments, and had new doors carved all over with elaborate ivy vines, twisting and coiling back upon themselves in a complex pattern.

I slam those doors behind me so hard the wall shakes. I hear wood splinter, but I don't stop to check Gaius' precious carvings. I need to get inside before I lose my shit.

"Where'd you go?" Victor calls from his spot in front of the PlayStation. He doesn't look up as his fingers mash the controller and he collects another high score. My friends are used to me slamming doors. "A car pulled up. I think your new stepsister is here."

"I met her," I growl, flopping down on the leather sofa next to him. My skin crawls with little bugs, and I punch my thighs because sometimes pain makes the bugs go away. But it's not working tonight.

I need blood.

I should be downstairs in my mother's basement lair, getting Fergie Munroe out of my system. But Victor says we have club business. And no one says no to Victor August, not even me.

"And? Is she hot?" Victor collects another high score. I notice he's knocked me off the top of the points table. Victor doesn't like to lose at anything. "Just because she's off-limits to you, doesn't mean I can't get a piece of the action. She's going to be the poor little new girl, *and* she's blind? They'll eat her alive at school unless I protect her."

"I never said she's off-limits to me." I pick up the controller. On-screen blood will have to do tonight.

"No fucking way." Victor swipes the controller from my hands and turns to me with that wicked grin of his. "Don't tell me you're planning to fuck your stepsister. Even for you, that's sick."

I open my hand and drop her panties into his lap. Victor picks them up and sniffs them, breathing in deep. I wonder if he smells what I do – that secretive, dangerous raspberry scent of her, so unlike anything else in our world.

"Don't be disgusting, Vic." His twin, Juliet, scolds him. She sprawls out across a red wingback chair, stretching her arms behind her like a cat, her dark hair brushing the carpet. A book lies open across her chest, and she jiggles her Manolo Blahniks from her toes. Both August twins inherited their dark hair, pale skin, and sharp cheekbones from their father, the singer Gabriel Fallen. But their ice-blue eyes and *I-know-best* attitude are a legacy of their mother, Claudia August.

Juliet's not an official member of Poison Ivy, but after what happened in freshman year, Vic won't let her out of his sight, which means Torsten and I have to endure her presence.

Victor tosses Fergie's panties over his shoulder, where they land on Torsten's notebook. He scowls and grabs them to toss back, but then he sees what he's holding. The hard line of his jaw softens as he leans closer.

Six months ago, a serious earthquake rumbled through Emerald Beach. Books flew off the shelves, and several expensive old busts smashed on the library floor. Victor and I huddled under the doorframe, using our bodies to shield Juliet from the falling debris. And Torsten kept writing in his notebook, oblivious to the chaos around him. It wasn't until *Anna Karenina* hit him on the head that he blinked and asked why we'd thrown all the books on the floor.

That's all you need to know about Torsten Lucian. He might live in this world, but he's always somewhere else. Vic and I are the only people who can deal with his poetic brooding and lack of social niceties. And yet here he is, staring at Fergie's underwear like they contain all the answers to the universe.

Hell, they probably do.

"What the fuck did you do?" Torsten growls.

I let my smile tell him everything he needs to know.

"You're sick." He tosses her panties back to me. I catch them midair and slip them back into my pocket. "She's your sister."

"We're not blood-related. No third nipples here." I stick out my tongue. "Although, I might be into that. You should see the way she purrs when you pinch her nipples. Imagine if she had three…"

Torsten slams his notebook shut. "Can we get down to business?"

With a sigh, Victor flicks off the TV. I drop the ledger into his lap and whip the bottle of Moet off the table.

"Hey, that's mine!" Juliet pouts. She holds her empty glass out for me to fill, but I ignore her and swig straight from the bottle. It tastes like My Little Pony Piss, but at least it's diluting the flavor of Fergie Munroe.

"Torsten, get my sister another drink. And one for me and yourself, too," Victor says as he flips open the ledger. Victor's one of the only people in the world who can tell Torsten to do anything, and he knows how to speak Torsten's ultra-specific language – if Victor doesn't tell Torsten to eat, Torsten might not eat. He'd just waste away, wearing his charcoal pencil down to the nub.

Torsten stands and moves robotically across the room to pour Juliet something from the drinks cabinet. As he mixes three whisky sours, his dark eyes flick back to the scrap of scarlet fabric spilling out of my pocket.

A growl rumbles in my throat.

Fergus Munroe is *my* problem, the thorn in my paw that needs to be removed before she poisons everything. And I'm not sharing her raspberry-scented pussy with anyone, not even my two closest friends.

"Geez, can you boys keep it in your pants?" Juliet throws her book down in disgust. "It's like a locker room in here. Vic, start the meeting already so we can go home."

"As you wish, princess." Victor flips open his leather-bound case and pulls out the extensive files he's already gathered. "With the applications for Early Decision and Early Action due on the first of November, we've been approached by three potential clients."

Ivy league acceptances are big business in schools like ours. Stonehurst Prep makes big promises about college admission to attract the elite families, who then shell out thousands of dollars on private tutors and essay coaches and years of therapy for those who don't make the cut. Ostensibly, every student in the country with decent grades stands an equal chance of getting in. In reality, the Ivies work like anything else in the world. It's all about who you know.

And our families – the Dios, the Lucians, the Augusts – are in the business of knowing the right people.

The Poison Ivy Club offers a second chance for the students who've blown it – the ones without alumni connections, with the public scandals, or the checkered family history. The ones who fail an important test or miss out on that team captain spot come to us as a last resort. And we make their dreams come true.

For a price.

We write it all down in our leather-bound ledger – who's on our list, what we do for them, what they owe us, and when their debt is called in. Torsten doesn't trust an online system not to be hacked by our enemies, so we do it old school.

Victor turns to a clean page and taps his pen against the crisp white paper. "First up is Bevan McManus."

Bevan's the captain of the Stonehurst Prep lacrosse team and the son of a prominent congresswoman. He's also one of the faces recorded on videos taken at a raucous party where two fifteen-year-old girls were drugged and assaulted. No Ivy will touch him, and it must hurt like a motherfucker for him to come to us, considering Torsten was the one who turned the footage over to the police.

"I'm not working with that prick. Period." Torsten's fingers dance across his notebook as he scribbles some abstract thing.

Victor taps his chin with the pen, waiting for my input.

"Do we take his money anyway, string him along? We might be able to squeeze a favor out of his mother before we turf him out." I think about the congresswoman's lips wrapped around my cock, but too quickly her face becomes Fergie, and I shake myself out of the fantasy.

Victor rolls his eyes at me, but he dumps Bevan's file in the trash. Rule number one of Poison Ivy Club – we don't work with a client unless we all agree.

"Next is Lucila Baskerville. Seven generations of her family have gone to Princeton, so she *should* be a legacy." Victor concentrates on his page. "Her grades are decent, but it looks like she blew her SATs and quit the field hockey team."

"We all know why that is." I glance over at Juliet, who's on the crew team and dumped Lucila in front of everyone at a party a few weeks back.

"What?" She sips her whisky sour. "She was getting too clingy."

"The problem here is that Eurydice Jones and Sierra Vanderbilt are also applying for Early Decision at Princeton," Victor says. "And neither of them have been on the receiving end of my sister's wrath."

No Ivy League school will confirm this, but it's an unwritten rule that they'll only take a certain number of students from each school. At Stonehurst Prep, we might have two students accepted to Princeton. *Once*, we had three, but that seems to be an anomaly. We'll never get four.

Without us, Lucila knows she's lost her spot.

I snap my fingers. "This one is easy. Judge Fredrickson is on the admissions board, and we've got dirt on him. I'll take care of it."

"No can do." Victor stares at the list. "Fredrickson left now. He might still have pull, but I think we're going to need to take direct action."

I rub my hands together. This is my favorite part of Poison Ivy Club. This is why my brother brought me into his circle in the first place, back when the club was just fists for hire. When it comes to *direct action*, I learned from the best.

"Who are you going to take out? Sierra or Euri?" Juliet sits up. "I vote Sierra. Euri is lovely. She's never hurt a fly."

"Sierra's also legacy," says Victor. "And that family name carries a lot of weight. So even if we bring her down, she might still take Lucila's spot. We're going to have to go after both of them. Cas, I trust you to come up with something creative. Creative and *non-violent*," he adds with a roll of his eyes.

"As you wish, Mother Superior," I say with a grin. "Who's our final client?"

"Chris Lawson. He's captain of the Acheron Academy basketball team." Victor makes a face at the mention of our rival school. Our very own Golden Boy is captain of the track, fencing, and basketball teams, so he's had that school spirit nonsense bred into him. "His grades are abysmal, his SAT scores below average, *and* he's from new money. No connections."

"Daddy's boy with something to prove?" I lift an eyebrow. He's going to be fun.

The people who come to us fit into two groups – swats who've spent their whole lives aiming for an Ivy but fuck it up in their senior year, miss out on their early placement schools and come running scared. We get the majority of those clients at Christmas, after ED results come back on December fifteenth.

The other type are the fucking fools who have no shot at an

Ivy but want that pretty school name because it proves something to someone, or to themselves. Chris Lawson fits firmly in that category.

Victor taps his chin. "I like a challenge. But I want to decide on his price."

"Done. And what's Lucila's price going to be? I was thinking prom date for Torsten?"

Torsten keeps scribbling in his notebook. He's not even listening.

"I know what I want from Lucila." Victor's tongue flicks his upper lip.

"Gross," Juliet moans.

"Mind out of the gutter, sister dear. That wasn't what I meant. And you only say that because you're not in on the action," Victor grins at her. "You want me to add your pussy into the bargain?"

Juliet perks up. "You forget, I've been there before. But she's got a mouth like a vacuum cleaner, so sure."

"How's that view from the moral high ground?" I smirk at Juliet.

"It's going to be grand with Lucila Baskerville eating me out," she answers.

Vic turns to me. "What about you, Cas? You're doing most of the work on this one, and you always have a thing for the smart chicks. What's your price?"

I try to picture Lucila's scarlet-painted lips wrapped around my shaft, but scarlet makes me think of the panties burning a hole in my pocket.

I shake my head. "I want a Sacramentum."

A Sacramentum is an IOU to a member of the Poison Ivy Club – it's an unnamed favor we can call on at any time in the future. It's called a Sacramentum because my older brother

Gaius is obsessed with Ancient Rome and Latin and shit, and he's the one who started the club.

Victor raises a dark eyebrow at me. The Baskerville family are perfectly respectable Emerald Beach old money. No skeletons in the closet. No connections to anyone or anything useful to us.

"What the fuck are you going to do with a Sacramentum from Lucila?" Juliet screeches.

Honestly, I don't know.

What I do know is that, for some reason, I don't want Lucila's lips anywhere near my dick. And that makes me stabby.

Victor sees me reaching for the knife I keep in my boot. Sensing I'm ready to go Michael Myers on his sister, he adds a final note next to Chris' and Lucila's names and closes the ledger. "It's decided. I'll give Bevan the bad news and talk to Chris and Lucila about their price. If they agree to our terms, we can get to work."

WE SPEND another hour or so fooling around in the library. I polish off two more whisky sours and throw my knife at a painting of our three mothers that hangs above the fireplace, while Torsten fills his notebook with doodles and starts another. The moment Juliet stifles a yawn, Victor starts shoving her toward the door. I watch from the window as they climb into his Jaguar XJ Sentinel and peel off down the street. They live just around the corner from us, but Victor feels safer with bulletproof windows between his sister and the outside world.

I lock up the library and Torsten follows me to my room, neck bent down as he continues to scribble. No light peeks from the crack under Fergie's closed door, but she's blind, so that doesn't mean she's gone to bed. I can hear my mom and her new husband moving around downstairs. Glasses clink. Her laughter peels through the stairwell.

Cali Dio *laughing?*

Everything is fucked up today.

I shove aside a pile of my clothes to make room in the bed for Torsten. He uses the bathroom first. He takes forever because he has a specific routine he follows every night. Torsten used to forget to shower or clean his teeth. He said the toothbrush felt disgusting in his mouth and he didn't see the point of standing under hot water for twenty minutes. Weird, but whatever. Victor did some research and made Torsten a bathroom routine, and now Torsten follows it like it's his religion. I got him an electric toothbrush when he moved in, which he finds easier. And I don't have to share a bed with a guy who smells like week-old sushi.

Everything with Torsten is like this – figuring out why his brain works the way it does so we can help him keep his shit together. All he wants is to be normal, but he doesn't understand what that is. Victor and I are the only ones who have the patience to help him – he's been there for us all these years, it's the least we can do.

Cali says Torsten can't keep living with us, and he can't go to Victor's for the same reason. If Livvie finds out he's here, it could cause a rift between the families, and rifts in our world tend to result in the Acheron River running red with blood. I know he needs to go, but he's *Torsten*. He needs a fucking routine to remember to brush his teeth.

He can't be on his own. He needs us.

"She's in her room," Torsten says as he returns from the bathroom, rubbing his damp hair with a towel.

"Fergie?"

He nods. "I can hear her moving around."

He throws the towel in the laundry and lies down on his side of the bed, on his back, crossing his hands over his chest like a mummy.

I enter the bathroom and close the door behind me. Torsten has put all his things neatly back into the tray beside the sink, arranged in perfect rows. I notice my stuff is all over the floor – Fergie's doing, I'm guessing. I cross the room and grip the handle on the other door. I press my ear to the wood and listen.

She's definitely in her room. She has music playing – some dark gothic metal thing – and I hear hangers clacking together. She's unpacking her clothes into the huge dressing room Gaius used to use for growing pot.

I twist the handle, but it stalls. I shake it, but it's jammed tight.

"Nice try, asshole," Fergie calls out to me. "You're not getting in here."

I laugh as I drop the handle. She must've jammed a chair under it. If my stepsister thinks she's keeping me out like that, I'm going to enjoy educating her. But not tonight. Let her have one night of peace so she builds up a false sense of security.

In the shower, I toss all her pretty-smelling products off the shelf, leaving them scattered on the floor. I brush my teeth and crawl into bed beside Torsten.

"Goodnight, man."

He doesn't answer, but I'm used to that. His long eyelashes flutter against his eyes.

I turn out the light, stuff Fergie's scarlet panties under my pillow, and shove my headphones over my ears. I scroll through my phone to find the loudest, angriest music I have – I need to drown out the throbbing in my cock at the thought of Fergie next door, folding her tight-ass black jeans, lining up her spike-heeled pumps on my brother's shelves.

I bet she has adorable pajamas with cats all over them.

What's happening to me? Usually, once I fuck a girl, that's it.

She's out of my system. Sex is a means to an end, another way to draw back the red mist when it becomes too much. I'm here to torture her until her and her father fuck off out of our lives, not to fantasize about her lips wrapped around my cock.

But Fergie's been eating away inside my head all night, which is ridiculous because she means nothing to me. Less than nothing. Fucking her was a chance to screw with her and her father's plans, nothing more.

My loathing for her burns in my veins, even as that raspberry scent of her invades my nostrils. I hate her for being here when Gaius isn't, when Torsten is going to end up living on the street.

And most of all, I hate her because she tasted so damn fine.

6

FERGIE

I lie in my new bed and stare at the ceiling. A blob of light streams in from the open windows – the city of Emerald Beach lit up at night. I'm able to see light and shadow, and my eyes are always drawn to bright sources of light.

The city light here feels different to back home in Witch-wood Falls (I mean, Cedarwood Cove. Gotta get used to that). It's louder, brasher, more... Californian. It's a *lot*, like this house, like my new stepbrother, like the ache rising between my thighs.

I do what I always do.

I listen.

I listen to doors opening and closing somewhere deeper in the house. I listen to Cassius' footsteps padding around the bathroom. I listen to the water running and the shower door clicking shut.

I try not to think about my stepbrother naked and dripping wet.

I fail.

I press my thighs together in a vain attempt to stop the tingling in my clit. My pussy still pulses with a satisfying ache from the pounding Cassius gave me earlier.

I think about how irresponsible I've been to have unprotected sex with a stranger, and how little I care about something that would've made Old Fergie break out in hives. Old Fergie never did anything reckless or impulsive. She'd never risk her GPA or reputation on a guy like Cassius Dio.

New Fergie just wants to feel something again.

I still have a month left on my injection, so at least there's no danger of getting pregnant. I'll sneak downtown this week and get an STI test because I bet that's not the sort of thing Cassius Dio thinks about.

And tomorrow, when I'm alone with Cassius on the drive to school, I'll tell him that I went temporarily insane yesterday and ask him not to tell anyone what happened, especially not our parents. And he'll agree, because he may be a cock but he's not a monster.

I hope.

Everything will be okay.

I can fix this.

I must fall asleep at some point because I wake to the buzzing of my alarm. 'It's 7:00AM!' the tinny electronic voice announces cheerfully. I debate throwing it across the room, but that didn't exactly work with Cassius yesterday. I hit the STOP button and drag myself out of bed.

My mouth tastes like dollar-store hummus. It's my first day at Stonehurst Prep. My head swims. I need coffee.

I stumble into the bathroom and knock several of Cassius' products into the sink while I search for my toothbrush. Geez, the guy has a lot of products.

"Looking for this?" a familiar dark voice calls. I don't need to see him to know he's holding my toothbrush hostage.

"I have another." I pull one out of my toiletries case and hunt around for the toothpaste, hoping he hasn't stolen that, too. "How long have you been standing there?"

"Since you barged in without so much as 'by your leave'." Cassius' fingers brush mine as he reaches across the vanity. A moment later, I hear him squirting shaving foam and whistling a jaunty tune. My resolution to talk to him like a sensible adult dies in a blaze of fury. Does he really think this is how it's going to be? We'll brush our teeth together and play happy families after he tricked me into fucking him?

You can't trick the willing, Fergie.

Shut up, brain.

Cassius' elbow jabs into my tit. "Ooops, didn't see you there."

Dick. I'm not going to let him see that he's got to me. Even though my legs are trembling and I'm aware that I'm wearing a giant Iron Maiden t-shirt and black cotton underwear and nothing else. It doesn't matter, he saw it all yesterday.

Okay, this is good. I'm alone with my stepbrother. I can get the grovel out of the way before breakfast.

I suck in a deep breath. "Listen, Cassius, about last night. It was a mistake, and not one I want to repeat. Dad didn't tell me that my stepbrother was my age, so I wasn't exactly expecting you, and—"

"—and yet, you opened your legs for me." Cassius' razor scrapes along his skin. My fingers itch as they remember the curve of his jawline, the little indent where his ear attaches to his head, the hoop in his lobe that I tugged with my teeth.

"Call it a temporary lapse of sanity. I'm better now."

"You keep telling yourself that, sis. The way you wrapped your legs around me, and your pussy clamped hard around my cock and milked every last drop, it seemed like you knew exactly what you're doing. Admit it – you liked it even more because it was filthy, devious, *wrong*."

Fuck him.

"Fine, dickweasel. You had your fun, but now we have to

deal with the consequences. Can you refrain from mentioning this to my dad? Or at school? Or to anyone?"

He taps the razor on the edge of the sink. "Want me to be your sordid little secret?"

"I just don't want the first thing everyone in Emerald Beach knows about me is that I slept with my stepbrother."

And I don't want to put my dad through more than I already have.

"Then why'd you jump in bed with me the minute you got to town?" Cassius taps his razor on the side of the sink. "Even if you believed my bullshit story, sleeping with my mother's pool boy within five minutes of arriving doesn't exactly paint a message of sanity."

"I don't have to explain myself to you. Will you keep this quiet or not?"

"What makes you think I'm inclined to do you a favor?"

I turn to leave. "I should have known this would be a fruitless conversation."

A hand snakes around my stomach, pulling me back against him. His body folds around mine, his thick shoulders hemming me in. My heart thuds against my ribcage as his cock rubs between my ass cheeks. He's growing hard again, and I have the bratty urge to wiggle my ass into him—

No. I'm not falling for his shit. I let my body go limp as I assess his hold on me, preparing a counter when he's off-guard.

"Don't worry your pretty head, little sis," he whispers. "I promise that I won't tell another soul."

My heart hammers in my chest. I'm not stupid. I know exactly where he's going with this. "But?"

"But in return, I want you to do something for me."

I sigh. "What?"

"Take off your underwear."

For fuck's sake. I blanch. "You already have my underwear."

His fingers slide over the waistband of my cotton panties. "Maybe I want to start a collection."

I bite my lip, contemplating taking him out with a flip, or raising my arms and straightening my back so I can pivot ninety degrees to grab his knees and trip him. That'd smash his head on the side of the basin. I love the idea of leaving him passed out in the bathroom. But then I wouldn't be able to get myself to school. Blind girl problems.

Plus, Dad probably wouldn't be happy if I took out my stepbrother on our second day.

Fuck it. If Cassius wants to hold onto a scrap of fabric because he thinks it gives him power over me, I'll indulge him.

I grin up at my stepbrother as I hook my finger in the elastic. My leg trembles, but I lock my knee so he can't see it. I keep my face angled up toward his as I wiggle my hips against his cock and squeeze out the huge, loud fart that I've been holding in ever since I stepped into the bathroom.

Cassius backs off me as I step out of my underwear and hold them up to him. The bathroom starts to heat up with a noxious smell. "They're all yours, bro."

Cassius makes a choking noise. "You farted."

"Damn right." I toss my panties at his head. "Enjoy the scent, you pervert. I'm going down for breakfast. Hopefully there are lots of beans."

Someone laughs. My heart leaps into my throat when I realize it's not Cassius. Some other dude is behind him.

I'm such a blind girl cliche, but I'll go all gooey over a hot voice, and the stranger's laugh is pure throat sex. It's rich and deep and resonant, and it bursts from him in a wild musical burst, like it's taken him completely by surprise. I might be wrong, but I detect the faintest edge of a European accent. *Mmmmm.*

I also detect his scent – it's mingled in with Cassius' carnation and musk, but it's distinctive – vanilla and orange zest and honeycomb. *He's* the one who uses the fancy products in the shower, the same ones I used last night.

How long has this guy been standing there? How much has Cassius already told him?

Did I just make a deal with the devil too late?

I don't know for sure, but I'm guessing the only way another dude ended up in our bathroom, using fancy products, is if he spent the night in Cassius' room. *Interesting.* I didn't peg my step-brother as bisexual, but he doesn't know everything about me, so I guess that makes us even.

"I hope you and your special friend are very happy together," I grin as I head back toward my room.

"We are," Cassius chuckles. "Oh, and Fergie?"

Don't engage don't engage don't engage—

My fingers pause on the door handle. "Yeah?"

Cassius' cocky voice shakes with laughter. "Anytime you want me to be the pool boy, you just have to ask."

I slam the door in my stepbrother's stupid face.

I PULL on the Stonehurst Prep uniform – blazer, scratchy pleated skirt, starched shirt, weird floppy tie thing – and fasten the buckles on my black patent Demonia ankle boots. At least we're allowed to wear our own shoes.

My old school back in Massachusetts – Witchwood—no, Cedarwood Cove High – didn't have a uniform. A year ago I'd have given anything to be able to go to a school like Stonehurst, where *sixty-five percent* of the senior class go on to T20 colleges. Now, I'm going through the motions, but I can't bring myself to care about school. None of it matters anymore. It'll pass the time until I figure out what the fuck I'll do with my life.

I don't want to start at a new school a month into senior year, but Dad's made it clear that dropping out completely isn't an option. And no way am I sitting in this stark, echoey house trying to motivate myself to complete coursework online. So school it is. Whatever. It's only terrible if I care what people think of me, and I give less than zero fucks. The fuck-pastures in my fuck-farm are barren.

Downstairs, I locate the kitchen again easily – my nose follows the delicious smells of spices and frying meat. Someone moves about, clattering pans and stacking plates. "Dad?" I call out. "Cali?"

"Good guess, but no," a new voice says. "You must be Fergie. Your dad and stepmother left a couple of hours ago for their tennis game. I'm Milo. Do you want your eggs scrambled or poached?"

"Huh?"

"Fried? Or perhaps you are a vegan? That's no problem. Vegans are a specialty of mine. I make a mean tofu scramble."

"No," I bark, then feel bad for snapping. "I mean, no thank you. I'm not a vegan, and I love a good poached egg with a runny yolk. But who are you and what are you doing in Cali's kitchen?"

Memories of falling for Cassius' pool boy trick assail me. I know there's an older Dio brother, Gaius. Dad told me I wouldn't meet him at the house, but I'm not willing to take my chances.

Just don't sleep with this guy, whoever he is, and you'll be fine.

My snarky inner monologue has a point. Besides, he sounds a bit too old to be another Dio brother.

"I'm the chef, at your service." Milo clinks the lid of a pot, and something delicious wafts across my nose. "Anytime you're hungry, day or night, I'm the doctor-in-residence to cure all ills."

I vaguely remember Cali mentioning a Milo. "You live with Seymour."

"Happily married eighteen years." Milo shifts something meaty and bready and garlicky on a griddle. "Seymour is out running an errand for Cali right now, leaving me to make sure you get off to school with a full stomach and a smile. But I'm happy to text him a shopping list if there are things you need. I noticed you didn't arrive with much luggage."

I hate to ask for a favor since they seem to come with strings attached in this house, but I'm desperate. "There actually is something. I'd like to install a lock on my bathroom door, to keep my nosy stepbrother out of my room. If Seymour could pick one up for me, and someone could show me where you keep the tools, I'll put it on when I get home."

"I had three brothers, myself," Milo chuckles. "I know how important it is to have privacy. Seymour will be delighted to assist. It will be done by the time you return from school."

"He doesn't have to do it. I can use a screwdriver—"

"It would be his pleasure. Please, Miss Fergie, it's our job to make sure you have everything you need."

My shoulders sag in relief. "Thanks, Milo. I appreciate it. I'm not used to having staff do things for me."

I've never liked people doing *anything* for me. I never wanted to be treated special. At my first school, they assigned me a teacher's aide, and I made it my personal mission to make sure I never asked her to do anything. I've always had to find my own way, even if that means making life a hundred times harder for myself.

You've only been in Emerald Beach for fifteen hours and you've slept with your stepbrother and given him and his boyfriend a show. I'd say you've made things plenty hard for yourself.

"You'll adjust," Milo says with a smile in his voice. "People always do. Before you know it you'll be calling me up in the middle of the night demanding my famous chocolate chili fondue."

I laugh. "Don't tempt me, because that sounds amazing. Speaking of which, what's that delicious-smelling thing you're making? Is it breakfast?"

"It is, indeed." Milo slides a plate in front of me. "I've made *gözleme* – it's Turkish flatbread stuffed with ground lamb, vegetables, goat cheese, and my own secret spice blend, baked on a special griddle called a saj, and served with a poached egg with a perfectly runny yolk. I'm on a Turkish kick at the moment. *She* gifted me and Seymour a vacation to Istanbul over the summer, and I'm still obsessed with the food we ate there."

He calls Cali She, *too.*

Isn't that a weird way for people to address their employer?

I tuck into the flatbread packet, which is a mouthgasm. While I eat, I ask Milo more about his trip to Turkey. The only time I've ever left the country was to go to Rio de Janeiro for the jiujitsu world champs, and that small taste of travel left me craving more. I was supposed to go to Japan over the summer for a martial arts camp, but I had to pull out after The Incident. Yet another part of my old life I had to kiss goodbye.

It doesn't help that fifteen hours in Emerald Beach in the company of my new stepbrother makes me desperate to punch someone.

As I clear my plate, footsteps pound on the stairs. "Hey, Milo," Cassius' smoky, gravelly voice calls from the doorway. "Thanks for the food. We'll eat on the go."

I guess by 'we,' Cassius means himself and his boyfriend – the mysterious man in the bathroom. The man with the laugh like satin.

"I've already wrapped up your gözleme for you. Careful, they're hot." Milo clicks his tongue as he hands over the packages, like he's indulging a child.

"You're wasted on us, Milo. You know that. You ready, sis?"

Cassius calls to me. Keys jangle in his hand. I sense the presence of his boyfriend in the room, but he doesn't say a word.

For the first time since I got into Dad's car to drive to California, the reality of my situation hits me like a punch in the gut.

I have to start over.

I have to drive to school with my stepbrother, who I slept with in a fit of self-loathing, and who is now in possession of two pairs of my underwear.

I have to go to a new school and sit in classes and smile and write essays like they actually matter and act like I give a shit about my future.

It'll be fine. Do the bare minimum you need to graduate and stay out of the spotlight. Don't get involved. Don't give away any more underwear. Cassius promised not to tell, so resist the urge to sleep with any more family members and you'll be fine. How hard can it be?

I grab my backpack from under my feet, pick up my cane, and lick the last trace of *gözleme* off my fingers. "Fine, let's go."

7

FERGIE

I follow Cassius and his silent boyfriend out to the garage, which judging by the lofty echoes of space is large enough to store an entire racing team, their pit crew, the girl who waves the checkered flag, *and* both her fake breasts. Cassius huffs with frustration as he waits for me to navigate around the other vehicles. He doesn't offer me a hand.

"This one?" I finally make it to where he's standing, my cane tapping the front wheel. I open the passenger side door and slide into the seat. I land on something warm and hard.

The seat's already taken.

"What the fuck?" I try to extract myself, but huge hands wrap around me and pull me into a lap. A lap made of Stone-hurst Prep uniform fabric and hard muscle. My heart races. I grab the edge of the door, but the owner of the lap pries my fingers from the frame.

"You can sit here," a voice purrs in my ear. This isn't the boyfriend's voice – it's someone else. A new guy, one who smells like dark chocolate and whisky and hazelnut – rich and sinful. His voice is smoother than the other two, the tone warm and convivial. *Too* convivial, like he and I are old friends and he's just having a bit of fun.

"That's illegal—" I start, but the door slams. When I try the handle, it's locked. The drivers' side door and back passenger doors slam shut.

"Are we all strapped in?" Cassius asks, wickedness dripping from every word.

The guy wraps the seatbelt around both of us, then belts his hands around my stomach, pinning my arms at my sides. "We're ready for a ride."

"You'd better not be fondling her," a female voice pipes up from the backseat. "Or I swear to the gods I will jump out of this vehicle."

I start to ask who the other passengers are, but Cassius stomps on the gas. Of course my stepbrother drives like a maniac. I'm slammed back into the strange guy's chest by the g-forces. He chuckles into my ear as he tightens his grip, and I hate myself for the flicker of fire that dances beneath my skin.

Nothing like making a resolution to live like a nun to make you wet for every guy within a twelve-mile radius. So far this morning I've given my panties to my stepbrother, had impure thoughts about his boyfriend just from hearing that deep, uncontrollable laugh, and now I'm practically drooling in this new stranger's lap. What the fuck is wrong with me?

What I thought was a harmless, no-strings-attached fuck has given another guy power he can wield over me.

How much worse can things possibly get?

At least here in California with Cassius and his friends, I feel *something*. It might be abject terror as Cassius takes a corner like a rally driver. It might be an illicit shiver down my spine as the guy holding me trails his breath along my collarbone, but it's *something*.

And that's addictive. And dangerous.

I didn't think I'd ever be able to feel again.

I reach for the dashboard, desperate for something to hold myself upright. If I think about it all too much, I'll be sick. Cassius cracks up laughing as he whips the car around another corner, slamming me and my mystery safety belt into the window.

I jump as a hand brushes my shoulder – someone passes something to Cassius from behind our seat. It's not the girl – she's sitting behind Cassius, but another person. It's the first indication I'd been given that anyone else was back there. And I have good hearing. They must've been very quiet.

It's got to be Cassius' boyfriend.

"Who the fuck is that back there? And who the fuck are *you?*" I wriggle against the guy's hold, trying to dig my hipbones into him and make this as uncomfortable for him as it is for me. We hit a speedbump, and my head slams into the low roof.

"I'm in heaven," answers that smooth voice. His hand squeezes my side, and I ignore the shooting sparks dancing across my skin. "And if you keep wiggling your ass like that, you're going to get a happy surprise."

"That better be your protractor digging into my hip," I snap back. "Because if it bothers me again, I'll cut it off."

The girl shrieks with laughter. "Omigod, Cas, I love her. Can we keep her? I don't want senior year to just be me surrounded by a bunch of cocks."

Fuck, how many people are in this car?

I can hear the silent guy back there now. He mumbles something, but it's too quiet for me to hear.

"We're not keeping her," Cassius growls. He fiddles with something on the dash, and a moment later, Nick Cave's sonorous voice howls from the speakers. Because apparently I love digging a grave for myself, I move my body along with the discordant squeal of guitars, nodding my head and wiggling my hips. The guy I'm sitting on groans, and I feel a flash of satisfaction.

Another *feeling*. Another moment where I'm something other than numb. What is happening to me?

"*I* say she should hang out with us." The girl leans over the seat and touches my shoulder. "I'm Juliet. Juliet August. I'm Vic's twin sister. Vic's the one you're grinding on. By the way, I fully support you making him a eunuch. In fact, all three of these guys could do with having their industrial-sized jizz factories unionized, so all their little workers could go on strike. If you're game."

I crack up. *Industrial-sized jizz factories?* That's genius and – in the case of Cassius and I'm pretty sure this Vic dude – accurate. "Who else is in the car?" I ask.

"I'm sitting next to Torsten Lucian," Juliet says. "But I wouldn't worry about him. He won't say boo to a goose."

"Claude Monet painted 'The Geese' after the first Impressionist exhibition, and the bright tone and thick strokes of color are typical of his experimental style during this period," says a male voice from the backseat. *Mmmmm, yes.* It's the exact same voice from the bathroom this morning. Torsten is definitely European – maybe Scandinavian? "Unusually for Monet, the painting is in a vertical format. But I'd never say boo to a painting—"

"I didn't mean it literally, for fuck's sake," Juliet yells. I hear a crash and a grunt as she hits Torsten with something. "Anyway, don't let the three hounds of hell here give you any trouble. Cassius is just pissed because his mommy won't let him carry a sword to school, Torsten never should be allowed outside his cage, and my brother is the biggest manwhore on the planet. They'll all giant teddy bears once you get to know them."

"Exactly," Victor says. "And if you rub this teddy bear in my special spot, you'll get a lovely surprise."

"In some cultures, cutting off a bear's cock and eating it will improve your sex life," I say sweetly. "And I am always looking for tips."

Juliet cackles. Victor's laugh tickles my ear. Cassius makes that insane growling noise that makes my insides go positively feral. And Torsten makes no sound at all except a scraping noise that I think might be a pencil drawing on paper.

"So, sis, why don't you tell us all about yourself." Cassius' voice sounds friendly enough, but I know when someone is baiting me.

I shrug. "Nothing to tell. My dad and your mom fucked on a business trip, eloped in Vegas, and now I live in your house and go to this school."

Saying it out loud doesn't make it any less wild. No matter what's happened in my life, I've always been able to trust that Dad would be there for me, stoic and dependable. He does crossword puzzles and reads the *Financial Times*. He's a *dentist*, for Satan's sake. He doesn't make rash decisions. As far as I know, he's never once had a night of drunken debauchery where he came home with a random piercing.

That is, until three weeks after The Incident, when Dad arrives home from a dental convention and tells me that he's married and we're moving across the country to live with a woman I've never met and her son who is definitely *not* twelve years old.

"We know all about John Munroe and his dental probe. But what about *you*?" Juliet prods.

I swallow the bitter taste in my mouth. "I'm pretty unremarkable."

"I don't believe that for a moment," Vic whispers against my ear. He shifts me in the seat so that I can feel his cock rubbing against my ass cheek. My whole body lights up like I'm a glowstick at a Blackpink concert.

First Cassius, and now this guy? Why is my body so determined to lead me down another destructive path?

Maybe because I'm ready to let it.

Maybe I have nothing left to lose.

Victor strokes my arm absently as the four of them settle into a conversation about a party on the weekend and kids from their school I don't know. Well, Cassius and Vic and Juliet chatter. Torsten remains resolutely silent, but there's a scratching noise, like a pen scribbling frantically on paper, and pages turning. *He's writing in a notebook.* From the sounds of it, it's something pretty intense.

I can sense Torsten's eyes on me, his zealotry sucking the air from the car. I'm tempted to ask him more about Monet's geese, but I don't dare.

We pull over and Cassius parks. I try the door again, but it's still locked. Victor's hands move up my arms. "Desperate to get away from me?" he whispers. "We were just getting to know each other."

The door flies open and a rough hand grabs me, hauling me from the car. "This is your stop, sis," Cassius growls. "We're driving around the back."

"But—"

A door slams and the car roars away. So much for Juliet 'keeping' me.

"Come back here, you bastards!" I yell after them, but they're gone, lost in the crush of unfamiliar voices and cars pulling up at a drop-off zone. I'm guessing I've arrived at my brand new school.

If this is their way of hazing me, then they're going to be disappointed. Being on my own suits me just fine. I don't want friends. I don't want to fit in at Stonehurst Prep. I want to graduate with as little fanfare as possible so I can get the fuck out of Emerald Beach.

I *want* to stay numb, because when I'm numb, I can't be betrayed again.

I tap the tip of my cane on the ground, trying to get my bearings. When I started at Witchwood Falls High (Cedarwood Cove, I mean), I went in every day for two weeks before it officially opened to do something called Orientation and Mobility. I worked with a specialist O&M instructor to create a map of the school in my head, and learned the way to all my classes and the library and offices, how to navigate the dining hall, and where all the steps and random pillars and other hazards were. By the time school started, I could walk around like I owned the place.

But since I've arrived in the middle of October, I'm being thrown to the wolves without a map or a tranquilizer gun. And I clearly can't expect my brother and his douchebag friends to help me find my way. I'll be sitting out first period for the next week to work with a local O&M instructor, but I need to meet the instructor at the Belasco building, and I have no idea where the fuck that is.

I grit my teeth in frustration as I tap my cane and turn in the direction of the school buildings. I use a technique called echolocation – if I tap my cane on the ground or make a clicking noise with my tongue, I can use the echoes to make out objects. I spent a summer in middle school on an immersive course through the Access for the Blind charity to learn how to do echolocation, and it means I'm able to 'see' the world beyond my cane – the location and configuration of buildings around me, steps or ramps coming up, trees and fire hydrants and overhangs. I can fill in the information my cane doesn't give me.

So I can find my way through the school buildings. I just don't know which is the one I need.

Independence is nice and all, but it falls apart within five minutes. No matter how clever I am, the world isn't designed for people like me.

I'm going to have to do my least favorite thing and ask someone for help.

I take a few steps forward. All around me, I can hear kids talking in groups, greeting their friends, telling stories about their weekends, swapping class notes. Mobile phones ping. Game consoles chirp, and in the tall trees flanking the front path, exotic birds serenade the chaos. I move along the path, trying to pick out a voice that sounds friendly to ask—

"Fergie. There you are!"

I turn in the direction of the girl calling my name. I don't recognize the voice. She sounds bubbly. *Great.* My least favorite kind of person. Why does she know my name?

She runs up to me, panting. "I'm so glad I found you. Cassius was supposed to bring you to the office, but I had a feeling he wouldn't do as he's told. Mrs. Emerson assigned me to be your student guide, so I'm here to guide."

"I don't need a guide, thanks."

"Oh, I'm sure. Obviously you're about to walk into that group of cheerleaders completely on purpose."

She says it with such earnestness I can't help laughing. "Okay, yeah, you got me. I've got to meet my O&M instructor in the Belasco building, and I've only taken five steps and I'm completely lost. So yes, please do your thing."

"Sure. Do you want my arm?" She offers me her elbow. I debate telling her no. I don't want students to think I need to hang on to someone to get everywhere, but the path is crowded and there's a lot of noise, and I don't want to make an ass of myself on my first day and walk into a tree or a cheerleader. I may be numb, but I still have *some* self-respect.

I slide my fingers into the crook of her arm, grateful she at least knows the proper way to guide a blind person and doesn't try to grab my hand or waist. She leads me toward the buildings, steering us through groups of students and up a flight of wide marble steps.

"I guess I should say, welcome to the hellhole that is Stonehurst Prep, home of the elite, pretentious asshole sons and daughters of California's most moneyed families. Although I'm sure you already know that, since you're living with Cassius Dio. By the way, I'm Eurydice Jones."

"Your name is *Eurydice?*"

"Don't ask," she groans. "My dad's a Classics professor with a terrible sense of humor. Everyone calls me Euri. I'm actually vision-impaired, too, which is probably why I got assigned to you. Shall we?"

"Yeah. Can we stop by a bathroom first?" Since Cassius hogged our bathroom this morning and didn't let me go after breakfast, I've been desperately holding in a pee.

"Of course. There's a bathroom down here, near the humanities block." Euri guides me through the crowds of people and under a portico into an internal courtyard, and I feel a tiny sliver of fear unraveling. Euri describes the layout of the school, the prime locker positions, and the cliques that we pass.

"—there's the basketball team. The cheerleaders hang out here, in front of the gym. Those guys over there are the TikTok stars. I'd stay well away from them – you don't want to get in the way when they randomly burst into dance. Limbs fly everywhere. It's complete carnage."

"Noted."

TikTok stars? This school is wild.

"...the wannabe actresses and musical theatre types hang out on the steps of the auditorium building." Euri pushes open the door to a bathroom and steps inside. "And the Poison Ivy Club take the prime spot by the fountain, because they like to have eyes on everyone and for everyone to have eyes on them—"

"The Poison Ivy Club?" I laugh. "What's that? Some kind of botany society biker gang?"

Euri lets out a hissed breath. "You don't know? It's—"

Her words cut off with a strangled gasp. She stops dead in her tracks, and I crash into her from behind.

"Euri, what's wrong? You're blocking traffic."

It's then I hear it. The wet sucking sound, the rhythmic panting. A rich, posh male voice *cooing*, "That's it, lick her hard, baby. You know how she likes it."

There's a guy in here. Victor August, judging by that distinctive voice. And from the sound of it, he's getting head.

"Now, Lucila, while I've got you here between my sister's legs, we have a little matter of the Cambridge house to discuss. Nod if you know which house I'm talking about, the one your father owns right next to the Harvard campus, the one that's... Good girl... no, don't stop. I know how much you wanted to taste my sister one last time. Well, I want that house. You're going to get your father to sell it to me at a price I determine. If I get that house, and Cas gets his Sacremantum, you get your Princeton acceptance letter. Do we understand each other? Nod for me... that's it, baby. As you were—"

"Shut the fuck up, Vic," a familiar voice snaps. "I can't come with you yammering on about some stupid property deal. That's it, Lucila, use that tongue, babe. Oh god, you're amazing."

It's not Victor getting head. It's *Juliet*.

But what the fuck is Victor doing in here with her? And what did he say about a house in exchange for a Princeton acceptance?

Euri starts to back up. Her trembling body presses against me. Personally, I don't give a fuck what goes on in the bathroom as long as I can deal with my imminent bladder situation, but she's clearly *terrified*. So I move back toward the door and of course, my elbow slams into the paper towel dispenser and sends the front panel crashing to the floor. Juliet groans with surprise, and Victor swears.

"The indomitable Euri Jones, hello," Victor says. ""Don't just hover in the doorway. Why don't you come over here and join in? I'm sure Lucila won't mind indulging you."

The wet sounds resume. Juliet grunts, her uniform rustling as she bucks her thighs against the sink and murmurs sweetly at Lucila.

Victor continues. "...unless you prefer to watch, of course. Come and stand with me, nice and close for a good view, since I know your distance vision sucks. I wouldn't want you to miss a moment of Lucila's tongue buried in my sister's pussy."

"I—" Euri stammers.

"Mmmm, yes, baby," Juliet moans. "Fuck, I've missed you. I don't know how I've survived without your tongue inside me."

"Go about your business. Don't wait around on account of us. Nothing unusual is going on. Lucila and I had a little deal to settle," Victor explains. "She wants to get into Princeton so very badly, don't you, doll? We'll be done any minute now, especially if she does that thing with her tongue again."

"You're the one in the girl's bathroom," I snap, moving in front of Euri, because I'm not going to let this dick with the angelic voice intimidate us out of here. I press my thighs together. I *really* need to go. "This doesn't seem hygienic. Isn't Juliet afraid she'll catch some disease and her pussy will turn green?"

"Why, Euri, I didn't know you had friends," Victor says with that achingly-sexy smirk in his voice.

"V-V-Victor, this is Fergie Munroe, from Massachusetts," Euri manages to get out. "Fergie, this is Juliet August, head cheerleader and school theatre star, and Victor August, class president, captain of the basketball and track teams, and member of the Poison Ivy Club."

I glower in Vic's direction. "We've met."

"Fergie got me so excited in the car this morning that I'm almost tempted to avail myself of Lucila's tongue," Victor says. "But I would never force myself on someone unwilling."

I snort. "That's rich, after what you did in the car."

"You sat on *my* lap, Duchess," Victor says. "I can't be held responsible for what happens when a gorgeous redhead writhes around on my gearstick."

"I didn't *writhe*," I protest, but it sounds a little needy. We both know I writhed.

I want him to call me *Duchess* again.

"Sure, you didn't writhe." Victor's voice darkens. "Don't be rude, Lucila – say hello to the new girl."

"H-h-hello, Fergie," the girl kneeling between Juliet's legs stammers out. Her throat sounds raw. "This isn't—"

She doesn't get to finish. Juliet groans and shoves Lucila's face back between her thighs. Lucila squeals, but the sound is muffled by Juliet's kitty.

The wet, sloppy, sucking noises continue, and I should be disgusted, I should whirl around right now and drag Euri out of there, but instead I press my thighs together because the wild ache Cassius stoked yesterday flares again, and I imagine myself where Juliet is now, sitting on the edge of the counter, thighs spread wide, groaning in pleasure, oblivious to the fact that anyone could walk in and see. Only, instead of Lucila between my thighs, it's Victor.

Old Fergie would never dream of doing something so demeaning, so filthy. But New Fergie... she's a monster who wonders what it would feel like to be on her knees with Victor August's fingers tangled in her hair...

Plus, I really do need to go.

Juliet squeals as she comes. The girl – Lucila – groans and sucks at her, swallowing her nectar. The sound is so intimate and so wonderfully filthy. Every atom in my body glows with the depravity of it.

Lucila gets to her feet. I hear clothing rustling and I imagine her tidying her clothes. "I have to get to my locker. Jules, I'll see you at lunch. Victor, I'll talk to my father about the house."

"Let's do this again, doll." Juliet slides off the counter. Her heels make a clacking noise as they hit the tiles.

I hear a thwack as Victor slaps Lucila on the ass. "Get me that house and your debt's paid. All yours, ladies."

As Lucila shoves past us, she knocks Euri into the sinks. "Get out of the way, freak."

Euri yelps as she hits the marble counter. Lucila's comment stings, even though it's not directed at me. I've been the Euri of my old school – the freak, the disabled kid that no one knows what to do with. That kind of offhand insult can't cut me anymore, but it doesn't mean I like knowing someone else is the punching bag for a mean girl's insecurities, especially when said mean girl will get on her knees for the August twins.

A zipper pulls closed. The tap runs. Juliet and Victor move toward the door. As he passes me, he deliberately brushes against me, leaning in close to whisper, "I'm going to think about you wearing those scarlet panties all day, Duchess."

What?

Cassius told him?

Bastard.

I whirl around, hands balled into fists, but Victor has already pushed through the swinging door. His posh laughter echoes down the crowded hall.

After I've done my business, I pull Euri into an alcove. "Are you okay? You seem a little shaken up."

"I'm fine. I just... I didn't expect to run into the August twins." Euri sucks in a deep breath. "Lucila isn't a nice person, and what you saw and heard in there, that's going to get her into Princeton. Fuck."

"What are you talking about?"

"I'm talking about the Poison Ivy Club – your stepbrother and his three friends, and their posse of ass-kissers and cum-dumpsters."

"That's a delightful and super-feminist way to talk about someone."

"Yeah, well, they're not my favorite people," Euri mutters.

"It's okay. I get it," I say quickly, because these are the girls who decided that Euri's on the outside, and I know that people like us have to find our ways to deal. "So Cassius is in this Poison Ivy Club?" My stepbrother doesn't strike me as the 'joining in' type.

I can practically hear Euri rolling her eyes. "You *do* know

you're sharing a roof with one of the most popular and notorious guys at Stonehurst?"

I've shared a lot more than that. "I do now. So this club is like a
popularity thing? What does it have to do with this Lucila chick
on her knees for Juliet or getting a real estate deal for Victor?"

"Poison Ivy is so much more than a popularity thing. It was
started by Cassius' older brother, Gaius – although back then it
was just a glorified gang where Gaius would beat people up for
money. Then Victor took it over and made it more... subtle. To
the teachers, Poison Ivy is a study group for SAT prep and peer
support for top students, but that's a front for their real mission
– to get their friends into the elite colleges, no matter the price.
If I were you, I'd stay well out of their way."

"Why?"

I can't help it. At the mention of *elite colleges*, my veins fizzle.
Old Fergie isn't dead yet.

"Victor might say that he doesn't go after unwilling girls, but
if you get in with their group, you'll end up on your knees in a
bathroom for him. Everyone else does. And if you're not one of
their friends, they'll destroy you. It's best to fly under the radar
at this school." Euri lowers her voice. "Three years ago, a student
named Bayleigh Laurent became a client of the Poison Ivy Club,
back when Gaius was running it. Bayleigh's parents wanted her
to go to Yale, but she didn't have the grades, and she lost out on
first chair in the school orchestra to my sister, Artemis. But once
Gaius Dio and his crew got involved, Bayleigh posted the
highest SAT score in her year, and my sister had an unfortunate
accident. She fell down the auditorium steps and broke her arm
in three places. She had to give up her chair. Bayleigh got her
spot and a ticket to Yale, and Artie has never been able to play
the cello again. *That's* the work of the Poison Ivy Club."

"Shit."

That's *despicable.*

I heard rumors at my old school about students sabotaging each other to move up the class ranking, but no one ever organized a *club*. Even though what they did to Euri's sister is completely shitty, I have to admire the enterprise of Cassius and his friends – if you have no morals, there will be a never-ending stream of business in underhanded college placements.

"Artie's not the only victim of Poison Ivy, either," Euri says. "Ask any senior with a legitimate shot at an Ivy and they'll tell you they've lost rankings or roles or competitions as the club moves their pieces around the board. But no one can do anything about it because the Poison Ivy Club has plausible deniability. That's Victor's influence. No one pushed my sister – she swears she slipped on something on the steps, but when the police checked them out, they were normal. Just a terrible accident. Well, there are a lot of accidents around here. And now they want to send Lucila to Princeton. *I'm* applying for Princeton. So that's terrifying."

"Do they know that?"

"I've tried to keep it quiet, but yeah, they'll know." Euri's voice trembles. "They may not be able to do much – my application is basically done. I'll get it finished and sent off early, and then it won't matter."

She sounds as though she's convincing herself.

I'm even more curious about Cassius' brother now that I know he started the Poison Ivy Club. If he made a career out of getting any student into the college of their dreams, where is he now? "What did Gaius do? Where is he?"

"In prison," Euri says. "And I hope he rots there forever. As for what he did, no one knows exactly. They didn't release a lot of details. I know more than most because I reported on it for the school paper, and all I could find out was that a Poison Ivy prank went wrong and a senior student got killed. Gaius admitted to the whole thing."

Shit.

Cassius' brother is in *jail*. And I'm living in his room. That's why Cassius was all weird about me being there. *Want me to eat out that tight little cunt while you come all over my brother's sheets? You don't belong here. You'll never be part of this family.*

Poor little rich boy. How utterly predictable. He hates me because he thinks Cali is trying to replace his brother with a brand new family. After all, I'm here and Gaius isn't. Cassius fucked me yesterday because he wants me to believe I'm worthless, because if he welcomes me then he betrays his brother.

Well, I won't let him take out his mommy issues on my body ever again, even if he does have a magical monster cock.

Cassius Dio can't get rid of me that easily.

I have nowhere else to go.

I realize that Euri's still talking. She's moved on from the Poison Ivy Club, and she's telling me about a college application panel she's putting together before ED applications are due. "— admissions officers from Yale, Harvard, and Princeton. I'm especially excited about Princeton because that's where I'm applying Early Decision. What about you? You going out for any Ivies?"

Her question burns through me like a forest fire. If she'd asked me three months ago, I'd be able to rattle off my ED school – Harvard, of course – and my backups for regular decision. But that was then, and this is now.

"No," I say. The words taste like sawdust in my mouth. "I'm not good enough for the Ivies."

Y ou don't need working retinas to know people are staring at you. Eyes stab into my skin as I walk with Euri to the Belasco building. They shoot arrows at me through open windows as I wander around with the O&M instructor, Katee. They gnaw holes with sharp, rending teeth as I walk the same areas of the school again and again, clicking my tongue and counting steps.

Katee drops me at my second-period class – chemistry with Mr. Dallas – and when I walk in, my boots tap-tap-tapping on the tiled floor along with my cane, the whole vibe shifts. I have to wait for the doddery Mr. Dallas to shuffle through his class list to assign me a lab partner, so I stand awkwardly by his desk like a show-and-fucking-tell display while their whispers grow fangs.

"That's her," a guy says to his lab partner in the front row. "She's Cassius' new stepsister. She's blind."

Yes, and she's not deaf, dickweasel.

Dickweasel is a word I learned in an interview with Faye de Winter, the violinist in Broken Muse, one of my favorite bands. It's a word for all occasions, especially this one.

"Shouldn't she be at some kind of special school?" his friend asks. "I didn't think they let people like that in normal school."

I didn't think they let people like you out of the chimpanzee exhibit, so I guess we both learned something today.

"My parents aren't going to like this," a girl scoffs. "She's starting mid-semester. She'll mess up the curve. If I lose my spot at Sarah Lawrence because of her, we're going to sue the school."

Your parents don't need to worry about that, since they clearly dropped you on your head when you were a baby.

Old Fergie would *never* think these things. Old Fergie had a smile for everyone and didn't mind patiently explaining about her eyesight and her accessibility needs again and again. She'd never get her rocks off imagining stabbing a room full of people through the eye with the heel of her stiletto boots.

New Fergie subscribes to the Jean-Paul Sartre view of the universe. *Hell is other people.*

"Thank you for waiting, Ms. Munroe." Mr. Dallas grabs my hand in his. I hate when people do this. The staff at Stonehurst Prep are supposed to have had training in guiding a blind student, but people say this all the time and it's not true. I don't want to make a scene in front of the class, so I grit my teeth and let him drag me to a table at the back of the room. "This will be your table for the rest of the year. I'll leave you to get acquainted with your lab partner. You have today's experiment listed in the folder on the school app. Sing out if you have any questions."

I sink into the seat, letting my backpack drop to the ground, and pull out my tablet, Braille note, and Braille labeler. I turn to where my lab partner slouches over the end of the table. "Hi. I'm Fergie. You're stuck with me. Aren't you lucky?"

No reply from my lab partner. A familiar smell wafts over me – vanilla, honeycomb, orange zest. It's the scent of the fancy bath products in the shower I share with Cassius, but richer and headier, mixed with something unique and intoxicating.

The same scent I caught in the bathroom this morning. The same scent from behind my seat in the car.

My heart hammers in my chest. I'm convinced I'm sitting with Cassius' boyfriend – the guy with the laugh like music who thinks Nick Cave is a good soundtrack first thing in the morning.

"Your name is Torsten, right?"

He doesn't answer.

Oookay. "Have you started the experiment yet? Where are you up to?"

Nothing.

I hear a page turn, a pen scrape across thick paper.

He's writing in that notebook again.

No, not writing. The strokes are too frenzied, too wild to be forming neat rows of letters. He's *drawing*.

I'm not supposed to care. I'm not supposed to care.

All I have to do is survive until the end of senior year. And that does not mean caring about this silent stranger with the sexy laugh and what he might've overheard between me and Cassius in the bathroom this morning.

But something about that rich, wild laugh of his that doesn't match this silent, obsessive scribbler, makes me *want* to care.

And I'm sick to fucking death of not getting what I want.

I slam my hand down on the table in the spot where I think he is. I catch the corner of his notebook. He tries to tug it away, but I hold it firm, splaying my fingers out so he can't draw around me.

"Hey," he growls. "What are you—"

"Good. You are alive. You can listen to me now," I say. "Here's the deal. I get that you don't like talking. I'm not a big fan of it myself. In fact, nothing would make me happier than if we both spent every chem lab hiding in this dark corner, doing our own thing. But to achieve that, we need to get Dallas off our backs, which means we got to finish the experiments and get at least a passing grade, and I am going to need your help because this lab is a death trap for a blindie. So when I call out the name of a substance, you pass me the jar or container or whatever, and then we spend the rest of the period in blissful silence, or you can tell me more about Monet's geese if that tickles your pickle. Got it?"

He doesn't say a thing. I don't even know if he's heard me. I let my hand slip away from his notebook, and consult the experiment on my Braille note.

"Hydrochloric acid," I call out.

Silence greets me.

I wait.

Okay, fine. Whatever.

I'm just about to get up and beg Mr. Dallas for another partner when something slams down on the table in front of me.

I pick up the jar and turn it in my hands. I can only *assume* it's hydrochloric acid. He could fuck with me easily by handing me the wrong chemical. That's the sort of juvenile thing kids at my old school did. But I don't think that's in his nature, and I don't have enough self-preservation left to care that I don't know this guy at all, and he's Cassius' boyfriend so I'm probably completely wrong about him.

I take out my labeler and punch out a quick label for it. As I'm sticking the label onto the jar, a warm hand closes over mine.

I hold my breath.

A dark voice whispers, "What's that?"

Curiosity tinges the edge of his voice.

I swallow again.

"It's a Braille labeler." I place the bottle on its edge on the table so he can feel the raised dots on the label I just stuck on. "I'm putting labels on all the bottles so that if you have a sick day I won't accidentally blow the place up."

Torsten runs his fingers over the label, sucking a breath

between his teeth as he feels the raised dots. His fingers slide over mine, curling between them and squeezing. He invades my space, his hand in mine, his knee pressing against my thigh. His breath warms my neck, and the pads of his fingers dance on my skin. "How do you read it?"

My skin tingles as I pry his fingers from my hand and press them over the raised dots. "That's the symbol for h, and this is c, and this is l. All the letters and numbers in the alphabet are made using different combinations of six dots in a cell, and they follow a pattern so it's easy to memorize. There are also some common contractions and shortforms, so I don't have to type three letters every time I use the word *the*."

"I like patterns." He leans closer, that vanilla and honeycomb smell invading my nostrils. His fingers rub at the dots between the letters. "What are these dots?"

"One single dot before a letter like that indicates that letter is a capital. I put them in front of the H and the C, but not the l. HCl – the chemical name for hydrochloric acid."

"Can you teach me?"

He sounds genuinely interested, that sexy European accent of his lifting at the end of the question. "Sure. But we have to do this experiment first."

"Why? It doesn't matter."

He's right. It doesn't matter. I've already done this unit at my old school, so I'm not learning anything. And a bad grade in chemistry won't hurt my chances of getting into college, because I'm not going to college. What matters is the way his lush voice pools heat in my belly, and his skin feels like butterfly wings where it touches mine.

I pass him the labeler and show him how to press down the keys to make the different letters in the cell. He hands it back, and I type a label with his name and slap it on his forehead.

"This is how you spell your name. That single dot at the beginning says that the first letter is a capital."

He laughs his beautiful laugh again as he reaches up to touch his forehead. "This doesn't make sense. It's all wrong—"

"That's because you're reading it backward, Netsrot."

Now we're both laughing. I hear someone at the table across from us mention Torsten's name, but they're quickly shushed. I'm aware that I'm being watched, that although every student is *pretending* to work on their experiments, they're hanging off every word and gesture between me and Torsten. I'm beginning to understand that from the moment I walked through the doors of Stonehurst Prep, I'm being judged on how I interact with the Poison Ivy Club.

It reminds me of when *He* welcomed me into the inner circle of Witchwood Falls High, and kids who tormented me in grade school suddenly wanted to be my friend. But this is different. I don't think Torsten knows or cares about anyone else in the room. And I don't think anyone wants to be my friend, or his. The air sizzles with danger as students shift and whisper – a school of piranhas stirring the water, waiting for that single drop of blood to spill.

I kind of like it.

"I want to write you a note," Torsten says. "Can you show me all the letters?"

"Sure." I tap out all twenty-six letters of the alphabet for him, plus a full-stop, comma, and question mark. He flips open his notebook and indicates a page for me to stick on the label.

"I see the pattern now," he says, running his fingers over the page. "I can't read it when I close my eyes, though."

"It takes years of practice to read with your fingers. I had to do exercises to make the tips of my fingers extra sensitive. But you can read it by sight, and if you write something for me, I'll be able to read it."

"And it will be secret," he whispers.

"Yes." I hand Torsten the Braille labeler and pretend to busy myself with my chemistry notes when Mr. Dallas comes by our table.

"Ms. Munroe, what's Mr. Lucian doing with your Braille machine?" He raps the table in front of Torsten. "I've warned you about treating other students with respect. Give that back to Ms. Munroe. Just because your mother is... who she is, doesn't mean you can do whatever you want in my classroom, is that clear?"

Beside me, Torsten doesn't react. He keeps tapping away with the labeler. A couple of tables away, someone stifles a giggle. Every eye in the room bores into me, gouging holes in my skin as they search for my weakness.

"What a pair of freaks," someone whispers near the front of the room, quiet enough that he assumes I wouldn't be able to hear. He's quickly shushed by a friend.

My ears ring. It's been so long since I've been the new girl. The blind girl. The *freak*. And as much as I've told myself that I've carved my heart out and replaced it with a lump of coal, hearing that one single word wrecks me. I shove my chair back until it hits the wall, wishing I could fall into the stones and disappear forever.

Coal isn't supposed to feel pain.

"Mr. Lucian," Mr. Dallas barks, oblivious to the chaos he's wrought. "Do I need to send you to Mrs. Jennings' office again?"

Torsten says nothing. His fingers *tap-tap-tap* on the labeler's keys.

"It's fine," I say, surprised by how clear my voice comes out. I sit on my hands so Mr. Dallas can't see them shaking. "He's helping me label the different chemicals so I can find them easily."

"He is?"

The incredulity in Mr. Dallas' voice annoys me.

"Yeah. Sorry if that's not allowed. I just thought you wouldn't want me to get the hydrochloric acid and potassium permanganate mixed up. Although, since the guy on our left is dangerously close to over-boiling his hexane, I think you have bigger problems than us."

"Oh, shit," says the student at the next table as he frantically scrambles to turn off his Bunsen burner. Mr. Dallas starts over there, but turns on his heel to speak to me again.

"Do you need some help setting up the experiment?" Mr. Dallas asks. "You don't seem to have started."

"Actually, sir, Torsten and I are all finished," I say. "When we mix the hydrochloric acid with $NaHCO_3$, we get table salt, water, and CO_2. And the aluminum foil gives us aluminum chloride and hydrogen gas, which is colorless and—"

"Excellent, very good." He moves on to help the next table, where the overheated hexane now emits a gasoline-like odor.

Torsten sets down the Braille labeler in front of me.

"How'd you do that?" he asks, lowering his voice to a whisper. "How'd you get Dallas off our backs?"

"Easy. We already did this experiment at my last school, so I remember the results." It's on the tip of my tongue to say that I should be in AP Chemistry, but I bite back the words. "I told you, if we work together, this can be our easiest class."

Torsten doesn't reply. He tears out a page from his notebook, peels the sticky back off the label and sticks it down, and slides the note under my fingers. This close, his scent overwhelms me. His knee grazes mine, and it's like the butterflies in my stomach turn into a horde of raging buffalo.

"Don't read it now," he says. "Later."

"Okay. I'll look later—"

The bell rings. Torsten grabs his notebook and bag, and flies out of his seat like his ass is on fire. All around me, stools scrape and phones beep as students make their way to their next class. I slide the page into my iPad case, my fingers trembling. I'm dying to look, but I don't want anyone else to see.

Whatever is in that note is between me and Torsten Lucian.

I make my way to my locker. It's slow going. The corridors crowd with students who are too busy chatting with their friends or fucking around to clear a path for the blind girl. I whack three students in the ankles with my cane to get them to move, but by the time I reach my locker, the second bell is already blaring.

I grab my power pack for my iPad and shove it into my bag. My heart thunders against my ribs as I block my locker with my body, slide the note out of the case, and run my fingers across the page.

> *DEGAS LOST MOST OF HIS VISION IN 1870.*
> *SO HE MADE SCULPTURES INSTEAD.*
> *CAS HAS YOUR PANTIES IN HIS LOCKER, BUT*
> *   HE WON'T TELL.*
> *YOU SMELL LIKE RASPBERRIES.*

10

FERGIE

"I heard Old Man Dallas gave you Torsten Lucian as a lab partner." Euri makes a gagging sound as she falls in step beside me. She promised to meet me outside my fourth period European History so we can eat lunch together. (We don't have any classes together because she in all the AP classes.)

A lunch date seems dangerously close to friendship territory, but I need to know how the dining hall works, so I agreed. I'm regretting it now. The last thing I want to do is discuss what happened in chemistry.

"Why do you say it like that?" I finger the corner of Torsten's note that peeks out from my iPad case. The note doesn't make much sense. But I get the feeling Torsten doesn't have a lot of experience engaging with people. He doesn't think or communicate like everyone else, and because of that, he chooses to stay silent instead. But for whatever reason, he *wants* to talk to me, to tell me about Degas and the way I smell, and I... I want to hear it. I want to understand him.

He noticed what I smell like.

"You're kidding, right?" Euri sidesteps us both around a

giggling gaggle of cheerleader types. "Didn't you notice how *weird* he is?"

"No, not really." I'm surprised that Euri – who is clearly on the fringes at Stonehurst – would make a comment like that. But I also understand survival instincts, and she's one terrified gazelle doing anything she can to avoid being eaten alive by the lions.

I actually had fun during chemistry. A tiny part of Old Fergie blanches at blowing off the assigned work to mess around with a bad boy. But New Fergie smiled all the way through European History at the memory of Torsten's strong fingers brushing over hers. "Isn't he a member of that super-secret club? So he can't be that weird if he's popular."

"It's a different kind of popular. I've had classes with all of them since middle school. People *like* Vic and Juliet. They're the king and queen – a smile from either of them is like being anointed. But people are *afraid* of Cassius and Torsten."

I can understand why people are afraid of Cassius. He's huge and he has this... *tension* to him. He balances on a knife-edge, a breath away from losing control and tearing off your head.

But Torsten's the opposite of Cassius in every way – he's not fighting with himself for control. He only knows how to be himself, even when who he is doesn't fit. I can relate to that.

Euri continues. "Torsten hardly says a word to anyone, rarely shows up for school, and when he is here, he barely does any actual work. He just scribbles in his notebooks. He's an incredible artist, but he doesn't even do well in art because he won't follow the assignments."

"What kind of stuff does he draw?" I ask.

"Oh, even that's weird, too. He copies famous paintings. You can show him a Monet or a Michelangelo or a Picasso for, like, ten seconds, and he'll go away and produce an *exact* copy of it. He can paint anything, but he never does original work. He can't *think* like an artist, and he resists anyone who wants him to try. I'm the editor of the school paper, the *Stonehurst Sentinel*, and I'm in charge of the yearbook, and Torsten does photography for both, and it's a nightmare trying to get him to listen to me."

"Are he and Cassius an item?" I ask. "He came out of Cassius' room this morning."

She laughs. "I don't think so, but who knows what those guys are into? Your stepbrother is a huge manwhore, almost as much as Victor. You're lucky you're his stepsister – you're safe."

Don't be so sure.

Euri continues. "Cassius is... not nice, and I'm not just saying that because of what he did to my sister. If Cassius is bi, he'd have slept his way through most of the guys and left broken bodies littered across the lawn. I don't know about Torsten – I've never heard of him being with anyone. Cassius and Torsten and Victor are like brothers – they've been friends since they were kids, and I think the other two kind of look after Torsten. In middle school, he used to sometimes show up with a black eye or huge bruises on his arms, and he never had to do PE class. One teacher tried to make him once, and I heard a rumor that Victor and Cassius *torched his house*." She steers me off to the side. "I've got to stop at my locker for a sec."

I wait, my stomach gnawing with hunger, while Euri jiggles her locker door. "Mine always takes a bit to get open. Last year your stepbrother slammed someone's head into it, and it's been a bit mangled ever since."

She says this casually, like slamming someone's head into a locker is completely normal. I'm *dying* to know more. "How is Cassius still in school? If he's done half the crap you say he has, he should be expelled and in some kind of asylum."

Euri hesitates before answering. "I told you, they're royalty around here, and not just with the students. The teachers look the other way and let the Poison Ivy Club do their thing, so it's best to keep your head down and stay out of their spotlight. So, I was thinking," she says with false brightness, changing the subject so swiftly, I wonder if there's something she's not telling me. "Are you interested in joining the paper? I've just had my features writer quit, and I'm *desperate*. It looks good on a college application."

I can tell from the waver in her voice that she's reciting a script she prepared earlier. The faculty *asked* her to get me to join the paper because they want Euri to become my new BFF. Because people who are blind want to hang out with other people like them, right? Because the *only possible interesting thing* about a blind person is that they can't see, and they couldn't possibly have their own life or passions or ideas.

Fuck them all. Fuck them right in the ear.

Especially since I used to be editor of the *Witchwood Falls World*, and I won a national journalism prize for a piece on ablism in the high school curriculum.

I move my mouth to answer Euri, but no sound comes out. I'd *love* to be on a school paper again. I miss hanging out in the newsroom after school, assigning stories, asking probing and uncomfortable questions of the faculty and board members, reading the online edition the morning it came out and knowing I helped put it together. I want so badly to say yes, but I can't, I *can't*. And I *hate* Euri for making me dredge up those memories of what can never be mine. I want to slam *her* head into her dented locker.

"No," I finally choke out. "I'm no writer and I'm not interested."

Get me out of here now, or I'm going to kick something.

"That's cool. But maybe—"

"Hey, sis," Cassius calls out over the din in the corridor. "We're going to lunch. You should join us."

Target acquired.

"No thanks," I call back as I pretend to arrange things inside my locker. It's completely empty apart from the spare power pack I left in there. Old Fergie decorated her locker with ribbons, fuzzy stickers, band patches, photobooth strips from her dates with *Him*, their arms around each other, their heads tossed back or tongues poking out or lips locked in a messy, passionate kiss... Old Fergie couldn't see the photographs, but she touched the glossy paper and *remembered* the way he made her feel.

Like she was special. Like she mattered.

But Old Fergie is *dead*. She isn't standing in this corridor with her stepbrother bearing down on her with that self-satisfied smirk in his voice. New Fergie slams her locker shut and turns to face Cassius down, because she knows he plans to destroy her in front of everyone, and she's not going to go down without a fight.

I'm done being the good girl.

"That's not a request, *Fergus*." Cassius' voice is pure sex and poison. I remember those filthy lips of his wrapped around my nipple, and I want to scream even as heat pools between my legs.

Beside me, Euri sucks her breath through her teeth. "You should go with them," she whispers. "No one says no to Poison Ivy."

"No time like the present to start." I know Cassius doesn't want to eat with me. He's not inviting me out of the kindness of his heart. His mother probably told him he had to, and he sees it as an opportunity to fuck with me again.

I slide my laptop and Braille display onto the empty shelf of my locker, in case I need my hands free. The conversations around us sputter out – everyone wants to see what the Poison Ivy Club has in store for the new girl.

I slam my locker shut. The *clang* echoes down the now silent hall, like a Cylon centurion storming in to destroy my enemies.

(Sorrynotsorry for the geek reference. *Battlestar Galactica* is my and Dad's favorite show. As a kid, I used to pretend I was Starbuck flying vipers made from the sofa cushions.)

I lean my back against my locker and glare up at the space occupied by my stepbrother's enormous, swollen head. My nostrils fill with plum and musk and carnation – a scent I've come to associate with danger, with *hunger*. How is it possible for so much heat to pool between my legs, for so much wetness to soak through my panties, over someone I hate with the fire of a thousand suns?

I lean forward a little, jabbing my finger into his hard chest and trying to ignore what that simple touch does to me. "I may be blind, but you're the one who's hard of hearing. Read my lips, Cassius. I'll even speak nice and slowly, and use small words so you understand. I'm *not* eating lunch with you. Or doing anything with you at this school. You stay out of my way, and I'll stay out of yours. That's the deal."

Cassius' fist whistles past my cheek and slams into the locker behind me. I wince involuntarily at the loud sound so close to my ear. He leans in close, so close I can taste him on my lips.

"Where's the fun in that, sister dearest?" he whispers, his lips almost brushing mine. His other hand grazes my throat, his fingers wrapping around my bare skin, locking my head in place and squeezing just enough that I know he's serious.

Every part of my body lights up like a space battle. *This is so messed up.* I'm aware that the entire corridor is watching us, waiting to see our next move. But Cassius isn't performing for them – he doesn't give a shit what people think of him. This little display of his is for me and me alone, but I don't yet understand what he's trying to tell me.

It's dangerous for me to play with Cassius, because while I also don't give a fuck, I don't want to hurt my dad, which means I've got to stay under the radar at this school. Word getting out that I slept with my stepbrother is definitely not staying under the radar. I can't forget that Cassius has two pairs of my underwear.

So Cassius and I dance together on the edge of chaos, both unsure what the other will do. He might tighten his fingers around my neck and squeeze the life out of me. He might kiss me, and make my body melt into his again. He might force me to my knees like Lucila or pull a dagger from his belt and twist it in my gut. I believe all these options are equally possible.

Is it crazy that I want to push all his buttons and find out *exactly* how crazy Cassius Dio can get?

"Didn't your mother teach you not to play with your food," I manage to choke out. "It might decide to play back."

To prove my point, I lean forward, pressing my throat against his hand so hard that my breath constricts. I stretch out my tongue and lick the tip of his nose.

"What the *fuck?*" Cassius growls as he jerks away from me. He rubs at his nose as if my saliva is burning him. Funny, he didn't mind so much last night.

Behind him, Torsten laughs his dark, twisted laugh.

"Fergie, stop this. You don't know what you're doing," Euri whispers. "Do you even know who your stepbrother and his friends are? Who their parents are?"

I consider her words. The truth is that I know very little about my new stepmother. I never asked Dad about her because asking meant acknowledging the woman who stole my dad.

I know Cali works in the fitness industry, and she must be successful because she has a huge house, the contacts to get me into this elite school, and the I'll-fuck-up-your-shit attitude of a self-made woman. But Euri speaks with real fear in her voice, like she's genuinely *afraid* of Cali, and I want to ask why, but I'm boxed in by Cassius' bulk and Torsten's laugh and Victor's sinful dark chocolate and whisky scent.

"Yes, Fergie," Cassius coos. "Listen to your friend. You should stay far, far away from Poison Ivy. In fact, you should fuck all the way off to Massachusetts and take your gold-digging father with you."

I'm about to retort when someone slams my locker shut behind me.

"Your *darling* stepbrother doesn't speak for all of us. Hello again, Fergie." Vic leans against my locker door, his shoulder brushing mine, his other hand reaching up to tuck a loose strand of hair behind my ear. He's casual about it, but he wants to make it clear that he's boxing me in. I have no escape. "I hope your day is going as nice as your ass."

"It *was* going well until I got ambushed by the three chipmunks," I grumble.

Behind me, Cassius roars, and I hear a sound that might be Torsten holding him back. But Vic only chuckles.

"Don't let the bear get to you. He's got low blood sugar and a beautiful girl's underwear in his pocket. We saved a seat for you at our table, and I promise I'll protect you from him," Vic says, twisting my hair around his finger, giving it a little tug. Sharp pain arcs across my skull, not so bad that I cry out, but enough that I know exactly what Victor can do to me if he's given free rein. How that silky voice and those powerful fingers can have me on my knees for him, and how some dark and secret part of me might enjoy it. "This is a once-in-a-lifetime offer, never to be repeated."

"No, thanks. I've already got a lunch date." I'll take Euri my forced friend over the three chipmunks any day of the week. Even if Victor does smell like dark chocolate and hazelnut and peaty Scotch and that scent does something wild to my insides.

Victor presses his chest against mine, leaning in so close I can feel his breath against my lips. The hallway shrinks away into nothing. All that exists is the impossibly small distance between his lips and mine.

"Help me out here, Duchess," he whispers. "I'm trying to diffuse this before Cas explodes. Are you afraid I'll bite?"

Victor leans forward and flicks his tongue over my upper lip, mirroring what I did to Cassius. Only Victor is slow and deliberate, his finger tracing down the edge of my face, making my knees tremble.

"Cas is the biter," he purrs. "As I think you already know. I'm the one who kisses all the pain away."

Victor tilts my head back, exposing my neck. He kisses a trail of fire across the sensitive skin, his fingers curling through my hair as his other hand grazes the edge of my breast, and the movement is so fluid and subtle that for a moment I'm not being kissed by Victor August in front of a crowd of people, but I'm back in Witchwood Falls, in *His* arms...

Oh, no you fucking don't.

I grip Victor's jaw with my fingers, turning it softly. Victor leans into me, thinking I'm going in for a kiss. Instead, I slam my palm into his ear, sending him sailing headfirst into the locker beside me. Before he has a chance to right himself, I slam my knee into his groin, get my shoulder in beneath his, and flip him.

Euri screams.

Victor sails over my arm. His back slams into the tiles with a sickening *crack*.

He doesn't move.

My ears buzz. Adrenaline liquifies my veins. The air fizzes with tension – a thousand bowstrings pulled taut, ready to loose directly at my heart.

At my feet, Victor groans. No one moves to help him. The hallway is deathly silent.

"I told you in the car today that if you weren't careful, I'd cut your dick off," I say, tugging down the hem of my shirt that had come untucked from my skirt. "I don't like repeating myself."

Victor groans and rolls over. I hear someone move to help him. "Vic, darling, you're bleeding," Juliet whispers, her voice a mix of awe and disgust. "Don't you dare get blood on my shoes."

Cassius yells, and there's a thump and a crash and someone whispering. I screw up my face, expecting his fist to fly at me, but nothing happens.

"Get off me, Torsten," Cassius cries. "I'm going to break every bone in her body."

Thanks, Torsten.

I don't know how long Torsten will be able to hold back my beast of a stepbrother. I step over Vic's prone body and grab Euri's arm. She's shaking like a Tickle Me Elmo.

"Let's go."

I don't even have to push through the crowd – they part to let me through. I'm Mosesing this shit. If only I had a Biblical plague I could hurl at them all. As far as they're concerned, I'm made of anthrax at this school now. Euri's nails dig into my skin, but she steers me in a straight line away from the carnage.

You said you didn't want to make friends. You didn't want to get involved. Well, congratulations, Fergie, you haven't even made it through the first day yet, and you've ensured you're a social pariah for the rest of the year.

"Still want to be my faculty-appointed friend?" I hiss to Euri as we round the corner.

"Are you kidding? That was *amazing,*" she breathes. "Stupid, but amazing."

As I walk down the hall, a smattering of applause echoes behind me. Maybe Euri is right – maybe the students at Stonehurst Prep don't love their three gods as much as I thought.

The adrenaline hums in my veins, reminding me of the buzz of a martial arts comp – the high of winning a bout against a skilled opponent. I miss the dojo so much. I could ask Euri if there's a martial arts club at school, or find a jiujitsu gym in Emerald Beach. Maybe I can—

No.

I can't do that.

Because the minute I start training again, I won't be able to hide how good I am. It won't take someone long to connect the new me to the old me – the blind girl they called Death Lily who won national competitions three years running.

I burned the sport I love, and I have to live with the rage of that eating away at my insides.

The burn of Victor's skin against mine just before I floored him does a little to calm that rage.

Euri leads me into the dining hall, straight to the front of the line. She dumps a bunch of stuff on my tray without asking me what I want, then leads me out a side door into a courtyard area, down some steps, through an overgrown garden, and into a long building. As soon as I step inside, hot, wet air clings to my skin, and the competing scents of hundreds of different plants and flowers threaten to overwhelm me. Water burbles from somewhere.

We're in a greenhouse.

Euri leads me to some wooden benches. I have to shove branches and vines out of my way to sit down.

"Is there a reason we're eating with the triffids?" I swat at a mosquito.

"That dining hall is about to fill up with students who were in the corridor, not to mention the club themselves in their private fishbowl, and you don't want to be there for that." Euri fusses around in her bag. The next moment, I hear a rhythmic clacking sound. "This greenhouse is for the horticulture students. Mrs. Maddock gave me a key. I eat lunch here sometimes when I need a break from all of *that*."

Clack-clack-clack.

Euri clacks something beside me while I fumble with the knife and fork on the edge of my tray. The adrenaline is starting to wear off, and I'm grateful for the cloying warmth of the greenhouse. Euri gives me a run-down of what's on my tray – clockwise from top: chargrilled zucchini with harissa, wild rice, beet hummus, green apple and macadamia dukkah, and smoked paprika potato skins covered in garlic yogurt.

Wow, this is world away from the soggy fries and mystery meatloaf at my last school.

The food makes me think of Milo, and *that* makes me remember that I now live in an enormous, sterile mansion with a personal chef, and that I'm very, very far away from Witchwood Falls (Cedarwood Cove, I mean) and The Incident. And even though I just made an enemy of my stepbrother and his powerful, popular friends, I can't help but be grateful that I can be whoever I want to be here. I've wiped the slate clean. New Fergie *can* be a girl who eats in greenhouses and hangs out with the weird girl and goes postal because a bully touched her tit.

My stomach growls with hunger, and I dig in while Euri clack-clack-clacks away.

"What's that sound?" I ask.

"It's my knitting needles. I like to knit. It calms me down. I'm finishing a scarf for my sister, and then I'll make you something. What color do you want?"

"You don't have to do that."

Friends knit friends scarves, and I don't want friends at Stonehurst Prep.

"Don't be silly. I have to knit something or I go insane, and my family is getting a little sick of the mountain of bobble hats and slightly crooked mittens I've made them. I just got this beautiful red alpaca wool – it's like an exact match for your hair, and it's *so* soft. You shall have a brand new scarf just in time for the Christmas holidays. So…" she stops clacking for a moment to crunch a carrot. "What've you got?"

I know exactly what she's asking. Blind people talk about their vision in a specific way. Sighties either make all these dumb assumptions about blind people based on watching *Daredevil*, or they tiptoe around our disability, thinking the very *mention* of our eyes will send us into a depressive spiral. I haven't been around another blindie since the echolocation camp three summers ago, and it's nice to know I'm not alone at this school.

Not that it matters. Because Euri and I are not going to be friends.

We're *not*.

It's just easier to have someone to sit with at lunch. It's easier to make nice with the one person who gets it. It's *easier*, that's all.

"I had retinopathy of prematurity," I say. "I was a preemie baby. I weighed under two pounds when I was born. The blood vessels that supply my retina with oxygen began to grow abnormally, and they bled and caused scar tissue. Most babies with ROP get a mild condition that corrects itself, but I wasn't so lucky. My retinas detached, and I lost most of my vision before I was three years old. My ophthalmologist performed an operation that was able to partially reattach my retina and save my remaining vision, so I still have light perception. Ever since, I've been the glorious creature you see before you. What about you?"

"Mine's genetic," says Euri. "I've got *achromatopsia*. It's this super rare and weird thing where my eyes have rod cells but no cone cells. So I don't see any color at all and I kind of walk around with night vision on all the time. During the day I get all squinty and weird, and I wear dark red glasses to help with that. I can see a lot, but I can't, you know, match my clothes or fly a plane."

"Color is overrated," I say. "Planes can fly themselves these days, and black goes with everything."

"Tell me about it. That's why my entire wardrobe looks like I'm an extra in an *Addams Family* movie."

"Nice. Mine's more Edgar Allan Ho," I laugh despite myself as I stretch out my legs, crossing my spike-heeled Demonia boots at the ankles. I wonder what shoes Euri's wearing, but then I curse myself for wondering because I *don't care*. "Must be a blind girl thing that Nick Cave and Andrew Eldritch speak to our souls."

Mentioning Nick Cave brings back memories of the car ride this morning, and Torsten's strange and lovely note from chemistry class.

Euri chews for a bit, then I hear her knitting needles clacking away. "Girl, what you did to Victor... that's the most incredible thing I've ever seen."

"You're visually impaired," I remind her. "You haven't seen much."

Euri laughs. "*Touché*. Look, I know the senior counselor and Principal Garcia want us to be best buds because of our eyes, but it's nice to have someone around who knows what it's like. Especially when she's some kind of badass ninja—"

"I got lucky," I mumble. I'm not comfortable with the turn this conversation is taking.

"I'm blind, Fergie. I'm not stupid. You've had martial arts training. If you only knew how many people in this school want to do what you just did," she drops her voice. "I think it's time the Poison Ivy Club got a taste of their own venom. And you might be just the person to help me do it."

"What do you mean by that?"

Euri's foot jiggles against the cobbles. Her whole body vibrates with energy. She doesn't seem so afraid anymore. "We could write an article for the *Sentinel*. Expose the truth behind what the club does at this school. Two students broke a sex scandal at Acheron Academy, and it got reprinted in the *New York Times*. That could be us. You wouldn't even have to help write it if you don't want – just get me the inside story from your stepbrother. Get us the smoking gun."

"If everything you've told me is true, that's a terrible idea."

"Yeah, I know. That's why I haven't done it yet. Because they'll destroy me and my family," Euri sighs. "But you're Cassius' family. If we put your name on it, they won't touch you, even if you destroy them."

I snort. "Did you hear him in the corridor? Being his stepsister doesn't protect me from jack shit. I don't want to lead any kind of crusade. I just want to make it through senior year."

"Don't we all." Euri's voice brightens. "Do you want some friendly advice?"

I pick up a piece of chargrilled zucchini and pop it on my tongue. "Let me guess what you're going to say – if I want to survive senior year at Stonehurst Prep, don't beat up the basketball star in front of everyone."

"Got it in one." Euri pats my knee. "You made Victor look stupid and weak. And they won't stand for that."

"Will they report me?" Now that the adrenaline has worn off, I realize how stupid it was to react to them like that. 'No violence' is top of the Stonehurst Prep code of ethics. Probably a dozen students videoed my little outburst. They'll already be circulating online. If anyone can identify me...

I don't want word getting back to Dad that I'm punching guys in the hallway. He's already worried enough about me going back to school. It took everything I have to convince him to let me go to Stonehurst instead of doing school online. And I'm not going to sit around all day in that creepy house answering multi-choice questions on my computer.

"That's not their style," Euri says, her needles *clack-clack-clacking* again. "Their revenge will be of the stealthy, sadistic variety. Your stepbrother and his friends can't allow you to threaten their authority and live to tell the tale."

I laugh at Euri's hyperbole, but she doesn't. My laugh cuts off. I can't help but think that Euri's dead serious. She's truly afraid that I might've damaged my stepbrother's ego so much that he'd actually *kill* me.

Which is completely ridiculous.

Isn't it?

12

VICTOR

I lower myself gingerly into my seat at our table, wincing as my balls throb. At least I can breathe without my whole chest caving in. Ten minutes ago, that felt like a very real possibility.

I peer over Cassius' head across the dining hall, searching for Fergie. Poison Ivy has our own special room off the end of the dining hall – it was built for the son of a Saudi Arabian prince who went to school here a few years ago, but now it's ours. Bulletproof glass doors separate our table from the rest of the plebs, and I see to it that the staff set our places with cloth napkins and fine silverware. It's important to maintain certain standards, to set ourselves apart from the rest of this town. My mother always taught us that a good leader has to be a little bit unattainable, a little bit godlike, otherwise people start to doubt their word.

Apart from the staff who serve our food – we don't wait in line – no one can just walk back here. You have to be invited. No one had ever turned down an invitation to dine with us before... not until today.

And Fergie Munroe did it with *style*.

I don't see that cascade of red hair anywhere in the cafeteria. Eurydice must've taken Fergie outside. She's smarter than her sister to stay out of our way. Especially today, because Cas is ready to start ripping heads off and turning skulls into drinking vessels. And he looks very, very thirsty.

"Poor Vic, are you breathing okay? Do you need painkillers? Should I have Galen look at you?" Juliet fusses over me, placing a sopping wet napkin on my forehead. "Bring him a *proper* drink," she barks at the waiter, swiping the iced tea from his tray and throwing the glass against the wall, where it smashes into a million pieces.

"I'm fine, Jules." Although, honestly, I'm still shaky. I've taken some bad falls during track meets, and of course the work we do isn't without its risks, but Fergie didn't just drop me. That move she pulled *slammed* my body into the tiles, not to mention pulverizing my boys into pancakes. I can only take shallow breaths. It's going to take a bit for all my organs to settle back into their correct places, and it's definitely possible that I've cracked a rib.

I've never been so turned on in my life.

"Of course you're fine," Juliet pats my face with the napkin. Water dribbles off the end of my nose. "You're Victor August."

"What did you think this is doing?" I yank the napkin from her hand and toss it over my shoulder. "I'm not a character from Jane Austen swooning onto the fainting couch."

Although... I kind of *am*.

The waiter sets a glass of Scotch in front of me. Yeah, I'm underage and injured and it's the middle of the school day, but I'm also Victor fucking August. What of it? I toss my head back and down the glass in one gulp. The waiter whips it away and sets down another glass.

Even though I know she's not here, I can't help scanning the room again for the red-headed siren who cast this spell on me.

Our table fills up with our court – the people we've deemed worthy of our presence. Juliet's annoying girlfriends. Members of the basketball team. A couple of girls I slept with whose names I've already forgotten, and Lucila – our newest client. Clients don't automatically become part of our circle – hiring us is not a ticket to popularity – but everyone in the school makes careful note of who gets an invite to our table, and we need them all to know that Lucila is untouchable. If anyone tries to stop our clients from getting what belongs to them, Poison Ivy may just pay them a visit.

The air inside our private room hums with tension. I know that outside these walls, every student in the school is talking about Fergie kicking me in the nuts and laying me on my ass. At our table, everyone *wants* to ask about the corridor but no one will risk our wrath. The only person acting normal is Torsten, who hunches over his sketchbook, furiously sketching the paintings from the Edvard Munch exhibit we took him to last weekend.

I stare down at my food, listening with half an ear to the inane conversation around me, my chest bubbling with the niggling sensation of *missing* something. All of this... our table, our status, our club, the twenty-five-year Scotch burning my esophagus – it's too *easy*.

It's boring.

I look over at my sister waving her fork at her friend Kate, and I remember the day I swore that I would rule this school, that I would do everything I had to do to keep her safe. I've done it. Juliet and I are untouchable, *invincible*. I've taken Gaius' little club and turned it into a lucrative enterprise that could go national, that could work alongside Mom's business until it's time for me to take over.

I can see my future mapped out in front of me, and it's filled with all the danger and excitement that should heat my veins, but it's a big fat *yawn*.

Something's shifted since Fergie kicked my ass. She's rattled something loose in my head. I think it's the fact that she's the first person who's ever said no to me. Who's ever backed up a threat with real action.

I like it.

I mean, I don't *like* the sensation of having my balls kicked into my spleen, or the feeling that I might throw up at any moment, but I like that she's strong. A fighter. I like that bold, defiant twinkle in her smile that says she doesn't give a fuck.

She reminds me of Cassius, only Cassius doesn't look as hot in a Stonehurst Prep tartan skirt.

Mmm. Everything about Fergie Munroe is addictive – the way she wears her tie just a little too loose, giving a tantalizing flash of skin on her neck, those spike-heeled boots she wears with her uniform, the *go-fuck-yourself* glint in her eyes, the way she squirmed on my lap on the drive to school, the vein in her neck throbbing as I ran my teeth over it. Her lips parting slightly, ready to accept my tongue. The taste of her skin, like raspberries, like desolation.

She wants me. I'm sure of it.

My testicles disagree, but what the fuck do they know.

Fergie Munroe wants me, and the feeling is *most assuredly* mutual.

Only one thing stands in the way of me letting that red-haired siren sing me to my doom, and he's slouched in a chair across from me, playing with a bone-handled knife.

Cas only fucked her because he's angry with his mother, because he misses his brother, and because he deals with feelings the way he deals with everything else in his life – by fucking shit up.

But I'm the only one who sees the need burning behind his

hatred. Fergie has got to him, too. And from the way Torsten held Cas back in the corridor, I think even our dark artist has been entranced by her. Or, at least, the *idea* of her.

Does that woman even *know* the power she wields? I haven't been inside her yet and already I know she's got a pussy that will launch a thousand ships.

Men will go to war over a woman like Fergie Munroe. But am I willing to launch an army against my oldest friend?

"What are you looking at, eunuch boy?" Cas growls at me as he splays his fingers open on the table and stabs the knife between them. He doesn't even look at his hand as he does it, utterly unfazed by the possibility of slicing his own finger off.

The knife slams into the table beside my hand, the tip quivering like Fergie's lower lip right before she pummeled my gonads. I look up to see a smirk twisting across Cassius' face. He leans back in his chair and slurps his organic juice through a metal straw, but his hands are so big and clumsy that he spills it down the front of his shirt. "How are you feeling, brother?"

"Like I'm in love."

The words fly from my mouth before I can stop them, but once they're out, I don't want to take them back.

They hit Cassius like a slap across the face. He leans forward and grips the knife handle, glaring up at me with the smile of a monster who's broken free of his cage.

Conversations around me die away to a trickle. Next to Cassius, Lucila's cheeks flush with pleasure.

How cute, she thinks I'm talking about her.

"Sorry, doll." I flick Lucila one of my patented Victor August smiles, the kind that's all teeth and cruelty. "This conversation isn't about you. I don't take my sister's sloppy seconds."

The truth is that Lucila's reputation for head should've made her tempting, especially after seeing her in action firsthand this morning. But I couldn't make myself care. Getting my dick sucked by hot girls is so easy now, it's *boring*. I wasn't even hard until Fergie walked into the bathroom. Then I'd leaped to attention like one of my mom's loyal little soldiers.

"Hey, Lucila. I'm not nearly as fussy as Vic." Xavier, our varsity center forward, leaps up. He grabs Lucila's hand. She looks to me, the question burning in her pretty blue eyes. I nod. Her cheeks burn red again, a mixture of pleasure and humiliation. Everyone at this school wants to be chosen by our group, even if it's just for a quickie. She lets Xavier lead her behind the mahogany bar at the rear of the room, where he shoves her to her knees. I hear a zipper tear open before my attention is diverted back to the table by the knife stabbing the table in front of me, dangerously close to my crotch.

"If you put any more holes in this table, we're going to be picking wood splinters out of our soup."

I try to pull the knife out, but it's stuck too deep.

Cas frowns. "Don't change the subject. I want you to tell me again what the fuck you just said about my stepsister. Did she mash your brain along with your scrotum?"

"You heard me the first time. The Titanic theme song is playing on repeat in my head right now. I think I'm in love."

"The fuck you do," he shoots back. "You stay away from her. You don't touch her unless I allow it, and I *don't* allow it."

He pounds his fist on the table. The plates clatter. Kate whimpers. From behind the bar, I hear wet, sucking sounds and Xavier moaning.

"Where's this protective brother routine coming from, Cas?" I ask. "You hate her, remember? So why do you care if I stick my dick in her?"

The whole table falls silent. The only sound is Torsten's pencil flicking across the page. He doesn't notice things like his two best friends having a staring contest over a girl.

Cassius' body shudders with rage. He reaches into his

pocket, and I know he's fingering the two pairs of Fergie's panties he has in there. His obsidian eyes turn crimson at the edges.

Once, I had to help my dad Eli move a bunch of white tigers out of a roadside zoo where they'd been trapped in cages no larger than my sister's shoe closet. Most of them came quietly, happy to be free of their prison. But there was this one breeding female who'd been so mistreated, so accustomed to cruelty that not even a double dose of tranquilizers could keep her down. She tore an arm off one of Dad's workers. In the end, we had to euthanize her. I've never forgotten that look of caged fury in her eyes... and that's exactly the look Cas gives me now.

Like he can no longer tell the difference between a friend and an enemy.

And I'm a terrible person, because all I want to do is poke the tiger through the bars of his cage.

"Fergie is off-limits," he growls, glaring at every male at the table before returning that fury-laced stare to me. "You all hear me? That bitch is not getting dick at this school, and any guy who tries will accidentally fall down the stairs and *tragically* break their neck."

It's going to be like that, is it? You're so fucking possessive that even though you hate her, you won't let another guy touch her. Grow up, Cas.

Now I want Fergie so bad my balls ache.

"Poor Cas... it must be so hard to resist that sexy little ass of hers, that waterfall of red hair, those full lips... sound asleep in the room next to yours." I'm walking a line, but he's being a dick and I don't care. I carefully cut a slice off my steak and raise it to my lips, taking my time to chew, letting Cassius stew in his rage. "I mean... there must be a reason you don't want your best friend to fuck your stepsister."

Cassius growls low in his throat. We both know why he wants me to keep my hands off her, but he can't say it out loud or he'll break the pact he made with Fergie, and one thing I can say about Cas is that if he gives his word, he'll kill to protect that vow. Not like me, which is why I'm dancing with death right now.

Cassius shoots me a final, warning look.

I swallow. "She looks like she tastes like raspberries."

SCREEEEEECH.

His chair legs scrape against the marble floor as he shoves it back. Without taking his eyes off me, he grabs the chair, swings it over his head, and slams it into the table.

Plates and food fly everywhere. Juliet screams. I throw myself in front of her as shards of ceramic and glass rain down on us.

Cassius storms off. After a few more glances, our court mumble their apologies and leave too, leaving me comforting a trembling Juliet, and Torsten, who still scribbles away in the journal resting on his knee, oblivious to the chaos I'd wrought.

Torsten looks up from his sketchbook. His shoulders shake with rage. *Okay, not so oblivious.*

"What are you doing?" His accent grows stronger when he's angry. "You knew he wouldn't let you have Fergie. Now no one can. He's got plans for her, and you're trying to ruin them."

"If Cassius wants to mess up the one good thing that might happen to his family because of his twisted loyalty to his brother, that's his business. But Fergie is woman enough for both of us, and she'll need someone to dry her tears after he's through with her." I shrug. "I'm simply volunteering."

"Do you not remember what happened last time the two of you tried to share a girl?"

"I can't forget," I growl, my jovial mood darkening. "This isn't the same."

"If the two of you hadn't been fighting over Gemma, she might've—"

"Don't say her name."

"—and at least Gemma knew what she was getting into—"

"I told you, *don't say her fucking name*."

Torsten's ocean-cold eyes burn into mine. He turns away from me and returns to his sketch. I've wounded him. Sometimes it's easy to believe that Torsten's made of ice, like the flecks of white iceberg that float in the deep, dark blue of his eyes. But he's the opposite – he feels things *too* keenly, and he doesn't understand why sometimes, because he doesn't see the world like other people.

He doesn't like it when we fight.

Cas and I have been clashing for domination ever since we were kids, and it always hurts Torsten. He should be used to it by now, but that's not Torsten's way.

I take a deep breath, willing my thundering heart to return to normal. I refuse to turn on Torsten, even if he just broke our number one rule. "Cas might've made Fergie untouchable, but do you think she's going to give a fuck? If that girl wants something, she'll go after it, and not even the Bear himself can stop her."

I uncurl my fisted hands and rise to my feet. I lean down and kiss Torsten lightly on the head, so he knows that I'm not angry with him. He continues his sketch of a William Windsor-Forsyth piece we saw at our mothers' museum a few months ago, his strokes vivid and angry. It's unusual for him to get this worked up over someone who isn't part of our club. I remember how he threw himself at Cas in the corridor to keep him off Fergie, and I wonder...

I glare at the wait staff as I exit the ruined room. The dining hall buzzes with faux noise as hundreds of eyes deliberately look anywhere but at me. Every student pretends to be deeply involved in conversations about SAT prep and college applications and the upcoming basketball game, anything but what they just witnessed through the glass. No one wants to incur the wrath of Victor August.

Cassius might've got to Fergie first, but he can't forget that I'm in charge. If we're Stonehurst Prep royalty, then he's the black prince, and I am the king.

He may be the muscle behind the Poison Ivy Club, the monster everyone fears, but I'm the brain.

People think that because I protect Juliet and I have my father's panty-melting smile, that I'm the nice one.

They're wrong.

13

FERGIE

The rest of the school day passes exactly as I expect. Word about me laying out Victor August spreads to every corner of Stonehurst Prep. Rando kids slap my shoulders as I walk past, which is fucking disconcerting when you're blind. Someone starts a wave for me when I walk into European Lit class. That *is* kind of cool. I'm presented with vegan cupcakes, a weird succulent in a clay pot, and three marriage proposals.

Even though people seem to like Victor and keep asking me if he's okay (as if I care), there's a fizzing undercurrent of sadistic delight in their congratulations, as if they're happy to see their kings fall.

Honestly, I think they're humoring me a little because I'm the blind girl and that makes me a novelty. I can't be the first person who's stood up to the Poison Ivy Club. Cassius may be a big scary dude, and Torsten's a little... off-center, and Victor has that easy manner of a guy who commands any room he enters, but they're just high school seniors. They might rule these halls, but they have no real power.

As I rest against a wall, waiting for Euri to go to the bathroom before final period, someone leans on the locker beside me.

"Hey, Fergie," says the stranger. He has a deep voice with a lilting Irish accent – a personal favorite accent of mine. "My name is Sean Montgomery. We have American History together."

"Hi, Sean. If you're here to propose marriage, you're about an hour too late. I already accepted an offer from Hannah Deloitte." I quirk the corner of my mouth into a smile. "However, I'm amenable to any counteroffer that comes with a designer handbag or a helicopter ride to a remote private island."

He laughs, and it's this lovely, musical sound. "My da taught me to never bring a girl to our private island until she's beaten me in a Battle Royale-style showdown."

A year ago, a sexy guy with a dark sense of humor talking to me would've made my stomach churn with excited nerves. Now, I feel nothing. The numbness settles across my chest, and all it makes me think of is when I fucked Cassius yesterday and felt *everything*.

My godawful stepbrother cannot be the only person who makes me feel something in Emerald Beach. I turn my body toward Sean and plaster what I hope is a realistic smile on my face, hoping my hormones will kick in and tell my coal-heart that he's hot.

"I'm intrigued." I match the flirting tone in Sean's voice with a little sass of my own. "When will this fight to the death for your affections take place? Do I have to bring my own rusty machete?"

"I'm having a party this weekend, to celebrate my eighteenth birthday. We rented out this new club downtown called Tomb. The party's kind of Indiana Jones themed, but you don't have to show up in costume or anything. I thought you might like to come with me. As my date. Full disclosure, though, there will be other fine women competing for my affections, so you might need that rusty machete."

He's asking me on a date. And he's funny and he likes Indiana Jones and I could listen to him recite train timetables in that gorgeous Irish brogue of his.

Surely if I spend some time with Sean Montgomery, perhaps in a dark corner of his party with his tongue down my throat, this bleak nothingness will lift and I'll feel *something*?

It's worth a shot.

"Can I bring Euri?" I ask. "She's kind of the only person I know at this school."

"You know me."

"True, although I may yet decide to run you through with my rusty machete. At some point during this birthday party of yours, you're going to ditch me to perform some embarrassing hip hop dance or chug twelve vodka-and-Tabasco shots and puke in a bucket. And I'd like someone to hang with while that's going on."

"What about your stepbrother?" Sean says. "You know him, right?"

More than I'd like to. "Yeah, but now that I've met him, I'm keen to stay as far away from him as possible."

"That's always been my motto when it comes to Cas and his friends," he says. "Vic's all right, but I can't trust him, y'know? Torsten's mother owns Tombs, though, so they might be at the party, if that's going to be a problem? I heard something happened at lunch, but I've been in the music suite all afternoon so I don't know all the details."

"The music suite?"

"Yeah. I play guitar, bass, violin, drums, flute, Irish whistle... I'm recording an album as part of my college application, and the bloody thing's doing my head in."

He's a musician? Be still my heart.

Only, my heart *is* still. Because even though hot, funny, Irish musician Sean deserves a page in the Fergie Munroe flickopedia, the only thing I feel around him is cool indifference.

Maybe I can change that at the party. Maybe I can obliterate the memory of Cassius' rough finger on my clit or Vic's teeth scraping my neck—

"There you are!" Euri appears beside me, out of breath. "Sorry, I'm late. Simone Kahn cornered me by the tampon dispenser to ask me about Cassius' ban on—" Euri chokes on her words. "Oh, hi Sean."

"Sean was just inviting us to his party on Saturday."

"He was?" Euri's voice sounds like someone just offered her a truckload of free puppies. "Um, is that a wise idea, after what Cassius—"

"I think it's the wisest thing anyone's said all day." I grin at Sean. "Euri and I would love to come to your party. We'll meet you there. What time?"

"8PM until late." Sean leans in close to graze my cheek with his lips. "See you then."

As Sean walks away, Euri loops her arm in mine and leans her head against my shoulder. "What are you *doing?* You can't go to a party with Sean Montgomery."

"Why not? Does he have a forked tongue or something? Because that could be fun—"

Euri drags me down the corridor like she doesn't hear me. "—and I can't believe Sean would break the *sacer.* Does he have a death wish? Because this is suicide..."

"What are you talking about?"

"...unless... he *doesn't know.* That's it, of course he doesn't know. It hasn't got all over school yet, and if he walks through the Atherton building, he won't see the mark. Which means it's not too late for you to turn Sean down, and maybe they never have to find out—"

"What mark? Who will find out what? You're not making any sense." I'm getting annoyed with her. "If you're high, I want some of what you're smoking—"

"Oh, Fergie. You didn't hear, did you?" Euri sounds exasperated. She yanks me through the crowd and slams my hand against a locker door. I can feel something painted on the door – the paint dry but still a little soft. "This is your locker."

"Someone painted graffiti on my locker? How very public school."

"Cassius did it." Euri's jaw is so tight I'm afraid she might break it if she talks much longer. "Or rather, he had one of his underlings do it. It looks like bear claws – that's Cassius' symbol. This is his *sacer*. It means you're untouchable."

"*Excuse* me? The fuck?"

What is she talking about?

"A sacer is like, a symbol. A mark. Painting this on your locker means you belong to the Poison Ivy Club," Euri says. "No guy in this school is allowed to fuck you, date you, or even *talk* to you without their consent."

"What the *actual* fuck?" I am going to *kill* Cassius. *Who fucking does that?* "That's insane. Not to mention stalkery and chauvinistic. What if I want to date a girl? This is insane."

"Oh, most girls will stay away from you now, too." Euri sounds sad. "No one wants to risk Cassius' wrath. It's dangerous to even be your friend now. It figures the one time I meet someone cool and get an invite to an *actual* party, we can't show our faces because your stepbrother will paint the walls with blood."

"Who says we can't go?"

"Fergie, you don't get it. If they find out you're Sean's date, even if all he does is hold your hand, they'll *kill* him." Her voice trembles. "I might not even be safe. This is *fucked*."

"You're right about that. No matter how many Paddington bears Cassius doodles on my locker, I don't belong to him. I'm not his fucking property." Euri yelps as I wrap my fingers around her wrist and pull her in close. "Listen to me, we are *going* to that party, and Cassius Dio and his fucking *sacer* can suck my lady boner."

14

FERGIE

"That was a crazy day. Do you want to hang out after school?" Euri asks as she swings through the door to my last period Government and Politics class. Her voice is back to her usual bubbly tone, completely oblivious to the students muttering insults at her as they try to shove past her to escape. "We could get some ice cream and wander down the beach and chill a bit, so you don't go home and knock Cassius' head off."

"I can't today." *Or any day.*

"Oh, okay." She sounds a little hurt, but she doesn't press. "Are you getting a ride home with Cassius?"

"I honestly have no idea." I don't have his number or any clue where to find him, and I don't exactly want to be stuck in a car with him and Victor after today. I do still have *some* sense of self-preservation.

"No problem. I can give you a ride."

Euri must be sighted enough to see the expression on my face.

"Relax, silly. I'm not driving, *obviously*. My sister's picking me up. We can drop you on our way."

I don't want to accept a ride from Euri. Things with her are already veering far too close to friend territory for my liking, but I *am* curious to meet her sister – the sister who Cassius and his friends absolutely did not push down the stairs. "Yeah, thanks. I'll just call my dad and find out our address—"

"No problem. I know where you live."

Okay, yeah, of course she does. If Cassius is one of the most popular guys in school, he's probably had a million parties at Cali's mansion. And I guess in a neighborhood like the ultra-rich and exclusive Harrington Hills, everyone makes it their business to know their neighbors and who their neighbors are fucking.

We walk out to the pickup zone, and Euri holds a car door open for me. I slide into the backseat, folding up my cane and slipping it into the pocket on the front of my backpack.

"I told you not to bring home any more strays," a bright, musical voice calls from the driver's seat as Euri climbs in front.

"I swear, this isn't like that puppy, or the Acheron Academy debate leader who smelled like moldy cheese, or the exchange student from Finland who turned out to be a bitcoin scammer," Euri weedles. "Meet Fergie. She's Cassius Dio's new sister, and I said we'd give her a ride home."

"Hi, Fergie. I'm Artemis. I'm the cool one." Artemis tries to sound upbeat. A sighted person might not notice the way her voice tightens, but I'm trained to listen to cues in inflection and tone.

Is it the mention of Cassius' name that's put her on edge?

"Hi, thanks for the ride. And if you're wondering, I'm not exactly thrilled to be sharing a house with my new stepbrother."

"You don't have to tell me," Artie says through gritted teeth as she pulls away from the school and lands us in the middle of a mess of chaotic traffic. "No doubt my sister's explained that I'm not Cas' number one fan."

"It's not as if it's some secret," Euri says. "Everyone at school knows what Poison Ivy did to you. And to Preston Bainbridge. And to Spencer du Pont. And all those others. That's the problem. Everyone knows what Poison Ivy does, but no one will talk. I'm sick of it, and if you'd seen what happened today you might see that I'm not the only one calling for their downfall."

"What happened?" Artemis asks.

"The Poison Ivy Club cornered us in the corridor," Euri's practically jumping in her seat. "They wanted Fergie to eat lunch with them, but she wanted to stay with me instead—"

Actually, I wanted all of you to leave me the fuck alone, but sure, we'll go with your version.

"—and they got all up in her face. First Cassius, and then Victor."

Euri launches into the story of me licking Cassius' nose, and how I sent Victor flying. "You should have seen Victor go down. *SPLAT.* Straight on his too-perfect face. It was *spectacular.*"

"It was no big deal," I mutter.

"It's a very big deal," Euri insists. "And all day people have been congratulating her. We even got invited to Sean Montgomery's party this weekend, although we can't go because Cassius put out a sacer on Fergie."

"You've been at school *one day* and they put a sacer on you?" Artemis isn't impressed. She sounds like she's ready to toss me out the car window. "You know you can't go to that party, right?"

"I don't want to live in fear of the Poison Ivy Club," Euri says in a small voice. "I think we should—"

"Euri, *drop it,*" Artie barks, her voice rattling with fear. It sounds like this is a conversation they've had a hundred times before. We stop at a traffic light, and her leather seat creaks as she turns around to talk to me. She tries to brighten her voice as she changes the subject. "What I can't believe is that Cali Dio actually got *married.* Is your dad an international arms dealer or something? An underground fight promoter? A mob boss?"

Why is she asking this?

"If my dad was a mob boss or an international arms dealer, do you think I'd just tell you?"

"Around here that's something to be proud of." Artemis turns back to the front as the person behind us lays on their horn. "For every kid at that fancy school who's a reality TV show star or movie executive's love child, there's one whose family money comes from more nefarious deeds."

"Nefarious deeds?" I laugh. "I didn't know I moved to a seventeenth-century pirate's cove."

"You practically did." Euri's knitting needles *clack-clack-clack* away. "Behind Emerald Beach's facade of glitz and glamor is a seedy underbelly of organized crime. And Cali Dio—"

"*Euri,*" Artemis barks. "Let's not discuss unfounded rumors about other people's stepmothers, shall we?"

Yes please, Euri. Let's discuss them all. For the first time since Dad announced he got married in Vegas, I'm *dying* to know more about my new stepmother. But Artemis has that *my word is law* tone in her voice, and Euri's needles *clackety-clack* with renewed vigor, so I'm guessing the conversation is dropped.

I shove my earbuds into my ears, pull up one of my playlists, and crank the volume loud so there's absolutely no way the sisters can talk to me.

I don't turn it down until the car pulls over and Artemis yells that we're at my place. I grab my backpack and almost make it out of the car before Euri asks for my number, but I pretend I don't hear her and make a run for it.

As I tap up the path to the front door, a cold ice shard twists in my chest. I *like* Euri. Dammit. I don't want to like her, but she seems cool, if not a little earnest. She gets being a blindie, and she seems to be on a crusade to bring down my stepbrother, which is a cause I can get behind. I'd love to get ice cream with her, or ask if she wants to go shopping, but—

That's the sort of stuff friends do together, and I'm not falling into that trap ever again.

15

FERGIE

"Miss Fergie, I'm glad to see you." Seymour throws open the door. "When Master Cassius showed up without you, I didn't know what to think. I was just about to head down to that school to find you."

"I appreciate it, Seymour. But I got a ride from a..." the word *friend* sticks in my throat. I can't call Euri that word, even if it's pretend. It feels too close to losing myself. "...a girl in my class."

"That's good. I know *She* will be pleased to see you settling in." Seymour steps back so I can move inside. "I've installed that lock on your bathroom door."

"You're a legend, Seymour," I yell over my shoulder as I trudge upstairs. I'm starving – I hardly touched a thing during lunch – but I can hear voices in the kitchen, and I don't particularly want a confrontation with my stepbrother and his friends.

Even though Vic's touch makes me hot and fluttery all over, even though Cassius' wild, destructive nature perfectly matches my own. Even though Torsten and I seem to speak a language no one else understands...

No. As tempting as it is, I'm not putting myself in the middle of that delicious sandwich. Not when Cassius Dio thinks he owns me.

I enter my room and check the brand new lock on the bathroom door. My shoulders sag with relief. At least I won't have to worry about Cassius sneaking into my room in the middle of the night.

I flop down on my bed, arrange the pillows behind my head, and breathe.

Day one is over.

It wasn't terrible. I floored a guy. I taught Torsten how to read Braille. I met a fellow blindie. I got asked on a date by a hot Irish musician, and my stepbrother drew a bear on my locker.

I didn't die.

And the best part is, I've been so distracted with everything that I've barely thought about college admissions.

Except for the thousand times I thought about it. Except for when Euri invited me to help her with the paper and her panel and I wanted to throttle her.

I flick through my phone and stick on an old Nick Cave album, *Lyre of Orpheus*. I shift on the bed, my skin itching. I'll never get used to lying around doing nothing. After The Incident, Dad took me out of school, and I spent a few lost weeks curled up in bed listening to true crime podcasts again and again, like *My Favorite Murder* and *My Dad is a Gerbil,* trying to lose myself in the stories of people who've had their lives ruined like mine. Now that I'm over the moping phase, I miss the busy schedule of extracurriculars and AP homework and college practice essays that defined Old Fergie's life.

What do normal kids do when they're not in a million clubs or desperately trying to add community service projects to their college applications? The rest of the evening stretches out before me. I have homework I can do, but what's the point? I've done most of it before.

I haven't explored the rest of the house yet. There's probably a TV room or something. Or...

I could find Dad.

We've hardly talked in the last couple of weeks. He's been busy packing up the house, closing his Witchwood Falls practice, and talking over details of the move with Cali in late-night phone calls that last hours. But it's more than that – since The Incident, we don't know what to say to each other. We haven't even really talked about his Vegas wedding, and why he didn't tell me about Cali or ask me to be there—

"Hey, Fergalicious."

As if I've conjured him with my thoughts, Dad appears in my bedroom door. He calls me by my childhood nickname – it's from some hip hop song that was big when he was young, seven billion years ago. "How was the first day?"

"How do you think?" I sit up, patting the bed beside me, suddenly so desperate for him that my bones ache. We used to be so close, but we don't know how to talk to each other anymore. Too many secrets stretch between us.

Dad crosses the room and sits down beside me. His thigh presses against mine, but he feels a million miles away.

"You don't have to go to school if it's too upsetting," he says. "You can take the rest of the year off, hang out here if you want to, figure out what you want to do."

Yeah, I bet my evil stepmother will love that.

"I can help you find a job," he continues. "Maybe doing something other than school would be good for you. You've had tunnel vision about Harvard for so many years, you might enjoy a chance to live in the real world for a bit."

"I've had enough of the real world, thanks." I'm pissed that he's offering now, when six weeks ago I suggested he take me on as the secretary at his new practice and he turned me down, said he needed someone with more experience, as if I couldn't have learned his stupid patient record system in an hour. "School's fine, Dad. I want to graduate and be done with it, then at least I'll have something to show for four years of work."

"Fergie…"

A hard lump rises in my throat. I swallow it down. "You might've told me my stepbrother was my age."

"I didn't?"

"No. You didn't. I thought he was going to be a twelve-year-old with a snotty nose. Instead—" I can't quite get the words out to describe Cassius, so I kind of gesture toward his bedroom. 'The Violation' by Fleshgod Apocalypse blasts through the wall, the bass making the wall shake.

"I'm sorry. I truly thought you knew, and you haven't exactly wanted to talk lately. You've been kind of spaced out ever since…" Dad swallows. "Since it happened."

Since The Incident.

'Yeah, well." I toy with the edge of the silk duvet, trying to think of something to say. So much happened today, but I can't tell Dad any of it. I can't say I took down the most popular boy at Stonehurst or that I got invited to a party at a club by a gorgeous artist, and *especially* not that Cassius banned every guy in the school from asking me out, or that I slept with my stepbrother on this very bed not twenty-four hours ago. So I settle on one thing I *can* tell him, one thing that might convince him I'm not going to fuck up our new life. "I made a new friend today. Her name is Eurydice Jones, and she seems nice."

Once again, my throat catches on the word friend. The lump rises closer, tickling the back of my mouth. I'm dangerously close to crying, and I don't know why. It's not as if I haven't lied to my dad before.

"That's good, Fergie." Dad's voice tightens.

"Yeah. She's a knitter. She's going to knit me a scarf. And she asked me to join the school paper and I…"

As soon as I say the words, I know they're a mistake. Dad sighs.

"You know you can't do that. What Cali did for you, for *us,* it's amazing. We wouldn't have been able to start over if not for her. But you know what it means, right?"

"I know, Dad." I have a clean slate. A new beginning. Which is more than I deserve. But new beginning means *new beginning.* Wiping away The Incident means saying goodbye to my 1540 SAT score, my jiujitsu gold medals and championship belts, my years of volunteering, my award-winning articles for the *Witchwood Falls World*. All of it wiped away, tainted by one stupid mistake.

A clean slate means that I have nothing to put on a Harvard application.

It means I'm out of the running for an Ivy League school.

And it means I can't give anyone in Emerald Beach a reason to look deeper into my life, to find the one Rio championship video we haven't managed to scrape from the internet or the old picture of me from the Witchwood Falls yearbook and blow our second chance. I can't do anything to stand out or rise to the top. I have to lie low, be a nobody. No extracurriculars, no top marks, no jiujitsu. Cali made it clear to my Dad that this is the only way her plan will work. And I get the impression it's the only way she'll accept me as her stepdaughter.

I agreed.

Because I've already hurt Dad so much.

Because the alternative is too hellish to think about.

I'm the girl who's had Harvard pennants on my bedroom wall since I was nine years old. And now I'll never get to step behind those ivy-covered walls.

If I graduate senior year with decent – but not top – grades, and take the SATs again, I *might* be able to pull a miracle and get into somewhere like Duke, if Dad even lets me go. Or I can wait a few years, get a job, and try as an older student. Maybe by then The Incident will be ancient history and no one will care. But who in the real world is going to hire a blind girl without a college degree?

Thinking about both those options makes me feel... nothing. Nothing at all. Where I used to see my future perfectly laid out, now it's just white noise inside my head. Like turning on the TV when the network is down.

Dad pats my leg. "We'll figure this out together, Fergalish. You've worked so hard for so long. It breaks my heart to see you..."

His voice cracks. I can't turn my body toward him, because I'm afraid I'll punch him.

You didn't seem like your heart was breaking in your wedding video. For your wedding you didn't want your own daughter to attend.

I get it. I fucked up his life. Why would he want me to celebrate with him?

Dad straightens his back and pats my knee, all traces of emotion wiped away. "I know there's a bright future out there for you. Sometimes things don't work out the way we planned, but we have to make the best of them."

I squeeze my eyes shut. I can't deal with Dad-plaititudes right now. "Did you *really* take up tennis?" I blurt out.

He laughs, but it sounds a little strained. "Cali wants me to stay fit. I think it's a good thing."

Since when has Dad ever wanted to be *fit*? He once joked to me that lifting the TV remote counted as cardio. When I was eight, he agreed to be a parent supervisor on our school camping trip, and half a mile into the first hike he got a cramp and spent the rest of the weekend in the cabin watching *Stargate SG-1* episodes on his phone.

Who is this person? He doesn't even *smell* like my dad

anymore. Instead of the mint and antiseptic scent that usually clings to his work clothes, he smells muskier, darker. Cali has to wipe away his old *smell*.

"It's a good thing," I say, because that's what he wants to hear. The lump of coal in my chest grows a layer of ice around it.

"Listen, I want you to get to know Cali, give her a chance. You hardly said a word to her last night."

"She hardly said a word to *me*."

"Fergus." Dad only calls me that when I've pissed him off.

"I'll *try*, Dad. But is it even wise for me to become best buds with her? Isn't she like, *really* famous? People at school know who she is. They talk about her like she's a mob boss or something—"

"You should know better than to listen to rumors," Dad snaps. I wince. I meant it as a joke, but I've struck a nerve. "Cali is a successful businesswoman in a competitive, male-dominated industry. She's tenacious and uncompromising, like someone else I know. I think if you got to know her, you'd come to admire her greatly. It's time for you to stop dwelling in the past, Fergie, and open your eyes to the new opportunities around you."

I tried that, and I ended up opening my legs for my stepbrother.

I raise an eyebrow. "But is it normal for 'successful businesswomen' to have access to people who can create false identities—"

"*Enough*." Dad shoots to his feet. His anger squeezes the air from the room. "I know you're used to having things your way, but your free pass for being an ungrateful brat stops *today*. We're a family now. You, me, Cali, Cassius. And you're going to start acting like it."

We were already a family, I scream inside my head as he slams my door and storms down the hall.

I skip the last classes of the day and head over to Cali's dojo. An advanced knife-skills class finished yesterday, so the place is crawling with fighters keen to have their turn in the ring of sweaty men brawling in the main gym. When I walk past, one guy has another in a headlock, but the victor isn't even focused on the fight – he's grinning at the mirrored glass that covers one wall of the gym.

"She's not even here," I growl as I storm past. The stench of sycophants hangs heavy in the air – most of these guys don't come here to learn new skills. They're here because they want to be recruited by my mother. She rarely picks her soldiers from the *hoi polloi* – most come through contacts and recommenda-tions – but every cocksucker signing up for a beginner Krav Maga course thinks they're good enough to catch the eye of Cali Dio.

I know better than most that Cali doesn't see what's right in front of her face.

On a normal day, I barely have the patience to deal with the meatheads at the gym. But today, the red mist closes in, and I know if I don't get my medicine soon, I'll make another fatal mistake. I crash through the doorway on the opposite wall of the gym, slip down a narrow hallway, and shove open the first of the private sparring rooms.

Inside, a Russian mercenary has a Philly street fighter in a headlock. *Excellent.*

I'm ready for my medicine, Doc.

They're so engrossed in the fight they don't even notice as I stride onto the mats. I pick up the Russian by the back of his thick neck. He barks something at me, but his words cut off as I slam his head against the wall.

Again and again and again.

The red mist crowds the edges of my eyes, creeping toward the center. It's been a long time since I've had to feed the monster that lives inside me.

I squeeze my eyes shut, but all I see is her face. Fergie Munroe, staring up at me with those unseeing, accusatory eyes.

That enticing flash of rage in her quirked lips right before she flipped Victor over her shoulder and slammed him into the tiles.

It was the same look she wore when I plowed into her, when she came apart on my fingers.

She lost control. She existed completely in the moment.

And when Fergie Munroe loses control, she burns everything down. I know because that's exactly what I do. Like recognizes like, and my darling stepsister and I, we're two peas in a fucked-up pod.

I had her once, but I lied to her, and I lied to myself. And now she hates me even more than I hate her, which was exactly my plan.

So why can't I stop obsessing over her? Why does thinking about Vic kissing her, touching her, fucking her, make the red mist descend?

Now that Fergie's glimpsed the real me, she knows the

monsters that lurk inside her new home. And she *should* run straight into the arms of Victor August. Because Cali and I will destroy her. That's what gets me hard, after all – the blood, the tears, the pain.

That's why Cali gave her to me. I'm sure of it. That's why she snarled at me this morning that I have to 'look after my new stepsister.' Because my mother needs me to hang on to my tenuous grasp of control.

With Gaius gone, she has no choice but to give me exactly what I want.

And not even my best friend will take that away from me.

I open my eyes. All I see is red. At first I think it's the mist taking over completely. But it's not. It's the Russian's blood spilling over my fingers, spraying the front of my black tank.

I unclench my hand from the Russian's neck. He crumples into a heap at my feet.

He doesn't move.

His blood streaks down the white plaster.

My muscles ache from the effort of gripping him. Blood dribbles from my fingers, creating gory Rorschach patterns across the mat. I kick him, and his body flops over, his face angling up to me, eyes glassy and lifeless.

I killed him and I didn't even *notice*.

Fuck.

Cali will *eviscerate* me. She just had these rooms renovated.

The red mist pulses.

Sensing the oncoming slaughter, Philadelphia lunges for the weapons rack along the back wall. He pulls out a katana, but before he can unsheath the blade, I'm on him.

A few minutes later, I stand over a pile of blood and gore and broken bones, my body heaving as I gulp in lungfuls of air. The red mist swirls in time with my heartbeat.

Fergie Fergie Fergie.

Her name pulses in my bloodstream.

Wait until she finds the little surprise I left on her locker.

My stepsister.

She's mine, not Victor's. Not anyone else's. *My* toy to play with. Cali gave her to me as a peace offering. I know that's what this is. There can't be any other reason for my mother to marry that boring dentist and bring them both into our home. Somewhere in her black heart, my mother loves me.

She knows exactly what I need.

I beat two more idiots into a bloody pulp before the red mist retreats and I'm calm enough to go home. My muscles scream, and the few hits and cuts my opponents got in sting so good.

As I head for the exit, smearing bloody handprints down the wall, I pass Cali, dressed in skintight leather pants and a sports bra, carrying a claymore on the way to her office.

Her eyes flick over my bloody physique with disapproval.

I know, I know. Gaius never lost his cool, not even in a fight. The perfect son did every job with the precision of a brain surgeon, without spilling a single drop of blood on his immaculate Armani suit. I'm everything he's not. But you and I are more alike than you think, Mother. You're starting to see that.

"There's a Philly street fighter in room 3 in need of Galen's expert hands," I say. "He's not half bad. He'd make a good soldier."

"Once he's healed," she murmurs.

"Yeah. Might be a few weeks. I think I broke his leg."

She narrows her flint eyes at me. "You're supposed to be at school. What happened to keeping an eye on your stepsister?"

No lecture about breaking her students this time. More evidence that I've worn down that stone veneer of hers.

"Don't worry, I've taken care of it." I think of the slashed bear claws I had Xavier paint on her locker. "No one will so much as touch her. You have my word."

"Your word is worth shit," she says. "I have enough to worry about without John freaking out about his precious daughter."

"You don't have to worry about Fergie. And, Mother?"

Cali narrows her eyes. She doesn't like the word *mother*, since hers sold her to Constantine Dio when she was eight years old. Cali never let me or Gaius call her that. We had to address her as Cali or ma'am or – as her soldiers do – simply *She*.

I bow my head to her, a sign of respect drilled into me from years of training. "Thank you."

She raises an eyebrow. "For what?"

"For my gift."

Cali nods and disappears into the gym, confirming what I already knew.

She meant Fergie for me.

Mine. Mine to have. Mine to ruin.

I walk outside. The crisp night air bites my wounds, and I love the feeling. I whistle to myself as I hop in the car and drive over the Acheron to Harrington Hills. No matter how many times I pull up at that fancy house, it never feels right to me in the same way the club does. I think Cali feels the same. That's why – despite its success and ample funds to move to a more prestigious location – the club is still across the river in Tartarus Oaks. Cali only moved to Harrington Hills to be close to Claws and Livvie. She didn't want her soldiers thinking the Augusts and Lucians had more than us.

I pull in beside my brother's beloved Bugatti Veyron, now covered in a fine layer of dust, and head up the back stairs from the garage. I don't want Seymour to see me. He'll freak about getting blood on the waxed floors.

It's not because I'm afraid of running into Fergie. Not at all.

I needn't have worried, because I hear loud music pounding from behind her locked door as I pass her room. I head straight to the library, not even bothering to shower. Muffled voices echo through the thick doors. As I suspected, they're all here without me.

I punch in my code and crack the door an inch, straining to hear. *I bet they're talking about the shit I pulled at school today.*

"—I'm telling you, Victor. It's a past participle."

"No, it's not. It should be a gerund," Victor shoots back in that pompous *I'm-right-and-you're-wrong* voice of his, the one that just begs for his face to be punched in.

"Shove your gerunds up your ass and rotate. If you're going to be a grump, you can finish my Latin for me, and I'll pour us another drink. Do you think Cas will mind if we crack open that twenty-seven-year-old bottle of Islay he's been hiding behind the Churchill biographies—"

"Don't you touch my Laphroaig," I growl as I step into the room. Juliet snickers.

"I *knew* you were there, Cassius," she sighs dramatically as she flops down onto the sofa. "I could see your hulking mass through the crack in the door. You're not exactly subtle."

Victor snaps shut his Latin book. "Cas, you—"

I storm across the room and snatch the book from his hands, tossing it into the bookshelf. It bounces off and lands on the drinks cart, smashing several crystal glasses onto the floor. Torsten looks up from his journal long enough to glare at me, a joint dangling from between his lips, then returns to his furious scribbling, his legs propped up against the window ledge. I notice he's stuck weird clear stickers over some of the pages in his book, but I'm not interested enough to ask what they are. I don't understand art.

"We need to talk," I snap at Vic.

"I think so."

Vic leans back in the leather wing-back – his favorite chair, I think, because it's where Gaius used to sit. Because as much as he's only in Poison Ivy because of me, Victor sees himself as my brother's heir. I let him because, honestly, I can't be fucked with the organization that goes into running our little enterprise. I just want to break things. Break people.

Right now, I want to break Vic's smug, aristocratic face.

I try to shove Juliet's legs off the sofa so I can sit down, but she shrieks and slaps me.

"Don't touch me." Juliet wrinkles her nose. "Vic, he's covered in blood and he smells like an abattoir. Make him have a shower first."

"Jules, can you give us a minute?" Vic lifts an eyebrow at her. He sounds tired.

She huffs, but she swings her legs off the sofa and flounces into the hallway. A moment later, the door slams so hard a couple of poetry volumes topple to the floor.

Vic stands and moves to the bookshelves. He reaches behind a set of gold-stamped volumes and pulls out a slim bottle of precious amber liquid. He breaks the seal, pours a dram into his glass, and hands me the bottle.

We know each other too well.

The leather crackles as Vic leans back again. He raises the glass to his pretty-boy lips. "What happened today?"

"You got the shit beaten out of you by a girl," I smirk. "I'm surprised you can talk with your balls lodged in the back of your throat."

"Cas..." he sighs. "You said you hated Fergie. You said she doesn't matter to you."

"She doesn't."

"You're lying to yourself."

I gulp from the bottle, tasting the Russian's blood mingled with the smooth whisky. "I don't know, okay? When you touched her, I realized the real reason she's here."

Vic crosses his legs. "Enlighten us."

"Cali gave her to me. Think about it, Vic. Why else would

she bring someone so goddamn *tempting* into our house, to live in the room right next to mine? You saw what Fergie did today. That wasn't a lucky move – she's had training. Our little blind firecracker can *fight*. Cali knows that, and she knows how much I'll enjoy breaking her."

"Cas, I don't—"

I hurry on. "It explains why Cali married the dentist – this is a job. Cali's been hired to torture the Munroes. She hasn't told me why, but that's not important. What's important is that she wants me to help. Fergie is my gift from her, my toy to break however I choose. And this time, I don't want to share."

Vic swirls his glass around in his fingers. "You may be right. That would be just the kind of sick mother/son bonding activity Cali Dio would come up with. But did it ever occur to you that maybe this isn't a job for your mother? Maybe she *fell in love?* I'm told it's happened before."

"Yeah, she fell for a ruthless killer who instigated a coup within the Triumvirate," I scoff. "My mother is *not* in love with that drip with the drill. It's a job, pure and simple."

"Okay, so let's assume you're right," Vic says. "So how about this? You go after your stepsister with that sadistic Dio rage, if that's what makes you happy. But when you break Fergie, I want to be the one who puts her back together again. Can you deal with that without going all wild bear on me?"

I spit my mouthful back into the bottle. *What is this shit?*

I assume that he's kidding, but when I look over at my friend, I see that he's deadly serious. He wears the same noble, tender expression he had on that day four years ago when we got Juliet back. Victor August *must* be the protector, the savior, the man holding everything together. No wonder he's fallen hard for our little blind dove.

He looks fucking *royal* in his immaculately-pressed school blazer and tailored trousers, artfully tousled dark hair flopping over one eye. He exudes poise and confidence and protectiveness – everything I'll never be.

Victor and Fergie – I can see them now. They fit together like puzzle pieces – his strength and her impulsiveness, his stoicness and her fire. They could rule this city together. That's what he's imagining right now as he sips my whisky with one Oxford scuffing my coffee table. He imagines Fergie wearing the August crown and ruling beside him, her belly round with his child.

Fergie is a queen and Victor is born to rule.

I stare down at my bloody clothes, at the whisky bottle in my trembling hand, at the scars and cuts on my hands and the bright-colored ink spilling down my arms.

All you do is break things.

My brother's final words to me echo in my head. My stomach twists, the pain sharp and heavy, like a blade tearing my flesh.

Devotion. Tenderness. Intimacy. Those things are for people like Vic. Monsters like me don't deserve love. My mother taught me too well. I'm not capable, not when my heart feel like it's made of teeth and bone. I'm too far gone for even a girl like Fergie Munroe to save me.

All I am is blood and dust and violence.

But, if she survives me, when I'm done with her, Victor will make her the queen she deserves to be. And *maybe* knowing that she'll never be mine will finally turn off that last shred of humanity inside me. Maybe I'll finally become the man worthy of my mother's legacy.

I raise an eyebrow at my best friend. "We have a deal."

17
_____

CASSIUS

After Vic and Juliet leave, I sneak Torsten back to my room. Cali is still at the club, but I don't know where the dentist is, and I can hear Seymour and Milo in the kitchen. I can't have the staff seeing Torsten and reporting back to Cali. Vic and I made plans to check him into a hotel this week but I'm too on edge to deal with that today.

We walk past Fergie's room. The music still pounds through her walls – it's an old Broken Muse record, the first they did with Gabriel Fallen on vocals. I once ripped a guy's fingers off to this song. She has good taste.

Thinking about my stepsister behind those walls, banging her little head to the violent beat, makes me hard for her all over again.

Fuck.

We enter my bedroom. Torsten collapses into the chair under the window, his hair curtaining his face as he flips open his journal again and continues scribbling. If he has any thoughts about the agreement Vic and I made tonight, he doesn't share them.

"I'm taking a shower," I say, tugging off my bloody shirt as I head for the bathroom.

"Don't," he says without looking up. "She's in there."

As soon as he says it, I realize I hear the water running. Steam curls from the crack under the door. Fergie's in there right now – in the shower, belting out the lyrics to 'Unleashing War.'

Naked.

Dripping wet.

And she can't see me.

My dick throbs against my zipper, hard as a preacher at choir practice. I think about my stepsister squirming beneath me yesterday, the way her warm body yielded to my touch, and then how she fought me like a gremlin the moment she realized I played her.

So fucking hot.

I know what people say about me. I know the rumors that spread like wildfire around Stonehurst Prep about what girls let me do to them. About the knives. About the bruises and the wounds no one can see. About how I need blood and violence to pull back the red mist.

Every one of these rumors is true.

I need more and more brutality to get my rocks off. Now, I can't even come unless I have their tears. Even the most enthusiastic girls – even the ones who come so hard they black out from what I can do to them – never return for a second go.

But all Fergie Munroe has to do *is* exist and I'm walking around with a permanent elephant eyelash.

My mother really does know what I like.

I glare at Torsten. "I'll do what I please with my gift."

My fingers grip the door handle. I push it open a crack and poke my head into the room. Steam obliterates the mirror and fogs the shower glass, but I can make out the shape of her standing under the jets, her long neck bent back in ecstasy as she runs her fingers through that flame-colored mane.

"I've sharpened my steel," she sings, loud and powerful and completely off-key. *"I've made my sacrifices. I'm unleashing war."*

And as beautiful as she was spread out on her bed for me yesterday, those long legs wrapped around me to draw me deeper, she's even more beautiful now that she's vulnerable, completely unaware of my presence. She can't hear over the thrashing music as I yank down my zipper and slide my stiff cock into my hands.

The cool air from my room de-fogs the glass a little as Fergie turns away from me and bends down to pick up the soap. My eyes rake across her long, toned legs before resting on that glorious plump ass of hers. I fist my cock and stroke slowly, keeping my breathing as silent as possible.

She turns, drops the soap, squeals with annoyance, and bends again. It's like my own private show. My cock pulses in my hand. My balls tighten. A hot, heady ache rumbles in my chest. *Any moment now...*

Fergie twists around to face me, but she can't see me. It's so fucking filthy. She sings a little quieter now as she rubs the soap over her torso, taking extra care around her breasts. Her nipples are hard, dark pebbles and I remember how she squirmed when I bit them. My stepsister likes a little pain.

I slam my other hand over my mouth as an involuntary moan escapes my throat.

I pump harder, my grip so tight I'm surprised I don't pop. Forget getting sucked off by Lucila Baskerville in the school bathrooms. This is where it's at.

My firecracker of a stepsister, dripping wet, her glorious body all mine for the taking.

She's completely oblivious that she's living in the den of a monster.

Fergie turns off the shower and grabs for the towel. I suck in a breath as I jerk my hand hard, thinking she's going to cover herself before I can finish. She rolls the towel up in her hands and steps out of the shower toward me, reaching for the hair dryer she placed on the sink. Before I have time to react, she flicks the towel through the air like a whip.

The towel catches the head of my cock. The pain is immediate and crippling. It arcs through my body like wildfire. I grunt as my cock explodes, the tension in my body released in a burst of utter pleasure. A rope of cum splatters across the floor.

"I knew you were here, Cassius," she hisses.

Fuck.

She draws the towel back to try again. I stand up, my cock still stinging, and grab the towel, tugging her toward me. Her wet, naked body presses against mine, and although her face sets in a look of utter contempt, her crimson lips part a little, and I know a dark and secret part of her *liked* that I was watching, and I...

...I'm flooded with a sensation that's so unfamiliar to me it's terrifying. A sickening, weak desire that Fergie Munroe might *crave* a monster. That I wouldn't have to give her to Victor to put back together again, because I wouldn't be able to break her.

My bones fizz with the impossible dream that there might be someone who could stare into the ghastly depths of my soul and see their own soul reflected back.

No.

I squeeze her naked body against me, cherishing every squirm and wiggle and disgusted growl, feeling how tiny and vulnerable she is, how breakable her bones are. I can't allow myself to drown in sentiment, in impossible dreams. Fergie may be stronger than most, but she will break. I always find a way to break them in the end.

I'm Cassius Dio, and I break the pretty things.

"Thanks for the show, *sis*," I laugh. "But if you want your pussy eaten so bad, all you have to do is ask. I'm always here for you, like a good big brother."

She uses a martial arts break to free herself from my grip and spin away. As she does, she slips on the jizz I smeared across the floor, and has to grip the edge of the sink to prevent herself from falling. Her chest heaves from the fright, and when she turns her head to me, her eyes are wide.

And I want so badly to run to her and gather her in my arms that I bolt back into my room and slam the door behind me.

Torsten drops his journal and watches me, a curious expression on his face.

What?

What the fuck was that?

I'm the Bear. I don't comfort frightened lambs. I tear them to pieces.

What's wrong with me?

Fergie's fists pummel my door. "I'll kill you, you bastard. Don't you *dare* watch me in the shower again. I'll tell my father. I'll tell your mother. I'll make them send you away to military school."

"It's adorable that you think you have that kind of power, sis," I call back. My voice sounds totally normal. But inside, I'm a mess.

She continues to bang on the locked door. I jump on the bed and pull the sheets over my head, rolling on my side so Torsten can't see that I'm rock hard for her.

Again.

Some monster I am. I'm supposed to get off on watching her in secret, on knowing she feels that crawling sensation on her skin that tells her she's not alone. I'm supposed to strip away everything that makes her feel safe. And yet, I'm the one lying in bed feeling like I've been set adrift in a dark, unforgiving sea.

Don't lose your head, my brother's voice soothes me as I plump my pillow and try to sleep. *You have a job to do. You're Cassius Dio, and you were born to bathe in blood and fire.*

That's right, my little firecracker, I think as my fingers trace the ghost of her touch on my skin. *I'm going to have so much fun breaking you.*

18

TORSTEN

I lie stiff in bed, staring at the ceiling while my mind whirs like a blender, chopping each individual thought into a gelatinous soup.

Finally, Cassius drops off to sleep. I turn over and watch his chest rise and fall for a bit, marveling that even a monster like Cas becomes human when he sleeps. Weak. Vulnerable.

I count backward from two hundred, and then I get up. Cassius doesn't know that sometimes when my mind is racing, when the sound of air whistling in his nostril and the smell of dried blood on his laundry and the chemical gloss of the paper of his porn magazine collection becomes an assault, I leave his room and go outside to have a joint, or wander around the house. I like it here more than at Victor's place. With Victor and Juliet and their four parents and all Eli's animals, there's too much noise. Too many smells. My brain can't take it. But Cali likes her house white and stark and clean. She barely even has any artwork on the walls. Sometimes, if I walk and drink in that white and flap my hands, I can quiet my mind.

If Cassius found out I'd been doing it, he'd kill me. Cali doesn't know I'm still living here, and if she found me, she'd tell

Livvie and it would cause a rift between them. Luckily for me, Cas sleeps 'like a corpse,' my mother would say. And she would know – she's buried a lot of them.

I have no hope of sleeping while Fergie's in the other room. The scent of her bath products wafts under the bathroom door, barricading me inside my head where all my monsters reside.

If I could just *see* her, maybe it would help. Like scratching an itch.

I creep through the bathroom. Her raspberry scent clings to everything. It's so thick that it has a weight, that it fills my lungs with rocks. I try the door to her room, and it's locked, but I studied the mechanism Seymour installed when I got home today, and I know exactly how to disable it. I take out the tools I hid under my pillow and get to work.

I don't want to do this. I know it's wrong.

Four minutes later, the lock falls out of the door onto the rug in her room. I push open the door, taking my time to make sure I'm silent. I step over the broken lock and creep toward the bed.

Now that I'm here, I don't know what I'm going to do. All I know is that I had to see her. And this way, I can talk to her. I can say all the things that I want to say.

Fergie.

She's so beautiful. Her hair fans out across the pillow – her long, dark eyelashes flutter as she experiences REM sleep. She's dreaming right now, and there's a slight smile on her lips, so I think it's a nice dream. She looks like a Titian painting – Danaë reclining in her bed, bathed in golden light.

"I wish I could paint what you dream," I whisper as I kneel beside her and place my cheek on the duvet. The fabric is soft and smooth and cool against my skin. It smells of Seymour's laundry detergent, fresh summer raspberries, and something deeper and darker, something I cannot define. "Do you see in your dreams? Do you dream in colors? I want to ask you so bad, but everything I say is wrong, so it's better if I don't say anything."

But I can say it now. I can say all the things bursting in my chest, and if they're wrong, if *I'm* wrong, then she'll only hear them as echoes in her dreams.

That's all I can ever be to her. An echo.

Cassius and Victor have claimed her. I'll never go against them. It would be wrong, a betrayal of their friendship. It would be pointless. Why would she consider me when she has them? Cas did exactly what he always does – he promised her pain and bloodshed, and she spread those long, sculpted legs of hers for him.

Victor wants her because he has to believe he can fix broken things, and he's sick to death of me – his failed project.

They'll do what they always do. Cas will break her, like a child pulling the legs off a spider because he doesn't know how to be gentle. He will crush her under the weight of his need for affection. And Vic, he will hold her up on a pedestal and worship her, and what can I offer her that's more desirable than that?

I don't even understand what desire is.

But I can't help it. I want her. Fergie doesn't look at me like I'm a freak.

If she is Cassius' gift and Victor's queen, why can't she also be my heart?

I watch her chest rise and fall, the questions burning inside me.

It's not explicitly written on Victor's list of things I shouldn't do in public because they scare people, but I think it's implied that watching someone while they sleep is not okay.

I'm not okay.

I lean over. I plant a kiss on her forehead. She stirs in the sheets, her pink lips parting a little. I can't help it. My hand trembles as I reach over and touch the tip of my finger against her soft lips. Her breath kisses my skin. It's so exquisite it makes my chest burn.

She parts her lips a little, letting out a soft moan. I slip the tip of my finger inside. Her mouth is so warm, so wet. Her tongue flicks over the end of my finger.

My whole body shudders. My dick hardens. I forget how to breathe.

What does it feel like to have lips like that wrapped around my dick?

I'll never know. It's too much, too much. The warmth and the wetness awaken every shame and insecurity inside me. They're soldiers, lining up in ranks to report for duty, to crush me beneath self-hate. Every inch of my skin *shrieks* – a sensation that is so visceral I jerk my finger from her lips and smash my hands over my ears. But I can't stop the shrieking. It's inside my body. It's me.

This is wrong. *I'm* wrong.

I fling myself away from her. I intended to replace the lock after I'd talked to her, but I couldn't do it now. I throw it on the bed beside her and flee into the bathroom.

I can't go back to bed with Cassius' whistling nostril, so I shut myself in the shower and sink to the floor. I turn on the water, ice-cold, and let it fall over me.

Even after sitting under it for hours, my skin still sizzles from the warmth of her lips.

19

FERGIE

I wake to the scent of vanilla, honeycomb, and orange zest.

The strange dreams that punctuated my sleep float in my subconscious. I haven't dreamed in colors since I was about seven – it usually takes a blind person around five years to lose visual memory. Instead, I dream noises, smells, and sensations. And last night, I dreamed about Torsten – the silent one, the artistic one, the one who learned Braille so he could talk to me.

I dreamed about his lips on mine, soft and firm and yielding. I dreamed about touching him, holding him close so he couldn't run. I dreamed about feeling safe in his arms.

And now my room smells like him. I lean back into the pillow and breathe deep. It's so *real*. It's as if he was in here.

I throw out my hands to pull off my covers, and my fingers graze something rough and metal.

I bolt upright. My fingers splay over the object. It's cold, hard metal.

It's the lock for my bathroom door.

Someone tore it off and smashed it to pieces, and left it in my bed for me to find.

"So, Fergie, listen," Sean Montgomery leans against the locker next to mine while I check the battery life in my Braille display. "About my party this weekend."

"Yeah?"

"I'm real sorry," Sean's voice swings as he looks over his shoulder again. "I didn't realize when I invited you, but the venue has a 400-person capacity limit, and you're number 401. So would you be okay just... not coming this time?"

"Is this about this stupid bear Cassius drew on my locker?" I slam the door shut and lean in close. "Because I'm not afraid of my stepbrother."

"You should be." Sean draws away. "So, don't come on Saturday, got it? Okay, bye."

He tears off down the hall like I have ebola.

Euri's distinctive sandalwood perfume appears at my side. "What's going on? I just saw Sean running away from you."

"We just got uninvited to Sean's party," I say.

"Um, yeah, of course we did." She sighs. "You can't blame Sean – he's practicing self-preservation, something you could learn."

"I can't believe people pay attention to some decree Cassius hands down like he's the Zeus of Stonehurst Prep."

"I told you, people are afraid of your brother. And for good reason."

"What about you? You're still talking to me."

She shifts awkwardly. "I am."

"So my brother can't be that scary."

"He is. I just..." she sighs. "Maybe I've been pretty lonely, okay? And maybe I've decided it's worth faring Poison Ivy's wrath to hang out with you."

"That's the spirit."

"Yup. So I'll see you in the greenhouse for lunch?" Her voice rises like a hopeful puppy dog.

"Yeah. Okay."

Euri bounces off. I slam my locker door and lean against it, hugging my books to my face.

I've been at this school one day. *One fucking day.* I met Euri. I even had a date for the weekend. I got a taste of being a completely normal teenager again. And then my stepbrother had to steal it away.

If Cassius thinks he can ruin my life, then he's got another thing coming.

He may have this whole school running scared, but I don't back down from a fight.

21

FERGIE

I n Chemistry class, I slide into my seat beside Torsten. He doesn't say a word to me. Instead, he grabs the Braille labeler from my bag and starts typing away.

I'm halfway through filling out a worksheet on gases when he sticks a message to my iPad. I'm impressed. He seems to have memorized the Braille alphabet and mastered using the six keys on the labeler to make the symbols.

HAVE YOU HEARD OF THE PAINTER GEORGIA O'KE-
EFFE? SHE PAINTED ABSTRACT VISIONS OF FLOWERS,
ROCKS, SKULLS, LANDSCAPES. SHE LOST MOST OF HER
VISION IN 1972, BUT SHE HIRED ASSISTANTS TO HELP
HER DRAW ON HER FAVORITE MOTIFS FROM MEMORY.
AFTER HER VISION LOSS, SHE FAMOUSLY SAID, "I CAN
SEE WHAT I WANT TO PAINT. THE THING THAT MAKES
YOU WANT TO CREATE IS STILL THERE."

I haven't heard of Georgia O'Keeffe, but then I've never had time for art. It's a sightie's lark, one of the many things in this world that are held back from me.

I am curious about what Torsten scribbles in his journal, though. Euri says that he doesn't draw his own work – he only copies others. I wonder why that is.

And I need his help, so I grab the Braille labeler from him and type him a note back.

THANKS. I HAVEN'T HEARD OF HER. IT'S INTERESTING THAT SHE PAINTS WHEN SHE CAN'T ENJOY PAINTINGS. MAYBE SHE SHOULD'VE TRIED SCULPTURE. WHAT DO YOU THINK?

Torsten spends a good fifteen minutes on his next note, and what he sticks onto the iPad next is a long list of facts about O'Keeffe and her life and her work. At the end, it says.

I BROKE THE LOCK IN YOUR ROOM. I'M SORRY. I WANTED TO TALK TO YOU.

I assumed it was Cassius trying to freak me out, but Torsten's admission makes me realize the scent of him on my sheets wasn't from my dream. It was real. He came to see me last night, while I was asleep. It should disgust me, but it sends a deviant thrill shooting down my spine.

I wonder what he sees when he looks at me. I wonder what he said to me. I wonder if that's why my dreams were filled with his lips.

I type back.

YOU DON'T HAVE TO BREAK INTO MY ROOM TO TALK TO ME.

I hear him make a strangled noise. A couple of minutes later, he slaps a label onto the back of my hand.

IT'S EASIER TO TALK WHEN YOU'RE ASLEEP.

And I think I understand. I have so many things I want to say to him, mainly about staying the fuck out of my room, and if his lips really are so soft in real life – but I'm on a mission, and I need his help. And right now, he seems to want to talk through Braille, so we'll roll with that.

IT'S OKAY. JUST DON'T DO IT AGAIN. WE CAN TALK LIKE THIS, ANY TIME YOU WANT. I WANT TO TALK TO YOU, TOO, ABOUT WHAT CASSIUS DID TO ME? THE SACER.

I stick the note onto his journal and slide the labeler over to him. I wait a few moments.

We haven't even got our equipment out for today's experiment, but Mr. Dallas is preoccupied with a table at the front who have a bunch of stupid questions. Torsten sticks a label to my hand. It's short.

YES.

Okay, then. Time for phase two. I tap out a note and stick it to his notebook.

I ALSO HEARD THAT YOUR MOTHER OWNS NIGHT-CLUBS AROUND EMERALD BEACH.

Torsten grabs the Braille labeler from my hand and heaves it across the room. I hear it crash into the wall and smash on the floor. A couple of people gasp, and Mr. Dallas yells Torsten's name.

"What the fuck did you do that for?" I snap. I need that labeler. I use it all the time.

"You're only talking to me because of my mother," he rasps, scraping back his chair.

"I don't give a fuck about your mother. I'm talking to you because I enjoy it, but if it's a big deal then I won't bother you anymore." I pick up my cane and stand up, just as Mr. Dallas arrives at our table.

"Mr. Lucian, you will apologize to Ms. Munroe right now. And report to Mrs. Emerson's office where you can discuss replacing her equipment that you so callously broke."

Torsten ducks around me and bends down to pick up the labeler. "It's fine," he says. "There's just a scratch here. It still works."

"Good." I snatch it out of his hands and stomp back to our table. I hear him sigh as he drags his feet toward the door. I slump down in my seat, holding the labeler in trembling hands. *I can't believe he did that.*

I thought Torsten was the most normal one out of the three musketeers, but I'm wrong.

"Why did you run away from me?"

I look up from the lunch. Euri makes a choking noise and drops her knitting needles. Torsten Lucian is standing in the greenhouse, agitation rolling off him in waves of orange scent. He tried to talk to me in my European Lit class, but I moved to another desk and ignored him. I didn't expect him to leave the safety of his friends in the dining hall to find me.

I move to stand, but Euri grabs my arm. "Don't," she whispers. "You don't know what he's capable of."

"I'll be fine. If I'm not back in ten minutes, alert the media."

I sweep my cane across the uneven cobbles as I join Torsten

on the other end of the greenhouse, near the lily pond. I can feel Euri's eyes on me.

"Why did you run away?" he asks again. His voice catches on the word *run*, and even though he sounds angry, I'm pretty sure he's distraught.

"Because I'm angry at you. Because you threw my Braille labeler at the wall. I don't just use that machine for writing secret notes to cute guys in Chemistry class. I need it to label things so I know what they are. I need to because I don't have eyes, because the world isn't made for people like me. And you tried to take that away from me. So I was angry. I'm still angry, and I still don't want to talk to you."

"I'm sorry," he says, simply and without hesitation. "I just wanted you to stop talking about my mother."

"Well, it worked." I turn to go.

"*Fergie.*" He speaks my name like an incantation, loading so much meaning and so much pain into that one word that before I can stop myself, before I can think, I've turned back around to face him.

I fold my arms across my chest, and shoot him a frown that I hope doesn't give away the thudding of my heart against my ribs. "What do you want from me, Torsten?"

"Back in class, you wanted to ask me something," he says.

"I did, but it involves the woman-who-shall-not-be-named, so forget about it."

"You said you use the labeler to send notes to a cute guy in Chemistry class..."

"I mean you, Torsten."

He sighs, and it's the sound of such raw, genuine pleasure that it clouds my skull with euphoria. I don't know what Torsten looks like, obviously, but I don't know how anyone can hear him speak and not think he's the most gorgeous man alive.

"Why were you asking about my mother?" he says.

"I thought that through your mother's contacts you might be able to get me something I need. I have a plan to show Cassius Dio he can't control me." I wave my hand in the air. "It's fine, I'll do it another way. I should probably leave you out of it, anyway."

He grabs my wrist, his fingers burning my skin. He doesn't squeeze or bend it like Cassius would. He doesn't try to move closer, to get further into my personal space. He simply holds my hand in midair, breathing so hard that his orange scent caresses my cheek. "I'll help you. I'll do anything for you."

22

TORSTEN

"I don't want you here any more than you want to be here." Cassius leans against the doorframe of my suite, staring at the red velvet furnishings and gilded mirrors with an expression of utter disdain.

"I know." I'd much prefer somewhere stark and modern, like his house, but while the decor at The Elysium would make Liberace avert his gaze, it's also one of the only establishments not owned by Olivia Lucian.

I kick off my shoes and sit on the end of the bed. I hate this room. It's large, with huge windows overlooking the boardwalk at Brawley. It would be quite pleasant if it wasn't crammed with so much stuff. My face glares back at me from three heavy gilded mirrors. There's even a stuffed peacock in the corner, its beady eyes following me around the room.

I hate myself more. I know I should tell Cassius about what Fergie asked me to do. That's what a friend would do. I open my mouth, but I can't form the words. I don't want Cassius to find out.

I want to help Fergie. I don't want Cassius to hurt her.

Cas is still talking, still justifying why he's brought me here.

"—if Cali catches you in the house, or Livvie sees you there and thinks Cali knows, it could cause problems for them, and that's the last thing Cali needs right now—"

"I know."

"Right. Of course you do. I've paid for the room until Christmas." Cassius removes a vase of flowers and several small animal figurines from the table by the door and tosses them into the coat closet. He knows this place must be hell for me. "So you don't have to worry. And if you run out of sketchbooks or charcoal, call down to the front desk and they'll run out and get you some. It's that kind of place."

I nod, because that's what Victor says I should do to let people know I've heard them.

"Okay, so you're good, then. I have to get to the gym. Cali's got me on this intense training schedule for Lupercalia. She doesn't want me to embarrass her. I'll pick you up for school, and for the party on Saturday? We don't have to if you don't want to." He grins at me. "We could call one of your mother's girls, score some blow, have our own party right here."

Cassius is always trying to get me to sleep with a prostitute. But I spent far too much time amongst them growing up. All that perfume, the sequins, their skin that always feels sticky. It's too much to think about.

Besides, I don't want to miss Sean's party. This time it might actually be interesting.

"I think we should do the party," I say. "Sierra is going to be there. You can take care of a bit of Poison Ivy business."

"You're better at this than you think." Cassius kicks a decorative urn into the closet and slams the door. "I'll come back with a drill and we'll take down the mirrors, okay?"

"Okay. Thanks, Cas. See you."

Cassius leaves, slamming the door behind him so hard that the entire wall shudders.

I'm alone.

Alone with my funhouse reflection and the smell of bleach and hotel soap and a thousand guests who've come before me.

Alone with the flowers on the carpet and the memory of Fergie's wicked smile taunting me with what I agreed to do.

I don't just use that machine for writing secret notes to cute guys in Chemistry class.

I light up a joint and pace the length of the room, smoking while I carefully step on the petals of the flowers and avoid the brown voids of space between them. The same thought spins around and around – I can't do it. I don't want to do it. She can't make me do it.

When I look up, two hours have passed.

I grab my phone and search her name. THE BITCH pops up. It's a small rebellion, labeling her that, but it makes me smile.

I hit CALL.

She answers on the second ring, her voice breathy. I can hear music in the background. She's at one of her clubs. "Torsten."

"Olivia."

"I told you not to call me that. I'm your mother—"

"You're not," I say, even though I know it will make her angry. I can't stand it when she lies, and she lies so damn often.

"I raised you. I fed and clothed you. That's what a mother is, Torsten, not a collection of DNA." She sniffs. "You're in a room at The Elysium, I hear. Is that where you've been all this time? Who's paying for that? August money? Or is it Dio? Is my son living it up off profits from the corpses dismembered by my dear friend Cali?"

I don't say anything. If I open my mouth, I'll tell her that Cassius is paying for me to be here, and that will get him in the shit, more than he already is.

"To what do I owe the pleasure of a phone call from my prodigal son?" Livvie demands.

It takes me a few tries to get the words out, but I explain what Fergie needs and when. It's a testament to my mother's parenting skills that she doesn't ask what I need this for.

"You can't ask Cassius or Victor for this? I'm sure they'd understand. I'm not the only source in Emerald Beach."

"It's not for me," I say. "It's for a friend. It's... a secret."

"Oh, a *friend*. She's a lucky girl." Livvie purrs into the phone, "Consider it done, my son. Now, I think that such a magnanimous gift deserves a little something in return."

"Then it's not a gift," I say. I knew all along that this favor would cost me.

"I want to see you again. You will come to dinner with your family, next Thursday night. And you will bring this *friend* with you. And I will—"

I hang up the phone and toss it on the bed. *Why?* Why did I call her? Why didn't I tell Fergie I couldn't do it?

Because she smells like raspberries, that's why.

With shaking hands, I pick up my phone again and type out a text to Fergie.

"I've got you what you need, but it's come at a price. I need you to come somewhere with me next week."

The rest of the week passes with little fanfare. Despite the school boasting a huge janitorial staff, the sacer mark on my locker is still there.

Despite this, I refrain from decking any other members of the Poison Ivy Club. No one except Euri talks to me (Torsten doesn't count – he still doesn't talk, but he does Braille notes), and even she avoids me in the halls and crowded areas now that I can make my way around with just my cane. We eat our lunch together in the greenhouse or in the *Sentinel* offices, and plot elaborate revenge plans for Victor, Cassius, and Torsten.

My stepbrother has made me a pariah at Stonehurst Prep. But he doesn't know that it's exactly what I wanted.

It's strangely peaceful having no responsibilities or expectations.

The gossip about me dies down by Friday, when the student body collectively realizes Victor isn't pursuing revenge and the Poison Ivy Club seems to have made up after their spat. All anyone can talk about is Sean's party. The club is supposed to be pretty wild, Sean's band is playing and – although we're all underage – there will be a fully-stocked bar.

Sean's even putting on a prize for the best costume – a photo-shoot with his father, the famed photographer Liam Montgomery.

Rich kids. I cannot *even*.

In amongst all the party excitement is chatter about the upcoming October SAT sitting, which I do my best to ignore. When Euri and her sister pick me up or drop me off, it's all they talk about – Euri's taking the SAT again to try and get a 1500. Even when I shove my earbuds in I can hear the drum of vocabulary words in my head.

But it beats being molested by Victor's cock in Cassius' car. Or maybe it doesn't. Old Fergie would be swapping notes with her new friend, safe in the knowledge of the 1540 she got in the August sitting. New Fergie won't even bother sitting the SATs and dodges the question every time Euri brings it up.

By Friday, my jaw hurts from gritting my teeth so hard.

Not even curiosity about dinner with Torsten's mother next week keeps me from dwelling on what I can't have. I'm ready for a party.

I'm ready to fuck shit up.

I ask Euri to grab me a container of paint from the art suite, and instead of going to final period I paint the entire bank of lockers sunflower yellow. I'm through with this shit.

AFTER ARTEMIS DROPS me home on Friday, I practically skip into the kitchen for one of Milo's after-school snacks. Milo's not there, but he's left warm slices of *baklava* on the counter. I grab two and turn at the sound of the front door, wondering if Dad's home early for once. He's been working late every night this week – which seems weird for a brand new dental practice, but what do I know?

Honey dribbles down my hand as I bite into the pastry. *Gods bless Milo and his Turkish phase.*

"Hey, sis."

I jump out of my bones.

Cassius.

I hadn't even heard him behind me. How long had he been standing in the corner of the kitchen, watching me devour sticky pastries? My skin prickles, like I'm a voodoo doll and Cassius is using me to curse an enemy he really hates.

Ever since I caught him jerking off to me in the shower, I've been feeling him everywhere, smelling his plum and musk and carnation scent in places he shouldn't be – the spot in the greenhouse where Euri and I eat lunch, the girl's gym lockers, the back of my closet where I keep my underwear drawer. But this time he caught me unaware, and I hate that.

Why does he have to see me covered in honey and pistachio crumbs?

Why do I care what he sees?

"Why are you talking to me?" I snap at my stepbrother. "Aren't you breaking your own rule?"

"Someone painted over my mark," he smirks. "Perhaps the rules no longer apply, *Sunflower.*"

I smirk at his stupid nickname. It's not exactly Death Lily, but I'll take it.

"We've missed you in the mornings," Victor says, his hand sliding over mine. Fuck, I didn't know he was here, too. I really did let my guard down. "The car ride isn't nearly as fun with Torsten on my lap."

I catch a whiff of vanilla and orange zest. *Great, all the merry men are here.* "Milo left us a snack."

"I swear he thinks we're still ten years old," Cassius says, but I hear him pick up the plate. No one says no to *baklava.*

"Milo was here when you were ten?" I ask before I can stop

myself. I know nothing about having staff. I assumed you had to replace them every few years after they got sick of literally cleaning up your shit, but then I remember that Cali sent Milo and Seymour to Turkey for their anniversary, which doesn't seem like the kind of thing my wicked stepmother would do for just anyone.

Cassius grunts, his jaw crunching on the hot pastries.

Victor's fingers curl around mine. I don't remove my hand.

"They've lived here ever since I can remember," Victor says. "Seymour built a treehouse for us in the garden. I think it's still there. I could show you—"

"Victor," Cassius snaps. "Let's go."

My stepbrother probably can't hear Victor's sigh, but I can. Victor drops my hand, his fingers lingering. "See you around," he whispers.

The three of them clomp upstairs, no doubt heading to their secret clubhouse – the room at the end of the other hallway, the one with the elaborately carved doors and the high-tech security. I know I won't be invited.

Fine by me. I have a fun evening planned. No boys allowed. I have an audiobook I'm enjoying. It's by this author named Steffanie Holmes, and it's about a girl who gets a scholarship to a creepy boarding school in the middle of nowhere and ends up falling for three of her bullies. All I need is snacks, booze, and my vibrator for the perfect Poison Ivy-free evening.

There's got to be some booze in this house somewhere. I open doors and root around in cupboards, but I can't find any wine or whisky or beer. Not even a single drop of cooking sherry.

Duh, of course. A house like this will have a fancy wine cellar.

I grab my cane from where I left it leaning against the island, and tap and click my way back through the dining room until I reach the staircase that leads to the basement. I've walked past it a few times and heard music blaring and Cassius grunting from a home gym down there, so I haven't ventured further because I'm not sick enough to willingly initiate an encounter with my stepbrother while he's in the midst of roid rage.

Now, it's blissfully silent.

I head downstairs and make the clicking noise with my tongue, getting a sense of the space. It's enormous, stretching the entire length of the house, I'm guessing, and divided into a few large rooms. I feel around, mapping out the main space containing rows of La-Z-Boy armchairs, a massive TV screen, a pool table and arcade games, even a popcorn machine, but it's all covered in a fine layer of dust. Why don't Cassius and the guys hang out down here? This room is *brilliant*.

On the back wall, behind the roulette table, I locate a fully stocked bar, complete with a wine fridge and shelves of spirit bottles and apparatus for making cocktails. I can't tell what anything is, so I toss two wine bottles and a random spirit under my arm and start back across the room. I'll drink anything. Not like my stepbrother, who judging by the pretentious conversation I overheard with Seymour the other day, has a thing for fancy Scotch.

I click my tongue to help me locate the edge of the pool table, and as I do, I realize there's a large door to my left. That must lead to the gym. I step toward it, curious about what equipment Cassius has down here. A sharp, cold breeze brushes my face. It's faint – a sightie probably wouldn't notice it, but I'm trained to notice these things.

A draft? That's odd. This house is sealed up tighter than a nun's proverbial. I don't hear any AC or a fan left running. Curious now, I step into the gym area and click my tongue again. My cane makes sweeping half-circles on the floor, and I navigate around weight benches and squat machines until I locate the source of the draft.

It's coming from between two panels on the wall. Judging by their smooth surface, I'm guessing they're mirrors so my step-brother can watch himself lift. I press my ear against the mirror. Cool air kisses my cheek. I rap my knuckles on each of the mirrors. The left one sounds different from the right, as if there's a space behind it.

What is this? Shoddy building work, or something else...

"What are you doing?" a sharp voice demands.

I jerk away in surprise. My head cracks against the mirror, and I drop my cane as I fumble to hold onto the bottles.

"I said, what are you doing to the mirror?" Cali's voice rasps with anger.

"Oh, I came down here to find something to drink." I hold up a wine bottle. "And I felt this draft from the gym, and I thought maybe there was some damage I should tell Seymour about or something."

"Seymour already knows about that... draft," Cali barks. "You can leave now."

I hate her. She's nothing like the soft woman in the floaty skirts who smelled like roses that I remember from childhood. I wasn't old enough when Mom died to have clear memories of her, and of course my visual memory is mostly gone now, but I know my mother was kind and good and fun. *I can't believe Dad fell for this woman. She's horrible.*

I have to give her a chance. For Dad. Remember, she did help me. She gave me a new life.

"Cali?"

"Yes?" she snaps.

"Um..." I had no idea how to start a conversation with her. "The woman who decorated my room – you called her Livvie. Is that Olivia Lucian, Torsten's mother?"

She grunts. "What about her?"

"I was just wondering, um, how did you two become friends? I've talked to Torsten at school and he's lovely, and he wants me to meet her, and I guess I'm hoping for a bit of background so I can make a good first impression—"

"My relationship with Olivia Lucian is none of your business."

"Right, okay. I was just trying to make conversation—"

"If you want to make a good impression on her, I suggest you convince her son to wear pants to dinner."

"Okay, but—"

SLAM.

I wince as the door to the gym bangs shut. Cali's gone.

24

CASSIUS

Torsten's mother's latest club is pretty much the same as all her other clubs – all flash, no substance.

But Livvie Lucian does love her flash, and she's gone all out with Tombs. The old warehouse has been transformed into a pharaoh's tomb, with towering columns decorated with gold hieroglyphs. The dance floor is on three levels, linked by staircases and secret passages behind old, crumbling pillars. More of Livvie's gold-painted girls dance from gilded cages hanging from the ceiling, and bring platters of grapes and cocktails to the VIP tables on level two. The crowd spills into the side rooms, where they find themselves locked in tight spaces with strangers and puzzles to solve to find the key. Judging by the number of patrons emerging with their clothing rumpled and lipstick smeared, they're finding a lot more as well.

Above them all, we chill in the VIP area, which is decorated like an ancient banquet with low couches to lie on, red and gold cushions, and even a couple of women to fan us with giant fronds, dressed in nothing but gold body paint.

Victor sips a milky cocktail served in a ceramic snakeskin cup. He's come in costume, dressed as Indiana Jones in a wide-brimmed fedora, khaki wool twill trousers and brown leather jacket, and a safari shirt with most of the buttons undone, revealing a smattering of ink across his pale chest. Lucila Baskerville sits in his lap, picking grapes from a platter and feeding them to him. Beneath her short toga-style dress, the curve of her ass bears red welts from where Juliet flogged her with Victor's whip.

He looks completely bored.

I knock back my third shot – I don't know what it is but it tastes like raspberries and has a candy eyeball floating in it. The alcohol courses in my veins. I may not have a girl writhing around on my cock, but I'm anything but bored. I scent blood in the air tonight.

"Don't drink too many of those," Victor scolds me. "We need the pictures to be in focus."

"Yes, mother," I smirk as I throw back another. The sugar raspberry sticks in the back of my throat. It reminds me of Fergie. But I'm determined to push her out of my mind tonight. I have a job to do, and besides, my stepsister is at home, holed up in her room with her metal music and her new nerdy friend Eurydice – she's exactly where she should be.

A smile tickles my lips whenever I think about that stunt she pulled with the paint. My stepsister has *fire*. It's going to make it that much more satisfying when I pull the petals off my little Sunflower, one by one.

Even though she painted over my mark, the *sacer* still holds. I don't have to spend all night making certain no one touches my property, so I can focus on other things. Maybe there's a girl in this room who'll hold my interest, make me forget about that fiery red hair and those long legs for a couple of hours. Maybe I'll take a video and send it to Fergie, another way to break her down, to mind-fuck her into submission.

But first, the blood.

Torsten leans over the railing, watching the crowd below. "Jason's on the move," he says, his words barely audible over the pounding music. "He's slipped backstage."

"Good. Where's Sierra?"

"She's at the bar, talking to Candice Fairbrother... no, now she's crossing the dance floor. And now she's backstage, too."

"Showtime." I rise to my feet, slide my phone out of my jacket pocket, and head downstairs.

The dance floor swallows me as I push my way toward the stage. Sean Montgomery and his band are up there, belting through their set. I heard Sean invited Fergie to be his date tonight. He's lucky he dumped her, because I'd hate to rip out the throat of someone with such a decent singing voice.

I push my way through the backstage door and press myself against the wall. *Jason said it would be just around this...*

"Is that all you've got?" Sierra's whiny voice breaks through the muffled music. "I have SATs coming up, and a flute exam, and varsity tryouts. I need more than this."

"I have other clients," Jason says. "If you want more, it'll cost you."

I lean around the corner, my phone poised. SNAP SNAP SNAP. Sierra grabs an unmarked pill bottle from Jason's hand, shoving a handful of cash at his chest. He fishes out a second bottle and dangles it in front of her face. She lunges for it, but he holds it out of reach.

SNAP SNAP SNAP.

Jason leers at her as he leans in close, whispering something in her ear. She blanches, and for a moment I think she's going to slap him. Her lower lip quivers. She tucks a strand of blonde hair behind her ear and drops to her knees. Jason's head tips back as she pulls down his zipper.

I stop taking photos. Jason's going off-script. We have strict rules about how we treat women. If someone wants our services then the price is always negotiable, a cost of doing business, but we don't use sex to blackmail. We have plenty of dirt on the Stonehurst Prep elite without resorting to that sickness.

I hope Jason enjoys Sierra slobbering all over his cock, because once I'm done with him, he won't have much use for it.

"Fuck yes," Jason moans. And I can't help but think of Fergie's soft lips and fiery glare, how she'd never kneel like that for anyone, and how fucking majestic it will feel when she finally kneels for me. Even though I'm disgusted by this entire situation, I'm also hard as a fucking rod.

I'm done with this.

I step out from behind the wall.

"Hello, Sierra," I grin. "Fancy seeing you here."

She screams and jerks away.

"Ow, fuck," Jason moans, collapsing against the door and clutching his crotch. "That was *teeth*, bitch."

"Serves you right for taking advantage of a woman," I growl at him. "You know our rules, and you broke them. I'll deal with you later. Now, get the fuck out of here. I need to speak to Sierra, *alone*."

Jason shoots Sierra a venomous look as he limps past me. He has no idea that his days are numbered. We don't allow low-life drug dealers to use Poison Ivy's reputation to get their dicks wet.

Sierra's still kneeling on the ground, the knees of her figure-hugging dress dirty from the dust and grime back here. I step up to her, grab her under the arms, and hoist her to her feet. She parts her swollen lips to whimper something, but she's so terrified all that comes out is a cute little moan.

"Naughty little lamb," I whisper, wiping a strand of hair from her eyes. "Don't worry, I'll never let him do that to you again. The next person we hire to supply you with your study drugs will learn proper manners."

Her face pales. The container of pills slips from her fingers and rolls across the concrete. She knows I have her over a barrel. "What do you want, Cas?"

"You know what I want," I whisper, my finger continuing to stroke her cheek. "I want you to withdraw your application to Princeton."

"What? I can't do that. Seven generations of my family have gone to Princeton. I can't—"

"You can do anything you want, Sierra. There are plenty of other good schools. Pick one. I don't care which. But you're not going to Princeton." I hold up my phone. "Or Mommy and Daddy see these pictures. Not the ones of you on your knees. Those I keep for my own enjoyment. But the ones where you're buying drugs to help you maintain that sexy GPA of yours. The press might be interested, too – a little drug scandal right when your father's insurance company is going through this merger—"

"You're a cocksucker, Cassius Dio." She spits in my eye.

"I think that's you, Sierra. This isn't personal," I say as I wipe away her spittle on her dress. "It's business."

"One day, someone is going to bring you down, and your stupid club," she snaps. "And I'll fucking cheer."

She runs past me, her heels clapping on the concrete. A moment later, the stage door swings open, leaking in an impressive guitar riff. Sean sings about the girl who broke his heart. I move away from the music, the party, the naive kids out there who have no idea about the real world. I shove through the stage door and into the alley behind the club, where Jason leans against the wall, smoking a joint.

He offers it to me. "No hard feelings, right, Cas? You saw her – she was gagging for it. And it's the whole point of the club, right? We're all out for what we can get."

I take the joint, grab him by the neck, and press the lighted end into his eye.

I told you the air smells of blood tonight.

"WHAT TOOK YOU SO LONG?" Victor demands when I return to the VIP suite.

"I had some unexpected business to deal with," I mutter.

"You have blood on your sleeve."

Instead of acknowledging him, I join Torsten at the railing and peer down into the surging crowd. He mouths at me that something's going on. I lean over, trying to see through the pulsing lights.

Something's definitely happening – people have left the floor to crowd around the club's entrance. The doors to the club bang open. People part like the Red Sea as a horde of guys crowd through the door. They're all naked apart from white loincloths and gold scarab beetles painted across their chests, and they're carrying something on long poles. It looks like...

It fucking *is*. It's a sedan chair surrounded by shimmering gold curtains. Someone is making a grand entrance.

I can't help myself. I lean over the railing as the men pull back the curtains to reveal their queen.

It's Fergie fucking Munroe.

My stepsister has dressed herself like Cleopatra, the dark kohl around her eyes making her shattered emerald orbs appear even larger. A beaded headdress circles her fiery hair. She wears a skintight gold lamé dress with a slit up to her navel that clings to every fucking curve, and a defiant smile that burns through my skin and shatters my icy heart.

She is a work of fucking art.

Two of the guys – two *dead* guys – lift her onto their shoulders and set her down on the floor. She runs her nails down one of their chests, smearing the paint and leaving claw marks behind. My cock leaps to life.

My little Sunflower. I have never wanted something as bad as I want to bend my stepsister over the stage and punish her with my cock in front of everyone.

Victor claps me on the shoulder. "Looks like your sister doesn't know how to obey the rules."

No, she doesn't. And that's exactly why Cali gave her to me. Because she needs to be broken. Because if I can break that fierce spirit of hers, then I can prove once and for all that I'm Cali Dio's rightful heir.

And I'll break every neck in this room if I need to.

How *dare* they all look at her, feasting on her body like she's a slab of meat. How *dare* those gold-painted jizzflaps touch her.

Don't they know she is *mine, mine, mine*?

The men reach into the sedan chair and pull out another girl. It's Eurydice Jones, only she doesn't look anything like the mousy dork we all make fun of. She wears an identical gold dress that shows off the curve of her ass, and with her face made up and her chin held high, she's actually kind of hot.

Beside me, Victor whistles. He's impressed, and very little impresses Victor August.

The guys surround Fergie and Euri as they strut to the center of the dance floor. Sean glances up at me from the stage, and he must see the rage on my face because the band scampers, leaving only little clouds of dust behind on stage. The DJ, though, doesn't know he's a dead man, because he spins a sultry, sexy dance number, and throws out a spotlight. And the crowd parts for Fergie and Euri to dance.

Fergie's head falls back, her hair spilling over her shoulders as she moves to the music. Her hands run over her hips, caressing that fine body. She grinds up against one of her naked servants before letting him flip her over her back to land perfectly on her feet.

She's completely in the moment in that way that only she can be.

Their hands are all over her, pawing at her as she dips and gyrates. I should be down there, making the floor run red with their blood, but I'm frozen in place, hypnotized by the way my sister moves.

Slowly it comes. The rage. The greed, the selfish need to keep her to myself.

The red mist descends.

I don't remember leaving the VIP area. One moment I'm standing beside Vic, the next I have a guy's throat in my hands and I'm squeezing tighter and tighter until he collapses on the floor. A couple of girls scream. The crowd backs up, pressing into the walls and running for the entrance, knowing that at any moment this place will become a bloodbath.

I reach for another gold-painted cumdumpster, but a hand circles my arm.

"Stop. What the fuck are you doing?"

It's Fergie. Of course it is. Only she'd be stupid enough to approach me now.

"I made the rules clear," I snarl at her as I slam my fist into the guy's face. Blood splatters the front of my shirt. "No one else is allowed to touch you. They touched you, therefore they must die."

"You're sick," she hisses. "You know this isn't normal, right? We slept together *once*. That doesn't give you ownership over my body."

"You don't make the rules, Sunflower."

She shoves me back. "I wish it had never happened. Because you're nothing but a fucking mistake, Cassius Dio. I was hurt and vulnerable, and I wanted to forget the fucking disaster that is my life for five whole minutes. It was supposed to be no-strings-attached quick fuck, but I didn't know I was sleeping with the world's biggest baby. I don't want you anywhere near me. Get. Over. It."

You're nothing but a fucking mistake.

Ain't it funny how words cut deeper than any blade?

I whirl away from her. All I see is red. I don't feel myself grab the gold dude, but I hear people scream as his body sails through the air. I hear the crunch as his body hits the wall.

You're nothing but a fucking mistake. Her words pound against my skull. I reach for someone. If I snap enough necks, maybe the words will go away—

I'm facedown on the ground. I don't know how I got here, but a heavy weight sits on my back. Someone else pins my feet. I thrash and yell and bite. Blood spurts between my teeth, and someone yelps. It sounds like Torsten.

"Get the fuck out of here," Vic yells at Fergie as he struggles to keep my arms pinned.

"Wah, wah, wah, look at the baby. His mommy got remarried, and so he's throwing his toys out of the stroller." Fergie taunts me as she pushes Euri toward the door. "Well, I'm not going to be a pawn in your games. Stay away from me, Cassius. You can make your little rules and throw your tantrums, but you don't control me."

"Don't you dare walk away from me," I yell.

Fergie's shattered emerald eyes look right through me, like I'm not even worthy of her fear. My cock throbs with need as she shoots me a final look of disgust, spins on her heel, and storms out of the club.

25

FERGIE

I wake up late Sunday morning, curled up in bed with a victorious hangover. I'm still wearing the gold lamé dress and some random person's tux jacket, although some angel of mercy has removed my shoes, closed the curtains, and stocked the bedside table with a bottle of Gatorade and some aspirin and...

I wiggle my toes on something warm.

Is that a hot water bottle?

It is. Someone made me a hot water bottle.

I've died of alcohol poisoning and gone to Heaven...

No, wait, that's not possible. if I'm in Heaven, my head wouldn't hurt so damn much—

Owwwwwie, my head.

After Cassius' fucking tantrum, Euri and I left the party with our entourage, or what was left of it. She wanted to go home, but I was high on making my point, so I had my boys carry us down the road to another club called the Flamingo. We danced on a table and drank pink Champagne until four in the morning. I vaguely remember some hot guy pouring our drinks and grinding up against me and putting his jacket over my bare shoulders and... holding my hair while I threw up on the DJ.

I haven't had so much fun in a long time.

And the best part of the evening – Cassius' stormy face when I walked away from him. No amount of alcohol could obliterate that victory from my memory.

Although I was definitely drunk enough that the rest of the evening is a blur. I don't remember how I got home. I have a vague flash of being in a car, of throwing up again on the leather seats, of a rich, dark voice chuckling and Euri's cheek pressed against mine...

There's a knock on my door.

"It's open, Milo," I call out. "You're an angel." The chef called up a few minutes ago, saying he'd make me his never-fail, hangover-cure tortilla Espanola with potatoes, caramelized onions, chorizo, and olive oil. Apparently, Milo's done with Turkey now and has moved on to Spanish cuisine.

"I'm not Milo," a familiar rich voice says. Cutlery tinkles as a tray is set down, and the springs groan as someone sits beside me, their warm ass grazing my thigh through the blankets. The scent of dark chocolate and hazelnut churns in my stomach.

It's Victor August.

And I have a sneaking suspicion that I know why he's here.

"What are you doing?" I snap.

"I brought up your breakfast and a hangover shake. Lots of electrolytes." His hand falls on my shoulder, and he pulls my limp body forward and tucks another pillow behind my head. I try to ignore the lingering heat of his hand. "And an ice pack for the bruise on your thigh. A little word of advice, Duchess. Next time you try to get an entire club to dance to 'Walk Like An Egyptian,' don't try to vault over the DJ booth. It doesn't end well."

"I did do that, didn't I?" I rub my temples. "You were with us last night…"

"I don't know what you're talking about."

That smirk in his voice tells me everything.

I groan.

"You were the guy dancing with us. You brought us all that Champagne. You…" I reach for the water glass. "I'm still wearing your fucking jacket."

"Hey, I tried to get that jacket off you when I put you to bed, and you *bit* me." His voice twinkles. "You're a mean drunk, Duchess. Hilarious, but mean."

I growl. More flashes of memory pound inside my skull. Me grinding up against Victor on a table, trying to tempt him into something more, to use his hands and his wicked mouth to quench the fire he stoked inside me. But even though I could feel his hard cock against my thighs, even though I was a fucking mess and would've done anything he commanded in that lush, sybaritic voice of his, he was a gentleman.

Now I remember clinging to him in the taxi after I'd thrown up on his shoes, gushing about how nice he is, how safe I feel with him, how I wish I'd slept with him instead of Cassius.

Urgh, how mortifying.

Victor rubs a finger along my burning cheek, leaving a trail of fire against my skin. "Don't worry about it, Duchess."

"I'm sorry I threw myself at you," I mumble. "How fucking pathetic. I didn't—"

"Don't apologize. You were adorable. And even slobbering drunk, you're extremely hard to resist."

His words rake over my ruined mind. "You… had to resist me?"

He gives me that dark chuckle. "Oh, Duchess. You were grinding that perfect ass of yours against me all night. You probably don't remember that I had to excuse myself to go to the bathroom. *Twice.* And it still took every ounce of self-control to leave you alone in this bed when you were begging me to fuck you like I hate you—"

My cheeks burn with fire. Did I say that? *Fuck, I'm never drinking again.* I yank the duvet over my face and burrow deeper into the silken sheets.

I'm going to hide here forever. I'm going to live in this bed and never face Victor August ever again—

Victor whips the duvet away. He leans in close, so close his breath dances against my lips. "I won't tell a soul about that, Fergie. Or that you destroyed a perfectly decent pair of Brionis."

I'm such an idiot.

I can't talk, can't *think*, when he's so close, when all the air in the room is tinged with dark chocolate and hazelnut. I swallow once, twice. "I appreciate that."

I expect him to pull away, but he doesn't. His fingers tangle in my hair, tugging the strands a little. His chest presses against mine, which doesn't help with the breathing thing. "You're a talkative drunk, too," he murmurs. "Who's Dawson? You kept asking me if I could make Cas kill him."

Shit. I didn't know I'd said *His* name aloud. I can't let Victor or Cas or anyone guess about The Incident. It's the only way this will work. "It's nothing," I mumble. "Drunk girl talk."

"Because the answer is yes. If this guy hurt you, we'll make him suffer."

"It's just a guy from a TV show. I don't even know anyone named Dawson."

"If you say so." Victor draws away. My heart leaps, and I'm ready to grab him and pull him back to me, but he shifts the blankets, grabbing my ankle and pulling my feet out the end of the bed. I'm ready to kick him in the face, but his fingers dig into the arch of my foot. A moan of pleasure escapes me.

"Wh-wh-what are you doing?" I manage to choke out, my

words dissolving into another moan as he rolls my toes between his powerful fingers.

"I'm amazed you danced for so long in those gladiator heels," Victor says, his voice light, teasing.

I roll my head back as he digs his fingers in again. "Wh-wh-why did you follow me? What about Sean's party?"

"I'm bored of Sean's parties." Victor rolls his knuckles into my skin. "But you're anything but boring."

This is a different Victor to the one who licked my neck in the corridor. He's more... normal. He's stripped bare of that Golden Boy image he likes to portray. And he did spend all night looking after us, making sure I got home safe. He never took advantage of me, even when I begged him for it. He made me a hot water bottle. He's giving me the foot massage of *doom*.

It's as if the king of the school *enjoys* looking out for me.

I'm... intrigued. And I won't admit it's because I like hearing Victor talk in that wonderful voice of his, or the hazelnut and chocolate scent of him clinging to the room, or the way his thigh pressing against mine through the blankets makes me dizzy.

I don't want to admit that this guy makes me feel something warm and happy and safe, because I can't ever allow myself to feel that way again. Oh, and because he's Cas' closest friend and what we're doing right now behind my stepbrother's back is *dangerous*.

But I remember him at school, leaning in close, whispering that he's trying to diffuse Cas, asking me if I'm afraid he'll bite. And I *have* to know...

"In the corridor at school... you said you were trying to stop Cas—"

"I've been around him long enough, I can see when he's about to go nuclear. And you rile him up like no one else."

"So then why are you here? With me? Why are your fingers... ooooooh... doing that to my foot?" I moan as he massages his thumb in exactly the right place. "You're his closest friend. Why are you protecting me from him, but at the same time, provoking his wrath?"

Victor drops my foot and leans over me, capturing my jaw in his hand, tilting my chin up so that our lips brush against each other. My breath hitches. I bet he can feel my heart pounding against my ribs.

"I don't know that anyone can protect you from Cas." Victor traces the line of my jaw with his strong fingers. His chocolate voice rumbles inside me. "But he's not the only monster in this town."

He kisses me.

The kiss isn't the explosion of need I experienced with Cassius. It's a slow burn. It's the kind of kiss that begins in your toes. It warms my entire body, and that warmth grows and burns until it is a fire that races toward its igniter, that flows and ripples and *consumes*.

I reach up and grab the collar of Victor's shirt, pulling him closer. I'm greedy, desperate for more of him, ready for something to obliterate the memory of what my stepbrother did to me on this same bed. And the fact that it's Victor, and that Cassius would kill both of us if he finds out, makes it that much hotter.

"Fuck, you taste so good." Victor breathes as he tastes my lips. His leg swings over me, and I buck my hips up, grinding against him, cursing the satin sheets that are tangled between us.

"Quit teasing me, August," I groan against his lips. "I want you inside me, *now*."

A wild groan escapes his throat. He tears himself away from me, throwing his body off the bed. He lies on the rug, panting like he's run a marathon or something.

What the fuck?

"Get back here," I yell.

"I... can't." Victor's voice sounds strained. "I made him a promise."

"For fuck's sake. For the last time, Cassius Dio doesn't own me. And he doesn't own you, either. You already kissed me. What does it matter what we do now?"

"I'm sorry, Duchess. You have no idea how sorry I am." Victor scrambles into the hall. He slams the door behind him, leaving me alone with my hangover and a raging ache inside me that not even my favorite vibrator will extinguish.

26

FERGIE

At school on Monday, I'm ignored by everyone. Even the teachers don't call on me in class. Honestly, after Cas' outburst in the club sent four of the male strippers I hired to the ER, I don't blame them.

I'm surprised to hear from Euri that no one's painted over the yellow lockers. Maybe Poison Ivy wants them to stay as they are – to remind everyone what they do to people who cross them.

My blood will show up better on sunflower yellow paint.

All weekend long, I've been hiding in my room. I expected my stepbrother to lose his shit, but I think this is part of my punishment. He wants me looking over my shoulder. I know he'll retaliate.

I tell Euri to stay away from me. I don't want him to hurt another innocent person because of what I did. Those strippers were just doing their jobs, and now one of them may not walk again. And I heard a senior named Jason has dropped out of school because he lost an eye that night. What did Jason do to deserve that?

The unfortunate thing about being an outcast is that with

nothing to distract me, I can't help overhearing conversations. And every conversation that isn't about me and Cassius is about the SATs and college prep and the admissions panel Euri organized.

The only class I look forward to is Chemistry. Torsten still won't say a word to me, but we fire Braille notes back and forth. He tells me about another blind artist and a woman with synesthesia who paints the music she hears. I love that he wants to tell me about these things. I ask him what I should wear to meet his mother, and he suggests the gold dress I had on at Tombs. I think that might've been a joke.

I ask him if Cassius knows about the dinner, or that he helped me, and he says no. I intend to keep it that way.

On Thursday, Torsten asks me to meet him at his mother's house. By some small miracle, Cassius doesn't seem to be in his room, but I still bolt both my doors (I got a new, fancier lock on the bathroom now, and one for his door, too) so he can't come into the bathroom while I'm showering and applying my makeup.

I shimmy into a red silk dress with a flared, A-line skirt, and chunky-heeled boots, and pin my hair off my face with shiny clips in the shape of ivy leaves.

Seymour told me he'd bring a car around when he finished watering the garden. I decide to get a cup of coffee while I'm waiting. I'm shaking with nerves, which is ridiculous because I'm just doing this as a favor to Torsten. It's not like it's a date or anything.

Because I'm not dating in Emerald Beach. Especially not a guy in the Poison Ivy Club. Especially not when it could bring the wrath of my stepbrother down on Torsten's head.

I enter an empty kitchen, realizing too late that I've never asked Milo where the coffee machine is. He always makes them for me. I grip the edge of the island and start moving toward the bench, and I crash into someone.

"Do you want something?" the person snaps, like it's a massive inconvenience that I dared crash into her, even though she's the one sitting like an Egyptian obelisk in the middle of her kitchen.

Cali.

How can she and Cassius be so silent? They're like freaking assassins, waiting in the shadows to pounce.

"I was going to make coffee," I say, keeping my tone even. I refuse to let Cali tell my dad that I've been rude. "I can get it myself if you point me toward the machine."

"Walk forward."

I step out into the room, cane sweeping over the floor. She doesn't offer any other instructions so I keep walking until I hit the counter on the far wall.

"Now left."

I feel along the counter until I find the machine. It's an enormous, complicated thing but I don't want to give my new stepmother the satisfaction of asking her how to use it, so I set about figuring it out.

"Your father and I will be away this weekend," she says as I tamp the grounds.

"More tennis?"

She doesn't answer.

"You know, I'd love to come with you this weekend, see you guys in action," I try as I steam the milk. "Back home, Dad wouldn't even lift a hand to swat a fly, so I'm so curious to see him jumping around in a tennis outfit."

Cali scoffs, no doubt at my use of the word 'see.' I want to throttle her. I'm trying here, but she seems determined to think I'm the invalid. Blind people use 'see' all the time – it's how everyone talks about shit.

A door slams.

"Oh, Fergalicious," Dad hums. "Where are you?"

"In here," I call back. *In the middle of another fruitless attempt at bonding with my wicked stepmother.*

"It's good to see your smiling face at the end of a long day." He pecks me on the cheek. He smells like disinfectant from the clinic. He leans across the counter to kiss his wife. "And my lovely wife, too. What are you two talking about? Not conspiring against me, I hope."

Perfect. "Actually, I was just saying that I'd love to come to tennis with you and Cali on the weekend," I say. "We haven't done anything as a family since we got to Emerald Beach. It could be fun."

Dad hesitates. "Oh, Fergalish, I don't think you'd like it very much. You won't be able to see the match. It will be boring."

What the actual fuck?

Dad never *ever* leaves me out of things because of my vision. He knows that I don't need to see the tennis game to enjoy myself – I like the energy of the crowd, the atmosphere, the food. I pretend to be hunting for something in a drawer so he can't see the hurt written on my face.

"I don't mind," I say. "I can always call Seymour to come and get me if I'm bored."

"Yes, well," Dad sounds squirmy. "The thing is, we play at the Olympus Country Club, and we haven't got a membership for you yet. It's a whole process. But they won't let you onto the courts unless you're a member. I'm sorry, babe. Another weekend, okay?"

"Okay, sure."

If I didn't know better, I'd say Dad was lying.

Because he doesn't want to spend time with you. Because he hasn't forgiven you for The Incident.

I'm shaking. Hot coffee sloshes over my hands as I place the lid on the reusable cup.

"Are you going somewhere tonight?" Dad switches to the fake-bright voice he's been using with me a lot lately. "I saw Seymour has the car in the drive."

"I'm having dinner with a friend."

"That sounds fun. Don't stay out too late," he says. "You have school in the morning."

I rush out to the car. In the backseat, I dab at my eyes and fight to get myself under control.

If Seymour notices that I'm upset, he doesn't say anything. I love him to the moon and back for that.

We don't drive for long before we pull into a house. "Would you like a hand to the door?" Seymour asks.

"No, thanks, Seymour."

I touch up my eyeliner and lipstick, check with Seymour that I don't look like a laughing clown, and slide out of the car. I go to shut the door, but Seymour leans over the seat and holds it open. I get the feeling he isn't sure if he should leave.

"Is there something else?" I ask.

"No, I..." he fiddles with the indicator. "Do you know whose house this is?"

"Um... yes?"

"All I'm asking is that you be careful." Seymour pats my arm. "Call me if you need *anything*. And it's probably best that you don't mention to *anyone* where you've been tonight."

"Why not?" I quirk an eyebrow. "You've been holding out on me, Seymour. I need all the gossip. *Now*."

"What about your date?"

"Oh," I punch the button on my phone, and it reads out the time. I'm seven minutes late. "Shit. You're right. I'll see you later. You'd better spill on the way home, though. I have a feeling I'm going to need something to cheer me up."

"Good luck, Fergie. And please, call me if you need anything."

I jog up the path, my cane sweeping in front of me. I click my tongue as I walk up the steps between two giant pillars. People in this neighborhood are nuts for pillars. It's like they all think they're Roman Emperors or something.

I go to ring the bell, but the door flies open. "You're late," Torsten cries. He sounds like he's on the verge of flinging himself off a tall building.

I put my hand on his arm. He's shaking. "I'm sorry. Are you okay?"

"I can't be here. This was a mistake."

"But you *are* here, so that's not true. And now I'm here, too. I'll protect you from the big, bad wolf—"

"Hello, you must be Fergie," a sultry voice calls from deeper in the house. "My son has told me nothing about you."

"I'm not your son," Torsten growls. His whole body tremors.

I'm about to ask him what he means by that, but the wind is knocked out of me by a wave of opium perfume. Have I walked into a Lawrence of Arabia-themed whorehouse?

But no, the cloying perfume announces the arrival of a woman in a rustling chiffon dress. She wraps warm hands around mine, her nails like talons scraping my skin.

"Hello. It's nice to meet you," I say, because one of us should be on our best behavior. Beside me, Torsten grunts, and I can feel that he's one wrong move away from losing his shit.

"The pleasure is all mine. You're the first friend Torsten has brought home apart from those two loud boys, Victor and Cassius. Come, come." Those talons grip me tight, leading me deeper into the house. Torsten drags his feet behind us. "You're our guest of honor. We'll take good care of you. I'm Olivia Lucian, but everyone calls me Livvie."

Livvie.

This is the woman who decorated my bedroom and is friends with Cali. As much as anyone can be friends with Cali. That must be why Seymour was nervous about taking me here. She knows this is going to get back to Cali.

And Cassius.

But Torsten doesn't seem worried. At least, not about his best friend finding out I'm here for dinner. I don't know if it's because the *sacer* doesn't apply to him, or if he just doesn't give a shit about Cassius' temper tantrums.

I kind of hope it's the latter.

"You decorated my room for me," I say to Livvie. I want her to be aware that I see the connection. "It's beautiful. The sheets are very soft."

"I'm pleased that you like them. Donatello's linens are an absolute *dream.* Do come to me if you need any more help with decor, fashion, that kind of thing. Fitting in at Emerald Beach can be a bit of a minefield, and Cali is absolutely useless at anything like that."

I smile. "She certainly is."

Someone tugs on my skirt. "Mommy, is this Torsten's girl-friend?" asks a girl – she's maybe six or seven, judging by the high pitch of her voice.

I start to answer, but Livvie jumps in for me. "Yes, this is Fergie, and we're very happy to have her with us tonight. Remember what I told you, Isabella. Fergie can't see, so would you like to show her to the dining room and make sure she has a drink?"

Of course Livvie already knew about my vision. I try to imagine Cali gossiping about her relationship with my dad and her brand new stepdaughter to this woman, and I can't see it.

Nothing about my stepmother makes sense.

Isabella grabs my hand. "This way, please, Fergie. Would you like some wine? We're all allowed a glass of wine with our dinner, because Mommy says it's important we learn about the finer things in life. Personally, I don't think wine is very fine, even though they rhyme. Hey, and that rhymes, too!"

"It sure does," I smile.

"I think wine tastes like vinegar. You can have orange juice instead. I like orange juice. It tastes like sunshine in my mouth."

I can't help but laugh. Isabella is adorable. "Do you know what? Orange juice sounds lovely."

Isabella leads me to a dining room that's even larger than the one at Cali's house. She marches me straight to the head of the table, and fusses over filling my glass with a big pitcher of juice. All around me, people talk and laugh and air kiss. There must be at least twenty people in this room. I didn't realize I was going to a dinner party. I smell Torsten lowering himself into the chair to my left, facing Isabella, and he reaches over and touches my arm. It feels both reassuring and desperate.

I lean over to Torsten. "There are a lot of people at this table."

"It's all my *family*," he says with a scornful emphasis on the word. "Sisters, brothers, in-laws, cousins, grandchildren. They all want to meet you."

"Why?"

"Because you're Cali Dio's stepdaughter. Because they think you're my girlfriend."

I don't understand why those two things are related. Of course Torsten doesn't elaborate. He squeezes my arm again. "I wish we had your Braille labeler," he whispers as he shifts in his chair.

He obviously has things he wants to tell me, but for whatever reason he doesn't feel comfortable in front of his family. And that tells me all I need to know. No matter how friendly this room appears, and how attentive Livvie is, I can't trust them.

Wait staff bustle in from the kitchen, placing down an array of delicious-smelling dishes. Livvie taps her glass and calls for silence.

"I'm thrilled to have you all here," she says. "It's been too long since we've had a proper family dinner with *all* my children."

Beside me, Torsten's fingers grip the tablecloth.

"I'd like to raise a glass to our loving mother, for bringing us all together," calls out a girl from the other end of the table, near Livvie. She sounds like she's maybe fifteen. How many children does Livvie have? "Mater mea, et vita mea. My mother, my life."

We're bringing out the Latin. How very Skull & Bones-ey.

"*Mater mea, et vita mea,*" we all say. Everyone, that is, except Torsten, who fists the tablecloth so violently he pulls over my orange juice glass. Luckily, a waiter swoops in to clean it up and hands me another.

"—hard year. There are those out there who want to see the Lucian family fail, who want our clubs closed, who want the people of this city to go without their bread and circuses. Not even my precious museum is safe, as if the preservation of human history is something that must be *quantified* and *regulated*. But these challenges are nothing compared to what we've faced before, and we have always emerged stronger and bolder and more imaginative. I want you to know that the Lucian family will find a place for you, no matter what you want to do in life. I'm always here for you, for whatever you need. Family sticks together," Livvie is saying. "Illis quos amo deserviam. For those I love, I will sacrifice."

"Illis quos amo deserviam," everyone chants. A shiver runs down my spine. When I used to go to *His* house, we had to wait to say grace before we ate, but I've never heard anything like Livvie's speech. Add in the Latin quotes, and it all sounds a little... *sinister.*

Beside me, Torsten practically hums with rage. He flaps his hand against his thigh under the table.

"Now, drink and be merry," Livvie cries. "For tomorrow we bathe in blood."

Okay, yeah, definitely secret society creep vibe.

Everyone roars their assent. Glasses clink, and conversation bounces back to life.

Oh, so we're just going to pretend that's a totally normal toast.

"Don't worry, she doesn't mean that bit about the blood," Isabella giggles as she heaps food on my plate. "It's just a thing she says because our grandfather used to say it. We like traditions around here, and honoring our grandfather and his grandfather and HIS grandfather. If you like, after tea I'll show you all the portraits... oh, but I guess you can't see them..."

"I'd love it if you wanted to show me the portraits," I smile at her. "You're right – I can't see them. But you can describe them, and tell me stories, and that's just as good."

I dig into the delicious Italian food, digging my bread through the thick, creamy sauce. I know Torsten isn't going to talk to me, and I won't force him to try. Instead, I listen to the conversations around the table, picking up snatches of sentences that make no sense to me. What's this about a museum? My stepmother's name comes up again and again, as well as the August family, which is Victor and Juliet's last name.

I guess rich families like this are all part of the same circle. Victor had said as much.

I wish I could focus on Livvie, but she's all the way down the other end of the table. Not even my well-practiced ears can pick out her conversation over the din of the others.

It turns out that I don't have to. "Fergie," Livvie calls to me, her voice silencing those around her. "I want to know more about you, since you're going to be part of our circle now.

Fergie's father married my dear friend Cali," she says to the room. "Were you at the wedding?"

"No." I try to keep the hurt out of my voice. "They eloped in Vegas."

"Ah, that's so romantic, but it's a shame. I do hope she will allow me to throw them a party to celebrate. We would love an excuse to officially welcome you and your father to Emerald Beach."

I think Cassius already did that. With his dick.

"A party sounds... nice. Thank you. I bet Cali would love that." She wouldn't, which is exactly why I want it to happen. I'm still smarting from her and Dad refusing to let me come to tennis with them. I know it's her influence – Dad would never say those things to me.

Torsten's foot crunches on top of mine. He's warning me about her, but I don't understand why.

Livvie calls a waiter over to top up glasses. "And has your father settled into his new life here?"

More than I could ever have predicted. A mushroom sticks in my throat. I have to gulp down my orange juice to dislodge it before I can speak. "Yeah, he's doing well. He's a dentist, and he's opened a new clinic in the city. I thought it would be slow to build a client base, but he's working late every night."

"Ah, yes. Cali will be sending a lot of people his way from her gym. Mixed martial arts, you know. Very dangerous. Lots of injuries. And he'll be the Lucian family dentist from now on, too. Young Isabella here has an appointment next week."

"I need a filling," Isabella sighs dramatically.

"I told you, darling, if you keep eating all those sweets, you'll make some dentist very rich," Livvie coos. "It might as well be Cali's husband. So, Fergie, what have you got up to around Emerald Beach? We have so many amenities here, especially in

Harrington Hills. I know you were at Tombs last week, causing all kinds of mayhem."

My cheeks flare with heat. "I'm sorry about all that. I didn't intend for my prank to get out of hand—"

"Please," she cuts me off. "If I had a dollar every time I've had to clean blood off the floor after a Dio, I'd own all of Emerald Beach. Go on, tell me what else you like to get up to?"

Torsten steps on my foot again. His hand flapping grows more insistent. I know that he's trying to tell me that his mother is digging for information, but I knew that already. Livvie Lucian is many things, but subtle isn't one of them. It occurs to me that I might be able to use this. "Oh, well, I was thinking about joining the country club. Are you a member? Dad and Cali have been playing tennis there and—"

"Tennis?" Livvie snorts. "Cali Dio is playing tennis?"

I nod. "They have a match this weekend."

Livvie sounds as though she's stifling a laugh. "I haven't been to the club in ages, but this I *must* see. Cali Dio prancing around in a tiny white skirt. Cali Dio playing a *team* sport? It's going to be carnage."

Livvie's not the only one who finds the idea amusing. Several people at the table titter. Does *everyone* here know my stepmother?

"I'd love to see it," I say, trying to keep my voice even. Beside me, Torsten buzzes with desperate rage. "But Dad told me they haven't had the chance to make me a member yet. Apparently, I might not be able to—"

"Oh, that's nonsense," Livvie scoffs. "Members are allowed to bring guests as long as they're approved by the club's committee. And with those cheekbones, you won't have any trouble. I'll put in a word for you next time I'm there. Did you know your driver is still here?"

"My... what?"

"Your driver is still waiting outside," Livvie says. "My valet informs me that he's frowning up at the house as if he might at any moment pull out a stake and try to shove it through my heart. I don't know what he thinks I'm going to do to you."

Wait, Seymour's still outside? He hasn't left?

That's kind of sweet. But also, *what?* Why does Seymour think I need watching out for when I'm in the home of Cali's friend?

Nothing about tonight makes sense, not least of which is how agitated Torsten's become as dinner progresses. I remember how he threw my Braille labeler across the room when all I did was *ask* about his mother. Tonight has been... weird, but so far, Livvie hasn't done anything that warrants his distress. Something's going on here that I don't understand, and I hope Torsten feels comfortable enough with me that he'll find a way to explain one day.

The staff serves dessert – some delicious panna cotta thing with chocolate mousse. I'm desperate to lick my plate clean but that doesn't seem like the vibe.

"Come, everyone." Livvie claps her hands as the table is cleared. "Esmeralda will put the little ones to bed. Those of us old enough can retire to the billiards room for coffee and brandy."

Chairs scrape and forks clatter as the family rush about to obey. Two of the children giggle as they play under the table, and Esmeralda swears in Spanish as she tries to fish them out. Beside me, Torsten remains bone still. He doesn't rise from the table. Livvie snaps her fingers. "Torsten, *come*."

His body shudders. A flicker of irritation passes through me. She's summoning him like a dog. I don't understand what's going on here, but there's some underlying trauma that has Torsten on the edge of losing his shit – and it's something

Livvie's determined to sweep under the rug for the sake of appearances. Torsten can't do that.

I lean toward him. "I think your mother wants us to go with her," I say.

"Yes." He doesn't move.

"What do *you* want? Because that's what I want to do."

Torsten grabs my hand. A lightning bolt jolts down my arm, like Zeus himself is dancing with me and he's feeling a little frisky.

He yanks me to my feet. Livvie calls after him, but he's not stopping. He pushes through the throng of siblings and cousins, and drags me from the room – down a wide hallway, through a series of large rooms, and into a lofty, echoing space. My heels clack against hardwood floors, and there appears to be very little furniture in this space. Torsten flicks a switch, and bright light dances in my vision – squares of warmth angled in different directions, casting interesting patterns that dazzle me.

I click my tongue, listening to the echo. I'm in a vast, empty space, so large it makes Cali's foyer feel like a phone booth. I'm facing a wall, close enough that if Torsten shoved me, I'd slam into it and break my nose.

"Look," Torsten growls, shaking my arm so hard it's in danger of falling off.

"I can't."

He sucks in his breath. I think he might've forgotten I'm blind. Or he hadn't quite articulated that being blind meant I couldn't see things. I'm starting to understand that his mind doesn't work like other people. He intrigues me, the same way he finds me intriguing, and that's why he's showing me whatever it is that's important to him.

"Okay," Torsten says. He grabs my waist and spins me around. I yelp in surprise as he twists me off balance. My cane drops from my fingers. Torsten's fingers dig into my skin as he presses my hand onto an object. My fingers touch hard ridges on a flat surface.

I realize what I'm feeling. Paint. The whirling ridges and soft dabs of paint swirled on a canvas.

I'm touching a painting.

I run my hand over the surface, my breath hitching as I take in the layers of paint. Art has always been useless to me – I've never tried to engage with it because like so many things in the world, it isn't made for me. But as Torsten moves my hand and my fingers graze ridges and trace swirls, my heart races. I feel something of what the artist was trying to convey in the thickness of the paint and the changing brushstrokes. The textures tell a story, the same way layers of music go together to create a song. Torsten's breath laces my ear. His body hems me in, his chest brushing my back lightly as he hovers behind me.

"What do you see?" he asks.

"Splashes and swirls," I say. "In this corner, they are jaunty, playful. Some of these are drips and dribbles. And then these ridges kind of form a lattice. This slash in the paint was applied on top of the others – it feels angry, like it's trying to obliterate what's underneath."

I let out a hiss. I'm not exactly well-versed in the art world, what with not having an appreciation of color, but that angry slash through the painting... when I touch it, my heart races, my pulse quickens.

Or maybe that's Torsten's breath on my ear, his hips brushing my ass, his lips dangerously close to my neck.

"It's a Jackson Pollock," Torsten says.

I try to yank my hand away, but Torsten holds it in place.

"I'm not sure I should be smearing my chocolate-covered hands all over it. That might diminish its value."

Torsten snorts. "Unlikely. I painted it."

"You... what?"

"It's a Jackson Pollock and I painted it. I painted everything in this gallery." He takes my arm and leads me across the room, pressing my fingers into another canvas. I feel bold, flat shapes with raised edges. "This is a Picasso. Next to it is a Cézanne. I've even done a few Renaissance works, but Impressionists are easier. The older you go, the harder it is to find the right type of paper or canvas, the correct pigments."

"You paint fakes."

Torsten squeezes my wrist. His body shudders against mine, as if he's reliving something painful. "This is what I used to do for my mother. There's more of my work in her museum in the city."

Sickness twists in my gut. "Does she sell them?" I ask.

Torsten doesn't reply. Instead, he draws my fingers across the paint, following one of Picasso's geometric shapes. "I wish you could see it. I wish you could see all of them."

"I wish for a pony," I say. "We don't always get what we want."

"This used to be my safe place," he says. "This used to be where I came when the noise and the smells and the emotions got to be too much. But then she decided to fill this place with my work. She got rid of all the real art, and now this is a shrine for her dead dreams for me."

I know that when he says *Her*, he means Livvie. My lungs expand, filling with air that tastes like vanilla and orange zest.

I want to say that I do it too – that it's too much for me to think about Dawson, so I reduce him to a pronoun, as if by taking away his name, I can banish his power over me. But I can't conjure the words.

I don't need to speak. Because the words are already here, resting between the layers of paint, more eloquent and poetic than anything I could say. Torsten *knows*. He's the first person I've ever met who might understand me better than I do myself.

We've only known each other for two weeks, and yet, it's as if he's always existed for me – a hollow inside my coal-heart. And now, finally, I am filled with him.

He nuzzles his face into my neck, his shoulders hitching. Every atom of me is aware of him, of the parts of him that touch me and the parts that still remain remote. There's so much I want to ask him, so many secrets he's hidden in the layers of paint. Soulmates have the same hiding places.

I retract my hand from the painting and knit my fingers in his. Torsten continues to hold me, his breath coming out in ragged gasps. He doesn't make any kind of move, and I know that we're already too close, that ours is the kind of closeness that hurts, that burrows under your skin and scars from the inside.

"You only draw and paint other people's work," I manage to choke out. "Why?"

"Because I don't understand," he says, his voice bitter. "I don't understand people and why they do the things they do. I don't understand why they turn away from me, or how they can find joy in things that are so repulsive to me. I don't understand why they like to touch, and laugh about stupid things, and do dumb assignments. And I think that these great artists spent their whole lives trying to understand people through their work, and so their paintings must have answers, and I can sit quietly and learn from them without them judging me, without them being repulsed by me. People made of paint aren't scary."

"They aren't so scary in real life," I say. "Not all of them."

Torsten spins me across the room and presses my hand to another painting. I move my fingers, feeling a central shape, with details painted in harsh, short strokes. Around that object are large, bold swirls and stripes. Something about the composition unsettles me, but I can't explain it.

"This is *The Scream* by Edvard Munch. He painted it after

walking at night with two friends. His friends walked ahead of him, and he stared out at a blood-sky over the fjord and sensed a scream tearing through nature." He sweeps my hand along the strips. "These art nouveau curves flowing around the figure indicate the way nature absorbs the scream, absorbs our petty feelings and fears, and so the individual becomes invisible. Nature consumes us until there's no feeling left."

"That's cheery."

Torsten's lips graze my cheek. His words come out in an excited rush as he talks about the art. I love him like this, so consumed by what he loves that he has no room for anything else, but he wants so badly to share his art with me.

"This painting is supposed to represent anguish on such a level that it floors anyone who sees it. Munch himself wrote in the corner that his painting 'could only have been painted by a madman.' Critics who saw it said that Munch had become mad himself. His sister spent time in a psychiatric ward, and they thought her illness had spread to him. They had no basis for that except for this painting. After he heard their criticism, Munch never, ever painted in this style again."

"I understand that." I think of the night I walked onto a bridge and screamed my own anguish into the night. I couldn't imagine tapping into that anguish every time I wanted to create something.

Torsten squeezes my fingers so hard that my pinkie goes numb. "When I look at this painting, I see myself. So I paint it, a kind of self-portrait, because I want to *understand*. Because I want to be able to feel things the way other people feel them. But I'm always on the bridge alone, screaming into the blood-red sky."

"I don't think you are alone," I say. "I'm no artist, but I think when Munch wrote that only a madman could paint this, he meant it ironically. He's taking control of his own life and his feelings. He's saying that we're all a little mad in the throes of anguish. If this painting didn't speak to something universally human in all of us, then it wouldn't be as famous as it is."

I don't move. Torsten doesn't move. Our bodies melt together under the weight of Munch's blood-red sky. Torsten's lips graze against my neck, so softly that I can almost pretend that didn't just happen.

But I don't want to pretend.

Like with Cassius and Victor, New Fergie takes over. The Fergie who knows she can do whatever she wants because her life is over anyway. The Fergie who likes the feeling of Torsten's soft fingers curled around her wrist, who's fascinated by what he sees when he looks at this artwork. And what he sees when he looks at me.

I lean my head to the side, my lips seeking his. But as soon as they brush together, he darts away, tearing his body from mine like I'm poison.

I reach for him, my body sick with his echo, clammy in all the places where he touched me and now no longer does. I'm a flame bending toward the air I need to breathe, to grow, to conflagrate.

"I thought you wanted this," I say.

"*Cassius* wants you," Torsten says from halfway across the cavernous room, as if he needs an entire ocean between us to make his point. "Victor wants you. They have an agreement. Cassius gets you first. He'll hurt you, like he hurts all the other girls. Victor will heal you. He's good at that. You'll be safe with him."

"Oh, is that so? They've agreed on all this, have they? Drawn up a lovely little contract, did they? Nice of them to inform me. And you?" I growl. "What part do you play in this deal?"

"I don't have a part." His voice cracks. "I like talking to you."

I cross the room, each stride a leap into the unknown

without my cane. I find him breathing heavy, one hand flapping, on the verge of exploding. And I know we're edging into a place where he no longer feels safe. I have to bring him back. I can't taint this room with more bad memories for him.

I rock forward on my toes, making sure no other part of me touches him but my lips. He's so tall that I can't quite reach his mouth, but I don't think he's ready for that. I kiss the skin of his collarbone, naked and exposed in his open collar. He tastes of fear and need and orange zest.

I run my tongue along the hollow of the bone. He shudders.

"Is this okay?" I ask. "Does it feel okay?"

"Yeah." He swallows. "It feels really good."

"Torsten..." I go back in to lick him again, slowly, gently, keeping my hands pinned at my sides even though all I want to do is tangle them in his hair and pull him close enough so I can crawl inside him. "I want to do more than just talk to you."

He lets out a feral moan that makes my coal heart squeeze in my chest. Hands grab me and shove me backward into the wall. The paintings shake on their mounts, but even if they fell I don't think I'd break this kiss. Because Torsten Lucian is kissing me, and it's hot and needy and filled with desperate longing. His hands claw at my hair, paw at my bare arms, shudder at the edges of my tits. I reach up and indulge my own wild beast. I rake my fingers through his hair, feeling how soft it is, how it's long enough to brush his shoulders, how it has a slight curl to it. I run my fingers over his shoulders, enjoying the wiry musculature of them, his Vitruvian Man proportions. I cup his chin and angle him closer as I probe every corner of his mouth with my tongue. I taste myself in his need – my own insecurities, my pain, my echoes.

I reach down and cup his crotch with my hand. As soon as I do it I know I've made a mistake. Torsten's body stiffens. I've gone too far, too fast. He trusted me and I...

A strangled groan escapes his throat. He tears himself away again. And this time I know he's not coming back.

"I can't," he whispers.

No, no, no. Tears clutch at the edges of my eyes. I haven't cried since that night on the bridge.

"Torsten? Please, I'm sorry. Don't—"

"Fergie, it's too... I can't."

He turns and bolts. His footsteps echo like gunshots in the vast room as he leaves me wet and panting and very, very confused.

Torsten doesn't show up at school again, so I can't even talk to him about what happened in the gallery. He kissed me and then he ran away, and I had to get down on my hands and knees to find my cane and wander the labyrinthine corridors of Livvie's mansion like a lost lamb until Isabella found me and helped me out to the car.

Since Euri's staying away from me for her own safety, and I'm not talking to Cassius or Victor out of spite, I'm spending another weekend alone in my room. Dad and Cali are at one of their tennis matches I'm not allowed to attend, so I have a hot date with my silk bedsheets, a pile of Milo's homemade desserts, a bottle of Cali's finest bourbon, a smutty audiobook, and my vibrator.

Because self-care should be prioritized.

It's amazing how many orgasms I have now that I no longer have a future to prepare for.

The only problem is that thinking about orgasms makes me think about Torsten, and how I fucked up that wonderful moment in the gallery. So many things puzzle me about that night. I know he took me to that gallery and showed me those paintings because he's trying to tell me something about himself. But he's Torsten, so he can't find the words. I had to go slow with him, but then he kissed me and he tasted like the sweetest sin and I couldn't go slow...

I find myself rubbing my wrist where he held my hand against the paint, feeling the ghost of those swirls beneath my fingers.

I've never *seen* art until that night. Until him.

And I want him to know that.

I've already texted him ten times. He's read them all but hasn't replied. I wrote him a long Braille note, explaining that I didn't mean to push him too fast, that I didn't want to fuck things up with his friends, but that I don't give a fuck about Cassius' sacer, that it's a free country and I want to kiss him again, but I'll respect if he doesn't. I could deliver it to the hotel where he's staying, but that meant I had to ask my stepbrother where he put Torsten up, and I'm not quite ready to do that.

I'm about to put my headphones on when I hear footsteps on the staircase and voices echoing in the halls. Cassius is home. And he's with someone. I think that's Victor's voice I hear, loud and aristocratic and overconfident.

Maybe Torsten is with them? I could give him the note in person.

I open my bedroom door a crack. I can hear the boys are on the landing, talking to Milo, who's pushing platters of tacos on them.

"Thanks, Milo," Victor says. "These look amazing. You know your cooking is the main reason I still love coming over here."

"Oh, I think a certain special lady might have more to do with it," Milo says with a knowing tone in his voice. I want to slap every one of them. "Please bring the platters back. I don't want that library of yours to get rats, especially since you won't let me clean it."

"I promise, we'll bring them back... when we need seconds." Cassius laughs. It's an actual genuine laugh, not that sick, monstrous thing. It cuts straight through my chest and pools in my belly.

Buried deep inside the monster is a human being, one who cares about Milo. *That's interesting.*

Milo heads back downstairs, and the guys walk down the opposite hallway toward their secret hideout with the carved doors. *The library.* How very *Beauty and the Beast.*

Before I know what I'm doing, I pad out of my room and follow them around the corner. I press myself into the wall so they can't see me.

The security panel on the wall beeps as it accepts their password. Cassius and Victor are talking. I still don't even know if Torsten is with them, but I catch a faint whiff of vanilla and orange zest, and it emboldens me. I shuffle forward, and as I move closer I can't help but overhead their conversation.

"...the client knows what he has to do," Victor says. "What he *doesn't* know is that a U Penn recruiter will be in the audience. He didn't even need to hire us. He could've made it on his own merit."

This is Poison Ivy Club business. I think about Euri's article, and how this might be prime information for her. But as much as I hate my stepbrother, as much as Victor tempts me and Torsten confounds me, I'm not going to get involved. It's rule number one of New Fergie's life – my prime directive. And I've already broken it too many times.

"Are you going to tell him?" Cassius asks, a gleeful smirk in his voice.

"Of course not."

I think about Euri's sister, but somehow I can't quite pair what she told me they did to Artie with the Victor August who looked after us when we were drunk, who massaged my feet and kissed me so, so sweetly. What did Euri even think about partying with Victor? I hadn't been able to get her to say much about it – I don't think she liked owing anything to Victor, not even gratitude.

I hadn't told her about the kiss.

"—we shouldn't talk about this out here," Victor says. He pushes one of the heavy doors, and it creaks as it swings inward. "You know how Cali feels about the club."

"She's not here," Cassius growls. "She took her new toy-boy husband to a party across town as part of a gig. Maybe he'll get shot in the crossfire and this will all be over."

Excuse me, what the fuck?

I lean forward, desperate to hear what he's saying about my dad, and I don't realize until it's too late that I said those words out loud.

"You spying on us, Sunflower?" Cassius storms toward me.

"It's a free hallway," I shoot back. As terrifying as he is bearing down on me, I stand my ground.

"Not this hallway." Cassius slams into me. He grabs my wrist, in the spot where Torsten held me in the gallery. Only instead of showing me something beautiful, my stepbrother smashes my wrist into the wall. I wince as pain shoots down my arm, as the bulk of him pushes into me, all fury and malice. I refuse to be intimidated by him.

I refuse to acknowledge how much my pussy sings at the memory of what this monster can do.

"Contrary to what you believe, *brother*, the world doesn't revolve around your swollen ego." I thrust out the paper in my other hand. "I came to give this to Torsten."

"Me?" Torsten squeaks.

I knew he was here.

"Torsten?" Cassius rips the card from my hand. "What could you possibly want to give him? What is this? I can't read it."

"Of course you can't. It's in Braille." I don't have the note anymore, so I turn to Torsten and hold out my hand. "That's for you. Please read it. I'll be in my room all night if you want to talk to me."

It takes all my willpower to turn my back on them. Victor calls out my name, but he can fuck right off into the sun. I stomp back to my room, put on my favorite scarlet bra and lace thong and crawl under the sheets. I turn my audiobook on low so I'll be able to hear a knock at the door.

Torsten never knocks.

28

FERGIE

"Are you going to the game on Friday?" Euri asks.

It's a Tuesday, and we're spending lunch period in the greenhouse. Victor seems to be holding Cassius at bay, so I've had no retaliation for my little Tombs stunt. Euri got a note from Victor, telling her that she won't face punishment if she hangs out with me. The Poison Ivy Club has decided I'm allowed a single friend.

Lucky me.

Ever since my dinner with Torsten, my life at Stonehurst has fallen into a strange, pathetic, lonely pattern. I go to classes, where no one talks to me, not even the teachers, and I go home and lock myself in my room and listen to audiobooks about people who didn't fuck up their lives at eighteen and get to go off and do amazing things. Lunches with Euri have become a bright spot in my long, boring days, and I hate myself for how much I look forward to them, because I'm not supposed to be making friends.

Even though Cassius hasn't pulled any more practical jokes, I tiptoe around the house in constant fear of what he might do next.

And all of that I can endure, if it weren't for the constant stream of SATs and college applications talk on top of it.

Blissfully, the torture's been dialed back in the last couple of weeks as the student body swarms with excitement about the upcoming basketball game between Stonehurst Prep's varsity team, the Sentinels, and our biggest rivals at Acheron Academy, and the blowout party that happens at Vic and Juliet's house afterward.

So, Euri's question isn't completely out of the blue. I shrug. "Spectator sports are kind of lost on me."

Especially not since my Dad forbid me from going to his matches.

"I can relate, but it's not really about the game." Euri's knitting needles clack together. She finished my scarf last week – it's a little crooked, but so soft and warm – and is now working on a matching pair of mittens. "I have to cover a lot of the games for the paper. They can be kind of fun. The whole school is there in costumes, and everyone chants, and the junk food is *excellent*. Plus, unlike football, even with fouls and timeouts, a basketball game only lasts forty minutes, an hour tops. So the actual sports portion of the evening is over super quick."

"What about the after-party? What's that like?" I have to admit that I'm curious about Victor and his sister.

"I wouldn't know," Euri says wistfully. "I don't get invited to these kinds of things."

Her words hit a nerve. At my old school, I *was* Euri, sort of. I was part of a group of friendly kids, sure, but people assumed since I was blind and class president and in charge of all the clubs and the paper, I was some kind of goody-goody who didn't want a social life. They weren't wrong. I remember eating my lunch on a Monday morning and hearing about all the crazy things that had gone down over the weekend and wishing I could be responsible for a tiny bit of that chaos.

It's partly why I've been excited about college. I want to meet people like me, people who have ambition and care about making a difference but who also want to get fucked up and do crazy shit. It turns out, all I had to do was move in with my new stepbrother. It also turns out that doing crazy shit isn't all it's cracked up to be.

Euri wants to go to that party, and I'm her ticket in the front door.

I sigh. I'm not doing this because we're friends, or because I want to spend the night hanging around Victor, Cassius, and Torsten. I'm doing it because I blew my own future, but Euri's is still intact, and I think every nerd deserves one bad apple friend to tempt them over to the dark side. "It's settled. We'll go to the game, and I'll get us into the party. But we bug out the minute it gets boring."

"Deal. Omigod. You're amazing." Euri wraps her arms around me in a huge hug. "You won't regret this."

"Try again."

"You will not have to buy your own booze."

"Much better." I stand up and perform a mock-cheerleading move. "Let's go to the game."

29

TORSTEN

O n the day of the game, school is even more obnoxious than usual. So much noise and excitement. Victor's surrounded by a gaggle of cheerleaders and sycophants. He will not shut up about how we're going to kick Acheron's ass, like it's something that matters.

I didn't want to go to the game. I've been skipping school ever since Fergie and I... since the gallery. I can't talk to her about what happened, so it's easier to avoid her.

But Victor made it clear that he needs Poison Ivy there in force, and if I avoid my friends much longer, they'll start demanding to know what's wrong. And I can't tell them. I *can't*.

They cannot know that I kissed the girl they both want.

They cannot know that I betrayed them.

Last night at Cas' place, I overheard Fergie telling Milo that she's going to the game with Euri. And even though the thought of talking to her again fills me with terror, I do something I've never done before and offer to photograph the game for the paper and the yearbook.

I don't have to talk to her. I just want to be near her. I want to see her laughing and having fun.

Euri hates me, but she agrees because all the other photographers on the staff are terrible. So I'll see Fergie at the game, and that thought helps me endure the droning teachers and the shouting students for another day.

Some dark, foolish part of me clings to the idea that Fergie can't even see Victor running around, 'like a stallion out to pasture,' (Cas' words). She can't see the other girls go all gooey whenever he winks at them. To her, the game will be a mess of noise and smells and sitting way too close to people you hate, like it is for me.

Maybe I'll even sit next to her. Maybe I'll hold her hand when they start those obnoxious waves...

Maybe Cassius will cut my head off and eat my brain with a spoon.

Maybe I'm playing with fire...

The final bell rings. Victor will head out with his teammates, but I'm supposed to meet Cas in the parking lot. He's procured some weed, which I desperately need to calm me the fuck down before I walk into that stadium. But first, I need to collect the camera from the newspaper office. Euri said she'd leave it beside the photocopier.

I round the corner, but before I approach the *Sentinel's* office, I hear two voices chatting outside.

Fergie. I'd recognize that don't-give-a-fuck East Coast accent anywhere. But the other voice sends a cold stake through my chest.

Drusilla.

She's back?

That's impossible.

She knows what we'll do to her if she sets one foot back at Stonehurst Prep.

I peer around the corner. It's Drusilla all right. I'll never forget that particular shade of golden blonde hair, and the graceful curve of her neck like one of Michelangelo's cherubs. She's wearing the Stonehurst Prep plaid-green uniform skirt over a tight white shirt with the top three buttons undone, and carrying a Hermes laptop case under her arm. Her other arm holds Fergie while she talks quickly.

"—and I just wanted to introduce myself. I heard you're Cassius' Dio's new stepsister, and that he put a sacer on you. You're not the first person to be victimized by the so-called Poison Ivy Club. Years ago, they hurt me, and now I'm here to take back this school. I'd love your help."

I know that Fergie doesn't like people touching her like that. She yanks her hand away. Drusilla winces, as though Fergie hurt her.

"Thanks, but no thanks," Fergie says. "I don't want a crusade. I just want to keep a low profile. But you should talk to Eurydice – she's out for revenge."

"No offense, but Eurydice Jones is a dork. A nobody. She's got no power in the real world. But you... I heard Victor and Cassius had a rather public fight over you. I heard you're talking to Torsten. I heard he invited you to dinner *at his house*."

How the fuck does she know that?

"—*no one* talks to Torsten," Drusilla continues. "You have power over the Poison Ivy boys. Let me use that power for the good of everyone at this school."

"Not interested."

"I can make it worth your while—"

I shove my way into the room. Drusilla's head snaps around. She tosses her hair and shoots me this look that I've seen on Cas' face a million times – she wants to gut something, and I'm within easy reach.

"Speak of the devil," she purrs. "Fergie, your friend Torsten is here. I wonder what his friends will think when I tell them who I saw kissing in the Lucians' private gallery..."

"Get out," I growl, my whole body trembling. I flap my hand frantically – it's the only thing that's going to stop me from wringing this girl's neck.

How the fuck does she know that?

If she tells Cassius, I'm dead.

"You don't own these offices," Drusilla says sweetly. "I came by to offer my services. I've spent the last three years writing a women's issues column at the *Acheron Academy Advocate*, and I came to offer my services when I got talking to my friend Fergie here."

"We're not friends," Fergie says quickly.

"But we *could* be. I'm a better ally than I am an enemy. Think about what I said." Drusilla pats Fergie's shoulder. She looks at me as she speaks, and I gather her facial expression is supposed to be meaningful in some way, but I don't understand.

All I know is that she has eyes in my mother's house, and she could ruin *everything*.

"You shouldn't be here," I manage to say.

Why are you here? Why did you come back to Stonehurst? Don't you know that's signing your own death warrant?

"Shouldn't I?" she asks sweetly. To me, she sounds completely innocent, but Victor and Cas have pounded it into me that I can never take anything Drusilla Hargreaves says as truth.

"You were warned never to set foot on this side of the river again."

"Torsten..." Fergie looks at me, her eyes wide.

"I'll go where I please, including to this school, and there's nothing you or the rest of your little club can do about it. And if you doubt my word, ask Cali Dio or Claudia August. Or better yet, ask your mother. Oh, that's right," Drusilla pouts her lips. "She's not even your mother, is she?"

Fergie shoots to her feet and shoves Drusilla toward the door. "I think you better leave."

"Poor little Torsten. You're not even one of them. I don't know how long they'll tolerate the silent freak ruining their street cred. Not that they'll have any for much longer." Drusilla waves as Fergie pushes her into the hall. "Toodles."

Fergie slams the office door shut. "Torsten, are you okay? Those things she said..."

The camera isn't beside the photocopier, so I move between the desks, hunting for it. I can't bear to look at Fergie. I'm afraid that if I say a word, I'll speak all my wretched dreams aloud and she'll laugh. She'll laugh because the idea of her choosing me over Cassius and Victor is laughable. I don't get humor and even I get that joke.

But Fergie's not ready to let me off the hook. She jogs behind me. "Torsten, who was that girl? Why does she know about the gallery?"

"That's Drusilla," I mumble as I pull open cabinets. It has to be here somewhere. Euri said she left it for me. "I don't know how she knows, but it's not good. Cas and Vic can't find out. I'm not supposed to kiss you."

"Oh, and they make all the rules, do they?"

"Yes."

She sighs.

"Torsten, look at me. I know you're not looking at me."

I can't refuse a command from her. Even though my hand is flapping like a hummingbird, even though it feels like she's punched a hole in my chest and is squeezing my heart in her fist, I look up into Fergie's green irises. She frowns, and an adorable crease forms between her eyes. "I *wanted* to kiss you, Torsten. And that has nothing to do with Vic or Cas. I like you a lot. I like talking to you. I like when you tell me about the artists you love. I'm not ashamed of what happened in the gallery, and I won't pretend I am. If Cas wants to kick your ass because you touched his property, then he'll have to go through me first. Okay?"

"Okay," I say, although I'm not calm enough to leave yet. It would help if I could find the camera.

"So this Drusilla…" Fergie lifts a perfectly-arched eyebrow. "Let me guess, old girlfriend?"

"No, I've never had a girlfriend—"

"I was kidding, Torsten. I know you have better taste." Fergie grins at me, and my chest lightens. I'm so used to not under-standing when people are joking, but she has this way of turning things around so I'm in on the joke, so I can smile too. I adore her for it.

I pull the camera out of the bottom drawer of Euri's desk. I'm able to stop flapping my hand now. I feel calmer. "Ask Vic or Cas about Drusilla. They'll explain."

They won't. But I can't say any more to her about it or I'll tell her things she isn't meant to know.

"I'm asking *you*—"

"Fergie, there you are!" A voice interrupts Fergie because she finds some nefarious way to draw the truth out of me. "You will not believe who I saw on the way over here. I know you don't know who this is, but Drusilla Hargreaves is back at Stonehurst, and—"

Eurydice Jones stops dead in her tracks as she sees me in her desk. "Oh, hi Torsten."

"I needed the camera." I held it up. "It wasn't beside the photocopier, like you said."

"No, because I was just coming to get it out for you."

"Hey, I didn't realize you two knew each other." Fergie gestures in Euri's direction. "Euri and I are going to the game together. I'm going to help Euri write her article, get a basketball perspective from the outsider."

"Torsten does some photography for the paper," Euri says, inching behind Fergie.

I don't say anything back. Eurydice Jones is uninteresting to me, so why acknowledge her?

For several long moments, no one says anything.

"You enjoy basketball?" I ask Fergie instead, because I *am* curious about this, about her, about why she'd want to sit in the smelly bleachers with everyone else when she couldn't even see.

"Not really," she admits. "I hate team sports on a good day, and the ball moves too fast for the commentary to be that useful. But Euri assures me the junk food is good."

"Are you kidding? The Grillennium Falcon food truck is gonna be there. They do these hot dogs with *everything* on them. I swear I could eat three." Euri peers at me with wide eyes. Victor tells me girls look like that when they're afraid. I don't know why she's afraid of me. I've never done anything to Euri. If anything, she's nice compared to most kids at this stupid school.

"Torsten's going to sit with us," Fergie says.

I am?

"He has to take photos of the game," Euri says.

"After that, though." Fergie grins at me. "Aren't you? Come find us when you're done. We'll hang and cheer Victor on together."

"I have to go." I grab the camera and flee the building.

Sitting with Fergie I could maybe handle, especially if she wants to leave halfway through and smoke a joint under the bleachers. But I can't deal with Euri. I don't know what to say to her. And I have to get to Cas. I need to tell him about Drusilla and what she said, before he hears it from someone else.

Drusilla Hargreaves is back at Stonehurst Prep. Which either means she has a suicide wish, or she's up to something.

My conversation with Drusilla and Torsten leaves a sour taste in my mouth as Euri and I walk out to the gym for the game. Something's gone down between Drusilla and Poison Ivy, that's obvious. I'm pretty sure Torsten doesn't lie, but his desperate need to get away from me suggests he's trying to hide something about this Drusilla girl.

But how does she know about the gallery?

I get why someone might hate the Poison Ivy Club enough to take them down. I've got no problem with that. In different circumstances, I might even sign up for the battle. But to walk up to someone she doesn't know, someone who literally shares a house with the chief cockpoodle of said secret society, and try to recruit them seems a bit... unnecessarily reckless.

And all those things Drusilla said, it was almost as if... as if she knew not only about me and Torsten, but about me and Victor.

About me and Cassius.

But that's impossible.

There's no way she can know I slept with Cassius and kissed Victor. She's not spying through my bedroom window. I'm on the second floor of a mansion surrounded by a security fence. She knows sweet-fuck-all. She's grasping at straws, making insinuations based on that one stupid fight they had in the hallway.

It's not my fault they're the *right* assumptions.

"You were telling me about this Drusilla girl?" I ask Euri as we mill about in the crowd waiting to get into the gym. I decide not to tell her about my conversation with Drusilla in the newspaper office, lest something unsavory came out about what I get up to with my stepbrother.

"Drusilla was the Queen Bee of junior high, and everyone thought she'd rule Stonehurst Prep," Euri explains as she shows me where the handrail is. "Freshman year, she had it out for this girl, Gemma, who was dating Victor at the time. Or Cassius, I can't remember? I think they both dated her at one point. Gemma was nice – we were kind of friends at one point, but also rivals. She wanted to be top of the class, captain of all her teams, class president. She was just so *perfect*, you know."

My veins turn to ice. I remember being that person. "What happened?"

"No one really knows, but Gemma ended up dead and Drusilla never came back to Stonehurst Prep. Officially she claimed she changed schools to get away from bad memories and negative people, but I heard that the Poison Ivy Club ran her out of the school."

"Hold on, Victor's girlfriend *died*?"

"Yeah. Suicide is the official reason. It's—" Euri's arm is ripped away as the crowd jostles us. Someone starts up a fight song, and the cry is taken up by everyone around us. "We'll talk about this later. When there are fewer meatheads about."

Even though school only got out an hour ago and the game doesn't start for ages, the bleachers are already packed. Acheron Academy supporters are here in force, their students cramming the student parking lot with the stretch Hummers they hired to transport them to the game. No smelly school buses for Emerald Beach's elite. They crowd the bleachers on the opposite side of the court, singing their own fight songs at the top of their voices and – judging by the smell of the crowd as we jostle for seats – getting drunk from their snuck-in flasks.

Euri finds us a spot near the top of the bleachers. Hopefully, Torsten will be able to see where we're sitting and join us when he's done. I spread out my favorite leather jacket to save our seats while Euri gets our food.

Of course, the conversation around me turns to, well... me. You get used to this as a blind person. People think you're invisible, an oddity to be commented upon. Although at least their commentary isn't just about my eyes.

"What's she even doing here? It's not like she can see anything."

"I think she's faking it for sympathy. I don't think she's really blind. Otherwise, she'd be in, like, a special school or something. It's why she gets away with doing no work in class."

"Nah, it's because she's fucking the Poison Ivy guys."

"I don't see why Cassius and Victor are fighting over her. She's not anything special. She can't even *see*. Victor should be with someone who can at least appreciate what a fine specimen he is."

"Like you, you mean?" her friend cracks up.

"Sure, why not? If I wasn't so afraid of Cassius, I'd hire Poison Ivy Club in a *heartbeat*. Did you hear how much dicking Lucila Baskerville is getting since she signed on as their client? Even sucking off Torsten is worth it to get a shot at Victor's golden cock. She told me he made her come *eight times* in one night."

My veins throb. For some reason, the idea of Victor August making some other girl orgasm fills me with violent rage. And that's not cool. We're all sisters here. As a gender, we've suffered through millennia of mediocre sex before men got it into their heads that they need to find the clitoris. We should celebrate whenever one of us gets a good dicking.

And yet, I want to curl my fingers around her (probably) scrawny neck and squeeze until her eyes pop out.

"...Mmmm. Can you imagine being the meat in a Victor/Cassius sandwich," her friend groaned.

"Not me. Victor knows how to treat a girl, but Cas is a brute. I've heard he can't even get off without pain. He slept with Lenora Hastings after last year's Spring Fling ball, and she says he carved his initials into her chest. Like, with a *knife*."

Why does that make me wet? I squeeze my legs together and lean forward. I want to hear every filthy, degrading thing my stepbrother has done to a woman. Some feminist I am.

"—and Peggy Braithwaite says he put these clamps on her nipples and tugged at them every time he thrust. She said that by the end of it she thought her tits would be permanently cone-shaped—"

My pussy throbs at the thought of it. I sit on my hands, wondering if I could run to the bathroom before Euri comes back.

"—blindfolded her and tied her up and used every hole—"

"Here." Euri dumps a heavy tray on my lap. "I got us one of everything. And two giant Cokes, as requested."

"A woman after my own heart," I say quickly as I hold the food while she gets settled, grateful for the distraction. What those girls were talking about was abuse. My stepbrother truly is a monster – a possessive asshole who forbids me from seeing Victor or Torsten, guys who actually might know how to treat a girl. And yet here I am getting ready to dial up the old rotary phone over him.

Euri pulls off the lids from sodas while I dig out my own

flask – an ornately decorated silver Victorian gentleman's flask *He* got at an estate sale and gave me as a gift when we started sneaking into concerts together. I pour a generous glug of Cali's top-shelf bourbon into each cup, and we clink in celebration.

This is how one forgets all about Cassius Dio.

"Hey, Euri?" I ask as I attempt to pick up my hotdog, which groans under the weight of a hundred gourmet toppings and needs to get in my mouth right now because it smells amazing.

"Yeah?" Her voice is muffled by her own dog.

I take a moment to chew my first bite and savor the caramelized onions and relish and tart pickles and spicy mustard. "How come you're not sitting with your friends?"

"Oh." She shifts uncomfortably. "Well, I'm not really sure I have any."

That hits me right in my coal-heart. "But you had people you hung out with before I got here, right? You don't end up class treasurer and head of the yearbook committee by being a loner freak."

"It's complicated," she says. "Artie and I are close, so I always hung out with her and her friends. They were this big group of music and theatre geeks across different grades – Sean Montgomery is kind of the leader of them now. They were heaps of fun. But after her accident, Artie was out of school for a bit, and then she moved to Acheron Academy to finish her senior year. At first, I tried to stay in that group, but it was weird without her. So I usually hang out with the computer science geeks and the paper staffers, but then people started hiring Poison Ivy and it got awkward, so I decided I was better off on my own."

"I feel that," I say between bites. Gods above, this hot dog is *orgasmic*.

"Honestly, I don't know how you do it, Fergie."

"Dowuuut?" I'm not going to stop eating to talk.

"Live with the *sacer*," Euri says wistfully. "I miss talking to people. No one's exactly mean to me, and I have my extracurriculars, but it's not the same. The night of Sean's party is the most fun I've had in a very long time. I wish—"

Our conversation is cut off by a holler as everyone around us gets to their feet and roars. A buzzer rings and the game gets started – a mess of dribbling balls and basketball shoes squeaking on the gym floor. I hear Victor's name on the commentary, but it goes too fast for me to follow what's happening.

"I've been so happy since you turned up," Euri yells over the din. "We don't get many senior students who transfer, especially not several weeks into senior year. So I guess I'm lucky that you're not an ax murderer or something."

See. That voice inside my head. *Even people like Euri who seem nice and lovely and trustworthy are out for what they can get for themselves.*

My morose thoughts are interrupted by a collective gasp from the crowd, followed by raucous cheers from our side and boos from the other.

"What happened?"

"The Acheron star player, Chris Lawson, just fumbled an easy shot." Euri's fingers tap on her phone as she makes notes for her article. "He must be nervous. I heard there are recruiters in the audience tonight, including one from U Penn, which is the school his daddy wants him to play for."

"How do you know about Chris Lawson's college recruitment? He doesn't even go to Stonehurst."

"It's my business to know all my competition in Emerald Beach," Euri says. "Just because I won't hire Poison Ivy like some lazy, cheating fuckers, doesn't mean I don't take getting into Princeton seriously."

I'm reminded again of just how much Euri reminds me of Old Fergie. We go back to eating in contented silence until a few minutes later when the crowd goes crazy again, the screaming and foot-stomping completely obliterating the commentary.

"Holy shit. Chris missed again." Euri's voice has changed. She sounds suspicious. "Something's not right here. There's *no way* he should've missed that shot. He was right under the hoop but he basically threw the ball at the wall and—"

She's cut off by a loud *THUMP* from the court and another roar of outrage from across the gym. All around us, students erupt into a chant of 'Victor, Victor, Victor!'

"What?" I grab Euri's arm. "Tell me."

"Shit. Holy shit, Fergie." She's shaking. "He's bleeding. They're carrying him off the court."

"Who's bleeding?" My mind immediately goes to Victor lying in a pool of his own blood. *Please, let him be okay.*

What? Why do I even care what happens to Victor August?

"Wes Bledsloe. He's another Acheron player. He was about to make a basket, and Chris just *pile-drove* him into the court." She slumps against me. "Chris attacked a member of his *own team*, and he's handed the game to Stonehurst Prep."

I don't need her to tell me because I *know* it. I overheard Cassius and Victor talking about it. This is the price the Poison Ivy Club demands. Chris is their client. I don't know how they fixed it, but this guy will be going to an Ivy League school.

All he had to do was hand the game to Victor August.

31

FERGIE

I follow Euri out of the gymnasium, my mind a million miles away.

Stonehurst Prep thrashed Acheron. 76-18. Their team never recovered from having Chris and Wes out of the game. All those Acheron players who wanted to impress the recruiters have had their hopes well and truly dashed.

Chris Lawson might've ruined his team's chances, but he'd guaranteed himself a place at an Ivy, thanks to Victor.

And I don't even blame him.

I got it. I *understood*.

More than anyone could ever know.

For most of my life, I wanted an Ivy so bad that it hurt some-times. School is super fun when you're a blind girl. It's just *filled* with understanding people who look past your disability and see the beauty inside.

Blah. That's sarcasm, in case you didn't pick up on that. School sucks if you're different. I mean, that's pretty much a universal truth. But at least I was born in the twenty-first century where I can go to school as a clever blind woman. I *do* have a future. I *do* have possibilities, and I intended to live up to them. I have shows like *Gilmore Girls* and books like Steffanie Holmes' *Pretty Girls Make Graves* (okay, that might be a bad example) and I've been waiting and waiting for my chance to step into my real life.

And my real life was supposed to begin at college. At an *Ivy League* college.

Nothing less than an Ivy would do. I set my sights on Harvard when I was nine years old, and I haven't stopped thinking about it for a single day.

My wall of jiujitsu ribbons. My work on the *Witchwood Falls World*. The hours of volunteer work I put in at the guide dog charity. All of it waiting to be written out on my applications for Harvard, Princeton, and Yale.

And then The Incident.

With a single, horrifying event, my entire future disappeared.

Everything I worked for burnt to ashes and dust in front of my eyes, and I had no one to blame but my own stupidity.

And I move across the country and fall straight into the arms of Cassius, Victor, and Torsten, the three people who have the power to place Harvard back at my fingertips. And I—

No.

Am I *crazy?*

Did I just consider becoming a client of the Poison Ivy Club?

It's not right. I'm not a cheater. What's the point of going to an Ivy if I didn't earn it? What could they possibly give me but a broken heart and an application filled with invented extracurriculars?

Someone will find out. I'd be humiliated all over again.

It's not worth it.

The Poison Ivy Club has been put in my path to tempt me. But I'm not going to fall into another trap.

I'm Fergie Munroe now, and I'm determined to have a

fantastic life *without* an Ivy League education. And that fantastic life begins with tonight's party.

As I'm swinging my leg into the back of Artie's car, a voice yells, "Fergie Munroe, where do you think you're going?"

"Hi, Juliet." I fold up my cane and tuck it by my feet. "That was quite a game."

"Wasn't it? My brother is an absolute legend. You're coming to my party, right?"

"Yeah. Euri and I are heading over to her place to get ready. We'll see you there in a bit."

"No." Juliet grabs my arm and starts tugging me out of the car. "Both of you, come *now*."

"But our clothes are at my place—" Euri whimpers.

"Whatever you were planning to wear, Eurydice, trust me that I have something better," Juliet declares. "I won't take no for an answer. Come on, are you afraid I'll bite?"

Beside me, Euri swallows. Her sister turns around in the front seat.

"Just say the word and I'll burn rubber out of here right now," Artemis says. "You don't even have to go to the party if you don't want to. We can hang out, watch movies—"

"No, it's cool." Euri shoves her door open. "We'll go with Juliet. Thanks, Artie. I'll call you when we need a ride home."

"Excellent choice." Juliet hooks her arm in mine and drags me out of the car. I barely have time to grab my bag and cane before she's dragging me over to her convertible. (Euri tells me it's a 2022 Porsche Boxster with a custom purple sparkle wrap, because in Emerald Beach even nerdy girls like Euri know about luxury cars.)

We squash in the backseat with three of her other girlfriends. Not legal, but I have the feeling we won't be pulled over. Juliet turns the music up to an earsplitting volume, and they sing along to some trash pop song I've never heard. Someone pops a Champagne bottle. When it's thrust into my hands, I drink. The bubbles tickle my throat.

We drive up into the Hills, twisting through the sprawling streets. We arrive somewhere surrounded by a tall stone wall. I can hear birds and smell trees and money. I remember Euri saying Victor had woods next to his house. I didn't know there were any areas of Harrington Hills left that weren't paved over with mega-mansions.

We stop at a security gate, drive into a tunnel (yes, a tunnel. Like we're docking on the Starship Enterprise or something), and park in a garage. Juliet grabs my arm and barely lets me unfold my cane before she's dragging me into the house.

"I'm so excited to show you the place," Juliet gushes. "You've never been here before, Eurydice?"

"I don't exactly get invites to your parties," Euri mumbles.

"Well, then that's an oversight," Juliet lets go of my arm to twirl around her marble-floored foyer. "All are welcome. *Per rectum ad astra* – from the asshole to the stars. Come on."

Juliet ushers us all up to her bedroom. It's on the second story, up a sweeping staircase that feels every bit as grand and not quite as cold as the one at Cali's place. Juliet's room is at the end of a long, wide hallway. One entire wall is floor-to-ceiling windows overlooking the house's back yard and – I assume, because this is a mansion in California – a massive pool.

There are at least six other girls in the room, all in various stages of primping. Hairspray fumes make my head spin. Juliet rushes around, filling mine and Euri's arms with designer clothing, seemingly oblivious to the fact that Euri hates her guts. But Euri accepts readily, and I pick up a hint of curiosity in her voice as she thanks Juliet and disappears into her en suite to try them on.

"You're the new girl, right? Cassius' stepsister?" a girl named Miranda asks. I want to scream. Every person in this room knows *exactly* who I am and that Cassius has a sacer on me. Miranda is fishing for gossip. "I love those boots you wear at school. Who's the designer?"

"John Fluevog," I say, fingering the edge of my red leather jacket. I've never before heard my heavy metal clothing described as a *style*.

"Jules has just the dress to match them." Another girl – Bernadette – dumps a mountain of fabric into my lap. "You *have* to try this. It even matches your Kate Spade bag."

"Does it?" I can't help sounding skeptical. I can't tell if these girls are teasing me or what. This must be what Torsten feels like *all the fucking time*.

"The dress is a beautiful red color," Juliet says. "And the beading is in black. Fergie, it looks amazing with your hair. Please try it on."

"Fine." I crowd into the bathroom with Euri and pull the dress on. It's practically a perfect fit. When I emerge into the room and everyone claps, I know I'm going to have to wear the dress.

"Fergie, please let me do your hair," Juliet gushes.

More Champagne bottles are passed around. Conversation flits between people I don't know, vacations in Martha's Vineyard and Cancun. I'm nodding off a little in my chair when something reaches my ears...

"You're Artemis' sister, aren't you?" one of them, a girl named Spencer who I vaguely remember from European Lit class, asks Euri.

"That's me." Euri's words are a little slurred, but I can't tell if it's agitation or alcohol consumption.

"Pity about her losing out on Yale," Spencer tsks. Euri's gonna cut a bitch, but she remains calm. "What's she doing these days?"

"She works as an orderly at Emerald Beach General," Euri snaps. "She empties bedpans. Do you want some more Champagne?"

BY THE TIME Juliet's ready to make her grand entrance, the party is in full swing. We sweep down the staircase in a v-formation, like a girl band on the red carpet at the Grammys. I can actually hear people snapping pictures. Stonehurst Prep parties go in the society pages. Rich people live on a completely different planet.

"Wow," Euri leans close, her nails digging into my arm. In a weird reversal of roles, she's clinging to me. "This is *insane*."

"Tell me about it." My feet scuff something gritty on the floor. "I'm happy to leave any time you need, especially if you have to fend off any more snotty comments about your sister, but in exchange, please describe everything you see in excruciating detail, because I don't want to miss a thing."

"It's a deal," Euri laughs. "Okay, so the whole place is decorated like... like the Russian Winter Palace. There's a white sleigh in the corner with taxidermied wolves and a professional photographer taking pictures. That stuff on the floor is fake snow. There are crystal snowflakes hanging from the ceiling, and the bar is made of *ice*. It's *October*. This is madness."

She gets the giggles. I can't help laughing, too.

We head to the bar and collect a couple of cocktails, then peruse the food selection. Milo did the catering (the twins adore his food almost as much as I do) and he's gone all out with the Russian theme – blinis, piroshki, caviar, even little shot glasses filled with borscht. We pile a bunch of stuff onto a plate and carry it around, doing the blind-girl version of people-watching: eavesdropping on conversations.

Everywhere we go, people talk about Victor's game, about the scout in the audience, the one who came up to him afterward and hugged him. Victor would be going to Harvard on a full-ride basketball scholarship, not that he even needs it. He'd taken the opportunity that might've gone to Chris, if Chris hadn't hired Poison Ivy to ensure his place.

The whole room buzzes with college talk. The final SAT sitting before the ED application deadline is coming up fast – it's the last chance to earn a score that will impress admissions officers at early decision stage, and even these rich pricks are taking it seriously.

And I hate them. I hate them all.

How easily the names of my dream colleges roll off their gilded tongues.

Euri's commentary doesn't help – she keeps up a steady stream of gossip about who has what scores, where they're applying, and their chances of getting in. She points out three people who she thinks will hire Poison Ivy in December if they don't get into their early decision colleges. "...and I know Peggy's slept with Cassius, but she's always had this thing for Victor, and I think she's only applied to Brown because she wants an excuse to knock on Poison Ivy's door—"

"I heard my name," a familiar, aristocratic voice interrupts us. "Euri, I hope you're telling Fergie how good my ass looks in these Rick Owens jeans."

"Victor." Euri's voice trembles.

If Victor notices her discomfort, he doesn't acknowledge it. How nice it must be to live in a dream world where your actions have no consequences.

"How about a kiss for the champion?" Victor leans in close.

His whisky, chocolate, and hazelnut scent is so strong it leaves a mark on my skin.

Euri makes a disgusted noise, but I can't help myself. I'm a magnet and Victor August is a giant, shiny fridge filled with delicious snacks. That metaphor doesn't make sense, but he's got me all twisted up, so who the fuck cares? My breath hitches as I allow my lips to linger a few moments before I press them lightly to his cheek.

His skin sizzles beneath my touch. I grip his arm and I remember how strong he is – not a wall of muscle like Cassius, but Vic could crush a windpipe or snap an arm without breaking a sweat and I'm into it. My body remembers Victor pressed up against me in my bed, all protective and cuddly. It remembers dancing with him on top of a table, even though my brain had left the building at that point.

And my body *definitely* remembers that – sacer and creepy agreement to 'put me back together' and all – I want Victor August, even if that's a fucking bad idea.

The longer I allow my lips to linger on his skin, the longer I drink from his whisky and chocolate scent, the more I lose any sense of self-preservation.

It takes all my self-control to pull back from him. I touch my fingers to my lips. They tingle with the memory of him.

"I want to show you something." Victor takes my hand. I let him. What the fuck is happening to me? This party, these people, they have me all twisted up inside. I don't even say goodbye to Euri as Victor pulls me away. "You're going to love it."

Victor leads me through a series of rooms that are distinctly less crowded, through a door, down a staircase, and into a basement that could rival Cali's. I sense the space is largely underground – there's a weight to the walls, as though they hold back a mass of dirt and secrets.

"We hang out here sometimes with friends when it's too cold

for the pool," Victor says. "Although if it's just the Poison Ivy Club, we go to Cali's place. There's a gym in here."

"You brought me down here to show me your gym? Do I look like a roid bro to you?"

"No." Victor pushes open another door and ushers me inside. "I brought you down here to show you this."

The echoes in this room feel strange and bright. I step onto a shiny floor, which slopes away beneath my feet. Subsidence? I tighten my grip on Victor's arm and move deeper into the space. My feet crunch over a thick layer of fine dust or... or sand... or *something*. What is this room?

"Can you tell what this is?" Victor asks.

"Some kind of indoor beach?" I lean down to touch the sand. I can't believe I've lived in Emerald Beach for over a month and the first beach I set foot on is in Victor August's basement.

No. Scratch that. I believe it. Rich people are fucking bonkers.

"Don't touch that." Victor grabs my hand, yanking it behind me in a controlling way that makes me want to push *all* his buttons. "You'll cut yourself. It's not sand – it's glass and ceramic and metal chips."

"What? *Why?*"

"This is my mother's rage room. When she was our age, she had a pretty traumatic life. It's a long story, but for a few years as a teenager she lived alone in this house. No family, no friends, just her and her cat. The loneliness got to her sometimes, so she turned the bowling alley into a rage room."

"I'll skip right past the bit where you have a bowling alley in your house. What does one do in a rage room?"

"You smash shit. Here."

Something slim and heavy presses against my palm. I run my fingers along the cold surface. It's a crowbar.

"Victor, why did you bring me here?"

Victor laughs that low, sultry laugh of his. "I've been watching you all night, Duchess. You look like you want to break something. I thought I'd save my testicles."

"So this is a purely selfish endeavor?"

"Oh, totally." Victor comes up behind me. His fingers drag over my hips as he twists me a little to the right. "Everything in this room is fair game, except my plums. About a foot in front of you is a stack of dishes. Go nuts, just not for my nuts."

He steps away, and I swing. The crowbar connects with the plates. The room explodes with bright sound as the stack topples over, plates fanning out across the space, shards ricocheting off the walls and raining down on me like sharpened hailstones.

I stand back, panting. My heart hammering against my chest.

This is *amazing.*

It's everything I've needed, ever since The Incident. All that hatred bubbles to the surface. In this room, with this Golden God, I don't have to hold back. I don't have to spare anyone's feelings.

I don't have to be afraid of the darkness inside me.

"Nice swing," Victor purrs. "To your right, about ten o'clock, there's an old wooden cabinet. It might be an antique."

I roar as I pound the crowbar into the cabinet. Wood splinters and cracks. The sound hums in my ears like a killer guitar riff, a soundtrack to destruction.

I whirl around and swing again, slamming the crowbar into another object. It feels like an armchair of some kind. I tear off chunks and throw them over my shoulder. My veins thrum with heat.

All the rage, all the righteous *injustice* of what happened, pours out of me. By the time I throw down the crowbar, I'm drenched in sweat and Juliet's fancy hairdo has come completely unraveled, strands sticking to the back of my neck and across my forehead. My arms sting from small cuts where shards flung up. My makeup is probably smudged. I must look like a car crash.

I haven't felt so completely *myself* in a long time.

Victor steps up to me, placing his hands on my forearms and pulling me close. His scent washes over me, that decadent chocolate and whisky that promises both indulgence and safety. I fall into him. He catches me. He holds me. I'm safe with him, and I haven't felt safe in a long, long time.

"I know what you want to ask," I murmur into his chest. Victor presses the back of my neck against him, and my hairs stand up where he touches me. "And I can't tell you why."

"Your home isn't the only one with secrets," he whispers into my hair. His fingers trail circles on my skin.

Tell me about it. Your mother has a rage room in the basement.

"If you can live without knowing mine, Victor August, then I don't care about yours."

He chuckles darkly – a sound that promises my destruction. His arm crosses my back, crushing me against him.

"Little word of advice, Duchess," Victor murmurs, every word stoking the wild hunger inside me, the one that smashing shit has fed into an angry beast. "You should run away from us. From me and from Torsten, and especially from Cassius. We're no good. We're trouble."

I lean forward, my chest pressing against his. "Maybe I'm trouble, too."

"Oh, I know you are."

Victor's hand slides behind my neck, and he pulls me in for a scorching kiss. My body melts into his. I love that hand on the back of my throat, so possessive, so uncompromising. Victor August knows exactly what he wants, and he wants *me*.

"Tell me to stop," he begs as he pushes me against the wall, as his hands tear at my clothing. "Tell me you don't want this. Tell me that Cassius will kill us if he catches us together."

"Why?" I pant.

Victor shoves the dress around my hips. He pushes my scarlet panties to the side and slides one finger into my cunt. I'm already soaking, have been since he brought me down here and handed me that crowbar.

He lets out a heavy breath as he slides a second finger into me. His teeth scrape over my collarbone as he fucks me with his fingers, stopping only to draw them out and wet my clit before plunging back inside me while his thumb rubbed evil circles over that bundle of nerves.

"Because when you take all of me into that hot, sweet cunt of yours, I'm not ever going to be able to give you back to him."

Back to him? Victor's words penetrate the haze of pleasure.

"To Cassius?" I growl. "For the last fucking time, I'm not his. I've never been his, and I want you inside me."

I know I'm playing with fire, that whatever bravado I have will fall to pieces under my stepbrother's cruelty. But I need to obliterate the memory of him inside me, and what better way to do that than with his best friend?

"Good." Victor's other hand tightening around the back of my throat as he plays with my cunt. "Because I'm well past the moment where I can say no to you. I'm owning you and all your secrets tonight, Fergie Munroe."

"You Poison Ivy boys, so obsessed with ownership. Did it ever occur to you that tonight I'm owning *you?*" I reach down and cup him through his designer jeans. Victor growls, like an actual animal *growl* that makes my belly go all gooey and my toes curl.

I manage to pop open the buttons one-handed and draw his length from his silk boxers. He's hard and fucking *enormous.*

As I explore him with my fingers, I'm surprised and

delighted to feel that the head of his cock is pierced. I give it a little experimental tug, and Victor moans.

"Oooh, you'll pay for that, Duchess." He tears his cock from my hands and drops to his knees in front of me. He places one hand on my belly, bracing me against the wall, and drives his fingers hard inside me. His tongue finds my clit, and he closes his mouth over it.

Whoa. *Whoa.*

Dawson *never* went down on me. Pre-marital sex was fine because he was the one getting off, but he thought giving a girl head was too obscene, that his God would have a problem with that, somehow. No guy has ever done this except in my fantasies, and I kind of thought I'd find it too intense and weird, but if I die with Victor August between my legs, I'll die happy.

His hot mouth sucks me in, and combined with his fingers stroking inside me, it's so intense that I kind of... lose myself. But just when I'm on the edge of the greatest orgasm of my life, he pulls back and uses the tip of his tongue to tease around the edges, not giving me enough pressure to fall over the edge. I don't even realize I have my hands on his head until I dig my fingers into his scalp.

"So impatient, Duchess," he chuckles as he plunges his fingers into me. "You'll get your orgasm. But first, I want to taste every inch of you."

He does, licking and sucking and nibbling at me like it's the peak of summer and I'm his favorite fucking ice cream. When he sucks my clit back into his mouth and scrapes his teeth over the surface, I scream.

An orgasm normally kindles slowly inside my stomach like a fire roaring to life, but this one *slams* into me like a fucking freight train. My ears ring. The lights in the room shudder and swim. Victor holds me as my legs collapse under me, pushing me back into the wall and kissing me as the pleasure rockets around my body.

"Who owns this pussy now?" he growls, cupping his hand between my legs. I almost come again from the raw possessiveness in his voice.

"You do," I whimper.

"Damn right. And now..." He kicks my feet apart. "You're going to come again, all over my cock."

"Vic..." I moan, my chest heaving, my breath rough and ragged against the wall.

"Don't worry, baby." He trails his fingers down my back as he lifts the fabric of my dress higher and pushes my underwear to the side again. "I'm clean. Augusts keep on top of that sort of thing. I have my paperwork on my phone if you want to see..."

Yeah, no way am I stopping so he can find his phone. "I'm clean, too. And I'm on birth control. But that's not what—"

"Good. Because you're going to want to be bareback when my piercing hits you."

The hot length of him sheaths inside me, and I forget my protests. I forget about my stepbrother and his stupid threats and sacers. I forget about Harvard and SAT scores and Dawson and everything except for Victor's dick pushing into me.

"That's it, baby girl," Victor whispers against my ear as he wraps one thick forearm around me. "That's it, take me deep."

He's so big, so goddamn *thick*, that it takes several strokes for him to get deep enough for me to feel that piercing. But when I do... holy fuck. Holy Jesus fuck shit cunt twatwaffle dickweasel bitchbadger it's amazing. It's like stars are fucking exploding inside me.

With one of his signature dark chuckles, Victor draws out of me slowly, making me whimper as I feel every inch retreating. Then he fills me with a single forceful thrust.

I arch my back, bracing against the wall and pushing back

against him, desperate to take him deeper, to make that piercing dance all over the dark and secret places inside me.

I scream and curse and whimper as Victor pounds into me, stretching me as that cold ball of metal works its magic. He's so fucking *smug* as he holds me upright, murmuring that he owns my cunt, that he's not done with me yet, and I almost don't want to come again so he doesn't get an even bigger ego about it, but there's no stopping this fucking locomotive. I fall to pieces in his arms, and it's a good thing he's huge, because his dick is the only thing holding me upright.

I'm going to be walking crooked tomorrow.

I wrap my arms around Vic's shoulders, falling into him as he lets himself fall over the edge, too. He comes with a grunt and a deep, shuddering thrust, sinking his teeth into my neck as he pumps inside me, marking me as his even as his cum drips down my legs.

If Cas sees me, there's going to be no mistaking what happened. Fuck Cas – I *want* him to see. I want him to know once and for all that he doesn't own me.

"Fuck, Duchess." Victor's chest heaves. Still inside me, still holding me against that wall, he cups my face with fingers that smell like me, and brings his lips to mine for a punishing, possessive kiss. It's a kiss that's about more than sex, a kiss that leaves me breathless and haunted and—

"Fergie."

A voice calls my name. It aches with hurt. It doesn't come from Victor's lips, but from somewhere behind us. I freeze, every lick of pleasure fleeing my veins.

It's Torsten.

No. No. No.

How long has he been there?

How much did he see?

It didn't matter. Vic's cock is buried inside me. There's no mistaking what just happened. I'm desperate to explain that what just happened has nothing to do with how I feel about the gallery, and what I want to happen between us. But I can't find the words, and I'm not sure they'd be true even if I *could* say them.

The way I feel about the Poison Ivy boys... it's complicated. They're intrinsically linked in my mind. I can't untangle Victor from Torsten from my monster of a stepbrother. I want them all. I hate them all. I need them all. But this dance of ours is going to end in shattered hearts.

"Victor, get off me." I shove him. He staggers back, his cock tearing from my entrance. Vic yells in surprise, but then he must see our guest because his voice turns to ash.

"Torsten? What are you doing here?"

Torsten's voice cracks as he pushes out the words. "You should come. Cassius is in a fight."

32

VICTOR

F uck.

Fuck.

The betrayed look on Torsten's face confirms my fear. He likes Fergie. He's fallen hard for her. I can't blame him, because she's fucking incredible, but I want to protect Torsten from more heartache. And from Cassius' wrath.

If Torsten loves her, he won't be able to watch Cassius ruin her.

If he loves her, he won't be able to watch me make her my queen.

If he loves her, it could tear the three of us apart.

From the way his face falls, I know that he's broken Cassius' *sacer*, too. I look at Fergie, but she's trying to pull her dress back over her hips and won't tell me even if I beg.

I've fucked up.

Now Torsten's forced to carry the weight of my secret along-side his own. Cassius *cannot* know that we've been with Fergie, not until he's finished with her.

If he doesn't know already. Torsten says he's fighting upstairs. And I can think of one thing that would set him off—

I should've been stronger than this. But seeing Fergie in the middle of that party tonight, looking so lost, looking like she needed a knight in shining armor, I had to do *something*.

"Torsten, wait—"

He spins on his heel and disappears. Cursing, I shove my dick back into my boxers and pull up my jeans. Fergie curses, and I see that I've torn the zipper on her dress in my haste to get inside her. Fuck it, there's no time to fix it, so I drop my shirt over her shoulders. She cinches it at her waist and draws it with the tattered braiding from the ruined armchair. She can even make *that* look good.

Cas will know what we did the minute he sees her, but it's probably too late, anyway. I have to come clean to him. I have to make this right.

I knit my fingers in Fergie's and head her back through the basement. Torsten's nowhere in sight, but I follow the shouting through the vast house and out into the garden. Kids are gathered in a circle on the patio, too near my greenhouse for my liking. They chant, "fight, fight, fight," and film with their phones. I shove through them, still holding Fergie, and find Chris Lawson, drenched in blood from a cut above his eye, with his arms locked around Cassius' throat.

Cas has gone blue. He's on the verge of losing consciousness, which I know is exactly where he wants to be. Even though he gasps for breath, his eyes glint with that monstrous mischief.

I burst into the circle. "What the fuck is going on?"

My voice stills the crowd. No one's yelling anymore, although phones are still raised.

"You ruined my life," Chris screams, spitting bits of tooth onto the ground. "How can you live with yourselves?"

Cassius' mouth flaps. He wants to say something smartass, but he can't breathe. I let Chris' comment hang as I feign disinterest.

"You knew that recruiter would be at the game," Chris continues as he tightens his grip on Cas' throat. "You may have got me into a good school, but no way will they ever let me on the varsity team now. My basketball career is *over*. And for what? So Victor fucking August can have another shiny trophy for his wall."

Chris glares at me in defiance. Cas' head slumps back. He's only got *moments* left.

"We had an agreement," I say. Although all I want to do is tear him off Cassius and let my friend breathe again, there are enough Acheron people at the party that this could descend into a bloodbath. I need to maintain control. "A signed contract. You knew exactly what you were getting into. When I told you my price, you didn't hesitate. Your teammates here should know that if they want to blame anyone for their devastating loss today, it's you. And you *dare* come to *my* house to tell me you're unhappy with how things worked out when you got exactly what you wanted? You're a sad excuse for a human, Chris."

Chris' teammates shift, their murmurs harsh, angry. It's only just occurred to them that Chris was the one who brought the Poison Ivy Club into this, that their own star player has cost them all their varsity hopes.

Cassius chooses this exact moment, as the crowd's sentiment begins to turn, to twist his body and bite a chunk out of Chris' arm.

Chris howls in agony as blood spurts over his Ralph Lauren button-down. Chris drops Cas like a sack of potatoes and scrambles away, clutching the messy wound in his arm. Cassius crawls to his knees, hawking and spitting a mangled clump of skin onto the tiles.

I rush to his side, but as I do, Chris lunges at me. A tactical error. Just as his hands go around my neck, Cas grabs him and slams him into the ground. Patio tiles crack. A sound like bones shattering fills the night.

Chris' keening wail rises like a banshee over the stillness.

No, not Chris.

Someone else is wailing.

I turn toward the sound just as someone rushes us. It's Sierra, her eyes wide from whatever drugs she's indulged in tonight. She swings a heavy Coach purse at Cassius' head.

Clonk.

"Ow, fuck." Cas rubs his head. His eyes are narrow slits. I need to get Sierra out of here, now. I need to get everyone out – no one is safe within a mile of Cas when he gets the demons inside him.

I grab for Sierra, but she ducks under me and swings at Cas again.

"You ruined my life," she screams. "My parents found out about the pills, and they're sending me to some Catholic convent school in the Swiss Alps."

"What are you talking about?" Cassius rounds on her, but I step in front of him, trying to give him the space he needs to cool down.

She thinks we told her parents.

"We never did that," I say. "You cooperated, and we kept your secret. Don't blame us because you were sloppy."

She swings the purse at me, but I dodge it easily. "Then how did they find out? How did a video of me on my knees for Jason end up on my dad's phone?"

That stops me dead. Because it's not possible.

A couple of days after that night, when he'd calmed down after Fergie's disobedience, Cas told me what Jason tried to do. He had a few seconds of video footage before he turned his camera off. I watched him delete it from his phone with my own eyes.

Sierra continues. "You act like you're such a good guy, Victor. You and your fucking morals. You wouldn't *dare* use sex as blackmail. Well, I'd say your reputation is pretty fucking shot. And what's a man like you without his reputation and his nice suits? Just a fucking lowlife criminal, that's what."

"Hang on, we didn't do that. Explain this to me—"

But it's too late. Sierra isn't in a talking mood. She screeches and lunges at me again. Cassius steps over Chris' prone body and looms over Sierra, and even though she's pissed, she's not suicidal. She steps away from him.

"Don't be so dramatic," he sneers, glaring at Sierra before fixing his wild eyes on everyone in the crowd. "You're all the fucking same. The only reason you're so pissed at me is because you didn't think to come to us first."

Sierra leaps at him. Okay, maybe she does have a death wish. She rakes her nails down his face while Cas laughs and laughs like a maniac. I manage to pull her off him and toss her to her friend, Peggy. "Get her out of here. Call her a cab. Make sure she gets home safe."

"Are you sure you wouldn't rather make her get on her knees for you, Victor? Make sure she really knows her place?"

What the fuck now?

When I turn around to face the dead person who addressed me, I don't see the whole of them all at once. They exist as a bunch of disparate pieces, like the geometric shapes of one of the Picasso paintings Torsten loves. Waves of golden-blonde hair. Heart-shaped face. Huge, swinging tits. Stony, aggressive gaze. Puffy, blood-red lips. The pieces fuse together, and I recognize my foe.

It's Drusilla Hargreaves.

At my house.

At *my* party.

Drusilla thrusts out her hip and glares at me with those cold, defiant eyes. "Hello again, Victor."

"Dru." I play it cool, although inside I'm a mess. This is the last fucking thing we need. I'm aware more than ever that Fergie is behind me, that she's listening to every word, that she might at any moment learn one of the secrets I've been desperately trying to keep buried. "Long time no see."

"That's your fault, Vic, not mine. You told me that I had to change schools or the Dio brothers would come after my family, and all because I bruised Cassius' fragile little ego." She tosses her golden waves over her shoulder. "I'm back now. And I see Cassius has a new stepsister, a poor little blind girl—"

"—ex-fucking-cuse-me?" Fergie shouts. Luckily, Cas is still too out-of-it to hear her in the crowd. I long to turn around to her, but I can't let Dru out of my sight and I can't let Cas see that Fergie's wearing my shirt. My Duchess has more than proven she can take care of herself.

"—she's just another toy for him to break, like he tried to break me," Drusilla purrs. "Well, not on my watch. I'm going to make sure that the Poison Ivy Club pays for every crime you've committed. I'm going to suck your poison right out of Stone-hurst Prep."

I laugh, because her threat is so pretty and so empty. "Dream on, little girl. How do you think you're going to do that?"

"Shouldn't you pay more attention to the wider issues in Emerald Beach?" she trills. "I'd have thought your parents would've told you. My mother has been sworn in as mayor of this city, and her first platform is to clean up organized crime, starting with three bothersome women who've enslaved this city. It's time for Emerald Beach to be free."

A few in the crowd dare to cheer quietly at that. Cas launches himself at someone, and the place erupts into chaos.

Fists swing. Glass and bottles smash. Someone breaks a lawn chair over an Acheron player's back.

"Fergie?" I kick Chris' body aside as I search the fray for that flame-colored mane. I need to protect her. I need to find Juliet and get them both to safety—

"You die now."

A rough hand wraps around my neck, lifting me off the ground. I claw at the hand around my throat, but it's made of rock. It won't move. I fight for breath as I stare down into the eyes of my attacker. My oldest friend.

"You reek of her," he growls. "I smelled that sweet raspberry cunt the minute you stepped into the fight."

"Cas—" I manage to choke out. Everything human has gone from his eyes.

"She's mine," he hisses. "You were supposed to wait your turn, but you touched her and she's *mine* and I'm going to flay your skin from your bones—"

I dig my fingers beneath his, granting myself a fraction of an inch of breathing space. "She's here," I gasp. "Do you want her to see you like this?"

"This is who I am," he growls back. "I'm the monster. And besides, she can't see me."

"No, but I can hear. And I can *feel*."

Fergie appears at my side, a fucking siren wreathed in flames. She glares from Cas to me, and although I know she can't see us, her shattered emerald orbs burn right through my chest.

"I'm *done* with both of you." Her voice is ice-cold. "Is there a single person at this party your little club hasn't hurt? A single life that isn't broken? And yet you parade around in front of them like you expect them to kiss your boots. And they line the fuck up. Well, not me. I won't be broken by a scared little boy, and I won't be saved by an arrogant prick. I'm out of here. Enjoy ripping Vic's throat out, Cassius. Enjoy breaking the only person who isn't afraid of you."

My eyes flutter closed. I can't bear to see the pain etched across her face. I watched her when she went off in the rage room. And I don't just mean that I watched the way her dress tugged over the curve of her ass when she swung that crowbar. I watched Fergie's lip twist with determination, her neck lengthen, her eyes come alive in a way they haven't before.

Something rotten is eating Fergie Munroe from the inside, and I *will* find it and pull it out and make it pay for hurting her.

And I have the resources to do that. This isn't like last time, with Gemma.

I'll save Fergie Munroe, if I can survive tonight. I'll save her and I'll save myself. *If* Cas would just let... me... breathe...

With a roar, Cassius hurls me across the patio. I crash into a deck chair, which shatters beneath me. I gasp for air, my stomach cramping. I know I'm in a lot of pain. I know I've landed on my arm and it might be broken, but I can't think of anything but the flames disappearing through the house as Fergie obeys the one sensible thing I've said to her and gets far the fuck away from us.

As I roll over and focus on gulping in lungfuls of air, I feel another pair of eyes boring into me. I look up, through the violent crowd, directly into Drusilla's contented face.

What is happening here?

Why is Drusilla back?

Are we losing our grip on Stonehurst Prep?

33

FERGIE

I spend most of Sunday in bed, nursing a mild hangover and trying to make sense of everything that happened at the game and the party.

Cassius' words dance over and over in my head. He's right. Every person in this school is out for what they can get. Even Euri uses others for her own ends. No one is innocent. No one fights fair.

The only difference between the Poison Ivy Club clients and everyone else is that they've made it official—

Stop it. You can't think like that.

They tricked that Chris guy.

They took footage of Sierra without her consent. They used her body against her. They ruined her life, and for what? So Lucila Baskerville could guarantee her Princeton spot.

They pushed Euri's sister down the stairs.

It's sick.

I can't stop trembling.

I need to talk to Dad. I need to tell him what Cassius did to Sierra, and about the fight he started at the party, and the way he choked Victor like he didn't even *know* him. He's out of control. I can't live in this house anymore. Maybe I'll have to come clean to Dad about what happened between me and Cassius. The thought of it makes me sick, but I have to make Dad understand that my stepbrother is out for my blood.

You can do this, Fergie. It's definitely not the most difficult conversation you've had with him.

Dad made a point of mentioning to me that he didn't have a tennis game this weekend, so he should be home. I pull on a baggy Octavia's Ruin sweatshirt and push my door a crack. Not a sound from Cassius' room. I can hear Milo singing along with his favorite Latinx radio station as he whips up something delicious in the kitchen. Outside, a leaf blower blasts as Seymour tends the gardens.

I pad down the corridor and stand at the entrance to Dad and Cali's private wing. "Dad?" I call out. No answer. I can't hear any snoring, and Dad's a terrible snorer. He must be awake already.

I head downstairs, calling his name. I pass the steps down to the basement and wonder if he might be down there working out, which would make about as much sense as anything Dad does these days. But I don't hear the machines running.

"Dad, where are you?" I call again as I wander through the endless rooms.

"He's not here, Miss Fergie," Milo says as I enter the kitchen. "He's at the clinic. He had to perform emergency dental surgery."

"He does?" My eyebrows shoot right up. Dad *never* went into the clinic on a weekend in Witchwood Falls. He never even brought paperwork home to do on the weekends. He kept that time sacred, just for the two of us.

Only now, he's got Cali and she doesn't seem to like to share.

Stop reading so much into this. He has to work harder to establish the new business. It's probably some uber-demanding rich client, one of Cali's friends.

I sag into one of the barstools at the counter, all the motivation to have a heart-to-heart leaving my limp body. Milo places something steaming and chocolatey in front of me. "Pain au chocolat, fresh from the oven. Please, eat, eat."

Milo's done with Spanish food now, and he's moved on to French pastries. I have no complaints.

I pick up a square and chew. It tastes like cardboard. I'm a mess. *Maybe I should go to the clinic and force him to talk to me. Before I lose my nerve.* "Did he leave a number where I can reach him?"

"He's only got his mobile, and he said he'd keep it off during surgery. And afterward, he and Cali are going out to lunch to celebrate."

"To celebrate what?"

"Oh, it's not important." Milo busies himself scrubbing the coffee machine. "*She* has been dealing with a difficult project, but it looks to have sorted itself out now."

Of course. Cali can't bear for me and Dad to have a single moment alone together. He's got work and emergency surgery and tennis and celebration dinners for things I know nothing about. He's so head over heels for my cold bitch of a stepmother that he can't see what she's doing.

I push away the plate. "Thanks for the pastries, Milo. I'm not hungry."

"Are you okay, Miss Fergie? You look a little pale."

"I'm fine," I whisper. The lump of coal in my chest aches, as if it has the audacity to *feel* my dad's abandonment. "I'm just peachy."

34

CASSIUS

I woke up on Monday morning with sore knuckles, a raw throat, and a throbbing head. Ever since the party, Fergie's been avoiding me – no easy feat for a blind girl, but my stepsister is nothing if not determined. She's had Milo send all her food up to her room, and she's added four more locks to the bathroom door. I break them all off but I still don't see her. I don't know if she's peeing in a cup or what, but she's made it clear – she doesn't want to see me.

Well, that's fucking great. I'm sick of her face, anyway.

Especially after the way she acted on Friday, like I'd fucking ripped the head off a puppy instead of putting Chris Lawson in his place.

She went behind my back to seduce Victor. Fucking pussy – he's called me a hundred times and tried to come over to talk, but I don't want to hear it. It's not even his fault, but I can't see his face until I've calmed down, or I'll break every bone in his pretty body.

Fergie knew exactly who she belonged to, she *knew* Vic would get her once I'm done, and she threw herself at him anyway. She did it because she knows Victor August is weak for girls like her. Poor Fergie with her mysterious past and her eyes that don't see. She needs saving. She needs a hero.

Blah blah blah.

Like fuck she does. She needs to be tied to my bedposts and spanked until she's red and dripping wet for me.

I have plans for both of them. But I need to deal with something else first. Drusilla's threat burns in the back of my throat. And Sierra claiming I shared those videos with her parents. Bitch can't be talking about the one of her sucking Jason's dick, because I deleted what I'd captured. And we never sent the evidence of her using study drugs to anyone, because as far as we know, she was playing ball and staying away from Princeton.

Every time Sierra's accusation rings inside my skull, the red mist descends over my eyes. I spent four hours in the gym trying to push it back, but last night, I cracked. I went to Colosseum. It wasn't even a championship fight, just some Sunday evening cage brawl, but I stove a guy's head in.

He deserved it – he's one of Cali's newest soldiers, but he thought he'd be clever and take jobs on the side for a Russian oligarch, depriving my mother of her cut. Word got back to Cali and she told me I could deal with him. I could feel her eyes on me as she watched from the VIP area with her new husband.

I wonder what Fergie will do when she finds out what Daddy Dearest gets up to when she's not around.

Breaking that soldier was supposed to help. Killing brings me back to myself, it draws away the red mist. But this time, as I stared at the guy's mangled body, all I could think about is her.

My stepsister.

A woman who's made it clear that she'll never willingly touch my dick again.

And now that I've had her, I can't bear the idea of her belonging to anyone else. I don't want her to *want* anyone else. Especially not Victor fucking August.

I don't just want her in my bed. I don't just want to make every one of her holes mine. I want her to *want* me, to give in to the demonic side of herself and beg for the carnage and depravity only I can give her.

I want her to see me.

I roll over in bed and listen as she moves around in our shared bathroom. The sound of her humming Ghost's 'Griftwood' as she showers is the most exquisite torture. I could break in there and join her, but I can't make myself do it when I know she doesn't want me.

Instead, I watch from my window as she walks to the front of the driveway, the red flame of her hair swinging down her back and her boots clacking on the stone. I grip my dick in my hands, willing her to turn around *just once*, wishing for a glimpse of her unsuspecting face as I jerk myself off. But Eurydice and Artemis Jones whisk her away just as a rope of white jizz streaks across the windowsill.

I slump against the glass, my chest heaving. Fuck, what is wrong with me?

I can't face school. What's the point? If I gave a shit about college I could get in anywhere, thanks to the Poison Ivy Club. But I know ivy-covered buildings and poetry readings and tweed blazers with patch elbows aren't in my future. I have responsibilities, and my mother is finally ready to let me take them seriously.

I know what I need to do.

I wait until the dentist heads out to his clinic and Milo and Seymour are occupied with yard work, then I head down to the basement, my veins still humming. I move through the gym and hit the secret panel on the wall. The mirror swings inward, revealing a short, soundproof passage that ends in an enormous steel door.

This door used to be part of an old bank vault. Cali rescued it from a fire that gutted one of Livvie's clubs, back before I was born.

I tap in the combination on the other side, turn the handle, and swing the door open.

I step into Cali's secret domain.

35

CASSIUS

She's hard at work. A man hangs from a hook in the ceiling, his eyes glassy. He's half-dead already. Precise cuts crisscross his back and buttocks, and my mother hums to herself as she selects a blowtorch from her rack of implements – the tools of her trade.

Cali looks up at me, her eyes a pair of flint chips amongst the dark red.

It might seem weird to someone who doesn't know my mother that she does this work in our basement rather than at the club, where she's also built soundproof and bombproof rooms. But then, anyone who isn't me who sees this room isn't leaving it again.

Cali's club is more important to her than anything in the world, and that includes her family, and it *especially* includes her youngest son. If she's ever raided, she wants to keep that place squeaky clean. But our house can be a den of sin, and no one cares. Any cop or FBI goon will think twice before descending on a Harrington Hills mansion. The director of the FBI lives just down the road. Think of what the neighbors will say!

I pick up my bear-paw glove from the rack and slide it onto my hand – I had it made special from toughened leather, with sick curved claws on the end of each finger. It fits perfectly, like a second skin. Finally, I'm on the outside the monster I am within.

With a nod from Cali, I slash my claws across his chest, leaving my signature bear-claw mark. The Dio symbol has always been an eagle, but I think in this business it's important to establish a personal brand. Inside and outside the ring, I am the Bear, and I'll be the most feared name in the world one day.

"Who's this?" I ask as the man screams.

"He's a city planner," she hisses.

"Interesting choice of entertainment."

"This isn't for *fun*." Her shoulders sheen with sweat. Torture is a tough workout. "This guy has personally blocked three of Livvie's applications for new clubs. He's allowed another club owner, someone named Zack Lionel Sommesnay, to move on her Tartarus Oaks territory instead."

"Weird fucking name," I mutter.

"Yup. And this isn't the first time we've seen this name. Claudia's ships have been raided three times in the last month. We lost the guns we needed to keep our hold over the West Oaks drug trade and fulfill our contract with the Mexicans. Of course, all Claws is worried about are the paintings. Ten portraits for the latest exhibit, all confiscated by the authorities. Livvie thinks they're putting together a case against the museum."

Cali tosses a bucket of ice water over our friend's head. The guy wakes with a shudder, his wide eyes fixing on Cali, and then me. He hangs his head and makes a low, keening sound. He knows he's not long for this world.

"We have a leak in the organization," she spits. "Whoever they are, they're working for the new mayor's office."

Shit. That's Drusilla's mother. This isn't a coincidence. This has to do with why she's back. That's what she was talking about at the party.

"That Hargreaves bitch has it in her head that she's going to clean up this town," Cali mutters. "As if she's not the tenth mayor who made such a promise. Only thing is, she's the first I believe might actually do it."

Various city officials have publicly threatened to get rid of the criminal families that run this city, but Cali, Livvie, and Claws have been playing this game a lot longer, and they're smarter. They know how to placate officials with bribes and deals, and to win the public with their free museum and their lavish gifts, and our family activities go on in the background as they always have.

Except now, it seems.

"Why am I just hearing about this?" I growl.

"Because you're nineteen years old," she snaps. "You're not the head of this empire, Cassius. I am. This isn't your problem."

"If it's about the Triumvirate, it is my problem."

I know I should say something about Drusilla, but I don't. If Cali knew Drusilla was back at our school, and if she thought that her latest round of trouble had anything to do with what went down three years ago, she'd shut down the Poison Ivy Club. And probably send me to a Swiss monastery to glare at Sierra from across a mountain valley.

A plan forms in my head. This is the perfect opportunity to show my mother what I can do. I'll use Drusilla. I'll play her like a fucking fiddle and use her to bring down her mother's little power play and get the mayor's office out of the Triumvirate's hair. And then my mother will finally see that I'm the right choice to take over the family business.

Me, not Gaius.

I've always been the son Cali trusted with the blood, the

gore, the violence. Gaius had no imagination for it. He was too... pedestrian. He treated killing like a job, not like the artform that it is.

Which is why it's so hilarious that he's the one in jail.

Gaius took the blame for what I did because he has a strict moral code. He's my big brother first, and a Dio second. And I may miss him every fucking day, but in the end, it's his own bloody fault.

I hold the guy's head up while Cali attaches some electrodes to his head and neck. She jolts him with several hundred volts, and he dances on the rig like he's in the cast of Riverdance. "Who is Zack Lionel Sommesnay?" she says, her voice cool and detached. One might mistake her for pedestrian, too. But I know my mother – I can see when bloodlust flares in her eyes.

She loves this just as much as I do.

The city planner blubbers and slobbers and jerks, but he doesn't give us what we need to know. Cali lets me crank the handle on the machine until he's nothing but a fried crisp. The air smells like BBQ pork. I'm starving, but I help her clean up.

"Can I ask you something?"

She grunts as she wipes down her knives. We speak each other's language.

"Why the dentist?"

"That's only half a question."

"I just want to be let in on the plan. You have your pick of the most bloodthirsty men in the world. You could've married that Russian spy, or that Italian assassin, or that British guy who makes those perfect little bombs. You could have made an alliance with someone important or useful, and yet, you marry the dentist. In *Vegas*. In a fucking *Elvis chapel*. I know it was a job, but surely you have better things to do with your time—"

"It wasn't a job."

I glare at her.

My mother glares right back. She's not lying.

"It's not?"

But that means... that means Fergie isn't her gift for me. That means...

I drop the medieval flail, narrowly missing my own foot with the heavy spiked ball. My head swims. I lean against the wall and try to pretend I'm slacking off and not that I'm about to keel over from shock.

"Why the fuck did you marry him then, if it's not for a job?"

Cali straightens her knives, arranging them according to size. "Because," she says. "I'm all sharp edges. Everything I know is pain and blood. But he talks about TV shows and spa vacations. He texts me funny cartoons. He holds me at the end of a long day."

My jaw falls open. Who the fuck is this woman? "He *holds* you?"

"I'm perfectly aware that I sound like a sappy Hallmark card," Cali says as she makes a long slide horizontally across the guy's abdomen. His guts spill out, and she collects his charred intestines into a bag. She'll use them later to leave a message for the mayor's office. "He came to me for help, but in the end, he's the one who helped me."

I narrow my eyes. "What do you mean, he came to you for help?"

Why the fuck would Fergie's dad need the kind of help my mother provides?

"That's none of your business. And so is my relationship with John. Whether you like it or not, John and Fergie are family now. And since you're so concerned about a *job*, I'll remind you that I gave you the job of looking after that daughter of his, *not* tormenting her."

"I haven't tormented—"

"Word of advice, boy. He loves that girl. She's his whole world. And if you hurt her, he will hire me to hunt you down and kill you." My mother looks me straight in the eye. She doesn't blink. "And I'll take the contract. Now, get out of here and get your ass to school."

36

FERGIE

For eighteen years, I've taken all the shit the world throws at me with bared teeth. I've come close to breaking so many times, and yet I've held on to a sliver of my humanity, to the part of me that believes there's a future out there for me worth fighting for.

And then... one tiny, insignificant thing flips the switch, and suddenly I'm barreling down a path I never expected to be on.

My tiny, insignificant thing comes in the form of Euri, who descends upon me at school on Thursday to *beg* me once again to help her with her college admissions panel. Sierra was supposed to work alongside her putting questions to the admissions officers on behalf of the student body, but Sierra's parents pulled her out of school.

And I agree, because even though it makes my skin crawl, I can't think of a legitimate reason to refuse. So I find myself sitting beside Euri on stage, in front of a packed auditorium of college hopefuls not just from Stonehurst, but from all the schools in the area. Across from us, seated at a long table, are admissions advisors from Yale, Stanford, Caltech, Johns Hopkins, and Harvard.

Harvard.

Euri emails me a list of the questions, and I bring them up on my Braille note while she introduces the panel. "I'd like to introduce my co-convener, Fergie Munroe, who will begin with our first question."

I stand, my voice perfectly clear as I angle my body toward the spot where the Harvard admissions officer sits, and I say, "Can you tell us what kind of student Harvard is looking for?"

And I *break.*

In one of those rare moments since The Incident, I feel something other than the terrifying numbness.

The first was when I fucked Cassius. Then there was when Torsten kissed me in the library, and Victor in my bed.

But now, I feel something else. Something I thought I'd never feel again, rising through my body like a black wave.

Something that Victor loosened inside me when he handed me that crowbar.

Rage.

I feel rage.

Raw, hot rage at the unfairness of it all. *I'm* supposed to be organizing workshops for Ivy hopefuls. *I'm* supposed to be nervously composing my essays and compiling my references for early admissions.

But The Incident took it away from me. *He* took it away from me. I took it away from myself. And now I have to stand here and help this auditorium full of students take my place at Harvard, and they don't even care about Harvard. It's all a stupid competition to them, another way to break the monotony of their privileged existence.

They hire the Poison Ivy Club to take each other down.

I've played by the rules my whole life, and what do I have to show for it?

"Fergie? You okay?" Euri's voice plunges through my thoughts. "You've gone all white."

"I'm fine," I choke out.

"Okay, good. You need to ask another question."

"Yes."

I stand, tucking a stray strand of hair behind my ear. In the audience, someone coughs. Students titter and whisper amongst themselves. I swear that I hear someone whisper, 'blind freak,' but it's hard to tell over the pounding in my ears.

When I open my mouth to speak, nothing comes out. I don't remember the questions. I don't remember the Harvard officer's name. I'm in a different auditorium as people's phones beep and my shame pops up on their screens for them to devour.

I reach down to grab my Braille note, where I've written down Euri's questions. Instead, my fingers brush my cane. Before I know what I'm doing, I race off stage. Cruel laughter follows me. Principal Emerson calls for calm. I've ruined Euri's panel.

"Fergie, wait," she calls from behind me.

I don't wait.

I burst out of the stage door and break march across the school. Right. Left. Right. Past the bay of sunflower yellow lockers. Past the *Sentinel* offices where I might've worked if I needed an extracurricular for a college application.

I crash into the nearest bathroom – the same bathroom where I found Lucila giving Juliet head on my first day of school. I listen, but it sounds empty. I lean over the sink and throw up into the sink.

It's not fair that they took it away from me. It's not fair.

But you can have it.

The voice whispers in my head. And as I stand there, spitting and gargling, letting the water run down the sink, the whisper becomes a shout and then a roar. It pounds against my skull.

I thought I lost my shot at the Ivies forever.

Maybe fate landed me in this school, with this stepbrother, with these dark desires I can't explain, for a reason.

Old Fergie would've called it cheating. She would have wanted to get in on merit alone.

But the Old Fergie burned to ashes in The Incident.

And New Fergie wants what she's worked for. She wants what the world owes her for enduring this shit.

And she knows exactly where to get it.

37

CASSIUS

I emerge from Cali's lair after another grueling three-hour session. My mother had another one of Mayor Harg-reaves' minions – a weedy office worker with a surprisingly strong disposition.

I only managed to break him when I made him eat his own thumb. But he couldn't give us anything useful. Barbara Harg-reaves told him to inform the authorities to get to the docks at certain times, and they always found one of Claudia's ships there. He has no idea where she got that intel from, and he's never met Zack Lionel Sommesnay, although he heard that the man is a wealthy German businessman with considerable connections.

While Cali makes some calls to her international contacts, trying to track down more information about Mr. Sommesnay, I shower off the blood in the industrial bathroom Cali installed downstairs so she wouldn't clog the upstairs drains with bits of her victims.

Bloody water circles my feet and flows down the drain, and I breathe deep as I lather up on fancy Susanne Kaufmann bath lotion. It feels good to have got my stepsister out of my system for the day.

She's not my gift. She was never meant for me. I'm not supposed to break her.

Cali's words play over in my mind. She *chose* to marry the dentist. Fergie wasn't a job I had to complete to finally win her approval. My stepsister is just... my stepsister.

I don't know what to think about that. I've been avoiding Fergie, avoiding dealing with it, even though it means that my every waking thought is filled with flame-colored hair and defiant emerald eyes.

As I wrap myself in a towel and head upstairs, I hear Cali on her phone, relaying to Claws what she found out. Cali holds the phone away from her ear as Claws shrieks her disapproval.

"Remember what I said," she growls at me as I walk past.

"If I hurt Fergie, my balls are on the line. I've got it."

Good thing she doesn't seem to know about the sacer, or the shower, or the fact I tricked Fergie into fucking me.

My stomach rumbles. Torture always made me hungry. I pat my hair dry as I emerge into the kitchen. "Milo, you'd better have some of those chocolate pastries left, because I'm so hungry I'll eat you—"

I stop dead in my tracks. Milo is nowhere to be seen. Victor and Torsten sit at the kitchen island, a plate containing only a smattering of pastry crumbs between them.

"You ate my cookies," I growl.

"You weren't at school again today," Victor says.

I shrug as I pick up the plate and move toward the fridge. There has to be something in here to eat. My friends – *ex*-friends now, I suppose – do not need to see what happens when they're around me with low blood sugar. "I've had things to do."

"You've been avoiding us ever since the party. I know you've got your panties in a bunch over Fergie—"

Victor ducks as I send the plate flying. It smashes into the wall behind his head, the shards falling into the coffee machine.

"It's got nothing to do with her," I shrug. "Cali needed my help. Of course, you'd know this if you weren't so distracted chasing blind girl pussy—"

"Jesus, Cassius, you're a mess." Victor's eyes sweep over me. His aristocratic mouth purses with a frown as he takes in my bloody clothing and the five days of stubble on my chin. "I need you to wake the fuck up. Drusilla's return is a massive blow to our power. I need you to be at school or the whole thing—"

"The whole thing will *what*?" I smirk. "Because I don't think you even care what happens to Poison Ivy anymore, not now that you've got your cock buried down Fergie's throat."

Torsten makes a growling noise in his throat. "Don't talk about her like that."

"About Fergie? Why the fuck do you care?" I round on him, but Victor shoves his way between us.

"Keep your voice down," he murmurs, gripping my shoulder, digging his fingers into my flesh. Purple bruises from my fingers circle his neck. His hands tremble as the tension fizzes down his arm. He's desperate to lay me out for what I did at the party.

Go on, Victor August. Give in to your monstrous side. Let me drag you down with me into the depths of Hell. Let me break you, because I have to break the pretty things.

"She's not here," I smirk at the pair of them. "She's helping Eurydice with that stupid college application panel at school. And if you must know, she's not talking to me, either."

"She talks to me."

We both whirl around to look at Torsten. He has his note-book open in his hands, but for once he's not scribbling in it. I squint at the picture. It's a drawing of a girl with a mane of fire, her eyes closed, her head tilted back and lips pursed in ecstasy.

It's Fergie.

I whip the notebook out of his hands. He whirls around and swings at me, but I duck it easily. It's been years since Torsten took a swing at either of us. When we first started hanging out, he'd get these uncontrollable fits of rage, like how I get when the red mist descends, but they'd be over *nothing*. At least, that's how it seemed to us. But over time we learned how to manage his triggers and let him do what he needs to do – we let him draw, we go with him to art galleries and let him bore us to tears with lectures about his favorite artists, we don't mind when he flaps his hand and we beat up anyone who comments on it. We don't force him to live every day in a skin that doesn't fit.

But now, for the first time ever, he's drawn something of his own imagination.

Or is it?

"When does Fergie talk to you?" I demand. I can't think of a single time we've left Torsten alone with Fergie.

"In chemistry class. We're lab partners."

"Oh, so you talk about penetrating her like a neutrino? Is she the Mohs scale because she makes you harder than a diamond?"

Victor snorts, but my crude puns are lost on Torsten's overly literal mind. He runs his fingers across a page in his notebook. I notice a clear label with little bumps, like the ones Fergie uses to label her bottles in the shower.

Victor leans in to look. "That's right. She taught you Braille. What does that say?"

Torsten snaps the journal shut. "I'm not supposed to tell anyone."

Hot, uncomfortable silence descends. I glare at Torsten. All this time I've been mad at Victor for going after Fergie behind my back, and Torsten's been playing with her, too. He's never, ever kept anything from us before. He doesn't really understand the meaning of a secret. Once, a police officer asked him where his mother hid her illegal prostitutes, and Torsten told him because he was asked a question and he knew the answer. That's how Torsten's brain works. And we're his *family*.

At least, we're supposed to be.

Fergie Monroe has messed everything up.

I glare at Victor. "You knew about this, didn't you?"

Victor sighs, confirming what I suspected. "We didn't come here to get into a fight, Cas. This is bigger than us. We need to figure out what to do about Drusilla."

"Fine." I stomp upstairs and open the library doors. Victor flops down in his usual spot on the sofa, while Torsten heads for the window seat. I stomp to the bar and fill my own glass. Victor lifts his eyebrow – his usual request for a drink. I finish mine and plop down in a chair opposite him.

Victor sighs again. "Do you want to talk about it or sulk like a spoiled little baby?"

"I'm fine with sulking."

"You're taking this surprisingly well, actually." Victor picks up the ledger from the table and flips through it casually. "It's almost as if you don't mind us sharing—"

"She's not my gift," I mutter. "Cali doesn't want me to break her. She wants me to protect her."

Victor whistles. "Yes, that's your forte. How are you supposed to protect Fergie Munroe from yourself?"

"Maybe I'm protecting her from the two of you," I glare at them both. "We had an agreement. You got her *after* me. And Torsten's not supposed to want her at all."

"Things have changed. I don't want to wait, and Torsten can't help what he feels." Victor throws a glance over his head, to where Torsten sat in the window seat, staring at the drawing of Fergie. "I think we should give him a chance, don't you? This doesn't have to be a big thing between us. We've shared a girl before. You don't even really like her, you just want her because she's forbidden fruit."

"Don't tell me what I like—"

KNOCK KNOCK

I jump out of my skin as a rapping sound penetrates the room. It's quiet, muffled, but it's there.

"What's that?" Torsten tears a page from his journal. "You got termites or something?"

"More like a rat." I strain to listen. There it is again. A faint tapping on the doors.

It *sounds* like someone knocking at the library door. It can't be Juliet, because she has the code. It won't be Milo or Seymour, because they know they're not to enter here upon pain of death. And it's not Cali. My mother wouldn't knock politely. She knows the value of privacy. If it was an emergency she'd force her way in. No reinforced wood-veneered, carved security doors are a match for Cali Dio.

So it must be...

I'm a fool as well as a monster, so I cross the room and hit the keypad. The locks disengage and the library doors swing open to reveal Fergie Munroe standing in the hallway, her shimmering red hair piled on top of her head in a loose bun, her eyes rimmed with red. She's been crying.

My veins boil with the urge to break something, to break someone. But it's not my stepsister – my rage is reserved for whoever hurt her.

"I thought I told you this area was off-limits," I growl, desperate to cover up this strange new sensation.

"You did." She tugs on the collar of her oversized men's shirt, which she's wearing with the tails untucked over a skintight pair of leggings that look like she was poured into them, a loose necktie, and the sleeves rolled up to reveal her narrow wrists. "Can I come in? I want to talk to you all about something."

"Fuck off." I slam the door, but it sticks. I jerk it hard, but it doesn't budge.

I glance down and see Victor's foot sticking in the gap, blocking me from slamming the door. "Come in, Fergie."

I glare at him. He raises an eyebrow, acting all innocent. "What? I want to hear what she has to say."

I growl, but in reality, I'm as intrigued as he is. Victor reaches around me and slides his arm into hers, allowing her to hold his elbow. I hate how fucking hot she looks on his arm. They fit together like two pieces of Lego. I know exactly why he wants all three of us to date her at once, because he knows she'll have to choose one of us, and she'll choose him.

"Come and sit down," he purrs. "I'll fix you a drink."

"Thanks." She lets Victor settle her on the sofa, in my fucking spot. She crosses her legs, those red lips pursing. "Is Torsten here?"

"Yes," says Torsten. He puts down his pen and leans forward in his chair.

Interesting. I think about that Braille label in his book. He's been talking. In class. To *her*. Torsten doesn't talk to anyone but us. He doesn't see the point.

For some reason, not even our most stoic member is safe from Fergie's charms. She's like a poison, seeping through our veins, spreading silently until no part of our lives isn't infected by her raspberry scent.

Victor goes to the bar and fixes drinks. He hands her a Scotch on the rocks, which she raises to her lips.

"Thanks. This is good."

She leans back in the chair and nurses her drink in silence for a bit. I know she can't actually see me, but I feel naked, like she's burrowing into my skin.

Vic raises his own glass as he leans back in his chair. "What did you want to talk to us about?"

"I know you have a little club. The Poison Ivy Club. Euri told me about it, and I put together a few things on my own."

Victor shoots me a worried look. I know nothing Eurydice Jones says about us will be good, but I'm not ashamed of what we do. We get the result for our clients and the Ivy Leagues get another scumbag, cheating lowlife – exactly what they deserve.

Those so-called Ivy League schools are built for one purpose, to take in bright, beautiful people, chew them up, and spit them out again as monsters.

Fergie draws in a deep breath. "I want you to get me into an Ivy League school."

38

FERGIE

Cassius grabs my arm and shakes me so hard that my teeth clang together. "You've got to be joking."

"I'm not joking."

This is a mistake. It's not too late to back out. I can leave this room and pretend I never said anything.

But I don't leave. And I don't take back what I said.

"But you..." Cassius sounds completely flummoxed. I admit that it gives me a little flush of joy to know I've left my step-brother speechless.

"It's what she wants," Victor says in that smooth, authoritative voice of his. I imagine he's already putting together a plan for me.

Cassius drops my arm and paces across the room, then recovers enough to snap at Victor. "Don't listen to her. She's bull-shitting. This is a trick. It's some way of getting me back for the sacer."

Victor ignores him, which is the right thing to do with Cassius. The leather sofa creaks as the Poison Ivy kingpin leans forward. His glass clicks as he places it on the table. I feel his gaze penetrating me, searching out my secrets. "Why do you want to go to an Ivy League all of a sudden? You're not exactly in the running. Your grades at your previous school were unremarkable."

"You looked into me?"

"Of course," Cassius says. "My mom might be blinded by her love for some nobody dentist, but I'm not going to let strangers into this house without a background check."

I have to clamp my hand over my mouth to stop myself from bursting out laughing. "And what did you find?"

"John Munroe ran a small clinic in Cedarwood Cove, Massachusetts," Torsten says from the window. He sounds a little proud. I gather this is his job for the club. In one of our Braille conversations, he said that he's good with computers. "Fergus Munroe is an unremarkable student at Cedarwood Cove High School, diagnosed with ROP at the age of three, lost her mother to ovarian cancer at age four—"

I don't like that they know even this much about me, but it's proof that Cali's work is *good* – not even her son and his friends can find the truth. "Then you know there's no dirt on me. Nothing in my past that will stand in your way."

"That's exactly it, Duchess," Victor purrs. "There might be no dirt, but there are also no assets. No achievements for an application. And no sign beyond you sitting across from me that you've ever wanted to attend an Ivy League college."

"Do you demand a reason from all your clients? No? Well then, sit on this and rotate." I hold up my middle finger in what I hope is Cas' direction.

Something hot and wet clamps around my finger. I scream and try to retract it, but moving it only gets it more stuck as something slithers around it. A tongue.

Cas' tongue.

"Don't tempt me, sister," he growls as he clamps his teeth around my fingers and licks and sucks it like... like how Victor sucked my clit in the rage room. And I am so fucking weak, because it makes a delicious, depraved heat pool between my legs.

"You should really keep my stepbrother on a leash," I say to Vic. "I want in. Your job is to get me in. Don't pretend like that's a challenge for you. I'm a blank slate. You've had far worse people for clients." A faint smile plays across my lips. "Think of me as a case study for your talents. I have no history before I showed up at Stonehurst Prep. And I want it to stay that way."

"What does that mean?" Cassius drops my finger. I can't help the flush of disappointment on my cheeks as I wipe his saliva on the couch.

"It means that whatever you do for me has to be about transforming who I am now. Leave my past alone. Don't try to dig up anything on me. If I find out you've been poking around in Cedarwood Cove, this deal is off."

It's a risk. I know that by saying this, I'm all but admitting that there is dirt to find. I can feel Victor's curiosity humming in his veins from the other side of the table. But I have to get them to make an oath. One thing I know about the Poison Ivy Club is that they will not break an oath.

"This isn't a negotiation," Cassius snaps.

"Everything's a negotiation." I lean back into the sofa and let a seductive little smile play across my lips. I need them to be intrigued enough to take this deal.

"We can abide by your terms," Victor says. "But can you abide by ours? We'll need to discuss payment."

"I can pay." I open my bag and pull out a box. I drop it onto the table. "Inside that box is my mother's jewelry. She inherited these from her mother, and I got them when she died. I don't know the street value, but the diamond necklace alone is insured for twenty thousand."

"We don't want money," Victor says, although I hear him

slide the box across the table and peruse it with interest. "All of us have money enough. If we take you on as a client, then you need to give us something of *value*."

"I don't understand."

"We trade in favors and secrets, Fergie."

My lips purse. "My secrets are my own. That's the only agreement I'll make. Take the necklace, or we're done here."

I start to stand, but Victor places a hand on my knee, pushing me back down.

"I know what our price should be," he says. "I want Fergie."

39

CASSIUS

"What the fuck?" I move across the room and grab Victor by the collar, hoisting him out of that wingback chair by the scruff of his Brooks Brothers shirt. I slam him into the bookshelf. Gold-edged volumes fly everywhere.

Victor's hands slide up my arms, gripping my wrists. His eyes bug out of his skull, and he tries to say something to me, but I'm crushing his windpipe. I'll do it this time. I'll get rid of him so Fergie can't choose him—

He can't have her. He can't have her because she'll never want me.

"No." Someone shoves their way between us. Torsten. He rips my hand from Vic's throat and shoves me. I'm too big for his shove to have any physical impact. My feet remain planted on the spot, but I look down at my two best friends and a horrible sensation crawls up my spine, the same feeling I remember when I watched the cops lead my brother away.

Shame.

This is who I am. All I do is break things.

"Fuck, Cas," Victor gasps, clutching his throat. "At least let me explain before you go all neanderthal on me. We all want her, don't we? Instead of letting her tear us apart, let's make her ours."

I stagger over to the nearest chair and slump into it. I'll listen to Vic's idea, and if I don't like it, I can always kill him later.

"What do you mean by 'you want me'?" Fergie asks in her low voice. She doesn't sound offended. She's intrigued.

"I mean, little Fergie, that we get you into a fancy school, but you become ours. Part of our crew. Part of the Poison Ivy Club. You hang out with us. You help us do what we need to do for our clients. You're *ours*."

"Is this the price you ask of all your clients?" Something unreadable flashes across Fergie's pretty face. "For all that talk about Victor August's morality, about what you won't make your clients do, you want me to open my legs for you."

She yawns.

"How boring. I thought the Poison Ivy Club had more imagination than that."

Fergie slaps Victor's hand off her leg and rises to her feet. She holds out her cane and turns toward the door, but Vic's too fast. He grabs her wrist and spins her around. She yelps as she drops her cane and he pulls her backward, flinging her onto his lap. His arms circle her chest, and he leans into her, molding his body around her and licking her earlobe. Fergie frowns, but her breath hitches and her mouth forms a surprised O. She doesn't struggle. In fact, she wiggles her hot little ass in Vic's crotch, and I meet Torsten's eyes, and he's just as mesmerized as I am.

I think my little stepsister enjoys being the center of attention.

Even though watching Vic put his hands on her makes me want to blood eagle him, I'm hard as a fucking rod.

Maybe... maybe we can do this.

Maybe it doesn't have to be me or Vic.

At least, not right away.

"Before you enter the hallowed halls of an Ivy League

university..." Victor whispers against Fergie's ear, "all three of us in this room will taste your incredible pussy. You will ride each of our cocks until your legs give out from exhaustion, and then we'll lick you until you come again. But we won't ever force you. By the time Poison Ivy is done with you, Duchess, you will be begging for us."

Fergie's eyelids flutter, her long eyelashes tangling together. My mouth goes dry as I remember the way she came apart beneath me. Every night since, I've jerked off with her panties wrapped around my cock. I want that again. I want to taste raspberries and awaken that sweet little deviant I know is hidden inside her.

And I don't just want her body.

I need her at our side. In our club.

I *crave* her secrets.

My stepsister can believe she's safe with us if she likes. Victor will make her feel like a queen, like nothing can touch her. But the minute she signs on the dotted line, she gives us full access. Torsten might obey her wishes not to go hunting for whatever darkness haunts her past, but I'll find a way to get them out of her. Inside and outside the ring, I fight dirty.

"I admire your confidence." Fergie snaps her body upright, leaving Vic sitting on the table with a tent pole between his legs. She spins on her heel and faces us, hands on her hips and a cruel smile playing across her lips. "I'm done sleeping with little boys, but that doesn't mean I won't play with you. You want me to be your dogsbody? Hang out with you, fetch your sandwiches, that sort of thing? And in exchange, you'll get me into an Ivy. Easy. Sign me the fuck up."

"We all have to agree," Victor says, folding his arms across his chest. He makes no move to do anything about his boner.

"I agree," Torsten pipes up.

Torsten has been the wildcard in all this. I'm almost not

surprised that Victor August has bulldozed his way into my business to steal my toy, but Torsten... he's never shown interest in a girl. *Ever.* We've tried to help him get laid on so many occasions, and he either runs away or goes psycho. But it turns out all this time he's been talking to Fergie. Torsten is talking to a girl. I don't know if they've kissed or fucked or what, but the talking thing is almost wilder.

She might fuck me, but she'll never talk to me.

My eyes remain locked on Victor. I know exactly what he's thinking. He wants Fergie to be his do-over for Gemma. For Juliet. She's his redemption. Well, Victor August can have fun being the savior, but he's not going to save her from all the perverted things I'm going to do to her.

"Cassius?" Vic lifts a dark eyebrow.

Fergie reaches out toward where she thinks I'm standing. "Please," she whispers. "I need this."

A groan escapes my throat. My stepsister's eyes are wide, pleading. Her long fingers reach toward me and that fiery-red hair spills over her shoulder, wreathing her face in fire. My cock is so hard, it's fucking painful.

Victor thinks he's holding her close, protecting her from me by bringing her into our circle. But I don't think Fergie Munroe needs protecting. I think she needs *schooling*. I'm going to have so much fun with her. I'm going to make sure she knows exactly what Poison Ivy is all about.

"Fine." I can't help the wild, monstrous grin that spreads across my face. I've got my toy back, and maybe I have to share her, but I'm going to be the one she chooses in the end. "We'll get you into the school of your dreams, sis. And you belong to us."

I swallow as the force of Cassius' words hits me. My pussy is on fire, and in a good way. In a 'shove me against the wall and make me call you Daddy' kind of way.

I'm *afraid*. I'm afraid of what I've agreed to. I'm mostly afraid that Victor is right. That these three dangerous guys will make me beg for them.

"Hand me a contract," Victor says. Torsten shuffles around in some books. Cassius grabs me under the arms and drops me onto the couch.

"Hey!" I kick at him. My boot connects with Cassius' shin, but it's like kicking a broken pencil – pointless. My stepbrother chuckles as he holds me down with one huge, meaty hand.

"It's too late to back out now, sis. Sit still so we can make things official, or keep wriggling and I'll bend you over my knee and show you how we keep the newest Poison Ivy member in line."

I freeze. *He doesn't mean that, does he?*

His dark, maniacal laugh rather suggests that he does.

"Torsten takes care of all the club records," Victor explains, spreading out pages on the table. He's all business, ignoring my stepbrother's threat. I don't know if that means I'm safe or not. "He's hacked practically every record system you can name – he can fix SAT scores, change recommendations, and invent whole identities for people. He's pretty good."

I don't like that. It feels too close. I don't want Torsten to go digging if he knows what to look for. But he did promise me he wouldn't, and Torsten can't handle lying. Besides, Cali assured me and Dad that we were safe. Dad wants me to trust her, and I don't have any other option.

Something slides across the table toward me. "This is the contract. Sorry, we don't have a Braille version. I'll read it to you."

Victor reads out the contract in his sultry voice. I'm so mesmerized that we get to the end and I realize I hardly understood a word.

Oh well. I already made the decision to do this. In for a penny, in for the entire fucking bank vault.

Vic hands me a pen. His fingers linger on mine longer than necessary. He directs me where to sign, and I scribble my name. Vic turns the paper toward himself and signs. Cassius storms over and adds his scrawl.

"You don't know what you're getting into," Cassius growls. There's a dangerous edge to his voice that should terrify me but only makes me wetter.

Torsten takes his time reading over the contract. His pen scrapes across the paper. When he's finished, his fingers brush mine in a handshake that feels impossibly gentle.

"Of all people, I never expected you," he whispers, closing his journal with a snap.

I'm their girl.

A Poison Ivy Girl.

I lay in bed, trying to sleep before school tomorrow, my eyelids half-closed against the onslaught of bright Californian sun through my open blinds, and run over everything that happened yesterday.

All the way home from the admissions panel, I'd tried to talk myself out of my decision. Old Fergie's voice battered against my skull, reminding me that I didn't want to be handed anything in life.

Old Fergie could go fuck herself. I *did* earn this. And then I made a mistake, and some rotten bastard took it away from me. Why does everyone else get to make mistakes in life, but not me?

I'm going to do exactly what people like Victor and Cassius do, what Cali Dio does – take what I want *because* I want it.

And damn the consequences, whatever they are.

I don't know what it means to be a Poison Ivy Girl, or why they want me to be that instead of taking my mother's things. It doesn't matter. Hell, if they demanded I fuck them, I'd probably have done it. I'm two-thirds of the way there already. Vic's words ring in my ears. "By the time you get your acceptance letter, you'll be begging for our cocks."

I've never begged for anything in my life, but the idea that he thinks I might makes heat pool between my legs.

"Get me that Harvard acceptance letter, and we'll talk," I say to the ceiling.

My Harvard letter.

There are only a couple of weeks left before the early decision deadline, a couple of weeks for them to make me Ivy League ready. On December 15th, I'll find out if the Poison Ivy Club lives up to its reputation.

If they worked their dark miracles and I get that Harvard acceptance letter in my hands and...

...my real life can truly begin...

I'd no longer feel this overwhelming numbness.

I could act on my own dark impulses.

Mmmm...

I reach down between the sheets, stroking my fingers down my thighs. I think about all three of them coming at me in that dark library of theirs, laying me down on that leather sofa and using their lips and hands and cocks to seal the bargain between us.

I push my panties down my thighs, imagining that my fingers aren't my own, but they belong to Victor August, and that he whispers something filthy and possessive in my ear in that sultry, posh voice of his. I imagine him licking slowly down my slit, the faintest hint of stubble on his cheeks grazing my thigh as he buries his face between my legs.

I dip my finger inside myself, feeling how wet I am at the thought of them. I'm messed up. But at this moment, I don't care. I open my knees wider and press them into the bed, imagining my stepbrother holding them there, demanding I take every inch of him with that cruel twist in his voice that drives me wild with lust.

I swirl my finger around my clit, slow and languid, just the way I imagine Victor would do it. That cruel bastard would take his sweet time. He's used to being in charge.

I think about the Harvard University letterhead at the top of an email. I think of falling to my knees, how good my Torsten's cock will taste after he gets me into Harvard, Harvard, Harvard...

I arch my back as I swirl my finger harder, faster. I remember Cassius' weight on me, the smooth planes of his muscles as he plowed into me. I claw at the sheets. The ache rises inside me. I gasp in a breath, and catch the scent of vanilla, honeycomb, and orange zest just as—

"Rise and shine," a soft voice whispers close to my face.

"Fuck." I jump out of my skin. My hand flies up and connects with a hard body.

Torsten laughs softly.

How is he in my room?

I put all those locks on the door. And how did he get so close to me? I'm practically impossible to sneak up on. Every tiny sound or subtle shift in the air alerts me to changes in a room. And yet, he'd snuck up on me while I was... while I...

My face flashes with heat. Beneath the covers, my legs are wide open, my cunt wet and aching. The mattress shifts as Torsten sits down beside me, his thigh pressing against my leg.

"What were you doing?" he asks. "You were breathing heavy, but you're not asleep."

"No—" I cry, but I'm too late. Torsten swipes back the sheets, revealing my panties pushed down my thighs, my pussy lips no doubt glistening with arousal. I yank my hand back, but it's too late, too late.

Torsten's breath catches. All I can hear is him puffing, trying to get himself under control.

"I was flicking the bean, okay?" I snap. "I was fanning the fur, visiting the bat cave, paddling the pink canoe, auditioning the finger puppets, getting lost in the pleasure catacomb, exploring the abandoned uranium mine of carnal knowledge."

Torsten makes a low growl. "I don't understand."

Of course. I know Torsten struggles with metaphors. He needs direct, literal language. My whole face burns with embarrassment. "I was masturbating, okay? I'm horny and I wanted an orgasm and I'm in my own private room where I'm allowed to do whatever the fuck I want to my own body, so—"

"Show me," he demands.

"Excuse-the-fuck-me?"

He leans closer, his body shifting as he rests his elbow on the bed between my legs, propping his head up so he can peer directly at my pink underworld (sorry, now that I started, I can't stop). "I want to see."

And maybe I'm sick and twisted, but the strain in his voice drives me wild. His eyes rake over my skin, and I feel it even more than if he were touching me – it's as if he's inside me, inside my veins.

I feel bold. Invincible. I'm a Poison Ivy Girl and no one can touch me... except myself.

I was horny before, but now I'm a fucking wet mess.

I flash Torsten a big grin as I slide my hand back down my naked stomach, brushing my fingers over my thighs. His breath comes out in ragged gasps. The bed creaks as he leans closer.

His breath brushes the bare skin on my thigh. His weight over one leg means I can't forget that he's watching, that I'm doing this intimate thing for an audience. I arch my back as the pleasure mounts inside me. I haven't even touched myself yet and I'm ready to come.

Torsten wants to see.

I push a finger inside my warm folds, getting it nice and wet.

My juices leak onto the sheets, but I'm so beyond caring. I touch my finger to my clit and slowly circle it.

"This is..." I croak. "This is how I like it..."

"What are you thinking about?" he asks. His words touch my skin.

"I'm thinking about my acceptance letter," I say, my voice catching. It's at least partly true. "The one you're going to get for me with that shiny Harvard crest in the corner."

"And that makes you wet like this?"

"Well, that and a hot boy is watching me," I pant as I stroke myself, trying to hold off a little longer, wanting to give Torsten a real show.

Yup, I'm *definitely* sick.

He shifts again, moving closer. His hair brushes my thigh. I almost leap off the bed. I'm so goddamn close...

"Can I try?" Torsten asks.

I'm teetering on the edge. My stomach pools with heat. I'd say anything to keep stoking the fire inside me. "Yes."

I draw my hand away, letting my legs fall completely open. My clit throbs and my pussy aches with desperation. Every inch of my skin tingles with the fire of his eyes on me. A moan escapes my lips, and I remember what Cassius said about begging. I'm *this* fucking close to begging Torsten to finish me already.

For the longest time, Torsten does nothing. He sits and he breathes, and each breath kisses my throbbing coastal floodplain (sorry, sorry), and it's the most exquisite torture.

Finally, *finally*, his fingers touch my stomach. His soft touch is an electric jolt straight to my pussy. He follows the exact path I laid with my own fingers, down, down, down. He makes this choking noise as he dances lower, moving his fingers down my slit, trying to find the spot.

Through the haze of sensation, something occurs to me.

"Is this the first time you've touched a girl?" I ask. It's hard to get the words out.

He whispers, "Yes."

"Do you want me to tell you what to do?"

"Yes."

Fuck me dead.

"Okay." I suck in a couple of deep breaths. I need to be calm and steady for this conversation and I. Am. Fucking. Not. "Well, you start by dipping a finger inside me. You want to get it nice and wet. But you have to be careful. Take it slow and only with short fingernails. Don't be too rough unless a girl wants it like that. And she'll tell you. Or you can ask her – she'll love that."

I reach down and take Torsten's wrist, moving his hand and straightening his finger. "Here," I breathe as I nudge him against my entrance.

Torsten's finger slides inside me. His breath comes out in a ragged gasp. I grit my teeth as I dance on the brink of orgasm.

"You're so wet," he whispers.

"Uh-huh." I bite my lip until I taste blood, and claw back a fraction of control. "That's what happens when a hot guy puts his finger inside you."

I pinch Torsten's wrist and remove his finger before I come all over it. I draw it slowly along my slit, up to my clit. Sweat sheens on my forehead, and I know I must be flushed and messy. I hope he likes what he sees, because I can't hold on much longer.

"Can you feel this little bud here?" I move his finger and whimper as he presses into the *exact* right spot. "That's this little lump of nerve endings we call the clitoris. It's like... like the tip of your cock – it's extra sensitive. If you play with this, you'll..."

I can't speak because his finger moves in slow circles, and I can't hold it anymore. I'm fucking *gone*. I throw my head back and howl as the orgasm claims me, as my knees rise up of their own accord and clamp around him, as pleasure rushes through my veins like Torsten turned on a happiness tap.

"And that?" Torsten whispers. "Was that…"

"An orgasm. Yeah, it was." I sink back against the pillow. "And quite a good one, too. Congratulations, Torsten – you're officially a man now."

"Can I give you another one?"

"Um, yeah… you can." I let my thighs relax again. My pussy hums with a mix of contentment and anticipation. It's been a long time since she was treated like the goddess she is.

Torsten starts again, stroking his fingers down my stomach and over my thighs in exactly the same way he did before. He pushes his finger into me to get it wet. He's a fast learner. I should probably tell him that he doesn't have to do it the *exact* same way every time, but it feels amazing and I'm rapidly losing the ability to speak, so…

"You can tease a girl's entrance, too," I choke out as he withdraws his finger from inside me. "Before you slide it in. Just run it lightly around the edges or push it in a little, but then take it away. She'll tilt her pelvis toward you, trying to push you inside."

"Like this?" Torsten's finger darts over the surface, so softly I'm not even sure I feel it. Instinctively, I tip my hips toward him, tasting the blood on my lip because I love the thrill of walking this edge with him.

"Exactly like that. Part of the fun is that you can give a girl exactly what she wants or…" I thrust my hips up to him again, desperate for more pressure, for more of him, "…or you can make her crazy. You can make her beg."

Torsten hums gently under his breath as he runs the very tip of his finger around my entrance, brushing it over my pussy lips. A deep ache pools in my stomach, and I know I'm going to come even harder this time.

I never thought having to explain what I wanted could be so

hot, but I feel powerful, like a conductor directing an orchestra. The music may come from Torsten's fingers, but it's mine to create.

He reaches my clit and sweeps slow circles until I'm achy and panting.

"And you can..." I gasp as my muscles clench. "You can kiss me. On my clit. You can stick your tongue inside me and do all the things I showed you, but with your tongue instead of your finger."

Torsten shuffles up the bed. A moment later, his slick tongue dances over my hole, where his fingers had been only seconds before. I moan and buck my hips, desperate for more pressure, for him to stop playing with me and let me come.

It's my own fault. I shouldn't have shown him how to be this cruel, how to draw out my pleasure until I'm a gibbering mess of limbs and heat and need.

He's such a diligent student. Torsten's giving my pussy all his attention. He plunges his tongue inside me again and again, licking and tasting until I'm leaking juices all over his face, until my legs clamp around him and I'm growling like an animal.

"Cassius is right," he whispers. "You do taste like raspberries."

He presses his tongue against my clit. He dips and swirls and shows me what a good student he is.

I come with a gasp, my legs clamped around Torsten's head. His long hair tickles against my chest. I see galaxies behind my eyelids.

As my muscles slacken, Torsten tries to pull away. I grab his collar. "Do you think you're done?"

"You want another?"

He sounds excited.

"I want you inside me. Now."

Torsten stiffens. "I... I don't know if I can."

"Why?"

His voice is tinged with sadness. "Because I feel *everything*. Every touch, every smell, every taste. And it's overwhelming, and I like you, and I don't know if I can—"

I prop myself up on one arm and cup his cheek in my hand. "I can't claim to know what it feels like for you, but what you describe is a little bit like being blind. Humans are so used to processing the world based on what they see that they barely use their other senses. But you and me, we're not normal, and I think that's awesome. We can figure out what feels good together. Would you like to try?"

"Yes."

I have an idea. "And we can make a safesign – like the safe-words people have in BDSM for when they want to stop. Only this won't be a word. It's a simple movement that each of us can use and 'see' with our bodies. Doing this movement means, 'stop,' and the other person *must* respect it. Okay?"

He says nothing. Which I know for Torsten doesn't mean he disagrees. I hold his elbow in mine and lightly pinch the skin on the inside. It's not something either of us would mistakenly do during fucking, and it's something that we can both feel if we need to.

"That's our safesign. If you want to stop, you pinch me in my elbow, and I'll do the same. So, how about it?"

He doesn't reply.

"Please don't make me guess, Torsten. It's okay if you don't want to do this—"

"I do," he whispers. "But Cas and Victor..."

"Fuck them, Torsten. Seriously. I'm a grown-ass woman and I decide whose cock is inside me. Look around. Cassius and Victor aren't in this room with us. It's just you and me. And I'm telling you that I want you to fuck me. What do you want?"

"We have to… go slow," he murmurs. "I don't know if I can… if it will all be too much…"

"Maybe I can put some music on? When it feels too over-whelming, you can focus on that instead of what's happening."

"Yes," he croaks. I lean over and fumble for my dresser, finding my phone and flicking on the Bluetooth speaker. I select a Spotify playlist of slow, pain-soaked Nick Cave songs. Torsten's body relaxes as the familiar music washes over us. I can see why he likes Nick Cave – their voices are quite similar – dark and lush and filled with emotion.

I pat the bed. "Now, get those clothes off and come here. Let me touch you. Let me make you feel good. I don't have to look at you at all if you don't want to. I'm right here with you."

Torsten removes his pants and shoes, and he climbs up into the bed and lies down beside me. I kneel and touch his legs. I take my time. I explore his calves. I feel bumps in his skin – a ridge of scars running down the backs of both his thighs. Like Braille on his skin, telling the story of his life. He leans back on the bed, deadly silent.

With a normal lover, everything we've done would seem strange. But with Torsten, it feels perfect. I can *see* him with my fingers, and he can experience being seen the way he wants to be seen.

I move to his thighs, dancing my sensitive fingers over every inch of him. Even though I can sense his cock near my face, and I know from his panting and the scent of pre-cum in the air that he's standing to attention, I avoid his genitals completely. I dance my fingers close and take them away again, letting him build anticipation at his own pace.

"Shirt off now," I demand. I crawl up beside him. Torsten takes his time undoing the buttons. I help him, entwining my fingers with his, doing it slowly so he gets used to my touch. I slide my hands along the inside of his arms, trace the line of his collarbone, count more scars. I want to ask about them, about what happened to him, but this is not the time.

I move to his chest. He shudders a little as I touch his nipples. I offer him the underside of my arm, but he doesn't use our signal to stop. I'm so into this. My body hums with need again just from the act of stroking him, exploring him, reading his life on his skin. It's time to step things up.

I slide my hands down and tease around his thighs, tracing over that cute trail of hair leading from his belly button, before rubbing my fingers just on the bottom of his cock. Torsten jerks a little and makes another of his strained noises, but he doesn't give me the signal to stop.

I run my fingers along his shaft, which jerks in my hands. I feel the veins and the ridge around the head, and pull the hood back to reveal the tip. I feel how hard he is, how his head is coated with pre-cum.

"Is this okay?" I ask. "Is it okay to touch you like this?"

He shifts a little. "Yes. Just... not too much."

"Okay." As much as I want to press myself to him, to feel the warmth of our bodies come together, it's not only about me. This is his first time, and I want it to feel good for him.

"You're doing great," I say as I stroke his dick slowly, getting him used to the sensation of my hands. "If you like, I'll be on top. You lie on the bed and you let me do all the work. And I won't look at you and it's okay if you don't look at me, because having a blind girl is awesome."

"Okay. I'd like that."

I scramble up, and Torsten lays down in the dent made by my body. Heat and nervousness radiate off him. I feel this mix of pride and awe that I get to share this moment with him, that we found a way to make it good for both of us, and that I get to reward him for being brave and honest.

"I'm going to straddle you now. I'll put my hands on either

side of your face for support. If you want more touching, just ask, and I'll touch your face or stroke your chest."

"O-okay."

I climb onto him, kneeling with my legs on either side and lowering myself over him slowly. Our skin brushes and he sucks in a breath. Nick Cave croons about the death of God.

I lower myself over him, sliding so that my pussy rubs against his shaft, just letting him get used to that first. I don't slide his cock inside yet, even though my pussy hums with need. Instead, I lean over him. Torsten sighs as the tips of my hair brush against his chest. I kiss him lightly on the lips as I wiggle my hips, teasing the head of his cock with my opening.

"We're here," I whisper. "It's you and me."

"You and me," he repeats. There's a hint of a smile in his voice, a little taste of that wild, unchained laughter I remember from the first day we met. The real Torsten shining through.

"We can stop any time if it gets too much. Is that what you want? Do you want me to stop?"

"Fuck no," he grits out.

"Good."

I sink down onto his cock. Torsten makes this noise that's more animal than human as he sheaths himself inside me. He's big and slightly curved, and he fits so perfectly it's like his cock is made for me.

My body wants to move, to fuck, to take the pleasure I've been denying myself for so long. But I stay still, listening to Torsten breathe through the new sensations, waiting until he's ready. I Mother Fucking Teresa that shit as long as I can because soon, things are going to get sacrilegious and I won't hold back.

His breathing calms, and I think he's ready. I draw myself up on my knees, sliding up Torsten's shaft so that only the very tip of him remains inside me. Then I slowly lower myself down again, letting him feel every inch of himself moving deeper inside me.

"You feel amazing," I tell him.

"You feel..." he chokes, "...like drowning in Monet's lilypond."

"Is that a good thing?"

"Fuck yes."

I keep my strokes slow, letting the music guide me. But as the guitars rise into a screeching crescendo, I pick up the pace, squeezing my thighs against him as I ride him hard. I toss my head back, not bothering to try to focus on his face the way I've been taught to do – apparently not looking at people when you're talking or fucking freaks out the sighties.

But not Torsten. He knows what it is to be different. We both live in the shadows, and when we come together, those shadows dance for us.

The music swells, and Torsten gasps. His hands reach out to grip my thighs. He bucks his hips, shoving himself up into me as I grind down on his cock. With every stroke, he drives himself deeper, and by the noises he's making, I know everything we did to make him comfortable worked. He's loving this, and so am I.

In this position, his pelvic bone rubs against my clit with every thrust, and it's not long until I come again. My pussy pulses around him as I ride through the orgasm, losing my rhythm completely.

That pushes Torsten over the edge. He comes with a roar of surprise, a giant hole blown in his universe. He rides through the wave of his pleasure, thrusting into me as his cock contracts and spurts. He doesn't stop thrusting even when he's done, because he doesn't know he's supposed to stop. I calm him with a touch, roll off him, and settle into the crook of his arm, not wanting to get too close in case it's too much for him. But he pulls me into his armpit and buries his face in my hair.

"Fuck," Torsten breathes. "Fuck."

"We did good," I smile.

Wow.

That was...

Wow.

I took Torsten's virginity, and it's the hottest thing that's ever happened to me.

42

FERGIE

Torsten pulls the covers back over me, tucking the edges in like I'm a mummy in a sarcophagus, which is weirdly exactly how I like to sleep. How does he know that?

Did it have something to do with that night I found my lock broken on my bed, and his scent on my sheets?

"You've been in my room before," I say as he pulls my curtains closed, shutting out the pale moon. "When I'm asleep."

He reaches down and touches my cheek, his finger tracing the line of my jaw. "I couldn't talk to you while you were awake," he says. "I didn't do anything bad. I just talked to you. I watched over you."

"It's okay." I smile as my weary body slips toward the wall of sleep. "I like you watching over me. It makes me feel safe."

"Can I watch you tonight? I'd like to be here when you wake up."

"Sure, Torsten." My eyelids flutter shut. "Goodnight."

"Goodnight, Fergie."

He sits down on the edge of the bed, and I feel his eyes trailing over me. He spills over with emotions I can't begin to comprehend. With the memory of his cock buried inside me and the sweet sound of his voice singing a Nick Cave lullaby, I slip into oblivion.

MY EYES OPEN RELUCTANTLY. I know instantly from the light pouring in from the gap in the curtains that I've slept in. I reach over with a languid hand and punch the button on top of my alarm clock.

"It's 9:45AM," the electronic voice chirps.

"I'm sorry," a sweet voice startles me. "I didn't want to wake you."

Torsten. I start a little. I'd forgotten I said he could watch me sleep. I guess I assumed he'd go back to his hotel after I fell asleep, but I guess not. The bed depresses as he sits gingerly on the corner.

"Did you watch me sleep all night?" I ask.

He doesn't answer. *So that means yes.*

"Waking up with you is so much nicer than first period American History," I smile. "Maybe we don't even go to school today. We could just hang out, you and me—"

"We have to go to school," he barks. He stands up and moves into my closet. I hear him shifting through my things.

"I thought you hated school. And what are you doing in my closet?"

"Cassius says I have to get you ready for school. That's what I was supposed to do last night but I got... distracted."

I hear a shoe hit the wall.

I sit up and throw off the covers. "This may surprise my stepbrother, but I've been able to dress myself and wipe my own ass for at least three years now."

"I believe you. But Vic and Cas say that if you're going to be our girl, you have to look the part."

Torsten hums as he sifts through my closet. It takes me a moment to realize he's humming Nick Cave's 'Red Right Hand.' He doesn't seem to require my help.

"So... I'll just shower then."

"Okay."

What the fuck is going on?

I didn't know being part of the Poison Ivy Club meant a dress code. And our school has a uniform, anyway.

I return, fresh-smelling and wrapped in a gloriously soft towel (Milo and Seymour are stars), to find Torsten sitting on my bed with a fresh school uniform, a pair of boots, and some jewelry ready for me. As I bend down to retrieve the boots he's chosen, he leans in close. "I like the way your shampoo smells," he says.

"So you should. It's your shampoo." I want to smell like him all day. I want to catch a whiff of vanilla and honeycomb and orange and remember what we did last night.

"I don't think I'll shower," he says, sniffing my cheek. "I like the way my skin smells like you."

I like that, too.

The shoes are an old pair of suede ankle boots, a little more demure than the wet-look Fluevogs I usually wore to school. Torsten fastens a necklace around my neck. It's a delicate chain set with jewels and made to look like a string of ivy, and it holds three charms. A little bear, a lion, and a sword. The stones set into each pendant felt solid – real gems.

"This is... interesting." I finger the exquisite lion. "But why the animal kingdom?"

"Victor had this made for you," Torsten says. "It represents me, Cas, and Victor. Our symbols. Cas is the bear, Victor the sword, and I'm the lion."

"You sure are." I pretend to bite his shoulder. "Does Vic just have random necklaces lying around?"

"He had this made last night, after you signed the contract. Victor knows a guy who can create some amazing pieces, and he works fast. He wanted to give you something to symbolize the club, our agreement, our... family. The stones are rubies. They're blood red. They match your nail polish. Do you have makeup?"

I think that's the most words Torsten's ever strung together around me that aren't about dead art dudes. He must be feeling more comfortable around me. Sex can do that, I've heard.

"Sure." I dump out my small case. I don't wear much makeup. Yes, I *can* do my own makeup perfectly fine as a blind woman, but I tend to use the same products that I know match my skin tone and look good. I don't experiment much because I can't exactly appreciate it, and one of the great things about not being able to see is how little you give a fuck about beauty standards.

Or maybe that's just me.

Bottles and tubes clank together as Torsten sifts through what I have and selects a palette. He gets to work on my face, brushing on foundation with deft, soft strokes.

"How do you know how to do makeup?" I ask.

"You met my sisters," he says. "I have six. Livvie works a lot, so I looked after the younger ones when I lived at her house. They liked it when I did their makeup. And I do Juliet's for her most mornings, too. Look up."

I do my best to make my eyes behave while he swipes on mascara and eyeliner with a deft hand. I guess he's so good at art that this is easy for him.

"Finished." He drops a lipstick into my hand. "I can touch it up during the day if you need."

Despite my protests that it belonged to my mother and has sentimental value, Torsten won't let me take my beaten-up Kate

Spade to school. He dumps all my things into some kind of designer quilted thing of Juliet's. Whatever. If being a Poison Ivy Girl means getting morning sex and makeup from Torsten, and free designer goodies, then sign me the fuck up.

I mean, this might all be an elaborate prank. He might have painted me up like a clown, but so what? If everyone in the school laughs at me, it won't bother me because I'm still numb. Nothing can touch me.

I follow Torsten downstairs. Juliet's staccato laugh punctuates the silent house. Sure enough, when I emerge into the kitchen, she rushes me.

"Omigod, you look amazing." She holds my arms out like I'm a semaphore operator. "The hair, the shirt, the necklace. I keep telling Torsten he's missed his calling as a makeup artist to the stars."

"I'm not a star."

"You are today."

Victor leans in and wraps me into his whisky-and-chocolate scent. "You look exactly like what you are – my Duchess," he whispers as he offers his arm to me.

I hesitate a moment, not sure how Cassius will react to the new me. But my stepbrother merely drops a reusable cup and paper bag into my other hand. "Coffee," he grunts. "And scones from Milo. He's moved onto British cuisine, God help us all."

We drive to school, eating our scones in the car and getting crumbs all over his seats. He's ready to eviscerate us all by the time we arrive at school, and I make things worse by crumbling the last mouthful of scone over his head. Being a Poison Ivy Girl has its benefits.

This time, they don't make me get out around front. We turn into the senior parking lot just as the bell rings for lunch. The place is crawling with people. Their eyes stab at us as we roll slowly to our parking space, Cassius' hip hop music turned up high.

The boys get out first, and Victor holds the doors open for me and Juliet. As soon as I slide out, the lot falls eerily silent.

"Everyone in this parking lot wishes they were you right now," Victor whispers as he slides my arm into his again.

He doesn't have to tell me. I feel the collective intake of breath, the raw envy in their gaze as they take in Fergie Munroe welcomed into the company of their gods.

So this is what it feels like to be powerful? To be coveted?

I'm into it.

I strut into school on Victor August's arm, Cassius and Torsten flanking us like two badass bodyguards. People jump out of our way or call out "Looking fine, Fergie" like we're friends. Like they haven't spent the last month acting like I'm a leper.

We march into the dining hall, and instead of heading toward the food, we turn toward the back of the room. Cassius holds a door open and we enter a lofty glass box. Torsten pulls a chair out for me and a literal *waiter* hovers behind me to take my order.

Euri told me all about the Poison Ivy Club's little private dining area, but I thought she was exaggerating. She wasn't. Victor introduces me to the group hanging out there – a bunch of guys from the basketball and track teams, their cheerleader girlfriends, a couple of girls I recognize from Juliet's bedroom before the party, and Lucila Baskerville. Lucila keeps trying to take Victor's other arm and engage him in conversation, but he's not having it.

Juliet holds court, dictating the conversation, which turned to the usual – SATs and college exams. "What school are you applying for early decision, Fergie?" Gillian Fosterque asks me as she hands around embossed invitations to a charity ball at the Olympus Country Club.

"Harvard," I reply instantly.

I love the way that word tastes on my tongue.

The bell rings. Victor offers to walk me to class. It's in the complete opposite direction to where he's going – we don't share any classes because he's taking all AP subjects. I point this out and he laughs.

"From now on, you don't go anywhere in this school alone," he says. "Especially not with Drusilla Hargreaves snooping around."

I have to go to my locker first to get my tablet, and as we walk down the hall, arm in arm, someone steps in front of me, blocking my path. I assume it's Drusilla, here to try and convince me to betray the Poison Ivy Club. I shift my weight on my heels, ready to bite back against her offensive.

They're offering me endless orgasms and a ticket to Harvard. Why would I turn that down?

Victor pats my arm. "Hello, Euri."

Shit.

I knew this moment would come. I've been dreading it ever since I ran out on Euri's panel, but I was hoping I'd get a couple of days to bask in my newfound popularity before reality came crashing back.

"Hi, Victor," Euri's voice drips with ice. "Can I speak to my friend alone?"

"No can do," Victor says. "Fergie is one of us now. I don't let her out of my sight."

A hand touches my shoulder. "How could you do this?" Euri sobs, her grip tightening as she gets more upset.

"Please, Euri, don't—"

"Don't what? Don't take it personally that you went to the

Poison Ivy Club? If you wanted to go to an Ivy League school so badly, you could have gotten me to tutor you. You could have joined the *Sentinel*. Hell, you could have actually done some work rather than slack off in class. But instead, you decided to cheat."

"Euri—"

"No, I get to talk this time," she snaps. "You know how they're going to get you a spot at your dream school, Fergie? They're going to *destroy* someone. They might destroy me. But you don't care. You don't fucking care about anyone but yourself."

I don't say anything.

There's no denying it. I made a selfish decision.

I'm not apologizing for it.

"You know what they did to my sister. They're evil." Euri's voice wavers. "How could you? I thought you were my friend."

I turn away. "I was never your friend, Euri. I don't know how to be one anymore." I tug on Victor's arm. "Let's go."

This is the hardest part about what I've done. I knew it would hurt Euri. But it's better that I did it. I was getting attached to her. I was starting to think of her as a friend.

And I can't have friends again.

"That's it, Fergie. Run away from me," Euri yells to my back. "You don't want to talk to me because you know deep down that you don't deserve to go to an Ivy. You know that I do, and if they take this away from me or anyone else who deserves it, I'm going to make sure that every single person in the world knows what the Poison Ivy Club is all about."

43

FERGIE

Euri's words pound against my skull all through my next class. I try to focus on the teacher, but all I can hear is Euri's hurt voice warning me that she's going to take us down.

It hadn't occurred to me that the Poison Ivy Club might actually *go after Euri*, that my spot might come at her expense. I don't think it will matter, because she's going for Princeton, not Harvard, but I can't help the gross churning in my gut.

What have I done?

You can't chicken out now, I admonish myself. *You chose this. You know what it means to hire Poison Ivy. Don't kid yourself that you're innocent. If you want your dream future, you're going to have to step on a few people to get to it.*

That's how the world works. They would all do the same to you.

My final class of the day is a free study period. I'd planned to use it to catch up on some of the essays I've been neglecting, but Victor drags me to a table in the corner of the library and plonks me down in a cushy chair.

"This is our table," Victor explains as he sits down at the head, because of course he does. He sets a container down in front of me. I smell Milo's cookies and dive right in. "From now on, you don't sit anywhere else in the library apart from here. It will always be available for you, got it?"

"Sure, duke." I chew on my cookie, smirking at my silly nickname for him. Ooooh, a fancy table. Big deal. The Poison Ivy Club isn't special. At every school in the country, the cool kids have a table just like this.

Okay, sure, but the student body at Witchwood Falls High weren't *afraid* of the cool kids the way they are of Cassius, and there's no club they could go to that would crush their Ivy League competition for a fee.

I'm reaching for another cookie when the chairs beside me scrape across the hardwood.

"How's your day, sis?" Cassius smirks.

"It's been great since your friend gave me the fuck of my *life* last night," I shoot back. "A good thing, too, because I didn't want the last dick in my bed to be my stepbrother's mediocre micropenis."

"August, you fucking *what?*" Cassius leans across the table, his body sizzling with rage. He's obviously still getting used to the idea of this sharing thing.

"Don't look at me," Victor says, a note of awe in his voice.

"*Torsten?*" I can't decide if Cassius sounds shocked or disgusted. "You actually *slept* with Mr. I-can't-kiss-a-girl-because-I-can-smell-her-nostrils?"

Victor sucks in a breath. On the other side of me, a chair pulls out, and I catch a whiff of orange zest as Torsten sits down. *He heard Cassius say that.*

"At least Torsten didn't have to trick me into fucking him," I shoot back. I could slap him for being so callously cruel to his friend.

"Oh yes, and why *did* my clever ruse fool the great Fergie Munroe?" Cassius says. "I wasn't even wearing my fake mustache. You were so desperate for cock that you'd believe anything I told you, and now it must've been so mediocre that you've come crawling back to me on hands and knees, begging for more—"

My hands ball into fists. "Our agreement is that I'm part of your gang, stepbrother. It's not open season on my pussy. And I will never, *ever* beg you."

"If you say so, Sunflower." Cassius' chair creaks as he leans back, and the smirk in his voice infuriates me. "Because as much as you enjoy bouncing up and down on these two cocks, you want what only I can give you."

All the rumors I've heard about Cassius flash in my mind – how he leaves women broken and bleeding, how he can make you scream with pleasure and pain at the same time. I grit my teeth as I squeeze my thighs together, but I can't stop the heat pooling there.

My stepbrother is rotten to his core. Why do I crave his cruelty so bad?

Because I'm rotten, too. That's the only reason why I'd ever make a deal with these three devils.

"Your cheeks are flushed," Cassius chuckles. "And look, Vic – her nipples are hard under her shirt. You're giving yourself away, sis. You want me to put clamps on those hard little nipples, and bend you over my knee and show you who's Daddy. You want me to cut you and lick up the blood as I fuck that tight cunt with my fingers and—ow."

He swears as he clutches his shin where I kicked him. I flash him a smirk of my own.

"You'd better guard your plums," Victor says, his voice strained from trying not to laugh. "Our girl is a lethal weapon with those heels of hers."

"I'd like to see her try," Cassius shoots back, but he shuffles his chair away from me.

"Please, don't fight," Torsten murmurs. "We need to make a plan for Fergie."

"Yes, we're here on business, not to prop up Cas' flailing ego. Which is your top choice school?" Victor asks.

"Harvard," I answer immediately. I can't help it. That old yearning rushes back to me. I've had Harvard paraphernalia up on my bedroom wall since I was nine years old. My mom went to Harvard, and I've never grown tired of hearing my dad tell stories about her college days. "But I don't really care. I'll take any one that will have me, as long as it's an Ivy."

Torsten's pen scrapes across his notebook. I love the sound of it – that deep scratch that scars the page with his words, like fingernails scraping skin, drawing blood.

"What program?" Cassius barks. Clearly, he isn't over the news about me and Torsten.

"Law."

"*Law?*"

"Yes, law." I fold my arms. "You got a problem with that?"

"Nothing," Cas has the smirk in his voice again. "I just didn't picture you as the type to stand up in court and defend drug dealers and murderers."

"I have no desire to be Denny Crane, or even Daredevil. There are lots of different kinds of lawyers. I want to work in employment law, as an advocate for disabled workers."

"How noble."

I wave my boot in his direction and smile sweetly. "Come over here and say that to my face, *brother.*"

"So if you want law, that's Harvard, Yale, Penn, and Cornell?" Victor sounds pensive.

"Not Cornell," Torsten says.

"Right." Victor taps his nail on the edge of the table. "Cas, remember what happened when we tried to get Darcy Rouge into Cornell drama?"

"That's right," Cas chuckles. "I don't think that midget will ever be the same again."

I'm dying to know what they're talking about, but I won't give Cassius the satisfaction of appearing curious.

When he'd stopped chuckling, Victor says, "I presume you have SAT scores?"

I screw up my face. "1410."

It's a perfectly respectable score, but respectable doesn't cut it for the Ivies. It also isn't anywhere close to what I actually got in my last test – a 1540. But when we came to Emerald Beach, Cali told me on no uncertain terms that my marks need to be mediocre – good enough to get into Stonehurst Prep, not good enough to stand out.

"1410." Torsten scribbles in his journal.

I bite my tongue. I want to explain that I really did get a lot higher, that they're not dealing with a person who gets a 1410 on the SATs. But that's my ego talking, and my ego needs to take a chill pill because I had to remain Fergie Munroe. It's the only way this would work. I just have to hope Cali's work stands up to the scrutiny of her own son.

"I'll take them again," I say quickly. "I have time before the advance placement deadline."

"The final sitting is next weekend," Victor says. "It's fine, we can work with 1410. When Torsten's done, you'll be in the 1500s—"

"I'll take them again," I say firmly. For some reason, my moral code won't allow them to fuck with my scores. Even if nothing else on my application will be real, not even my name, my SAT score *will* be my own.

"Okay. You'll take them again." I sense Victor's mind whirring, already planning what they'll do if I get another mediocre score. I'm going to enjoy surprising him. "And I'll work with you on the essay section, so we've got that covered."

"Victor's been writing college essays for Gaius' clients since he was in eighth grade," Cassius says with a sneer.

I swallow. "Right."

I didn't particularly want Victor August to write my essay, either. I love writing. I've been on the school paper since junior high. But I'll concede that point if it will get me in. He's gotten more people into Ivies than I have.

"The biggest hole on your application is going to be your extracurriculars. Or lack thereof. But that's also the easiest to solve. Most admissions officers don't bother to check if you were *really* the head of the Model UN or founded your own charity. Torsten will make you an app that does something useless, and you can say you built it. College applications love an app."

"That's it?" I ask. "This is what people bargain away their secrets for? Some essay prep help and a useless app?"

"No," Victor's silken voice caresses me. "That's not all. You might not be aware that there's an unofficial quota for spots in the most competitive schools. At a school the size of Stonehurst Prep, two students will get into Harvard. Maybe three, but never four. So you're competing for those two slots against every other classmate who also wants to be a Crimson, and those classmates *have* extracurriculars and 1500 SAT scores and top the class lists. You hire Poison Ivy to ensure you're not overlooked."

"Victor is already taking one Harvard slot," Cassius says. "We need to figure out who's after the other and make them... reconsider their options."

I swallow. And there it is. Sabotage. It's not like it doesn't go on in other schools. I've heard rumors about students spiking their competitor's sports drinks with laxatives the day before a crucial test or planting drugs in bags to get their rivals kicked off teams. But I've never heard of anything like the Poison Ivy Club. Nothing so... organized.

"Luckily, we've been working on our intel for years,

compiling the lists of top students and their first and second choice schools." Victor turns a page in their ledger. "In our class, the students gunning for Harvard are Meredith Forsythe and Eurydice Jones."

Shit. Euri. Of course. She did tell me that Harvard was her backup school if she didn't get into Princeton. I'd forgotten about it because I make a habit of tuning out as much college talk as possible.

"I don't want to go after Euri," I say. "If it's between her and me, I'll go to another school."

"I told you she didn't have the stomach for this," Cassius growls at Victor. "You want to go to Harvard, sis? This is how you do it."

"Fine. I just don't want to... to hurt her."

"Euri's first on the class list, so she's your steepest competition. We won't make it so she can't go to any school. We just close the door to Harvard for her. Meredith is less of a threat, but we still need to take care of her, too."

"And we need to talk to Renaldo," Torsten adds.

"Renaldo? Is he like the fixer? Does he do the kneecapping?" My voice drips with sarcasm.

"No outsourcing. We do our own kneecapping," Cassius says, and something in his tone makes me believe he's serious. "Kamilla Renaldo is the school's college counselor."

"*One* of the college counselors," Torsten corrects. He likes things to be exact. "We have five."

"Yes, but she's the only one who matters to us. A recommendation to a college from her is basically as good as getting in."

"I'm not assigned to her," I say. At the beginning of senior year, every student is assigned a college counselor to help them navigate their choices. Because I came late and my grades were average, I was given whoever had a gap in their schedule. "I have some guy named Russell."

"Christ on a cross, Munroe," Cassius snorts. "What do you think you hired us for? We'll get you Renaldo."

I stand. "Okay then. What are we waiting for? Let's go see this Renaldo."

Let's do this before I get cold feet.

A hand clamps around my arm, forcing me back into my seat. "Sit down, Munroe. Take a load off. Let Victor invent some extracurriculars for you, and Torsten can get started on your app. We don't talk to Renaldo here. Meet us at the car after school. We're going on a little class trip."

44

FERGIE

After the final bell rings, I head out to the parking lot with Cassius and Torsten. Victor can't join us because he has a Model UN meeting. I can't see how Victor can be in the Model UN with a straight face while also rigging basketball games in his favor.

Or maybe I *can* see it. Victor August is a walking contradiction.

Cassius drives with terrifying speed. We head across the city, past the rolling Harrington Hills and into Brawley, a more middle-class suburb. Here, the houses are closer to the street, with fences instead of high security walls. I hear children playing and lawnmowers rumbling. A perfect picture of suburbia.

We stop in a quiet street and get out of the car. I can tell from the change in echo that we're parked in front of a row of townhouses.

I start to walk toward the front gate, but Cassius grabs my arm. "Where do you think you're going?"

We walk around the other side of the house. Cassius and Torsten boost me over a fence. I stand with Torsten in a patch of fragrant flowers while Cassius grunts and swears and throws tools on the ground. A few minutes pass and then he yells for us to get inside.

I follow Torsten into Kamilla Renaldo's home.

"Is this really the way to ingratiate myself to the lady who'll give me a college recommendation?" I ask as I stand in the woman's living room. I click my tongue, discerning a low sofa on my left, a small coffee table, and the distinct aroma of cat litter.

"Are you going to question everything we do?" Cassius growls.

"Yes."

Is this what being a Poison Ivy Girl means? We break into the homes of college counselors?

Okay, then.

I perch next to Torsten on Ms. Renaldo's sofa, trying not to get my fingerprints on anything, because I'm pretty sure being arrested for breaking and entering counts as 'drawing attention to myself.' Cassius bangs around in her kitchen. I hear him crunching on something. Potato chips, judging by the crinkly sound of the bag. He doesn't offer any to us. A cat wanders into my lap and settles down in a ball to sleep. Cats have no loyalty.

I stroke the cat, because it's impossible not to stroke a tiny, purring ball of cute that's made its home on your lap.

Some time passes. Cassius munches through the entire bag of potato chips and starts flipping through the woman's book-case, muttering about the pompous titles. Keys jangle in the door. A woman walks into the house, places her keys on the hall table, kicks off her shoes. "Manuéla?" she calls.

The cat raises its head and yawns, but doesn't bother to get up.

"Hello, Kamilla," Cassius says as the woman enters the room. "Did you miss us?"

She lets out a string of Spanish. Cassius groans as she grabs some item from the kitchen counter and whomps him with it. I like this woman already.

"Can't you use the front door like normal people?" Kamilla shoves Cassius out of the kitchen and opens the fridge. I hear a glass hit the counter, and a wine bottle opens with a hiss. Kamilla pours herself a glass and brings the bottle and more glasses to the coffee table. She doesn't acknowledge me or Torsten.

I hear Cassius pick up the wine bottle and take a long gulp. "Where's the fun in that? We have business."

"You brought a friend with you?" Behind Kamilla's icy voice, I sense her fear. "*Eres tan pendejo.* I told you this arrangement has to remain absolutely secret—"

"Fergie is one of us now," Cassius says. "You'll be seeing a lot more of her. I thought you'd like to meet your newest student bound for Harvard Law School."

"*Her?*" The counselor's voice rises an octave, obviously taking in the cane leaning against my knees. "They'll eat her alive at that school. But you know I can get her in. What's her SAT score?"

"I'm right here," I snap. "And I got a 1410, but I'm resitting next weekend."

Kamilla whistles through her teeth. "*¡A la Verga!* She's going to resit." She says this to Cassius, like she doesn't know what to do with me. "You truly believe this little club of yours is invincible, don't you?"

"By the time we're done with her, she'll be Ivy League material," Cassius says.

I'm already Ivy League material, I want to shout. I bite my lip to keep the scream inside.

Kamilla sighs. "What do you have for me?"

I hear a thump as Torsten drops something on the table. "Courtesy of Livvie Lucian."

There's a rustle of a package being opened, and Kamilla's voice fills with awe. "These are..."

"Yes. These are Dante's Inferno – the latest designer drug from Southeast Asia," says Cassius. "They aren't even on the streets here yet. There are three pills – Inferno, Purgatory, and Paradise. You take Inferno first – it allows you to cast aside the expectations of the world and experience the ecstasy of sin. Purgatory comes second, and it fills you with a sense of righteous poetic justice, an ability to see the world as it truly is. The third, Paradise, fills body and soul with unimaginable pleasure. From placating helicopter parents to wrangling their entitled brats and marking midterms for hours, all the mundane chores of a meaningless existence suddenly become beautiful works of art, pieces of a vast tapestry of life."

Cassius sounds like he's quoting from a catalog and loving every moment of it. What is this? Is Livvie Lucian a drug dealer? In the gallery, Torsten implied that she had him forge art for her. I can almost believe *that* of her – with her fine clothing and exquisite taste, and her high-end clubs all over the city. She even owns a museum, so of course she'd be deep in the art world. But drugs? It sounds like the plot of a James Bond film or some kind of mafia romance novel. This isn't really how drug deals work, is it? And yet...

...and yet, Kamilla Renaldo makes approving clicking noises with her tongue as she riffles through the package of Dante's Inferno.

"Ms. Renaldo supplies the Stonehurst Prep faculty with whatever they need to get them through the day," Cassius says. "How do you think the teachers deal with our selfish, entitled asses day in and day out? They're flying high on the latest designer drugs. We're practically performing a public service."

"You don't have to justify it to me," I say. I'm not exactly in a position to judge how other people make it through the day.

Kamilla seals the package. She grabs the wine bottle from Cassius and shoves it into my hands. "Well, then, girl. Drink and let's seal this deal. Tomorrow I will make you one of my students, and you will go to Harvard."

That easy, huh?

I gulp a mouthful of wine. It burns all the way down.

The three of us finish the bottle (Torsten abstains), and when we walk out of Kamilla's house, I'm lightheaded and floating, and not just from the alcohol.

I can't believe I just sat through a drug deal and bribed a college counselor to recommend me.

There's no turning back now.

"Recommendation, check." Cassius throws his arms around my shoulder. "I hope you're ready for my favorite part, sis. We're taking down the competition."

45

FERGIE

I t's Saturday.

I'm a Harvard-bound high school senior and I have nowhere to be, no early-morning jiujitsu training or gym session, no yearbook meetings, no last-minute study prep session.

The day is wide open.

Life is good.

It briefly crosses my mind what Euri might be doing this weekend, but I toss that thought out of my head. I can't care about Euri now. Victor is right – she's going to get into Princeton anyway, so it doesn't even matter if I take the second Harvard spot.

I call down to the kitchen and ask Milo if he could bring my breakfast upstairs, hating myself for turning into a spoiled lazy rich person, but too lazy to change. I sip my Turkish coffee as I listen to an audiobook. It's this author named Steffanie Holmes, and she wrote this duet about a secret society at Blackfriars University in the UK. I've heard of Blackfriars – it's a real school, one of the most prestigious colleges in Europe, and the buildings are ancient and gothic, and the whole place sounds like my Hogwarts dreams come true.

During a quiet passage, where the heroine George is trying to convince herself that she's not falling in love with the gorgeous and slightly eccentric college priest, I hear the sound of splashing from outside.

I pop out my earbuds and pad to the window. I lean across the overstuffed armchair and shove the glass open. I'm greeted by more splashes and Juliet's delighted squeals as someone dunks her underwater, and Victor yelling at Torsten to stop drawing and get in the pool.

The Poison Ivy Club are poolside.

"Morning, Sunflower," Juliet calls up, using Cassius' nickname for me. It's not the nickname I would have chosen, but it's growing on me. "Come and join us! I made piña coladas."

"Isn't it a little early for drinking?"

"What a silly question."

I wrinkle my nose as a blast of frigid air hits my face. "And isn't it a little *cold?*"

"The pool's heated, and this might be our last chance to use it before winter really sets in. Get that cute ass of yours down here."

I pull out my bikini from my drawer and put it on. I wrap a towel around myself and pad downstairs. The house is deserted, like usual. Neither my dad nor Cali are anywhere to be found. *They're probably at another of their tennis matches that I'm not allowed to see.*

It takes me a couple of tries to locate the right patio doors, but I'm getting more familiar with the house. Another few weeks living here and I won't need my cane inside anymore.

I push open the doors and navigate around the furniture to find the pool gate. Victor comes running over to offer me his arm.

"There you are." He wraps a damp arm around my shoulders. His hair drips water onto my tits. "We were just about to send a search party."

"Victor wanted to swoop you off your feet and carry you out here, like a knight in shining armor," Juliet says.

"Yes, and then drop you in the pool." Victor nuzzles my neck. He smells like chlorine and dark chocolate – a strangely erotic mix.

"Do it and die, August. I heard something about a piña colada?"

I locate the nearest lounger and plonk down into it.

"Hands out," Juliet commands. I stretch out my hand and she places a drink in it. I pull down the brim of my huge black pilgrim hat and tug nervously on my black bikini. It's strange – I've been naked in front of all these guys before, and yet, I'm nervous. I feel exposed out here, with them, doing this perfectly normal California Saturday activity.

It's probably because I'm their client. And because at Kamilla's house, they let me see a piece of themselves. I saw Cassius blackmail a college counselor. I saw Torsten do a drug deal. They've given me a glimpse behind the gilded curtain of Poison Ivy, and I'm terrified of what they'll want in return.

"Such service." I sip my drink. The alcohol pools warmth in my gut. And it might not be just the alcohol. It might be the proximity to three guys who confuse, irritate, and intrigue me. It might be the fact that I haven't spent many days of my high school life hanging out beside a pool like a normal person.

But that's exactly why I have to keep my guard up. The last person I did normal people things with betrayed me. And the Poison Ivy Club have shown me that they're not exactly angels.

I raise the piña colada to my lips again, but this time I only pretend to sip. I need to stay sober. I'm not quite ready to trust them yet.

We sit around and talk about people at school. Victor and Juliet discuss some trouble their mother's having with her shipping company. Cassius holds Juliet under the water until she comes up sputtering curses.

"You bastard. You could've drowned me!"

"You swim for the varsity team, Jules. You're fine." Cas dunks her again. Cold pool water splashes my feet. I'm reminded of the first day I arrived at this house, and the mystery man in my room who smelled of chlorine and danger. If the Fergie that day knew she had another shot at Harvard...

...or that her stepbrother was determined to corrupt her...

"Come on, Fergie." Juliet places her hand on mine, pushing my glass to my lips so that I have no choice but to gulp at the drink. "We're all ready for round two. You have to keep up, girl."

"I'm going for a swim." It seems the safest way to keep my head around Juliet's piña coladas. I shove the towel off my legs and get up. My cane leans against my chair, but instead of grabbing it, I inch forward little by little until I can feel the very edge of the pool with my toe. I'm about to sit down on the edge when a hand thrusts from beneath the water and grabs my angle, yanking me off-balance.

I scream as I fall into the abyss. My arms flail. I try to turn my body so I don't hit the edge. I don't know exactly where it is, but then it's too late.

I hit the water. Hard.

The air drives from my lungs. I gulp a mouthful of water. The hand yanks my foot up, shoving me to the bottom.

My other foot bursts with pain as it crashes against the side of the pool.

I swallow more water as I claw at my attacker, trying to get him to release my foot. My lungs burn for air. My movements slow. I try to swing my arms, but they're made of concrete. Everything's muted, far away, getting farther...

I break the surface, coughing and spluttering. I grip my churning stomach and gasp for air. The hand releases my foot and someone swims up beside me, roaring with laughter.

Cassius.

Of course it fucking is.

"Why did you do that?" I lunge at him, but he darts away. He laughs even harder. "I didn't know where the water was, what shape the pool was. I could have hit my head and *drowned*."

"I wouldn't have let that happen, sis."

"How do I know what you will and won't do?" I pound his chest with my fist. "You've done *nothing* but torment me from the moment I walked into this house. Even when we slept together, it was just your way of having power over me. So I'm not going to trust you not to smash my head open on the side of the pool."

Cassius isn't laughing anymore. He catches my wrist and lifts it high above his head so that our bodies swing together. His chest presses against mine, and I'm aware now that only my thin scrap of bikini fabric separates us. As if reading my thoughts, Cas reaches down and cups my breast with his other hand, his finger playing with my hardened nipple. He rolls it between his fingers, then pinches it.

Hard.

A whimper of pleasure erupts from my mouth before I can stop it. I *hate* what this man does to my body, that I can detest him so goddamn much and yet I'm gagging for his hands to be all over me.

The water around us feels like it's boiling against my skin. It's too hot, too much. He's too close.

I grit my teeth as Cas twists my nipple a little harder. He chuckles in that infuriating way of his that makes me want to slap him. But I'm not sure if it's because I want him to stop, or because I want to see what he'll do to punish me. "You're *mine*, little sister. You're part of this family now, which means I'll protect you with my life. You got that? I'll only make you bleed if you beg for it, and you *will* beg for it. I can see the little deviant glowing behind those sightless eyes of yours. You like when I do *this*."

He slaps his hand across the top of my breast. It stings a little, and I gasp. But it's not a gasp of pain.

"It hurts," I growl through gritted teeth.

"Exactly. It hurts and you like it, because you're a filthy little slut. You're *my* little slut. Mine and Victor's and Torsten's. And I am going to have *so much fun* showing you just how much pain you can take."

His words burn through my veins.

A threat.

A promise.

A wish.

"No thanks," I manage to bite back. "Now that I have Vic and Torsten fucking me raw anytime I want, I have no use for you."

My stepbrother thinks that he sees inside me, that he can cut me open and bleed my secrets on the floor. Well, I've seen inside him, too. I know that the one thing he hates more than anything in the world is feeling inferior. So I poke the bear with his own insecurities.

I am a redhead, after all.

He leans in, his breath hissing over my cheek as he whispers quiet enough so the others can't hear. But he doesn't say a word. He *growls* at me, like an animal. The sound is low in his throat, and it's fucking terrifying, but it heats my blood past boiling point. I'm going to melt into a Fergie soup that they won't even be able to scoop out with the pool skimmer.

I open my mouth to bite back, but something slams down on top of my head and I'm pushed underwater.

My lungs heave as my mouth fills with water. I manage to

hold my breath this time, but I'm being pushed down, down, down, and I can't get a grip on Cas to get him off me. He shoves me right down until my knees scrape the bottom of the pool, and my mind clouds with panic and I forget every jiujitsu move I know that could get me out of this.

My stomach cramps and heaves. My ears shoot with pain like he's stabbing me through the skull. The edges of my consciousness cloud over. *This is it. This is when he kills me—*

Cas' hand tightens on the back of my head. He forces my face against him. His lips crush against mine.

The water boils against my skin. Cas forces my mouth open, and more water rushes in. He pushes a mouthful of air into me, the remaining air in his lungs, and it's enough, enough for our tongues to tangle together and our souls to scream for each other.

And then the air is gone. I can't breathe. My throat's on fire. I'm drowning. My lungs scream for air, but I can't stop. I don't want to stop.

I'm on the edge of death, and I'm kissing him, and I've never felt more *alive*.

Every atom of my body is in magnificent glow. My whole body feels like it's falling backward into an abyss with only my monstrous stepbrother to hold me back. I cling to him. I want him to fall with me.

He's the one who breaks off the kiss. He shoves me, hard. My back slams into the wall and I fight my way to the surface. My chest bursts with pain as I gasp in breath after breath of beautiful air. Every gasp is exquisite agony. My skull blooms with a vicious headache, but every other part of me *hums* with heat and adrenaline.

That kiss... I had no air. My head spins wildly. We both could have died, and...

...and I loved it.

"See?" Cassius paddles over to me and rubs circles on my back while I cough and splutter. "You crave the darkness. You want just enough poison to feel good. But you'd better be careful, Sunflower, because if you take in too much of me, I'll get into your blood, and I'll rot you from the inside out."

46

FERGIE

"I'm bored," Juliet says as she picks at the tray of sandwiches, cheeses, and exotic fruits that Milo set down for us for lunch. "Let's go to the club."

Cassius groans. "Talk about boring…"

"It's only boring to you because you're not taking over your family business," Juliet says. "It's the best place to find all the gossip."

I hear the now familiar smash of Cassius breaking a glass. I don't know what the deal is about his mother's business, but Juliet hit a nerve. "I don't care about gossip."

"You should." Juliet's phone beeps. "For example, right now I can tell you that Meredith Forsythe is booked on a tennis court. A *private* court."

"That's the other girl who wants to go to Harvard," I say from my safe space on the lounger. I haven't been back in the pool since Cassius kissed me. I've tried to stagger my drinks, but I feel a little lightheaded.

"Exactly, and she's only booked a private court if she's with someone she doesn't want anyone to see. Those courts are reserved for the richest, most private clients at the club. You can put security on the doors, and they have tunnels so you can get in and out without anyone seeing you. And I bet we'd all *love* to know who Meredith has brought along."

My stomach churns. I don't know if I'm ready for what comes next.

Someone splashes in the pool. "How do you know that?" Victor demands. He treads water down the deep end.

"I told you. I pay attention to gossip," Juliet says. "You don't have to do everything with fists and threats, brother."

More splashes. Someone grabs the towel from under my feet. "We should get there now," Victor says. He leans over me, dripping water on me as he picks something off the tray and chews it.

"Relax, Kingpin, we've got time to finish our drinks." Juliet pats my leg. "What do you say, Fergie? Want to hit the club with us?"

"I thought we *were* the club?"

"No, silly. We're talking about the Olympus Club. Don't listen to what these heathens tell you – it's loads of fun. We can get the scoop on Meredith, hit the beauty spa, and then the bar."

"I'm not a member." Dad hasn't mentioned doing the paper-work for me, and after the way Torsten reacted around her, I'm not inclined to go back to Livvie for a favor.

"That's fine. We can bring guests. No one is going to refuse any of us."

So why did Dad tell me I couldn't come? I need to confront him about it, but that would require him to actually be at home occasionally. "I have nothing to wear."

Juliet smiles. "We can fix that."

❧

JULIET PAWS THROUGH MY CLOSET, making disapproving noises at my collection of vintage heavy metal t-shirts, leggings, and leather skirts. "Hasn't anyone ever told you that the grunge look went out like, thirty years ago?"

"Sure they have. But when it becomes cool again, I'll be the height of fashion."

"This is a square-necked plaid *shirtdress.*" Juliet tosses a garment across the room in disgust. "It's never going to be in fashion. Next weekend, we are burning all these clothes, and then we're going shopping. No arguments. If we're going to be friends, I need to not be embarrassed to stand next to you."

If we're going to be friends...

First Euri, and now Juliet. It doesn't matter what I want, people in Emerald Beach are determined to get under my skin.

Juliet summons Seymour. She hands him her keys and instructs him to go to her house and bring back a specific selection of her clothes. Much to my surprise, he does this. He returns twenty minutes later and dumps an armload of fabric on my bed. Juliet flings clothing everywhere before she finds what she's looking for.

"Tada. I'm a genius. Put these on."

I shimmy my ass into a silk Diane von Furstenberg wrap dress and shove my feet into a pair of black patent leather pumps – the only pair of my shoes Juliet deems "acceptable." She spends another forty minutes having Torsten paint my face while she jabs at my unruly hair with bobby pins.

"By the time we get to the club, it'll be closed," I complain. This is *exactly* why I don't bother with all this nonsense. Who has got the time for this every day?

"Be quiet and take your makeover like a good girl," Juliet says as she stands back. "We're done. It's a shame you can't see it – you look incredible and totally not like a drunk hobo anymore.

I'm a genius. And Torsten is not too shabby with an eyebrow pencil, either."

I touch my hair. "It's... unique."

"*Unique?*" Juliet screeches.

"It feels like a wombat had sex with a beehive."

"Omigod, Fergie. You're ridiculous. You look amazing, and you're going to the club like this. End of story."

When I walk downstairs, the other two guys are waiting in the foyer. Victor sucks in his breath when he sees me. "You look incredible, Duchess."

Cassius doesn't seem as impressed. He barks at Juliet. "Why did you have to dress her up like a mini-you?"

"What? You prefer her looking like a mini-*you*?" Juliet shoots back.

"No. But I like her enormous band tee-shirts and those stompy boots of hers."

"Those faded tents with the gross pictures on them?" I imagine Juliet is wrinkling her nose right now. "The one she had on this morning had a goat-demon fingering a mermaid."

"Damn right," Cassius squeezes my arm. This time, I don't shy away from him. After that kiss, I don't know how I feel about my stepbrother. What he did was dangerous and reckless, but I think it's the only way he could make his point – there is something about the forbidden with him that I can't ignore, not even when I have Vic and Torsten to sate my every whim. "That's hot. If Fergie wants me to dress up like a goat-demon and do unspeakable things for her, I'm game."

"Noted," I say with a laugh.

Victor drives us to the club in his giant truck thing. Cas takes charge of the stereo, and he puts on a heavy metal playlist and growls along at the top of his lungs just to piss off Juliet. My head feels like I'm being stung by a hundred bees, but no way am I pulling out of this adventure. Victor slows the truck and turns underneath a tall gateway, and I wind the window down to get a sense of the place. Everything smells fresh and floral. And *expensive*.

I couldn't describe it to a sightie, but you can smell money. Certain places and people reek of wealth and excess. It's a thing, and I smell it everywhere in Emerald Beach, but it's a particularly potent stench at the Olympus Country Club.

We pull up and Cassius hands his keys to a valet. Juliet links arms with me and drags me up the steps into an enormous building. We stand in a foyer that's almost as large as the one in Cali's house. People rush in all directions, and I catch snatches of conversation about rich people things – stocks, galas, business deals, art, gossip.

"So, where's Meredith now?" Victor asks.

"According to my source, she's still on a private court." I hear Juliet tap her phone. "You won't get in there, brother. She's posted two security goons at the door. And she's booked service for the entire day. That girl's not coming out until she's been bent over the net and fucked in every hole."

"So what are we doing here?" I ask, my chest tightening with nerves. In the excitement, I'd mostly forgotten we'd come here to work on the next part of my Ivy League plan. "Because if Meredith is sleeping with someone, we can't use that against her. I thought you had rules and—"

"We *do* have rules, but if Meredith is hiding a paramour, she's probably hiding other things as well. We'll be taking turns staking it out," Victor says. "We should be able to get *something* we can use. Cassius, can you talk to the staff, use your wit and charm to get us behind that door. Torsten and I will take first shift."

"Fine. I'm going to the bar." Cassius heads down the right hallway.

Juliet drags me in the opposite direction. "We're getting the full treatment at the spa. My treat. And then we'll have a steam and meet the guys for dinner. Those private courts have fully stocked bars and little cabana houses. I bet Meredith won't even emerge until well after midnight."

"You want us to have a steam? What about my hair..."

"Don't worry. I can fix it after."

That's what I'm afraid of.

At the on-site spa, Juliet signs us up for a barrage of treatments that sound like they were invented by the Spanish Inquisition. After being poked, prodded, scraped, submerged, and pummeled, all while Juliet chatters beside me about how wonderful her brother is, I finally emerge – a butterfly from the chrysalis, a new, more radiant Fergie.

After twenty minutes admiring herself in the mirror, Juliet checks my spa robe is wrapped around my naked body, then pushes me down another corridor that smells like lavender. "Steam time."

"Okay, but I don't have—"

"Have fun!" She shoves me through a door. I stumble over my own feet and crash into something large and warm and hard.

Not something. *Someone.*

"Why, Duchess," Victor purrs. "I'm not sure if you're aware that this is the men's steam room."

"Maybe our little Sunflower has got all hot and bothered thinking about what Meredith's been up to, and she wants a piece of the action," a dark voice whispers in my other ear.

Cassius.

Shit.

I whirl around, but as I do, the door slams in my face.

"Enjoy your steam," Juliet giggles from the other side of the door.

"Juliet." I jiggle the handle, but the door's locked tight. I bang my fists on the window. "You're absolutely hilarious. Now let me out. We're supposed to be watching Meredith, remember?"

"Oh, don't worry. I've already taken care of that," Juliet cackles. I hear her footsteps retreating down the hall. "Have fun, Fergie."

Great. I turn back to Cas and Vic. "She locked us in."

"My sister," Victor sighs. But his hand slides up my arm. He trails his fingers over the underside of my wrist, and I don't think he's that sad about this at all.

"Step aside. I'll break the door," Cas growls.

"It's fine." I pull the strands of my fluffy robe tighter around my chest. "Juliet says Meredith isn't going to come out of her private bunker until later. I've just been submerged in a mud bath and had some kind of weird molasses slathered all over me. We're in a sauna, and I'm game for any rich person tradition at this point."

Especially if it involves two hot, naked, sweaty Poison Ivy members.

Cas comes up behind me, pressing his chest into me. He scrapes his teeth along my neck as he plays with the hem of my robe. And I'm suddenly very aware that he's my stepbrother and we're at his country club and that only this fluffy material stands between me and his *very* rigid cock.

Old Fergie would stop this right now, before it went too far. But Old Fergie has left the building.

New Fergie stands in her place, with her stepbrother's huge hands pawing at her while his best friend pushes her robe off one shoulder and tenderly kisses her skin. I swallow into my raw throat.

New Fergie wants to find out exactly what these two will do to her.

"We'll show you the sauna. It's right this way, ma'am... oh, *shit.*" Vic's hand tightens on my arm as he hauls me back around a corner. He lowers his voice to a whisper. "It appears we're not the only ones here."

"What?" I whisper back.

Behind us, Cas whistles low in his throat.

"It's Meredith. I guess Juliet must've done something to force her off the private court. And she's doing some extra credit work with Coach Franklin." The grin in Vic's voice is unmistakable. "My sister really does come through for us."

"Coach Franklin, from school?" I have Coach Franklin for PE, but he mostly leaves me in the weights room while he teaches team sports to the sighties, which works fine for me.

I hear the click of Victor's phone camera. Cassius moves beside me, and I'm positive he's taking a video. I listen into the room beyond, and I can hear sucking sounds and a male voice moaning, "That's it, baby doll. Take it all the way in."

My whole body goes numb.

Cas feels it. He squeezes my shoulder. "Relax, sis. You just got one step closer to Harvard Law."

Harvard Law. Just the name on Cassius' lips makes me hungry. Or maybe it's not the Ivy League I'm lusting after. Maybe it's being trapped in this hot room wearing only a robe, with my stepbrother and his gorgeous friend threatening to do all kinds of filthy things to me.

But the hunger tastes rotten. I know that this girl is my main competition for that Harvard spot. I know that she's just handed us all the ammo we need to take her out. And I know a teacher taking advantage of a student like this is all kinds of fucked-up, and that should be exposed.

But I can't do this.

I reach out and knock Victor's phone from his hand.

"Duchess, what are you doing?"

I grip his arm. "You can't use those images. Or that video."

"What the fuck are you talking about?" Cassius growls.

"Delete it. *Now*." I grab for my stepbrother's phone, but he tears it from my hands.

"We're not going to use this stuff," Vic whispers. "We'd never do that. We'll delete it as soon as we get them to agree to our terms. But he's a teacher – he deserves to pay for this."

"And what about *her*?" My voice rises. I'm dangerously close to losing my shit. "What about what happens to her? What about your rules?"

"For you, Duchess, we'll break every rule."

"Did all that hairspray Juliet put on you kill your brain cells?" Cas snaps as I try to wrestle the phone from his hand. "I thought you hired us because you were willing to do anything to get into Harvard. Well, let us do our job."

The panic rises up inside me. I'm no longer in the steam room at the Olympus Club. I'm back in the newsroom at my old school, listening to a video on my phone as my own moans play back in my ears.

And before I even know what I'm doing, I leap out from our hiding spot and shove my shoulder into the sauna door.

"Fergie, fuck!" Cassius yells.

It's locked, but my weight breaks the lock easier and I burst into the room. The sucking noises abruptly cut off.

"What the fuck?" Coach Franklin cries out.

"Get out of here," I yell.

"No," a girl whimpers. "Please don't tell anyone."

"It's okay," says the coach. "She goes to our school. She's blind. She doesn't see anything."

"Maybe not, Coach Franklin," Victor says from behind me. "But we've seen it all."

"No." I hear a thump as the girl slides to her knees. "No, no, no, no."

I drop to my knees beside her. I'm shaking all over. It's like it's happening all over again. I reach for Meredith and wrap my arms around her naked body as she sobs.

This is for Harvard.

Harvard.

Harvard.

Harvard...

"It's okay, Meredith," Victor says. "We're not going to say anything. The last thing we want is for this to come out. All we ask for in return is a simple favor."

"Anything," the girl cries. "I'll do anything."

I have to do this. I have to. I'm a Poison Ivy Girl now.

I can be just as ruthless as they are.

"We want you to change your early decision application from Harvard."

"Fine!" she sniffs. "I want to go to Oxford anyway. It's my parents who want me to go there."

"Then we have an agreement," Victor sounds a little sad as he steps closer. "I know you can't see it, Fergie, but I'm deleting the photographs. And Cas is getting rid of the video. We trust you to hold up your end of the bargain, Meredith."

"Yes, I will. I promise. Thank you." Meredith scrambles out of my arms, grabs her clothes, and races from the sauna.

"Thank you for your discretion, Victor," Coach Franklin says as he moves around behind me. I'm guessing he's frantically pulling on clothes.

"No need to thank us, *Coach,*" Victor sneers. "We're not done with you yet."

The coach makes a strangled noise, but he shoves past me and runs as well. Now I'm all alone in the sauna, and it's too hot and it reeks of sex and desperation, and I need to get the fuck out of here.

"I need some air," I murmur. My head swims. The steam

presses in on me from all sides. Everything smells like Victor and Cassius. They're too close. I'm too close.

I don't know what the fuck I'm doing anymore.

I launch myself toward the door and emerge into the shower rooms. I feel my way down a row of lockers to a series of shower cubicles. This isn't like a school locker room – each cubicle is basically a hotel bathroom with marble tiles, freshly laundered towels, expensive bath products, and a large walk-in shower with a hundred different jets.

Nothing in the whole world sounds as good right now as standing under a jet of water and blasting away the horror of what just happened, of what I did.

I grab a towel from the basket and a bunch of bottles of things – the spa range they use has notches on the lid for blind people to indicate whether the bottle holds shampoo, conditioner, or body wash – and step into the shower. I locate a panel of buttons and dials to work the jets and hit one.

A spray of boiling hot water hits me right in the face.

I yelp and stagger back. I lean my back against the shower wall as the spray pummels me. I burst into hysterical laughter.

How did I get here? How the fuck did I end up in a Star Trek shower at a country club, doing the same thing to a girl that was done to me? Is this who I am now?

Is this who I want New Fergie to be?

Is Harvard worth blackmailing Meredith Forsythe with her mistakes?

Tears sting my eyes. I go to wipe them away, but then I think fuck it, who am I putting a brave face on for? Certainly not my father, who's forgotten I exist. And definitely not for those two broken boys out there who'd probably be perfectly happy to ruin my life the way they've ruined countless others. So I sink to the floor of the shower and let the tears fall. They cascade down my cheeks with the water until my stomach twists and my nose burns, and still they come.

"Fergie."

I jump at the voice. It's Victor.

"How did you get in here?" I murmur. I don't turn to face him.

"I broke the lock. I wanted to see if you're okay."

I sigh. "You don't need to rescue me, Victor August."

The jets turn off. Hands grab me under the arms and lift me to my feet. He touches my cheek, brushing away the tears gathering beneath my eyes.

"Why not?" he whispers, his voice a promise, a curse. "You're clearly so adept at saving yourself."

I don't know what to do, but I need to distract myself from him, because when I'm near him, when he speaks to me in that posh voice and I breathe in his whisky and dark chocolate scent, I forget who I am. And that's dangerous. So I jab my hand onto the panel of buttons. Victor yelps as ten streams of water slam into him from all directions, plastering his designer clothes to his skin.

"Argh," he yells. "I've got shampoo in my eyes."

A shaky grin finds its way to my lips. "I feel better now."

Victor growls – a sound that always makes me think of Cassius. But the way Victor does it is less about losing control and more about... *claiming* it. He grabs my wrists and slams them into the wall above my head, pinning my chest against the wet tiles with one hand. The other hand snakes down my body, stroking fire along my skin.

"I know what will make you feel even better," Victor murmurs against my lips.

He's not wrong. When I walked into this shower, I wanted nothing to do with either of them. But now that he has me pinned to the wall, and his erection presses against my thigh and his heady scent fills my lungs, I want him. More than anything. I want to obliterate this horrible day with his cock.

But I have to say something. Before I lose myself completely.

"I don't know if I can do this." The words taste like rotting fruit.

"You managed to in the rage room," Vic chuckles.

"*No*. I don't know if I can blackmail Meredith with those pictures. I thought you wouldn't—"

"We deleted the photographs, Duchess." Vic's thumb traces across my cheek, catching another tear before it falls. "We were never going to use them. But sometimes people don't need to know about our moral code."

"But she's going to change schools, and it's because of what we did—"

"We gave her *permission* to be brave and do what her heart desires," Vic says. "I've been at school with Meredith since we were in diapers. Her parents put *insane* amounts of pressure on her. I knew how badly she wants to get out from under their control. She'll tell them that the Poison Ivy Club has something on her, and that's why she's changing schools, and they'll call me and I'll confirm it. Call it a little club charity project, if you like."

I rest my head against his shoulder, breathing in his scent. I consider what Vic's saying, how he *planned* this so that both Meredith and I would get what we wanted. "I still don't like it—"

"Let me get this straight, you're okay with faking extracurriculars and bribing a counselor for a recommendation, but *not* with encouraging Meredith to apply to a different college, even if it's the college she actually *wants* to go to?"

"Yes. I'm a complicated woman."

Vic's body presses me into the wall. He leans behind and turns the tap on – not all the way like I did, so it's just a steady stream of perfectly warm water cascading over us. Victor cups my cheek with one hand and tilts my face to his. His breath caresses my lips. "I've never met anyone like you before, Fergie Munroe."

"Is that so?"

"It's not every girl who'd agree to be shared by three guys." Vic's lips brush mine again, hinting at a kiss. "Especially not three guys like *us*."

"I can't imagine that Cas knows *how* to share."

"We've done it before," he murmurs as he kisses a trail along my jaw. His lips are pure evil. "It was fun for a while. Don't you worry about what goes on between me and Cas, Duchess. We'll sort our shit out the same way we always do. We're brothers, first and foremost. We may snipe at each other, but we're used to sharing our toys."

I raise an eyebrow. "Is that what I am? A toy?"

"You are so much fucking more than that," Victor groans. "I don't even have a word for what you are. You are a tsunami crashing through our lives, destroying everything in your path. But maybe it's good to tear the world down, so we can build it anew."

Such pretty words. But I have no use for poetry. I grab Vic's shoulders and yank him against me. I want to crawl inside him and lose myself.

Vic kisses me like a madman as he kicks off his soaking wet clothing. When he's as naked as I am, he hefts me up the wall, scraping my back against the tiles. His lips crush mine, dominating and possessive. I kiss him back with everything I fucking have, wishing and hoping that a taste of him will leave me sated, will set me free of Poison Ivy's thrall. But there's no hope left for me. I'm utterly under the spell of this man.

He barely gives me a moment to draw breath before entering me in one deep stroke. I latch my legs around him, my head falling back against the shower as the water sluices over us. It's a similar angle to when we fucked before, in the rage room, and it rubs his piercing in the perfect spot and oh... and *oh*... and...

I don't realize how close to the edge I am, and how much sadness and sex are connected in my mind, but I come almost immediately. My body convulses around him as I ride through the orgasm. Fuck me dead. Fuck me into the sun. Cock piercings are *brilliant*.

"That was fast," Vic moans, his lips grazing my shoulder. "Don't think you can get off that easy, Duchess. We're not done with you yet."

His words register through the fog of pleasure as I squirm under him. "*We?*"

"Hello, Fergie," Cassius' wicked voice pulses through my veins.

My stepbrother is in here with us.

When did he come in?

I'm in a shower, naked, with one guy's cock buried inside me and another guy, my stepbrother...

Crap. Shit. *Sound the fucktrumpets.*

I'm in for it now.

"Flip her around, Vic," Cas commands.

I cry out as Vic yanks his cock out of me and spins me around, moving me so that I'm on the glass wall of the shower and facing Cassius through the glass. My hands press against the shower as Vic moves in behind me, trailing the head of his cock down my cheeks, teasing the entrance to my ass.

I never thought I'd be into that *at all*, but right now, as my body squirms under my stepbrother's hot gaze, I'd say yes. I'd say yes to anything they want to do to me.

Cassius steps into the shower and moves beside me. My arm brushes against his bare skin, sending my stomach into the flutters of a butterfly migration.

He's naked too, or at least, he's topless.

His plum and carnation scent mingles with Victor's smell, threatening to overpower me. Vic hums under his breath as he trails his fingers down my back. He kicks my legs further apart and rubs the hot tip of his cock over my entrance.

This is so goddamn hot.

An object *CLANGS* as Cassius removes it from the wall. "Hit the button, Vic," he commands.

Vic does something on the panel behind us, and a hot spray of water hits me right in the nipple. It's not a wide, gentle spray like the shower nozzle, but thin and concentrated so that it stings my sensitive skin. Cassius aims that stream of pain right at my nipple, punishing the tiny bud while I squirm and squeal.

"You like that, don't you, little sister?" he purrs. "You like me punishing your nipples."

The pain of it is like nothing I've experienced. It fucking *hurts* having my nipples battered with that stream of water, but it's like my pain reflex is connected in a direct line to my cunt, which hums and aches and begs for release as my stepbrother moves the stream around, punishing every part of my poor nips.

Without warning, Cassius' fingers plunge between my legs, pushing inside me as he moves the stream to the second nipple. Vic drives his cock back between my ass cheeks, grunting as he slides his hot length between them and pressing them together around him.

"You should feel her, Vic," Cas says, and there's a hint of awe in his voice. "She so goddamn wet for us. So tight."

"I *know*, Cas," Vic grunts as he slides his cock down my cheeks again. "I *was* inside her before you rudely interrupted us."

But there's a hint of teasing in his voice that makes me think he knew Cas was there the entire time.

"Forgive me, brother." Cas moves the stream away from my

ruined nipples. I breathe a sigh of relief. "I know how filthy our little slut is. I want to make sure she's nice and clean for you."

And with that, he aims that stream of death right against my clit.

I scream.

I *howl.*

I paw at the glass and claw at Cas' chest, and all he does is laugh like a fucking madman as he attacks my poor, sensitive clit. But I can't stop the orgasm that slams into me at the same time that Vic plunges himself back inside me. My legs give out and Vic has to hold me upright while he rocks his hips into me. But Cas doesn't let up. He holds that stream between my legs, gripping me under my shoulder with one rough hand so I have nowhere else to go. For the second time today, I'm completely at my stepbrother's mercy.

I love it.

I come and I come again and I am not sure where one orgasm ends and another begins. Just when I think I can take no more, when I'm no longer made of flesh and bone but of jelly and raw, destroyed nerve endings, Cas removes the stream. *Thank fuck, praise the angels, holy hell I didn't even know it was possible to come so hard.* But I know better than to expect that he's done with me.

I brace myself against the glass, relaxing into Victor's thrusts as I gasp in breaths and await the next punishment.

Just when Vic begins to build up steam, and I start to think that maybe my stepbrother is spent for the day, the stream comes back again, spraying between my ass cheeks. I yelp and try to wriggle away, but that only makes Vic press me into the wall and buck his hips faster.

Cassius' lips brush my ear again.

"I love watching him fuck you, sister," Cassius says. "I love watching my best friend touch what's mine. We share everything, you know. And soon, we'll be sharing all your holes."

He grunts, and I know he's jerking himself off with his other hand while he keeps that stream aimed straight between my cheeks. Vic makes a strangled noise, and his cock jerks inside me. I know he's not far from coming.

"But not today, Sunflower," Cassius purrs. "Because you don't get my cock inside you until you beg for it. And I know you're not ready to beg."

"Damn right," I manage to choke out.

"Such defiance," he chuckles. "It doesn't matter. You will come to me on your hands and knees one day soon. But today I'm going to come all over those gorgeous tits of yours while you take my friend's dick. You look so pretty taking his cock. Doesn't she look pretty, Victor?"

"She's beautiful," Vic murmurs. He runs a hand through my wet, matted hair.

"That's right, she's beautiful, laid out like this for us. She's our gift. Hold still, little sis," Cas coos in my ear. "Let us take care of you. We know how to make you feel good."

At his words, Vic slides one of his hands around my front, rubbing the tip of his finger lightly over my ruined clit. At least *something* about this is gentle—

SMACK.

I yelp as Cassius' hand comes down on my ass cheek. The sting of it brings tears to my eyes even as it makes my pussy flare with greedy heat.

"One day, little sister, I'm going to have your ass," Cas growls against my ear. "Are you ready to begin training for that day?"

I want to yell at him that I hate him, that he'll never get within a hundred miles of my rear entrance, but he's just given me seven bajillion orgasms in a row and I... I don't want to say no. So I nod.

I fucking *nod.*

New Fergie, who the fuck *are* you?

I have no time to debate that existential question because a beefy finger dives between my cheeks and pushes through the ring of muscle into my ass. It feels rude and odd and deviant and filling and *perfect.* And then Vic's finger rubs a slow circle on my clit as he draws back and thrusts deep inside me. I can feel Cas' finger pressing against his dick through a thin wall of flesh, and it's... it's fucking *everything.*

They move slowly at first, Cas fucking my ass with his finger while Vic thrusts into me, his finger just brushing over my clit every time he pushes forward. They get into a rhythm, working together so that it feels like it's one long cock sliding through me, and they get faster and faster as the pleasure builds and the butterflies have a fucking party in my stomach. I can't move, can't speak, can't do anything but breathe through the pure wanton *abandonment* of it as I give my body over to them and they make me feel utterly *worshipped.*

"See, I told you she's a dirty slut," Cas puffs out. Through the haze of pleasure, I'm dimly aware of the wet sound of his hand pumping his dick. He's close.

"I don't think she's dirty at all," Vic replies. "Look at her laid out for us. She's perfect. She's our queen."

Damn right I am.

"You don't know, Sunflower," Cassius whispers against my ear as he pushes his finger deeper inside me. "But there are about ten mirrors in this bathroom, and you're in all of them, your eyes rolled back in your head, your pussy leaking, those gorgeous tits of yours pressed against the glass while he punishes your pussy and my fingers claim your ass. You're completely at our mercy, Fergie. You've never looked more beautiful."

"Fuck you," I growl out.

"That's right. You *will* fuck me again, sister. But not yet. I want my friend Victor to make you feel so good. I want him and Torsten to make you ready, because when it's time for me to have you again, you're going to get on your knees and beg for my cock, and I'm going to split you in two."

Cassius shoves a second finger in beside the first, and goddamn it hurts so good. I come again, hard and fast, my body being split apart on Victor's cock as my stepbrother has his way with my ass. With a groan, Vic jerks and spurts inside me, slumping against my back as he finally gets his release.

Cassius leans against the shower and grunts as he pumps himself a few more times and then comes. True to his word, he squirts across my tits, and I know it's filthy, but I love it. Vic turns on the other shower jets and helps me stand upright while he scrubs down my body with beautifully scented things. Cas is strangely silent, waiting his turn while Victor fusses over me.

By the time Victor has wrapped me in about six towels, my stepbrother still hasn't spoken. "Cassius?" I call out, not sensing him anywhere in the cubicle.

The door bangs shut.

Vic touches my cheek. "He's gone, Duchess. He doesn't stick around for the aftercare. But I've got you. You're safe with me."

I snuggle deeper into the warm towels as Vic lays out my clothes and massages the bottoms of my feet. But I can't stop thinking about all those filthy things Cassius said to me while he had his finger in my ass. Why is he so determined that I'll beg for him? We've agreed that they're sharing me, so why does he still have to make my body into a competition?

Why can't my stepbrother face me as he truly is, stripped of all his posturing and pretense?

Why did he run?

My thighs burn from the pounding Victor gave me as I walk out to meet the others in the bar. Juliet's hairpins jangle in my pocket. My hair spills down my back, loose and tangled and dripping wet on the expensive carpet. But fuck it. I don't belong here, anyway. What's the point of pretending?

Victor orders drinks for everyone. It irks me that he assumes he knows what I want, but when he hands me a whisky Old Fashioned, I have to grudgingly admit that he called me right.

"Look who's here," Juliet coos as she bumps into our circle with Torsten and another person in tow. "Fergie, I don't know if you've met Lucila."

"Hi." Lucila shakes my hand. The other Poison Ivy client. I wonder what brought her to the point where she considered this, and I wonder again about that conversation I overheard between her and Victor in the bathroom. *Why does Victor want a house her family owns?* "I've seen you around school. Oh, I'm sorry, I mean—"

"Don't apologize for using words like 'seen'," I say. "I use them all the time. It's not offensive."

"Oh." She sounds relieved. "Cool. Well, in that case, I've seen you around school, and I love those boots you wear. I could never pull them off."

"Lucila and I are playing Guess-Who," says Juliet.

I frown, confused. "The kids' game?"

"No, silly. Lucila's father is the top plastic surgeon in Emerald Beach, so she has all the gossip. How it works is that we all take turns guessing who has had plastic surgery done, and Lucila will tell us if you're right."

"Fergie can't play," Torsten points out.

"Oh, right, of course not," Juliet says. "We'll have to think of another challenge for you…"

"How about I try to guess the fake accents?" I pipe up. "Rich people always talk in these affected faux European accents, like they have this complex about sounding American. I bet I can tell you who's really a Russian oligarch and who's faking it."

"Okay, that's perfect. We can check origins on the club directory." Juliet taps on her phone. We move away from the bar and sit around a table in the center, giving us eyes and ears on every conversation in the room.

"Mrs. Dudley has her boobs done," Juliet announces as a lady wearing overpowering floral perfume breezes past.

"One point to Juliet," murmurs Lucila.

"Too easy," Cassius scoffs.

"Only because you slept with her and bragged about them," Juliet shoots back. "Don't be sour because I beat you to the point. And what about Lavinia Bainbridge, Preston's mom? Do you think her nose is a different shape?"

"Not her nose," Lucila says.

"It's her ass, isn't it?" Victor says. "She's had something done there."

"One point to Victor," Lucila says.

I strain to drown out their conversation and the clink of ice cubes in glasses, listening to the voices around me, searching for something that reeks of play-acting. "Over there," I nod my head toward the bar. "There's a man with a deep voice. He sounds slightly Southern, but he's really German."

"Oooh, I see him," Juliet says. "He's yummy. Golden-blond curls, ice-blue eyes. I don't usually swing that way but I'd be persuaded for him. Eins *zwei*, eins *zwei*." She slaps the table suggestively.

"Foul," Cassius says. "He looks like he could be your brother."

"Don't pretend you're not into that kink, Cas. Besides, we'd look so darling together in the society pages. What do you think, Fergie? Should I go over and introduce myself to our German friend?"

"He's got a date already," Victor says with a shudder in his voice. "That's Drusilla Hargreaves on his arm."

"Even more reason to—"

"Excuse me, ma'am," an officious-sounding voice cuts into our conversation. "I'm Norton, the head of security on duty here at the Olympus Club. I'm afraid we're going to have to ask your group to leave."

"Excuse me?" Juliet shrieks. "I think you're new here, because I certainly don't recognize you, and that's the only way I'd forgive such an error. You obviously don't know who I am, who we are—"

"I know *exactly* who you are, ma'am. You are Juliet August. I've been instructed by the new owners of the Olympus Club to inform you that neither you, nor your brother, nor Mr. Dio or Mr. Lucian nor anyone associating with you is welcome in this establishment. I'm here to escort you to your vehicles."

48

VICTOR

Juliet remains quiet as we exit the country club, but I see the simmering rage burning in my twin's eyes. She grips Cassius' arm as we're escorted out by security, the two of them acting as a buffer for each other – her steady hand preventing him from beheading everyone in the room, and his powerful frame giving her the strength to hold her head with dignity.

She looks so much like Mom right now. Which means the whole world better watch out.

Juliet climbs into the passenger seat and beats her tiny fists against the dashboard as we pull out of the club. "What the fuck just happened?" she growls.

"We got kicked out," Torsten says in his usual literal way. He fumbles in his pocket for a joint.

I throw out an arm to hold Juliet back before she decks him.

"This is about Mom, isn't it?" Juliet yells. "We all know what's going on. The stings. The red tape. The stuff at the museum, and now we're not allowed at the Olympus. It's a conspiracy."

I cast a gaze back to Fergie, who's smushed between Torsten and Cassius in the backseat, making herself very small and unobtrusive. But I'm aware she's listening to every word, and there's so much that she cannot know.

I pinch Juliet's arm. She yelps and turns to slap me, then sees my finger pressed to my lips. She slaps me anyway.

"Mom is going to fix this," she snaps. "Whoever this new owner is, he'll wish he'd never been born."

There's nothing much more to say after that. We drop Torsten off at the hotel first. He won't want to talk to his mother about this. Next, I pull the car into Cassius' driveway. "Out," Juliet barks.

"Why?" Cassius demands. "The day's not over just because we can't play golf."

"Get the fuck out of this car *right now*. We need to talk to our mother," Juliet says. "And you should probably have a word with Cali, since this concerns all of us."

As Fergie slides out of her seat after him, Juliet places a hand on her thigh. "You should stay," she says.

"That's not a good idea," I say. Juliet is right – we need to talk to our mother, and Fergie needs to be protected from this.

"Whatever's going on, it's not any of my business," Fergie agrees.

"You're in Poison Ivy, right? That's what Vic told me. That means it *is* your business. This little club only has power as long as our families have power, you got that?" Juliet glares at me as she talks. "And you're safer with us than with Cas, anyway."

"If this is about our families, then Fergie is a Dio now," Cassius growls. "She's coming with me."

"No, she's not," Juliet trills sweetly. She slams her foot down and tears out of the driveway before Fergie can get out of the car.

"Jesus *Christ*." Fergie throws herself back into the car and manages to pull the door shut as Juliet tears down Harrington Hills drive toward our place. I dare a glance out the back window. Cassius stands on the driveway, fuming. His glower slices into my marrow.

We circle back through Harrington Hills and pull into our driveway a couple of minutes later. Fergie perks up as I park the car in the garage. "You and Cassius live close to each other, too. I didn't realize how close when I went to the party the other week."

"Yeah. And I guess you've been to Torsten's house, so you know he's the next block over."

She freezes. "He told you."

"He's not great at keeping secrets. But it doesn't matter anymore. You belong to all of us. And it's by design that we're close. Our mothers wanted our families to grow up together. My mom and Livvie already had homes here, and Cali moved to the neighborhood after she had her kids."

"Your parents are all friends?"

"I don't know if 'friend' would be the word they'd use." I think of the story Mom told me once about her and Cali fighting to the death.

I turn into the long tunnel that leads from the back entrance of our house into the underground garage. Juliet bursts out of the car before I've even turned off the engine, and takes off toward the house. I move to the backseat to help Fergie out. She rests her hand on my arm, sweeping her cane in front of her and making that clicking noise with her tongue. "You have a lot of vehicles," she says.

"Yeah. Juliet and I have our own cars, plus Mom has a couple of different ones for work. And each of my dads likes their own specific model."

"*Each* of your dads?"

"Yeah," I smile. "I've got three. My mom is sort of... unconventional."

Fergie licks her lip, and I know she's thinking about what

happened in the shower at the club. "I'd be interested to learn more about your unconventional family."

"Mo—om?" Juliet calls as she crashes through the house ahead of us, kicking open doors and peering around corners. "We need to talk to you, *now.*"

"She's not here," a deep voice calls back, punctuated by the unmistakable howls of a pup desperate for attention. "She and Noah are at the docks, trying to figure out how the shipment dates keep being leaked. She'll be back for dinner, though. We're having meatloaf."

Juliet grabs Fergie's hand and drags her through the house, following the excited howls and jibbers and barks to the ballroom, which has been converted into a shelter and hospital where Eli tends some of his rescue animals.

Eli's one of my three fathers. He's not my biological dad – that would be Gabriel Fallen, famous rockstar and singer for Broken Muse – but he's probably the one I'm closest to. We're a lot alike – Eli ran track at school and was on all the different teams and committees. My mom still jokingly calls him the Golden Boy of Stonehurst Prep.

After Juliet and I surprised Mom by being twins and nearly tore her vagina in half during birth, she shut up shop for babies, so Eli and Noah don't have biological kids of their own, but they treat us like we're theirs. Honestly, Gabriel is basically like having another teenage boy in the house, so I can see Mom's point.

Gabriel's on tour in Europe with his band right now, and our third dad, Noah, is Mom's chief bodyguard. He barely leaves her side. Eli doesn't entirely approve of the family business, so he hangs out with his animals and tries to stay out of it as much as he can. He's not the one who needs to hear what went down at the Olympus Club, but he's in the unfortunate position of being in Juliet's line of fire.

"Daddy, you won't *believe* what happened. We went to the Olympus Club and they kicked us out!"

"Aw, honey, that's too bad," Eli says in a teasing voice. "I'm sure you deserved it. What did you break? Which senator's daughter did you seduce in the steam room?"

Juliet throws herself dramatically on the sofa, narrowly missing crushing a tiny puppy. "Don't laugh at me – it was *humiliating*."

Eli smiles when he sees Fergie on my arm. "Who's this?"

"This is Fergie Munroe. She's Cassius' new stepsister," I say. "Fergie, this is my dad, Eli August."

Fergie holds out her hand, and Eli shakes it. Fergie moves her head around the room, and I know she's processing the strangeness of her surroundings. Everything she can hear and smell must seem strange – Eli had cleared the animals out of the house when we had the party, so she had no idea what to expect. "This room is... full of animals."

"Correct. We've got a few puppies on their way to foster homes, a troupe of tiger cubs from a roadside farm, and a bunch of monkeys some stockbroker was keeping in his Manhattan apartment until they escaped and killed a baby."

What *actually* happened with the tigers is that Mom and Noah went out and made it *very clear* to the owner that he'd be selling the zoo and all its animals to them. The owner didn't approve of the price, so Mom had Cali go out there and persuade him with her knives. The owner's wife, who was in charge of his estate after he accidentally brutally stabbed himself, sold in a hurry. We've got most of the larger animals to various sanctuaries, including the Everlasting Hart Ranch that Eli's company runs, but the cubs are waiting to be picked up by an animal welfare charity.

"Boring," Juliet rolls her eyes. She can't focus for very long if the conversation isn't about herself. "Daddy, you have to *listen* to me. I didn't seduce anyone. Cassius didn't break anything. We got kicked out of the country club *for no reason*."

Eli rolls his blue eyes. "You must've done something, honey."

"Nothing, I swear," Juliet whines. "We were in the bar, minding everyone's business, when the security guard came up to us and said we're no longer welcome."

"I know it sounds odd," I say. "But this time she's not being dramatic. That's absolutely what happened."

Eli flicks his gaze to Fergie, raising his eyebrow in a question. *How much does she know?*

I shake my head.

"The security guy, Norton, said the club is under new management," Juliet adds. "Is it someone Mommy pissed off? They don't want Lucians or Dios in there, either."

"Perhaps." Eli pats my twin's knee. "I'm sure it's nothing, but when your mother comes home, I promise we'll look into it."

"At least you're taking this *seriously*," Juliet wails. She drops the puppy in Eli's lap and flounces out of the room.

"Fergie, since my kids are terrible hosts, would you like to meet the animals?" Eli asks. "I have a new litter of kittens in an enclosure outside, and they love cuddles."

"I'd love that," Fergie says. "I always wanted a cat, but my dad's allergic."

I shoot Eli a nod of thanks and take off after Juliet. I find her in Mom's office, twirling around in the giant leather chair while she waits for something to print.

"Look at this," she says, tearing the sheet off the printer and flinging it in my face. "I found a press release about the new owner of Olympus. His name is Zack Lionel Sommesnay."

"That's the same guy who's been blocking Livvie's clubs," I say, suddenly more interested in this whole strange incident. "I don't think that's a coincidence. And did you see Drusilla hanging off his arm? I wonder if this Sommesnay fellow is why she feels safe returning to Stonehurst Prep—"

But my twin isn't paying attention to me. She stares out the window, a scheming smile playing across her features.

"What?" I demand.

"Nothing," she smirks as Eli opens the cat enclosure for Fergie to walk in. "Just that everything is going according to plan."

"*What* plan? Juliet, why did you make Fergie come to our house? Come to think of it, why did you lock me and Fergie and Cas in the sauna?"

"Because I'd paid off two staff members to tell Meredith and Coach Franklin that the sauna would be locked for their exclusive use," she says sweetly. "And I want you to get my new friend Fergie into Harvard."

"Don't play coy with me, sister."

"Fine. I did it for you, brother." She leans back in Mom's chair and folds her hands behind her head. "I did it because I want you and Fergie to go to Harvard together. I want you to live in that big house you're trying to buy from Lucila's family, and get your fancy degrees and get drunk at college parties and develop pretentious liberal world views. I want you to have the future that's supposed to be yours, Vic. Can't you see that Cassius has her in his sights? You may have this agreement now, but he won't be able to share her for long. And I'm not going to let you give her up for him, like you do with everything else."

"I don't do that."

"Yes. You *do*. You always have to put everyone else first. But this is about more than Cassius. It's about the future of our family. Of the August name." Juliet's dark eyes bore into mine, and suddenly she looks so much like our father when he sings about love and sin and salvation. "There's a fire inside Fergie

Munroe that matches your own. I haven't seen you interested in anyone since Gemma."

Juliet's the only person I'd allow to say her name, and even then it scrapes my skin raw.

"Don't be like that," I say. "Mom *specifically* said that she'll choose a successor based on talent. That might not be me. Our parents changed the rules, so succession doesn't have to be about blood—"

"Naivety doesn't suit you, Vic. She wants us to take over the business. Which means she wants *you* to take over, because I don't want the hassle." Juliet spins Mom's chair around, throwing her arms wide. "I want you to marry me off to some rich, impotent old oligarch who will shower me in diamonds and let me have as many affairs with hot Russian pole dancers as I want. But that can't happen if you don't have a queen, and Fergie is your queen."

"She can be my queen and still be with Cas and Torsten."

"No. She can't," Juliet snaps. "He's determined to turn this into a competition. And I want you to win, brother. Now go out there and fight for her."

49

FERGIE

After we finish snuggling the cats and he shows me the birds in his outdoor aviary, Eli leaves me beside the pool. "Victor will be right outside," he promises. "I'd better go and try to get hold of my wife."

Now that the yard isn't filled with brawling kids, I can explore it at my leisure. It's large, surrounded by a high wall, and beyond the wall is that wooded area I've been told about. My cane sweeps over the tiles as I look around the immediate area, finding some small garden beds and, further from the house, a couple of raised stones on the grass. The patio door slides open, and I catch a whiff of Victor's distinctive chocolate and hazelnut scent as he rushes over and offers me his elbow. My stomach flutters with nerves. This is the first time we've been alone since the shower, and I don't know what to say.

"What are you doing?" he asks as he steers me away from the pool.

"I'm just looking around. The tiles are uneven over there," I say. "By the pool."

"Oh yeah, that's because my mother killed her arch-nemesis

there. Well, one of them. She likes to leave it like that so every time someone trips, she remembers how badass she is."

I raise an eyebrow. "You're serious?"

Victor doesn't answer, and I have no idea what the fuck to believe now. Instead, he turns me toward the two stones. "Those are our first two cats," he says. "Gizmo and Queen Boudica. Remember when I told you that my mother lived in this house alone for five years with her cat?"

"Yeah."

"Well, Queen Boudica was that cat. She was quite something. Definitely lived up to her name." Victor's voice sounds pensive. "She died a few years ago, and Gizmo not long after. Mom was heartbroken, even though they were both like a hundred and sixty in cat years and they'd lived a life of luxurious excess."

"Your mom sounds *fascinating*," I say.

"That's one word to describe her. I hope you'll get to meet her sometime." Vic sounds like he's not so sure this is a good idea. He hugs my arm tight to his chest. "Want to see something interesting?"

"Um, sure?"

He leads me past the kitty gravestones, toward the back of the garden. The shower hums in the air between us – the touch of our bodies reminding us of what we did only a couple of hours ago. Out here in the peaceful, enclosed garden, it seems impossible that it happened. But my pussy remembers. She clenches and aches, and my thighs scream with every step I take.

Victor pushes open the door to a long, low building. From the brightness of the echo, it sounds as though it's made out of glass. "Okay, stay behind me, and don't touch anything. We're going inside."

"Inside what?" I let Victor lead me into the structure. It's warm inside, warmer than the fading Californian sun. A fan blows in the corner, and I hear branches wafting and leaves rustling as they brush against each other. *I'm standing in a greenhouse.* It's similar to the one at school, but not as large. And this one has a strange scent in the air – a cloying sweetness that makes my head spin.

"What is this place?" I ask.

"It's a Poison Garden," Vic says.

"And what exactly is that?"

"Every plant in this greenhouse is deadly poisonous. I grow them all myself. I got the idea from my dad's bandmates. They all studied at the Manderley Academy of Music, and the family who built that house in the 1800s used to collect specimens of poisonous plants from all over the world and keep them in a greenhouse. When the ancestors died out, no one took care of the greenhouse, and the plants took over until it became this ruin filled with monstrous tendrils and giant deadly flowers."

"Isn't Manderley Academy the creepy school that burned down, and it had the ghost in the walls—"

"That's the one. Gabriel – he's my biological dad – showed me photographs of his bandmates and their friends partying at the glasshouse. It looked like something from the Day of the Triffids. I liked the idea, so I thought I'd try it here. Watch out," Vic moves me to the left. "There's a wall of poison ivy there."

A faint pain throbs behind my eyes. "I never knew you had a green thumb."

"Didn't your friend Euri tell you that I'm top of the horticulture class?" Victor says. "Then again, it's the only class where she can't beat me, so I suspect she's sore about it."

"Euri's not my friend," I say. The words taste bitter on my tongue. "Why grow poisonous plants, though?"

"I think they're interesting," Victor says. "If it makes you feel better, I also grow lovely tomatoes over the summer. Eli uses them to make pasta sauce."

"I'd love to try it someday," I say. "The pasta sauce, I mean. Not the poisons."

Vic chuckles. He takes my hand and lets me stroke a leaf.

"It was a serious question, Vic. Why poisons?"

"I gave you a serious answer. I think these plants are beautiful. People are afraid of them because they can kill you. But *anything* can kill you if you have too much of it. Even water can be poisonous. Sometimes, a little bit of poison can even save your life. I think they're beautiful. They remind me of you."

They remind me of you.

His words might not sound like a compliment, but they dredge up a memory I've been trying to forget. I'm holding up my ribbons from the Jiujitsu World Champs as my teammates chant my nickname, "Death Lily, Death Lily!" That's what they called me – pretty to look at, but deadly.

Vic snips something and places a branch with a few berries in my hand. "This is *Aconitum napellus*, or monkshood. It's got pretty blue flowers and berries, but every part of it will kill you. It used to be fed to criminals, and small amounts were a medicine for curing fevers. And this one... feel the leaves..."

He drops something into my other hand. The leaves are larger and kind of curl over into dramatic fronds.

"That's *Ricinus communis*, or the castor oil plant. It's quite beautiful with these architectural leaves. But if you have a laboratory and you know what you're doing, you can use this plant to extract ricin, which is the deadliest poison known to humans."

"Wow."

"And this is *Brugmansia*, or angel's trumpet. It has these beautiful trumpet-shaped white flowers." Vic holds my fingers out and lightly brushes them over the flower so I can feel the shape. "It's hallucinogenic. Victorian ladies used to keep angel's trumpet plants on their tea tables, invite all their friends around, and then shake the pollen into their tea to get tongues loosening."

"Sounds like something Juliet would do," I say with a smile. "Is this how you seduce all the girls? With your creepy poison flowers?"

"I wanted to show you what I'm passionate about," Victor says. "This is why I'm going to Harvard. I want to study plants like these, try to reclaim their sordid reputations a little. Many of them are so useful and so beautiful, I want them to have their time in the spotlight."

"How noble of you."

I say it sarcastically, but actually, I think it's so Victor. He can see the beauty in what others dismiss as dangerous, wrong, evil. That's why he's so protective of Torsten and Cas.

"We should get out of here. You can't spend too long inside the greenhouse or the fumes will make you ill." Victor leads me back outside and shuts the door. I suck in a few lungfuls of fresh air.

"What now?" I ask. "Don't tell me – you have an Egyptian mummy for us to unwrap together."

"Maybe for our first actual date," Victor says, and I'm not sure if he's joking or not. He leads me over to a wrought iron table and chairs. As I sit down, I run my hands over the table's surface, and see that he's set it with his laptop and some pens, pads, and books. "Right now, I thought we could take a stab at your Harvard admissions essay."

"*Now?* Surrounded by poisonous plants? Don't you have to help your sister talk to your mother about what went down at the country club?"

"That's not as important as getting you into Harvard." Victor uncaps his pens. "Okay, so for an Ivy League essay, we have to begin with a deeply personal experience that highlights a specific set of values that you want to showcase. We need to draw on specific details and use strong imagery, and avoid cliches..."

"Thanks for the BuzzFeed article, Professor Obvious. I know how to write a college essay," I snap before I can stop myself. I clamp my hand over my mouth. "I mean, I've heard Euri reading hers aloud to me so many times I'm pretty sure I can recite them in my sleep. I understand what the admissions officers expect."

"Mmmm." Victor makes a sound like he doesn't quite believe me. He scribbles a little on his paper and then reads back what he's written. It's a completely fabricated story about experiencing discrimination because of my blindness, and how my disability has taught me to 'see' the world in different ways.

"I don't want to use my blindness in the essay," I say through gritted teeth.

"I don't want to, either. You're so much more than what you can't see," Victor says this pointedly, and I curse myself for my slip with the essays. He suspects... *something*. But suspecting and figuring out the truth are two different things. And he made me an oath that he wouldn't dig into my past. "It's the simplest way to address the essay prompt without needing to provide specific details about extracurriculars that you're not actually involved in. It speaks to your desire to become a lawyer, and it means you don't have to remember a complex invented backstory in your interview. Lies that are closest to the truth are always preferable."

I understand that all too well.

Together we craft an essay and polish it, arguing over every word and comma placement until we're happy. Victor reads it aloud one final time, and I have to admit that it sounds like it could be quoted in every 'Ivy League Essay Examples' article.

"I think this will do the job." Victor leans back in his chair and puts his feet up on the table. "We make a great team,

Munroe. I could've used you in the club years ago – Cas and Torsten are terrible essay writers, but they do have other skills."

"You can say that again." I think back to Cas bribing Kamilla Renaldo. "Although I'm surprised that Torsten alters people's records. He's usually so brutally honest."

"Only about things that matter. Torsten doesn't see why standardized tests are important. Or college. Which is stupid. I keep telling him that he has to go to art school, but he won't even consider it." Victor pauses. "So, you and Torsten..."

"Don't you *dare* take that tone," I snap. "I didn't sleep with him out of pity."

"I didn't mean to imply otherwise. I only meant that Torsten doesn't feel things the way the rest of us do, and he's been through a lot already with his family—"

"I don't intend to break his heart," I say. "He told me that his mother made him paint faked artwork for her to sell."

"That's not the half of what she's done to him," Victor's voice is dark. "Don't be fooled by Livvie Lucian's bubbly exterior, she's a ruthless woman. Almost as ruthless as Cali."

"Tell me about my stepmother. I know almost nothing about her, except that she owns a gym and a fitness empire."

Vic snorts. "Is that what they told you?"

I jerk my head toward him. "What are you implying?"

Vic sighs. "I shouldn't have said anything. Look, Cassius gets his personality from his mother. She's kind of notorious in this city. No one crosses Cali Dio and lives to tell the tale."

"You mean she destroys people's businesses, takes out the competition, like how Poison Ivy works?" I know that Cali has the resources to create fake identities, but I'd been so preoccupied with being numb and sad about leaving my old life that I hadn't considered what other nefarious deeds she might be involved in. "Is this why Cassius is such a caveman? What happened today..." My skin flushes thinking about it. "It was amazing, but I don't understand why Cas gets off on acting as though he's gifted me to you, like I'm a toaster or a library book."

"I think it's the only way he can make sharing you work in his head," Vic says. "Cassius struggles to share because to him, sharing means that he loses."

"Explain."

"You heard that Cas and I shared a girlfriend once. Her name was Gemma. She was... a bit like you, actually. Bright, funny, beautiful. She was a walking ray of sunshine, far too fucking good for either of us. But she died. She killed herself, actually. And it's all because of his brother, Gaius."

My breath catches in my throat. I think of a time I walked that same edge between life and death, weighing the worth of my heart in my hands and finding it so, so wanting. Maybe this Gemma and I *are* alike.

Vic continues, "You never met Gaius, but he's quite somebody. He's the kind of person who can walk into a room and have every person eating from his hand. Cali adores him. She's been grooming him his entire life to take over her business. And Cas worships him. That's why he hated you when you first moved here – because Gaius is in prison and you're in his room, and even though that's not your fault, he blamed you. It's probably Gaius whispering in his ear. If Gaius told Cas to jump off a cliff, your stepbrother would throw himself over without hesitation. But what Cas wants more than anything, more even than his brother's love, is to have Cali look at him the way she looks at Gaius."

"What did Gaius do? Why is he in jail?"

Victor shifts in his chair. For a long time, he doesn't say anything. "He's there because he's Gaius Dio," he says. "And that's all you need to know about why Cas is the way he is."

Cryptic answer times is interrupted by Eli, who brings us a pitcher of lemonade. He's followed by a trail of kittens, all mewling for attention. Vic and I play with them for a while, and then I call Seymour to come and pick me up.

I leave Victor's house more confused than ever. Who is my stepmother? What fucked-up household has my dad married us into?

Does he *know*?

He has to know.

He can't know. He'd never marry someone if they were crooked and evil.

Would he?

Between actually handing in assignments for class and cramming for the SATs, I hardly see the guys for the next two weeks. I only close my books to sleep or send down to Milo for snacks.

I put off the only other chore I have to do until the last possible minute. Before we had our falling out, Euri asked me to write a feature article for the paper about test prep anxiety. I didn't want to leave her hanging, so I wrote the damn thing – some of my best work, in fact – and emailed it to her. But she never got back to me with edits or final approval, and with the deadline tomorrow I need to suck it up and talk to her.

Yay. That's going to be fun.

At lunch, I try the greenhouse, but if Euri's in there, she does an excellent job of hiding from me. Next, I stop by the *Sentinel* offices. As I push open the door, I hear Euri's voice. She's on the phone, and her voice is hoarse like she's been crying.

"—but this isn't fair. We've been working toward Princeton since freshman year. I can't change now—"

I clutch the Braille printout of my article to my chest. I know exactly what this phone call's about.

"I don't want to go to *Brown*," she shrieks. "Have you ever heard of any famous journalists who've attended Brown? No, you haven't, because there aren't any. How can you do this to me—"

I can hear Kamilla Renaldo's voice on the other end. "I'm sorry that you're upset, Ms. Jones, but this is how Ivy applications work. And quite frankly, I'm sick of spoiled students like you thinking you can get whatever you want, whenever you want it. Every Ivy League school has the same pool of top applicants, with the same GPA, the same SAT scores and extracurricular activities. The difference between you getting in or scraping gum from underneath chairs at the Denny's on the corner is a recommendation from me. And if I tell you that you're not suited somewhere, then you'd better believe that I mean it."

Yikes. Kamilla Renaldo clearly hadn't had her Dante's Inferno today.

"You need to learn to accept setbacks instead of running to Mommy and Daddy to make everything better," Kamilla continues. "Because I don't send students to their top colleges if they're still wearing diapers, got it?"

"But I—"

"Instead of wasting your energy yelling about things you can't change, how about you get started on your Brown application essays. Because I don't have to write you a recommendation at all. I can tell you to apply to Duke. Do you want to go to Duke, Miss Jones? I have an application right here—"

"I don't want to go to Duke," Euri sobs. Her voice wavers. "Please, just tell me what I need to do for the Brown application."

She listens for a few more minutes, making little strangled sobs, then she hangs up the phone and begins to cry in earnest. Her sobs echo through the empty room. I'm suddenly very, very aware of how kind she'd been to me since I arrived in Emerald Beach, and of how much she reminded me of Old Fergie.

And I've done the same thing to her that was done to me. I remember the feeling of my heart turning to coal in my chest when I realized my dreams had been dashed. And now Euri's heart is turning to coal right in front of me.

I move back toward the door, but of course I hit some books off the edge of a desk. They clatter onto the tiles. Euri's cries cut off as she realizes she's not alone.

"Hello, Fergie." Her voice strains. She's trying to hold it together.

"H-h-hi, Euri. I just came to check if you got my article, and if you had any editing notes so I can make changes before the deadline. But if it's a bad time, I'll—"

"I didn't use your article in the issue," she says, her voice flat, awful. "I didn't trust that you'd give it to me on time, given the company you keep and your general lack of concern for anything and anyone, so I wrote it myself."

"Oh."

Her comment stung, but I can't blame her. Everything she said about me is true. I back toward the door. "Okay, then, I'll just leave you alone, then."

"You know, it's the strangest thing," Euri says in her awful flat, emotionless voice. "All year I've been working with Ms. Renaldo on my college applications, and suddenly she's telling me that she won't be recommending me for early admission to Princeton *or* Harvard. Do you know anything about that?"

"Not a clue."

"Right. Obviously not," Euri snaps. "Well, I hope you have a fucking *amazing* time at college, Fergie. I hope it's all your dreams come true. Oh wait, they can't, because those dreams aren't yours – you stole them from me."

"Euri, I wish I could explain, but I—"

"I hope you fall down the stairs and *die*," Euri hisses as she shoves her way past me. The office door slams behind her.

SAT DAY PASSES IN A BLUR.

Last time I was a bundle of nerves, daunted by the size of the room and the importance of each answer weighing on my future. But this time, I'm just... empty. And in that emptiness, the answers come easily.

I breeze through the questions and finish with twenty minutes to spare, plenty of time for me to replay Euri's words over and over in my head until I want to scream.

Maybe betrayal *is* the recipe for success.

A WEEK LATER, when I get my results back, I have to read them three times to believe them.

I long to run downstairs and tell Dad, but he can't know about this.

Not yet.

Not unless it works.

He pulled so many strings to get us here, to get me Cali's help, and what I'm doing goes directly against her instructions. I'm not supposed to stand out, to draw attention to myself. And these scores are *definitely* attention-grabbing.

But I know who will appreciate them. I can't wait to see the look on their faces. And I'm starting to get used to that fluttery feeling in my stomach – the butterfly migration every time I think about seeing them.

I'm starting to get used to being a Poison Ivy Girl. Sometimes, I even enjoy it.

EURYDICE

The strip light above my desk flickers. I glance at my watch. It's past 10PM and I'm still in the *Sentinel* offices, finalizing the layout for next week's issue. Torsten was supposed to be here to help me, but I told him not to bother.

I can't face a member of the Poison Ivy Club right now.

Ms. Renaldo won't give me a recommendation for Princeton or Harvard. She says she has other students more suitable for those schools.

What the fuck? How are there students more suited to those schools than me? I'm first on the class lists. I'm the editor of the paper, a prize-winning writer, the organizer behind every school charity event, and class treasurer. I'm the perfect candidate for my top-choice schools, and I'm done stepping aside and handing shit to people who don't deserve it.

I know who's behind Kamilla's rejection.

The Poison Ivy Club want to get two of their clients into my schools. They want to give my places away to kids who don't deserve them, who haven't worked as hard as me or sacrificed as much as me. Kids like Lucila Baskerville who messed up their chances and decide to take the cheater's way out.

Or like Fergie, who pretended to be my friend and then betrayed me.

They took away Artie's music – the one thing she loved more than anything. Artie wasn't even aiming for an Ivy League – she had her sights set on a full ride at Manderley Academy, this hyper-exclusive music school in New York. Manderley had this big scandal twenty years ago – I didn't know much about it... something about a fire and a ghost – but they were under new management, and it's *the* place to study Classical music in America. But Artie was first chair of the orchestra and they needed Bayleigh Laurent to be first chair, so my dear sister paid the price.

And then they took away my one friend.

They already have everything – the looks, the money, the cred, the grades. They don't have to constantly look over their shoulders, hoping they don't stand out *too* much. I was a fool to assume I was safe because they've kept away from me so far.

And I can't count on Fergie to rescue me. Not now that she's one of them.

I've been hoping she'd come to her senses and get out from their influence. I want her help with my article. She could have gotten all the dirt on her stepbrother – and maybe even on his mother and the rumors about where she really makes her money. But I'm going to have to do it on my own.

I pull over my laptop. I let the Poison Ivy Club walk all over my sister. I was too young to do something about it then. I had no power. But it's time that Poison Ivy learned just how powerful my pen can be.

Besides, Harvard loves stuff like this. If I break a major corruption story in my high school paper, the *Harvard Crimson* staff will cream themselves. It won't even matter that I don't have

Ms. Renaldo's recommendation. Maybe I could even submit the piece to the *Atlantic*—

Stop daydreaming, Euri. I can't go off on a tangent. I have to focus.

I pull up a new file and start writing my notes. I make a list of all the students I know who've been victimized by Poison Ivy, and all the students from previous years who got into Ivies where they never would have normally stood a chance. I add Lucila, Chris Lawson, and Fergie. I think about the fight at Victor's party, and I add Drusilla's name to the list.

Someone on this list will talk.

If it's the last thing I do, I'm going to bring down the Poison Ivy Club.

Fergie slides into the seat opposite me and slams her phone on the lunch table. "Read it and weep, August."

"Your SATs?" I slide the phone across, careful not to touch the screen so her voiceover software doesn't read aloud her results. I don't want to embarrass her in front of everyone.

It turns out, I don't need to worry.

"A 1590," I snort at the obviously fake results page. "Go on, Duchess. Tell us what you *really* got."

She taps the corner of the screen, letting her software read aloud the official letterhead.

I'm glad she can't see my jaw hit the ground.

Fergie got a 1590 on the SATs. That's so close as makes no difference to a perfect score.

How the fuck did she *do* that?

I know our girl is whip-smart. I know she hasn't been 'living up to her potential,' (as all of Torsten's teachers are fond of saying) at Stonehurst Prep. But a 1590? She's been cramming for two weeks, but you can't pull your score from a 1410 to a 1590 by reading a few books.

"Phew," Cassius leans over my shoulder. "What did you get,

Vic? A 1560? Sunflower kicks your ass, both literally and brainally."

I peer across at Fergie, who digs into her chicken Kyiv with gusto. A 1590. That's the best score in our class. How the fuck did she end up here, at Stonehurst Prep, with nothing to show for all her years of schooling? How can she get the grades she gets and end up with a 1590?

Something's going on here, and I don't like it.

AFTER LUNCH, Juliet and Fergie head off to their European History class, and Cas slumps off to fuck knows where. I grab Torsten as he's heading toward the art suite, and pull him into a supply closet.

"What?" he glares at me as he shoves a joint between his lips and lights it. Great, now we'll both reek of weed – no one will call us out on it, but I'd rather not reek of the stuff. I'd never tell Torsten not to light up, though. Sometimes he needs weed to get through the day.

"I need you to look into Fergie."

"I already have, remember? Born in Cedarwood Cove, to John and Bethany Munroe—"

"Yes, Torsten, I remember. But that was before she got a 1590 on her SATs."

He shakes his head. "We promised we wouldn't dig into her past."

"I know what we promised, but..." I glance over my shoulder, as if I can sense our monstrous friend standing behind me. "She's living in Cas' house. And since she and her father showed up, all this weird stuff has been happening with our parents' businesses."

"It has?"

I sigh. "Yes, Torsten. It has. A lot of it is bureaucratic nonsense – Drusilla's mother is trying to 'clean up this town,' and unlike all the other mayors that have made that promise, she's actually had some success. And then there's the fact that Sierra's footage was sent to her parents, even though I know we deleted it. I'm starting to think it can't be a coincidence. And then there's that name that keeps coming up. You remember when we got kicked out of Olympus?"

"Zack Lionel Sommesnay."

"Yes. Call it a hunch, but I think he's that guy we saw Drusilla with in the bar. The one Fergie said is German. He's connected to all this somehow."

Torsten twists the sketchbook in his hands. "What do you want me to do?"

"Look over her history again. See if you missed something. And check out this Sommesnay guy. That's all I'm asking." I grip his shoulder and stare into his eyes – today they're the cold, bottomless blue of an ocean. I hate asking him to do this. He'll feel like he's betraying Fergie. But we don't have a choice. Our loyalty is to Cas. *Always.* "I just have... a feeling."

"Okay."

He goes to leave, but I stop him with a hand on his arm.

"And Torsten? Don't say anything to Cas about this. I know it's hard for you, I know I'm asking a lot. But if he thinks we suspect Fergie is someone other than who she says she is, then he'll turn on her. And we both... we both don't want him to hurt her."

Torsten stares down at the notebook in his hands. His face is stricken. He nods, once, and flees.

~

I HAVE basketball practice after school, and Juliet has clarinet lessons, so we meet up afterward and drive home together. She will not stop talking about Fergie's SAT score.

"I mean, she got a 1590 on her SATs. What does she need you for?"

"That's exactly what I'm asking myself," I murmur.

Juliet glares at me dead in the eyes. My twin may get on my nerves, but we can read each other like our favorite books. "Victor, *no*. Just because she aced one test doesn't mean she has some nefarious purpose here."

"You don't get a 1590 by accident, Jules. And the timing of this with everything else going on... I don't like it."

"Do you mean the stuff with Mom's shipments? That's nothing." Juliet opens her compact and checks her makeup is perfect. "She's a crime lord, Victor. There's always something going down in her world. You're reading too much into this. Don't you trust your sister's instincts? When I look at Fergie, all I see is a girl who's just as smart and sassy and driven as you – the kind of girl who'd make an excellent queen."

"I'm nineteen. I'm too young to be thinking about that," I say. "And you shouldn't be, either. I'm going to Harvard and you're going to fashion school, and we're going to live in the beautiful house I bought from Lucila's dad, and we'll see what happens with the business after that. Mom wants us to make our own choices. A lot of people died to give us that right. And as for Fergie, I don't date liars. She's hiding something. I have to find out what it is. And you can't breathe a word of this to Cassius, or—"

"Cassius is a big boy," she says. "He'll deal. He doesn't need you to swoop in and save him."

Yes, he fucking does.

I turn into the road where we access the tunnel.

Wait.

Something's odd.

The lights are all off in the house. Usually, our place is lit up like the Blackpool illuminations with all of us going about our activities. But tonight it looms in ominous darkness. Po, the most senior member of my mother's security force, stands guard at the entrance to the underground tunnel. He waves us through, a stern expression on his face.

We drive through the tunnel into the garage and park up. I notice the cars have been shifted around – the Jag XK150 is in the spot closest to ours, meaning someone used it today.

Gabriel's back.

My stomach twists with nerves. It's another sign that something's not right. Our father is only halfway through the European leg of his tour with his band, Broken Muse. He wouldn't return to the States unless...

...unless something terrible's happened.

Juliet notices the car, too. Her hand flies to her mouth, muffling a frightened squeak.

I grab Juliet's hand and yank her toward the door to the house.

"Ow, Victor. You're hurting me." She tries to wrench her hand out of my grasp, but I'm not letting her go. Not if there's any kind of danger threatening our family.

I won't make the same mistake twice.

"Mom?" I yell as we crash into the opulent foyer. "Gabriel? Noah? Eli?"

"Kids, can you come in here?" Mom calls from her study. "We need to talk to you."

Juliet and I exchange a glance. *At least they're alive.*

We enter the large room on the ground floor. In the twenty years our mother has managed the August empire, she's kept this study pretty much exactly as it was when the house's previous occupant, Howard Malloy, used it to oversee his pharmaceutical company. The shelves that line one wall are filled with gilded leather-bound books on Ancient Rome and Greece, nestled between busts of Julius Caesar and Cicero. Her vast mahogany desk is usually strewn with papers – shipping forecasts, printouts of acquisitions for the museum, contracts and deals and favors owed, and the old-fashioned ledger book Eli uses to keep the family's accounts. But today, the desk is empty – the papers pushed into a haphazard pile on the floor.

The only thing on the desk is a single parcel box.

Our mother sits behind it, her golden-blonde hair impeccably smooth, framing her heart-shaped face. My own icicle eyes reflect back at me. Our three dads flank her – Gabriel slouches on the corner of the desk, his dark eyes crinkled at the edges. Eli stands behind her chair, his hand resting protectively on Mom's shoulder. We're so alike – we need to hold the things we love close.

Noah paces by the window, a semi-automatic rifle bouncing across his shoulder as he peers suspiciously into the darkened garden.

Anyone who passes my mother in the streets would see a typical Californian housewife – sun-kissed skin, golden hair, the perfect little smile. They wouldn't know what she's capable of, and that's always their last mistake.

And they would never guess that right now, she's pissed *as fuck*.

"Sit down," Noah barks. He gets all drill sergeant when he's afraid.

Juliet flops down onto the sofa opposite the desk. I perch on the arm, keeping my hand on my twin's shoulder. "What's going on?"

Mom shoves the parcel across the table toward us. "Earlier today, someone sent this parcel to the house. It's addressed to you, Victor."

"Cool." Juliet leans forward, reaching for the box. She loves getting things in the mail. "What is it?"

Noah bats her hand away.

Mom folds her arms and shoots me a glare that could turn me to stone. "It's a parcel bomb."

"**S**ay that again," I growl.

"Someone sent you a bomb, Vic. It's been disabled now." Her fingers grip the edge of the desk. She's beyond pissed. "If Po hadn't insisted on his parcel screening procedure, we could've had a very different ending to the day."

Juliet nods, even though she's been complaining about Po's security checks for years. He always holds on to parcels for an extra day, which is apparently hell when your new Prada purse has just arrived.

"Who sent it?" I demand, moving so I can read the label, but it's typewritten. No return address.

"Po's trying to trace the package, but it's probably a dead end," Mom says. "So we went looking through social media, trying to find a reason why someone might be targeting us. And we didn't have to look far before we found this."

She clicks a button on her desk panel. A video flickers on the TV behind her head. It's footage from the Acheron Academy game of Chris Lawson fouling his shot. Then it cuts to another clip of mobile phone footage – the fight at our place. Chris

Lawson is yelling that I ruined his life, and Drusilla is declaring that it's time Poison Ivy pays for our crimes.

"This basketball game was a Poison Ivy stunt," Mom says. It's not a question.

"Yes."

"Jesus fucking Christ," Noah snaps.

A white cat wanders in and jumps on Mom's lap. She strokes it like an evil Bond villain while she continues to glare at me. "For someone who wants to take over the business one day, I'm surprised at you. We've told you time and time again that we don't approve of this club of yours. Taking money to beat up other kids, pushing girls down stairs, all so some rich asshole kids can get *another* leg up in the world."

"Those things happened under Gaius. Things have changed now," I say. "We have rules. Standards. We only work for favors, so anyone can hire us. We don't throw people down stairs anymore—"

"No, you just incur the wrath of people like the Lawson family and get parcel bombs sent to our house. You sent this kid to hospital with serious injuries. He's only just been released. You put your sister in danger. You put this *whole family* in danger. And for what? To win some stupid game?"

"You can't honestly blame Victor for that?" Juliet shoots back. "You don't even know if Chris is responsible. It's not as if you don't have enemies, Mom. Or it could be some crazed fan of Gabriel's—"

"Unlikely," Gabriel says. "My fans usually send underwear, not homemade parcel bombs."

"Jules, it's okay…" *Please, shut up, sis. You're going to make this worse.*

"Oh, I have plenty of blame to go around," Mom tosses her hair over her shoulder. "When I catch the person who sent this, I'll pull out the Brazen Bull again, mark my words. But that's not the issue here. The issue is that someone tried to blow up my son today, and I'm not going to stand around and let them make a second attempt."

"We'll be careful. We're always careful. The club might be an open secret, but nothing we do can be traced back to us. I learned this from you."

"Do you want me to play that tape for you again?" Mom slams her fist on the desk so hard that the parcel wobbles. Juliet winces. "There's nothing fucking *careful* about it, Vic. And the person who sent this package agrees. We're beefing up security, and I've spoken to Cali and Livvie about keeping the Triumvirate secure, especially during Saturnalia, but we need you to take precautions, too. From now on, I need you to promise me that you won't pull any more of this bullshit. No Poison Ivy Club."

"I can't do that. I have clients who expect—"

"Not anymore." Noah grabs me by the collar. His eyes flash with rage. But Noah's rage isn't like Cassius' – it's not a red mist that descends and drives him to chaos. It's a rage born of fierce protectiveness for the people he loves. "Tell your clients that you're officially out of business. And if we hear of *anything* going on at that school that your mother hasn't officially signed off on, you'll all be in trouble. Got it?"

"Got it," I growl. I break his grip and storm out of the room.

Juliet races after me. "Victor, wait."

I hear the panic in her voice. I'm halfway up the stairs. I turn, and she throws herself into my arms.

"Someone tried to kill you," she whispers into my neck.

Someone tried to kill me. But who? And why?

"Ssssh. It's going to be okay." I stroke her hair.

She sniffs. "What are you going to do?" she asks.

"I'm going to do what I've always done," I say. "What Mom expects me to do."

"But Mom said you can't do anything. You have to leave this to her."

I kiss the top of my sister's head. "I am my mother's son, Jules. I'm going to keep us safe. And if that means disobeying Claudia August, then that's what I'll do."

54

FERGIE

The early admissions deadline comes and goes. I expect to feel *something* as I listen to Victor loading each section of my application into the online portal. He clicks SUBMIT. I expect fireworks to go off in my head. After years of hard work, it's finally done. My Harvard application is in.

But instead, I feel nothing.

It feels like someone else's life, someone else's future.

More than anything, I wish I could talk to Euri. But I overheard a conversation between her and Drusilla at our lockers. I think I was supposed to hear it. Euri applied Early Decision to Brown. She isn't even trying for her dream schools, and it's all because of the Poison Ivy Club.

All because of me.

I hoped to at least do something to celebrate with the guys after school, but Victor has another basketball game, Cassius disappeared during fourth period and I haven't seen him since, and Juliet has clarinet and drama club. I decide to head to the art block to see if I can find Torsten.

The art block occupies a suite of rooms at the far end of the gymnasium, so I have to walk around the sports fields and swimming pool to get there. Hearing the grunting from the guy's track team as they run laps gives me a pang of longing for jiujitsu. The most exercise I've had since arriving in Emerald Beach is riding Poison Ivy cock, and I miss the adrenaline pumping through my veins as I achieve a perfect rear mount and the satisfying smack of an opponent's hand tapping out.

As I pass the natatorium, someone calls out, "Miss Munroe."

I stop. It must be a teacher, as his voice sounds older. I haven't quite got over Old Fergie's desire to please teachers. "Yes?"

"I wanted to congratulate you. I heard about your 1590 SAT score." The voice sounds familiar, but I can't place it. I'm certain that he's not one of my teachers. "That's very impressive."

"Thank you." I narrow my eyes. "But how did you hear about my score?"

SAT results are confidential. The only people who know about them are the student and their college counselor and the schools you're applying for.

"Oh, I have my own contacts." The guy steps closer to me, and his chlorine smell invades my nostrils. The truth hits me like a brick.

I do know him.

He's Coach Franklin. He smells the same as he did when we found him in the sauna.

"Um, I have to go." I turn to leave, but he grabs my wrist and starts dragging me into the looming shadow of the natatorium. I swing my cane up to hit him in the head, but it hits the wall and bounces out of my hand.

"Not so fast, Ms. Munroe. You and I are going to have a little talk."

"Let go of me!" I yell, trying to twist myself out of his grip. But Coach Franklin holds me tight and pulls me off-balance. He moves too fast for me to gain leverage, and I have no choice but to be dragged along by him. He shoves me through the swinging door into the natatorium. The air grows hot. Chlorine stings the back of my throat. He pulls me through the pool area and into a small, dark room. He shoves me, hard. I fall into a stack of kickboards and water polo sticks. I try to untangle myself, but he slams the door shut and grabs me by the hair.

"Ow, you're hurting me," I cry out as I claw at his hands. My scalp burns with bright pain.

"Now we're all alone," he whispers, his breath hot and stale against my ear, "I'm going to do so much more than hurt you, you little bitch."

I kick and thrash, but my skull screams as he drags me up by my single braid and shoves me against the wall. He holds one hand at my throat, his fingers pressing just hard enough so I know what he can do. I go limp. It's a great defense technique – if you're limp then you can save your energy and make your attacker think they've won while you search for an opening.

"You and your friends have video of me and Meredith," he growls, his spittle drenching my cheek. "I want them."

"We destroyed them," I whisper.

"Now, why don't I believe you?" He squeezes my neck a little, letting me know he's in control. "Those boys are too smart for that. Those videos were uploaded to the cloud the moment they made them. I know, because they sent one to my phone this morning."

"That's not true. They wouldn't—"

I yelp as he cuts me off with a sickening kiss on my cheek.

"You know, I've taught at this school a long time, and I remember when Gaius Dio started this little club." His fingers tangle in my hair. "And there were girls then, too. Pretty little girls just like you willing to do anything to get ahead. Gaius made sure we all had a lot of fun. But then Victor August took over and the fun stopped. Well, I think it's time the fun started again. You see, my little birdies have told me all sorts of stories about you, Fergie Munroe. I wonder what the Harvard admissions people will think if I tell them what you and Mr. August did to enter those hallowed, ivy-covered walls? I wonder if all the Ivies will rescind their offers to the students at this school, just in case they accidentally admit a Poison Ivy client? And what about your friend, the lovely Eurydice? She'll be the first person in the firing line – they'll—"

"Euri has nothing to do with this." I thrash in his arms, but he holds me tight.

"Tsk, tsk, you should know better than anyone that we never let the truth get in the way of a good story. I'm going to the school board with everything I know. I'll make sure that neither you, nor your boyfriend, nor dear little Euri or anyone involved with the Poison Ivy Club even makes it into *Bakersfield*, let alone an Ivy. That is, unless you give me what I want."

"I can make them delete the videos," I say. I don't know if I can, because Vic swears they don't have those videos anymore.

Which means either he's lying, or...

"That's not good enough," he tsks, his slimy tongue licking my cheek. "I have no way to know that they won't have them saved somewhere else. No, what I want is a guarantee that you'll never use them. I want mutually-assured destruction. Which means..."

He removes his fingers from my hair and fumbles in his pocket. I hear the click of his phone screen unlocking.

"If you want to keep your Harvard spot and save your friends a lot of heartache, I'll tell you what's going to happen now. You're going to open wide for me, Fergie. You're going to take my dick between those pretty lips of yours, and I'm going to film you doing it. If you ruin me, I'll ruin you. It's as simple as that."

He breaks the hold on my neck to shove my shoulder down. I try to resist, but my legs have gone weak.

My knees hit the cold tile. The pain ricochets up my thighs. But it's nothing like the pain behind my eyes.

Is this what they expect me to do?

Is this why they want me to be part of the gang? Do they want me to suck off a teacher to save their asses?

I think of Cassius' cruel laugh after he tricked me into sleeping with him. I think of Victor showing me his garden of poisonous flowers. I think of Torsten's beautiful gasp when he entered me for the first time.

"Don't you cry out or try anything stupid," Coach Franklin growls as he unzips his pants. His smell slams into me – sweat and chlorine and something rank and rotting. Bile rises in my throat. "Not unless you want to kiss Harvard goodbye forever."

I can't do this to Euri. I can't take her whole future away from her.

His fingers dig into my collarbone.

Tears roll down my cheeks as I open wide.

His phone makes a clicking noise as the video starts recording.

No, please no. I can't believe this is happening.

Couch Franklin shoves his cock inside my mouth.

I nearly retch, but I manage to hold it down. He tastes worse than he smells. *I can't do this. I can't I can't—*

He fists the back of my hair and lets out a moan like a sunbathing walrus. "Oh, god, you're amazing. You have such a tight little mouth. Maybe when we're done here you'll let me stick it somewhere else."

I let him shove his rank fucking dick all the way into the back of my throat.

This is what I deserve.

This is who I am.

I'm a Poison Ivy Girl.

I'm...

I bite down.

Hard.

I'm so, so sorry, Euri. I couldn't do it.

Blood squirts between my teeth.

I don't stop.

I work my jaw, tearing my teeth through his flesh even though it's the most disgusting thing I've ever tasted. His cock flails in my mouth, becoming this limp, dead thing flopping around in my mouth as he claws at my face, trying to get me to let go.

His scream becomes my reason for living.

The blood bubbles from my mouth, dribbling down my chin. It's so wet and slippery and foul-tasting that I need it out of my body *now*, but I hold on with everything I have, ripping and tearing with my teeth so that he'll *never* be able to shove his cock anywhere warm and fun again.

"Bitch," the coach gasps. His mangled dick slips from my mouth, and he sags against me. I know exactly what to do with someone in that position. I execute a perfect roll, pinning his body and slamming his hand into the lockers behind me with enough force that I hear something snap.

He howls with fresh agony. Yup, I definitely broke something.

"Your mistake was assuming that because I'm blind, I'm helpless," I whisper. "I'm a black belt in jiujitsu. It's going to be pretty hard for you to coach, or wank, with all your fingers broken. Oh, but I guess that won't be a problem for you anymore, either."

I step back, and he drops like a stone. I spit a glob of his own blood at him, turn around, and fumble for the door. I unlock it. I don't have my cane, so I have to move slow, keeping my hand on the wall as I find my way back through the pool area, even though I'm desperate to run. Once outside, I stumble onto the grass as the tears start to fall. They fall thick and fast, and I can't walk anymore. I collapse on the ground. I bury my face in my hands.

I scream.

I hear voices calling out to me. They must see the blood staining my uniform. Maybe they're drawn by my cries or by Coach Franklin's agonized screams, audible even from out here. I try to say something, but all that comes out is another scream.

I can only think of one thing. *Get to Torsten. Get to Torsten.*

"Something's wrong," I hear a voice cry, but they sound muffled, like they're underwater. "She's covered in blood."

"Torsten—" I cry out.

And then, the world becomes nothing.

I'm walking across the fields toward the gym, psyched for the game, when I notice a group of students crowded on the grass outside the natatorium. Suddenly, a figure bursts from the group and runs full speed toward the art block, carrying a lump in his arms.

It's Torsten. And that lump...

It's Fergie.

Her white button-down is stained with blood.

No.

My heart leaps into my throat. I think about the parcel bomb sitting on my mother's desk.

I should have been protecting her. I should've been with her every moment of the day. She knows she's not supposed to go anywhere alone.

I run after Torsten faster than I've ever run in my life, and catch up to him just as he bursts into one of the art studios. Three students look up from their stations as Torsten swipes a bunch of paints and oils off a table. They roll across the floor, spreading a rainbow of colors down the middle of the room.

The guy working at the table leaps up. "Hey, what the fuck—"

"Go away," Torsten yells. "*Go!*"

The students scatter. The door to the art suite swings as they flee Torsten's wrath. He sits Fergie on the edge of the table, then climbs up beside her and props her head on his shoulder. He looks at me with large eyes – a crystalline blue today, sparkling with emotion.

He doesn't know what to do. He needs me to help her.

I kneel down in front of Fergie and take her in. Dried blood coats her lips and neck, and trails down the front of her shirt, but I can't see any signs of cuts or wounds, and she doesn't seem to be bleeding now. So not her blood, then. Her eyes are shut, and when I hold my hand in front of her nose, I feel her breath rushing over my skin.

"Duchess?" I try. I place my hands on her knees, rubbing small circles on her thighs. "Can you hear me? It's Vic. I'm here with Torsten. Please, wake up."

She murmurs under her breath. Her eyelids flutter.

"Duchess, what did you say? What happened?"

She murmurs again, louder this time. It sounds like she says, "I bit his dick."

"You bit someone's dick?" I pick up one of her limp hands and squeeze her fingers. After a few moments, she squeezes weakly back, and her eyes open properly and she sits up. "Vic?" she whispers.

"It's me. And Torsten's here, too. He found you in front of the natatorium. Fergie, you're covered in blood, and you passed out. We're worried about you. Can you tell us what happened?"

"Coach Franklin..."

But before she can get another word out, the door to the studio slams against the wall. Cas barges in. "Where is she? Is she okay? I found her cane on the ground. Who hurt her, because I'm going to skin them alive and feed them their own testicles—"

"Calm down, Cas," I snap. "She's awake, and I think she's fine. She's trying to tell us what happened."

"Franklin cornered me," she says, her whole body trembling as she recalls the ordeal. "He dragged me into a supply room and he said that one of you sent him the video from the sauna—"

"We didn't," I say. "We deleted those files."

"That's not what he said." Her voice rises a little as the panic seizes her again. Torsten pulls her head back into his shoulder and wraps his arms around her. He glares at me like he wants me to back off, but I can't. I have to know what that bastard did to her.

"He said that he wanted mutual... um... mutually-assured destruction. If we ruin him with the video, he needed a video that would ruin me. So he..." her body shudders again, "...he forced me to my knees and shoved his dick in my mouth and I... I *bit* it."

"You what?" I stroke her cheek with my thumb.

"I bit his dick."

"That's my girl," Cas purrs from behind me.

I chuckle as I lay a kiss on my beautiful, brave, bloodthirsty queen's forehead. "Fergie, you're something else."

"I mangled it up pretty bad with my teeth." She sounds a little clearer now, a little more like herself. She clings to Torsten as though he's all that holds her upright. "And then I broke his fingers and I ran out of there and I think I blacked out..."

Cas shoves me out of the way and throws his arms around her. He buries his face into her hair and her entire body seizes up.

"What's wrong with her?" Cassius growls. He shakes her roughly, but she's a stiff corpse in his arms.

"Jesus Christ, you animal." I rip her from his arms and settle her into my shoulder, rubbing her back until her stiffness relents a little. "You have to be gentle. She's had a traumatic experience. You grabbing her like that probably made her panic."

Cassius slumps down in a chair, staring at his hands. His shoulders tremble.

I know exactly how he feels.

We weren't there.

We weren't with her, and that asshole hurt our girl.

And she may be a fighter who can look after herself, but she's broken by this, more broken than anything Cas has tried to do to her, and none of us – not even me – know how to put her back together again.

I don't have time to worry about soothing Cas' shattered ego. The only person I care about is Fergie. I stroke her hair while she clings to me, and a million questions swirl around in my head.

How could we let this happen? How could we allow Franklin to be so bold? I assumed our presence in the sauna was enough to keep him in line, but I wonder again if we've lost our grip on this school.

And where did Franklin get those photographs? It makes no sense. We deleted our versions, including the backups. I promised Meredith, and I always keep my word.

I didn't send Franklin the video. The only people who could have are in this room with me, and I know they didn't do it, either. They're my brothers. I trust them with my life, with Fergie's life. I meet Cas' eyes, and I know his mind is following a similar path to mine.

It *can't* be a coincidence that this happened now, when our parents tied our hands. We can't retaliate. We can't make Franklin pay for what he did to our girl—

Cas pulls his lips back into a smile that's more beast than man, and leaps to his feet.

Shit. No.

I grab for him, but my arms are still full of Fergie and he slips under me easily. Torsten peers at me with wide eyes.

"Go after him!" I yell. Torsten runs out. I clutch Fergie to me, my heart hammering. Hopefully, Torsten can catch Cassius before he makes this so much worse.

"Victor," Fergie murmurs, her lips grazing my neck. "I was so afraid."

"I know. But you did everything perfectly. You know that you're amazing, right?"

"You don't understand. It was too much like last time. I couldn't—" her eyes flutter closed again.

"Last time?" I stroke her hair, but she's fading away, going someplace inside her head where I can't follow.

I wasn't there. I couldn't save her.

Just like with Gemma. Just like with Juliet.

No matter what I do, the people I love get hurt.

Everything is spiraling out of control.

"Don't worry, Duchess." I hold her against me, squeezing so tight I worry I might break her. I'll never let her go, ever again. "You're safe with me. No one will ever hurt you like that again. I promise you."

I have to believe that. I have to believe I can keep you safe.

Torsten returns with Cassius storming behind him.

"He's gone," Cas thunders. "That cowardly little eunuch did a runner. Good. That's good. We'll get him when he's off school grounds. We'll torture him nice and slow. Cali showed me this cool Viking thing called a blood eagle and I've been dying to try it..."

"Cas, we *can't*."

He stares at me blankly, like he doesn't understand. "He touched her. He hurt our Fergie."

"Yes, *exactly*. If you torture him, then everyone is going to know who's responsible. And whoever sent that parcel bomb might do something worse."

Realization dawns on Cas' face. I think he gets that our hands are tied, but then he says, "You mean you're going to let Franklin get away with putting his dick in her mouth, in *our* queen's mouth, because you're afraid of what Mommy might do to you?"

"No, you idiot. I'm afraid that we might put our families in more danger. This happened because of the Poison Ivy Club." I wring my hands. "I've been thinking that we were careful, that we were safe. But I've been kidding myself. We *ruin lives*, Cassius. We take pride in it. Every stunt we pull, every oath we make, every powerful family we piss off paints a target on Fergie's back. And someone finally decided to act."

"So you think she deserves this, out of some twisted sense of martyrdom?" he yells back. "And you think because you're an August that you get to call the shots. Well, maybe I'm *just a Dio*, but my family has honor, too. That coward doesn't get to touch what's ours. I'll make sure of it."

TORSTEN

"I brought the down pillow you requested, sir." The concierge stands in the doorway, holding out a pillow as if it's a bomb about to explode.

Bomb. Explode.

I think about the parcel bomb sent to Victor's house. Addressed to him. Just waiting for him to open it in his careless way and explode all over the walls.

Who's sending bombs to Victor?

I take the pillow. The man hovers in the doorway, his hand poised awkwardly at his side. I shut the door on him. I asked for a pillow. He brought the pillow. I don't see what else he's waiting for.

This is why I need Cassius and Victor. They'd know why the concierge is hanging around with that expression on his face.

Bomb. Explode.

I drop the pillow behind my head. Now that I've been at the hotel for a month, I kind of enjoy having my own space. When I lived with the Lucians, the only place I liked was the art gallery, and when Livvie found out what I could do, not even that remained safe for me. My sisters were always in my room, moving my things. Livvie got so angry when I drew on the walls or moved the bed into the middle of the room. She wanted me to be *normal*. She wanted a son she could bring to her clubs and show off at her parties.

I liked living with Cassius. I liked hanging out with him every day. I liked that we could sit in his room for hours, and he'd let me play whatever music I liked and draw, and he made me talk to him. I liked that sometimes he'd take me down to the basement and get me to tell him about famous painters while he punched bags and lifted weights. I especially liked when Fergie showered in the bathroom and her scent lingered on everything.

I liked sneaking into Fergie's room and watching her sleep.

I liked touching her silk duvet and remembering what we did.

But even with Cassius, I had to be careful I didn't cause offense and ruin our friendship somehow, the way I've ruined so many evenings and parties and business deals for Livvie. Everything I do causes offense. But here... no one cares what I do as long as the bill gets paid, and my friends have taken care of that.

I've told housekeeping I don't want them in the room. All the surfaces I can't draw on, I've covered in cartridge paper. I tacked up a picture of Fergie. I took it at lunchtime – she's eating spaghetti, and there's a little spot of sauce on the tip of her nose, but she has her eyes closed like the spaghetti is really good.

I'm painting her on the ceiling so I can look at that little speck of sauce before I go to sleep.

At the thought of Fergie, my dick grows hard. It's been doing that a lot lately. Especially in chemistry class. It's so painful sometimes that I get short of breath. But I won't touch it. I like when it's painful. When I think about having sex with Fergie, I want to do it again.

When Victor took over the Poison Ivy Club, one of our first clients was a girl named Marcella, who wanted to get into the

Royal College of Art. She was in my art class – she made these Antony Gormleyesque sculptures where she'd create molds of her body in all different positions, and then fill them in with cubes and angles. She used to get me to help her bend the metal armatures around her naked body.

Victor kept telling me that she wanted to sleep with me. He and Cassius were so excited about it. They kept forcing me to work together alone with her on her application. One day she kissed me, but all I could taste was her toothpaste and the fries and mayonnaise she had for lunch, and all I could smell was the inside of her nose, and the scents and smells closed in on me like a sticky mucus all over my skin. The need to wipe it all away was visceral, but I tried so hard not to do it. I let her swirl her tongue around and around in my mouth and tried not to throw up.

Her hands groped over my skin, lighting up every nerve ending with all the old traumas and indignities I suffered at the hands of the woman who isn't my mother, and the mother who gave me away. Self-hatred bore down on my chest, suffocating me.

In the end, I couldn't do it. I pushed her off me. She told me I was a loser and left.

She was right.

Something's wrong with me.

I'm far more broken than they think.

Bomb. Explode.

Who wants to hurt Victor? It can't be Fergie, no matter what Victor believes. She doesn't have it in her to hurt. She didn't even want us to go after Euri, even though Victor explained a hundred times that Euri could take Fergie's Harvard spot.

Who sent Coach Franklin and Sierra those videos? I've swept our phones and checked our backups. We don't have a security breach, and without seeing the material, I can't determine if they're really our footage.

My phone rings. I stare at the screen as the words 'THE BITCH' appears. I hang up the call without answering.

I have work to do.

I pull over my laptop and log into my VPN. I've been looking for information on Zack Lionel Sommesnay, but apart from the deed of sale for the Olympus, he's a ghost. I've found nothing. Which has me more convinced than ever that he's the key to all this. But he's not who I'm looking for tonight.

Fergie told us we weren't supposed to dig into her past. That it was part of her agreement. But Victor says that we need to know what we're dealing with, in case Fergie is some government spy or part of a rival gang trying to take out the Triumvirate.

Victor always knows what's best, so even though bugs crawl over my skin while I do it, I'm looking into her past. Again.

I already have a file of information on Fergie from when Cali announced her marriage. I start by reading it over. It's all exactly as she says – she was a mediocre student at Cedarwood Cove High in Cedarwood Cove, Massachusetts, and her dad had a clinic on the main street of the town. Her school records check out, and so do John Munroe's patient records and her mother's death certificate.

But I remember what Victor said, and I know I have to go deeper.

I switch over to Google Maps and pull up the street view of Fergie's old house. It's a pretty standard New England Colonial – a pitched roof with narrow clapboard cladding and grey shutters. I wonder if the dormer windows were Fergie's room.

Then I flick over to the street view of the dentistry office.

I stare at the screen.

I locate the date when the street view pictures were taken. I stare some more.

Interesting.

Now that the first clue has dropped into place, I go back through the records I'd already found. And as I dig and dig, I discover something that shatters the fragile happiness that has marked my life since she arrived in Emerald Beach.

Fergie Munroe is not who she says she is.

"**A**re you sure about this?" I stare at the screen in disbelief.

"I'm positive." Torsten waves his laptop in my face. "I found her old house in Cedarwood Cove. A Turkish family has lived there for the last eight years. They run a little tailor's shop. There's no way Fergie ever lived in that house. And I checked out the patient records from her dad's old dentist clinic. Every single one of them is dead."

I stare at the pictures and records flashing on the screen. It's all going too fast for me to process. *Please, let this be a misunderstanding. I don't want to be right about this.* "Okay, but maybe he's just a terrible dentist..."

"This guy died in 1984." Torsten taps the screen. "Fergie's entire history is fake."

I frown. I *hate* that I'm right. "I believe you. What does this mean?"

"For the valedictorian, you're being very stupid." Torsten smiles – it's a sad smile, a smile that says he's trying his best to make a joke because he knows I'm upset, but he doesn't know how. "It means Fergie and her father hired someone to make them new identities. This is a professional job – it's better than anything I could do, and I'm good. This will fool most people unless they dig as deep as I did. It nearly fooled me."

I ran my hand through my hair, a habit I picked up from Eli. "So..."

"So... whoever the girl is living in Cassius' house and hanging out with us, she's not who she says she is."

Oh, Fergie. Why did it have to be like this? "Then who is she?"

"I have no fucking idea. That's the point." Torsten snaps his laptop shut. He hates it when he feels like he's been clear but we don't seem to understand him. "Whoever did this went to a great deal of trouble to make sure they were never, ever found out. Is it a coincidence that Zack Lionel Sommesnay starts making trouble for us just as Fergie and her father show up in Emerald Beach?"

This is why Fergie didn't want us to ask about her past.

"We have to tell Cassius," Torsten says.

Fuck.

I sink into the chair opposite Torsten's opulent hotel bed. "We can't. You saw how he got when he thought she was simply a gold-digger. And now she's under his skin. He's willing to risk bringing down war and ruin on our families to avenge her, and I don't know how much longer I can hold him back. If he thinks Fergie betrayed him, he'll end her. And we don't even know why they changed their identities. It could have nothing to do with the Triumvirate."

"But what if it is?" Torsten's dark eyes bore into mine. "What if she sent that parcel bomb? The postmark was Cedarwood Cove, Massachusetts."

I hadn't seen that. That can't be a coincidence. I wring my hands. No. I'm not going to rush into this thing believing the worst. We're going to go about this in a calm, collected way. We'll find evidence. "Chris Lawson has family up there, too. My mother's people found that out. So that doesn't mean it's from Fergie. If she's behind this, I'll hand her over to my mother herself. But I'm not going to without evidence. We've both had enough of that in our lives."

"Agreed," Torsten says.

"But this has to remain between you and me for now. Can you do that?"

Torsten nods.

"Good. Now, any ideas how we can find out why our duchess might have an assumed identity?"

"But I promised Fergie—"

"I know what we promised, but Cassius and Cali are more important. If Fergie and her dad are dangerous, if they've been sent by an enemy to spy on the Triumvirate, then we need to know." I steeple my fingers together as my mind whirs through this puzzle. "And we need to take them out."

58

CASSIUS

"There's a stray cat in the restaurant. I want you to get rid of it."

I grab a towel and wipe the sweat from my face. My veins still burn with adrenaline. I've been at the gym for four hours. I can barely stand upright anymore, but I don't want to stop fighting.

Officially, I'm in training for the Saturnalia fight – a big night with lots of money to be won and an endless parade of arrogant fucks wanting their throats punched in. Unofficially, my step-sister is lying catatonic in her bed for the third day in a row, barely responding to my presence, barely eating a thing. Those shattered emerald eyes that usually sparkle with life are vacant. She's broken.

Not even Milo's famous chili hot chocolate can help her, and that stuff is legitimately magic.

Ever since she stepped foot in my brother's room, I thought all I wanted to do was see her broken. To know that this larger-than-life person is made of flesh and blood and mushy stuff like all the rest. I needed to believe that she was nothing special, when she stormed into my life with her fuck-off boots and her scarlet panties and turned my whole world upside down.

And then he broke her. And all I want to do is put her pieces together again. But I don't know how. All I do is look at her and see the mess I've made of the one good thing that's ever happened to me.

I can't help her. I can't do anything except bleed the world for her.

I've been plotting how to kill Coach Franklin, but Victor stepped in. He spoke in his sensible big brother voice – the one that makes me want to smack his head in – and he reminded me that we can't make a move now. Cali told me the same thing his parents told him – no more Poison Ivy Club until they figure out who's pushing the mountain of shit on top of us.

Vic is right. There's a leak in our system somewhere. And until we find it and kill the fucker responsible, we can't do a thing. As much as it fucks me off, I agreed to let Franklin go free. Cali needs to believe she can trust me.

But that was before the fucker got out of the ER and showed up at school today. He uses crutches and winces visibly as he hobbles around. I heard that he has a special tube for peeing now. Fergie did that to him. She took care of it because I wasn't there to do it for her.

The story Franklin told the school is that he was attacked, and Fergie saw it happening and tried to save him, but she got hurt. He *strongly implied* it was Poison Ivy who maimed him, and Drusilla Hargreaves has picked up that rumor and flown it to every corner of the school.

Fergie looks at me like she might not ever smile again, and I feel helpless, just like when Gaius went to prison, just like when Gemma died, and I *hate* it.

So I'm in no mood to chase a stupid cat.

"Get someone else to do it," I growl into my phone.

"I'm not asking someone else. I'm asking you." My mother sighs. "We've had an incident at Livvie's new club, and I need to get over there with my soldiers. It wouldn't surprise me if the health inspector makes a surprise appearance, and this fucking cat is not going to get the better of me today, you got that?"

I got it. The city officials know what goes on at the Italian restaurant beneath Mom's gym. They know the restaurant is a front for what's happening upstairs – a legitimate business like Mom's gym and the museum to help funnel illicit funds to our offshore accounts. And usually a well-placed bribe in the right hands is enough to keep the officials out of our hair, but ever since Mayor Hargreaves got her panties in a twist about the Triumvirate, she's hit us with every bureaucratic trick in the book, trying to catch us out.

She will not bring down Cali Dio's empire over a fucking cat.

I let myself into the restaurant and corner the little ginger menace in the walk-in pantry. It scrabbles against the wall, trying to crawl up the bricks or some shit. I grab it by the scruff of its tiny neck and haul it up to my face. Let it stare death in the eyes before I sent it to kitty hell.

It's been in the wars. Its fur is matted in places and caked with dirt and dried blood. One eye is swollen shut and the other is crusted with grime. I hold it closer to my face, and the scrappy little bastard punches the air with giant, awkward paws. It reminds me of Fergie – cornered, blind, but always fighting.

I pick up a butcher's knife. "Sorry, little dude. Cali's orders. It's light's out time."

He swipes me across the nose.

The pain is instantaneous. And *mighty*. I drop the knife and press my hand into my nose. The pain blooms so sharp that it makes my eyes well.

Fuck. Evil bastard cat.

I was punched once by a guy with a razor blade between his

fingers, and this is a not dissimilar feeling. I stagger back, caught off-guard by the pain, and the kitten takes the opportunity to wriggle around in my fist, execute a perfect backflip, and perform a Matrix jump onto the top of the freezer, where he glares at me and lets out a defiant, "Mew."

"Oh, no, you don't." I scoop up the cat, holding it tightly against my chest. It digs its claws into my pec and hangs there, it's one working eye closed, whiskers twitching. It lets out this happy little purr, and it reminds me of that sound Fergie made when I slid my cock into her.

I stare down at the knife.

Something inside me snaps.

I throw the knife into the sink.

Fuck this.

I go to stroke the kitten's tiny head, but at the last moment, I pull my hand away. It's so tiny and delicate. It's not safe with me. I'll probably crush its skull with my finger.

It's just like Gaius said, *you break everything you love.*

What the fuck is happening to me?

I'm supposed to be a monster. I have one job to do for our family, and it's to kill things. To snap the neck of anyone who crosses my mother. And this kitten crossed her.

But I stare down into one wide, round eye, and all I can think about is my stepsister lying in her bed at home, broken by someone's hand other than mine, and how fucking sad it is that I'm all she has to help her.

"Mew?" says the kitten.

"Okay, buddy," I whisper as I clasp it in my arms, certain I'll hold it too tight and accidentally break its tiny bones. "Hold on. I'm going to take you somewhere safe."

～

WHEN I GET HOME, I discover that Fergie's not in her room. A note in our group chat says that Juliet took her shopping. I guess it's a good thing that Jules got her to get up.

I set the kitten down on the rug, next to where Gaius kept his drumkit before he decided that the Poison Ivy Club was more interesting than music. It wanders the perimeter, stopping to sniff every piece of furniture before burrowing its head into the duvet and making a nest for itself. It purrs like a little buzzsaw, its' matted fur trembling with contentment.

I can't bear to look at it any longer.

I leave it there and go back to my room. I pick up my laptop and google 'how to care for a kitten,' since I know nothing about helping tiny things stay alive. I learn that we need food, a litter box, and toys, so I order a bunch of stuff online for overnight delivery. The website even has little harnesses and leads, and there's one that's the same color scarlet as Fergie's underwear, with gold sparkles, so I buy that, too.

I picture my stepsister walking around with her cane and a little guide cat on a lead, and the image is just so *Fergie* that it makes me smile for the first time in a long time.

I click over to another website about cat behavior, and *then* I start down the rabbit hole of whether it's possible to die from a cat scratch, because my nose really fucking hurts. I'm so involved in my cat research that I don't even notice that it's past 1AM until I hear the front door open and Fergie stomp upstairs in those heavy boots of hers. I move into the bathroom and lean against the door, waiting to hear her reaction.

She's going to love him. She's going to—

"AAARRRRRREEEEGGGGGGHH!"

Her scream shakes the windows. I tear into the room, surprised. Maybe she's afraid of cats or something.

Or maybe Franklin's back to finish the job—

"What's wrong?" I snarl, searching the room for intruders. *Nothing. He's not here.*

"I told you to stop fucking with my locks!" she yells. Her chest heaves. "You put something furry in my bed."

The kitten peers one-eyed up at us from its nest. Its whiskers twitch with amusement.

"What is it?" she demands, sounding more like the old Fergie. "A rabid bat?"

"It's not a bat, although I'm noting that idea for later." I lean against the doorframe and smile at the little ginger furball. It's funny – the dark fur down his spine almost perfectly matches her fiery hair, and their eyes are the *exact* same shade of emerald. It's as though they're *made* for each other. "Why don't you pick it up and find out?"

"Why don't I pick it up?" Fergie screeches. "Because *you put it in my bed.* I touch that thing and it'll bite me and give me rabies and I'll die and then you'll win."

"Trust me, Sunflower. You have my word that it won't hurt you." I touch my finger to my tender nose. "At least, not much."

She screws up her face, and I know she's taking my request seriously. I've given her no real reason to trust me. But she knows I consider an oath sacred.

Fergie reaches down, slowly, tentatively. Her finger hovers just above the kitten's nose. He reaches up and buts it with the side of his face. "Mew?"

"It's... a kitten?"

"Excellent deduction, Einstein," I say.

"Oh, he's beautiful," she coos, picking it up and holding it against her cheek. It nuzzles against her skin, purring frantically. "*Is* it a he?"

I shrug. "I actually don't know. We can look it up on the internet. I found it at the club. I thought you might like to have it, as a pet or a guide cat or whatever, but if you'd rather me wring it's neck, then—"

"Don't you dare." She cradles him against her chest. "And you can't have a guide cat. Cats are too stubborn and independent."

"So basically like you, then."

"Basically." She sits down on the bed and loosens her grip on the kitten. I expect it to be afraid and dive into the covers, but instead, it gets up shakily on its giant feet and headbutts her hand again, then leaps onto her arm and uses her sweater like a climbing wall to scamper onto her shoulder. He peers at me with one-eyed triumph and makes a satisfied *chirrup* noise.

"He thinks he's a parrot," she laughs, and it's the first genuine laugh I've heard from her in such a long time. My chest tightens at the sound of it.

She's laughing, and I did that.

"I think he likes you," I say.

"I think so." She flops down on the bed and scratches its tiny nose. It grabs her finger and tries to chew it off, but all it manages to do is look adorable. Fergie laughs again, and my mind flashes back to when Gaius had this room, and I used to run in during the middle of the night as a kid, when I had a nightmare, and he'd tell me stories and make me laugh so I'd be able to sleep again.

Seeing Fergie in my brother's room doesn't make me seethe with hatred anymore. I feel something else instead. Tightness crushes against my ribcage. I feel like... like I want to make her laugh and hold her until the nightmares go away.

"Can I really keep a kitten?" she asks. "My dad's allergic, but the house is so big he won't even notice, but your mother..."

"You'll have to leave him with Seymour and Milo when you're at school. Cali isn't into furry animals. And I'll get them to talk to the maid so she doesn't freak out and go running to Cali."

The kitten takes the opportunity to turn his back and wiggle his bum at me, so I snap a picture of its junk with my camera and Google it to be sure.

"He's a he," I say. "A boy kitten. I've already ordered him some food and a litter box, but we might have to see what we can do tonight."

She pats the bed. "Sit down. I think he needs two friends to play with."

"I don't think—"

"Jesus Christ, Cassius. You've spent weeks pulling the locks off my doors, and now I invite you in and you want to stand around like a gormless idiot. *Sit down*."

"Can you crack a whip and drive a stiletto into my ass when you do that?" I grin as I sit on the corner of the bed. I'm afraid to get too close to the kitten. And to her. They're both putting on a brave face, but they're tiny and fragile.

You break everything you love.

"So..." Fergie trails her finger across the duvet, and the kitten pounces on it, but he sort of runs out of steam after a couple of tries and flops over. "Juliet tells me that Coach Franklin will be transferring to Acheron Academy, and I guess I should be happy about that. From the sound of his injuries, he's not going to hurt any other girls."

I grit my teeth. If our mothers hadn't laid down the law, that guy would be in a bodybag now. And I bet Fergie wouldn't have those tears pooling in the corners of her eyes.

"Fuck, look at me," she sniffs, wiping her eyes with her sleeve. "I should be celebrating. But I can't stop playing it over and over in my head. I lost my *shit* in that room, Cas, and not in a good way. I *panicked*. I *never* panic. And it was all because he pointed that phone camera at me."

"You also bit his dick in half, so if that's you panicking..." I squeeze her knee, not willing to do anything more. I feel like she's a skittish horse, and I have to approach carefully or she'll bolt.

This time, I don't want her to bolt. I want to stay on this bed with her and the kitten forever.

"At my last school, I was a bit of a... well," she laughs bitterly. "I was basically Euri. Most kids knew me, and apart from a few dickweasels, they were always friendly. But when you're blind, people just sort of assume you're not like them. I never get to be a normal teenager, you know? I didn't get invited to parties or on shopping trips with friends, which means I had plenty of time for studying and being involved in all the clubs."

"My sister, the super nerd."

"Exactly. Anyway, there was this guy... fuck, I can't believe I'm telling you this." She wipes her eyes. "But I have to talk about it, or I'll take myself to a bridge again."

"A bridge?" I don't like the sound of that. "You're not going anywhere without Vic or Torsten or me with you, and that's an order—"

"Just shut up and listen for a moment. I'm telling you about this guy, Dawson. He was basically the Victor August of our school, a bit less of a scoundrel, but everyone loved him. He was captain of the football team, class president, and volunteered at his parents' church every weekend. A real golden boy. Anyway, he joined the school paper, and I was the editor, and so we ended up hanging out a bit after school and bonding over writing, and I don't know... I couldn't believe someone like that paid attention to me. I..." she swallows. "I've never admitted this out loud – not to Dad, not to my therapist, not to anyone. But I fell in love with him. Completely and utterly. I wrote terrible poetry. I Brailled his name inside my iPad case. I had our future all planned out – college and then a wedding, and then we'd get jobs at law firms in New York City and spend our weekends going to underground music clubs and pretentious cocktail bars."

"Sounds like a fucking nightmare," I say, and she swats me playfully on the arm. The kitten thinks this is a great game and takes a swipe at my elbow, removing a chunk of skin.

"Dawson and I dated for six months. He was my first boyfriend. He met my dad. He took me to prom. We lost our virginity to each other on prom night like a high school movie. We spent every spare moment together – not that I had that many spare moments between college prep, 5 AP classes, and all my extracurriculars. And because he was popular, I kind of became popular, too. For a little while." She wiggles her finger for the kitten, but he's slumped over again, and he's wheezing softly. I wonder if we should clean all that dried gunk from his eyes, but I know nothing about kittens. "Anyway, it turns out, he'd been spending a lot of those moments with someone else – a long-term girlfriend at another school. He thought he could hide it from me because I'm blind. I found out, and I dumped his ass. Kind of publicly."

Fergie flashes me a smile that's so broken I want to punch something. But there's a little Fergie sparkle in her eyes, too. I *have* to know this story. "How did you dump him?"

"I faked an STI test, gave him like ten different venereal diseases, and posted it all over school with a note on it that said 'I don't date dirty, cheating, skank boys. Xxoo, Fergie.'"

I laugh. "That's my girl."

"Yeah, well." Fergie turns away. "Turns out I poked the bear. The other girlfriend found out about the STI test, thought it was real, and broke up with him, and then he became kind of a butt of the jokes in the football crowd. And I guess his poor, fragile ego couldn't take it. How dare the blind freak dump *him*? I think he felt like he'd made me into this popular girl, and he wanted his social currency back, so he..." she takes a shaky breath.

"What?" I growl, my blood already beginning to boil. "What did the dead guy do?"

"He had some footage of me. And him. Together. And he put it up on the school's social media for everyone to see."

"I want his name," I say.

"Cas, that's very sweet, but I—"

"His name," I growl. "I want his name. Dawson, right? Last name, please. Spell it out for me. I want to make sure I get it right on his tombstone."

She smiles that broken smile again. "Cas—"

"I'm serious. He dies tonight. We'll take the Tesla, drive all night, show up on his doorstep, and drag his scumsucking ass into the woods. You want to kill him? I can tie him up and we can torture him together. I'll let you be the one to cut his penis off, since I know that gets you wet."

She squeezes my knee. It's one of the first times she's ever initiated a touch between us, and it's so unexpected and lovely that my heart feels like it's going to fall out of my chest.

"That's literally the most romantic thing anyone's ever said to me."

Me? Romantic?

I grin. The thought makes me giddy.

"As much as I love the sentiment, I don't want you to get into trouble on my account, and I don't want to go anywhere near that place and dredge up the memories," she says. "Dad and I fought hard to get some kind of justice, but Massachusetts doesn't have revenge porn laws. Dawson was the *quarterback*. In a town like mine, that's like being a god. No one wanted to ruin his 'bright career' over this one little mistake, so he got a warning from the school and had to take the video down. The principal said I'd learned an important lesson, as if the sharing of an intimate video without my consent is somehow *my* fault, and because of the coverage of the case in the media, my college counselor said no Ivy League school would touch me."

"Keep talking, Sunflower. My list of people who need to die is growing longer," I growl.

"It's fine." She cradles the kitten in her arms. "I'm over it. Or maybe I'm not. That's why I hired you. I thought I could handle senior year as an ordinary student, but all the Ivy League bullshit at Stonehurst got to be too much."

So Victor *was* right – Fergie's high SAT score was because she'd been a nerd at her last school. She was supposed to be Harvard bound, before this Dawson cocksucker messed it all up. No wonder she came to us.

We've never had a client as righteously deserving of their place at an Ivy as Fergie Munroe.

Fergie continues. "The battle against the school and the website and the press was destroying my dad. He decided we needed a new start, and he met Cali and she asked him to move here, and here we are. My new start." She shudders. "I've already fucked it all up again."

"You haven't. You bit a guy's dick off. I'd say that's a great start to the year. What happened to the video?"

"We got it taken down," she says. "Although it's probably still circulating in certain corners of the internet. Please don't look for it."

"I'm not going to look for a tape of you that's out there without your consent. That's not how we roll."

"But Coach Franklin—"

"We have no idea how those videos got sent to him, or why Sierra's parents saw hers. Vic's got Torsten looking into it, but if we find out the coach is lying about any of this... I'll nail him to a cross for you. Hell, I might do it anyway."

"Don't take this the wrong way, Cas." She peers up at me with those wide emerald eyes. "But why haven't you? You nearly *killed* three of those male strippers at Tombs just for dancing with me, and yet Coach Franklin is still walking."

"Trust me, if I was in charge, he'd be a blood eagle." My hands ball into fists. "It's complicated. There's some other stuff going on."

"What other stuff? I thought I was supposed to be a member of Poison Ivy. Not a client. I was supposed to be in this. So tell me what's going on?"

"I—" I notice the kitten's head slumped in Fergie's lap. "What's up with him? He was all bouncy a second ago."

"Oh, he's probably tired himself out." She picks him up and holds him up to her face. "Cassius, he's wheezing. He's struggling to breathe."

No.

He can't die on us now.

"What do we do?"

"He needs a vet," she says. "But it's nearly 2AM. We'll have to find an after-hours vet, and even they aren't usually open after midnight—"

"I'll take you," I leap to my feet. "I know a guy. He's the best in the business, open all hours. Get your coat on, sis. Let's get this little guy to a doctor."

59

FERGIE

I slide into the passenger seat of the Tesla with the kitten wrapped in my arms. Cassius takes off at a surprisingly sedate pace. He doesn't want to jostle the kitten too much. The electric car pulls silently out of the house and hums onto the freeway. It doesn't take me long to guess where we're heading – across the Acheron, into Tartarus Oaks.

"Isn't there somewhere closer?"

The kitten makes a strangled noise in my lap.

"Nowhere that I'd trust. Eli takes all his animals here." Cas yanks the car around a corner. The tires squeal, but I'm too scared to be impressed at how the car grips the road. "Besides, we're here."

"*Where* are we?" I ask. Cassius swings the car through an impressive set of stone gates and drives around the back of an enormous, imposing building. And yes, I can tell that kind of detail by hanging my head out the open window and *listening*. Blind people may not have Daredevil powers, but we are pretty clever.

"This is the oldest hospital in the city. It used to be an

asylum. It now houses several different businesses, including a veterinary clinic."

"But this building is dead. No one's working now."

"Don't be so sure about that."

Cassius parks the car and comes around to my side. He opens my door and takes the kitten from me, letting the little guy nestle into his hoodie. The kitten's wheezing even worse than before, his tiny little body convulsing with each ragged breath.

My stepbrother leads me away from the building, through the garden, and into a humming maintenance shed. Behind a bunch of pipes, he pulls open a trapdoor and leads me down a narrow stone staircase.

"What the fuck, Cas? Why are we in some ancient tunnel?"

"Trust me, sis. Come on, we need to hurry."

We head down, down, down. Water drips from pipes above our heads. Stale air clings to me. Inside Cassius' hood, the kitten sneezes.

I swipe a spiderweb out of my face. "Seriously, what the fuck is this place?"

"We're almost there." Cassius squeezes my hand. "Okay, we're going up some stairs now. Hold on to me, sometimes they're slippery."

I brace one hand against the wall as my feet fight for purchase on the worn stones. At the top, Cassius grunts as he struggles to move something heavy. A square of light penetrates my vision and we emerge into a large, low-ceilinged room. I can hear medical equipment beeping and a few murmured conversations. In the distance, someone grunts with pain.

"Cassius Dio," a cheerful male voice greets us. "I've got a full house tonight. I don't have time to shove someone's guts back inside his body just because he put the wrong song on the jukebox at whatever dive bar you frequent."

"It's not an asshole with unfortunate taste who needs your help tonight, Galen." Cassius drops my hand to lift the kitten from his hoodie. "I found this little guy in the kitchen at Mom's restaurant. He seemed happy enough, although his fur's all matted, but then he got all weak and started wheezing."

The man makes a clicking noise with his tongue as Cassius hands over the kitten. "No wonder. The poor guy is very dehydrated, and he's probably got some kind of worm. And look at his poor eyes. He's been living rough. I'll get some fluids and antibiotics in him, and then we'll clean him up and see what else is wrong."

The kitten gives a weak mew, and I reach for him. Cassius takes my hand and squeezes it. "Don't worry, sis. He's in the best hands now. Galen will make him good as new, won't you?"

"We make no promises in the medical profession, Cas." The man says as he moves away from us.

My heart thuds against my chest. *Please let the kitten be okay.*

Cassius takes my hand and leads me into a smaller room. He shuts the door, blocking out the sound of the medical equipment, and helps me sit in a cushy chair. "We'll wait for Galen to work his magic. There's a pile of magazines. I can read one to you. Do you want to know the top tips for getting your baby to sleep through the night, or whether handkerchief hemlines are back in fashion this season?"

"Cas... where *are* we?"

"We're at a vet clinic," he says, with a hint of a smile in his voice. "Sort of."

"No. We're not. *People* are being treated here. I heard them. And why did the doctor—"

"—his name is Galen—"

"—fine, why did Galen assume he'd be patching up a guy that you *cut up*?"

My infuriating stepbrother doesn't reply.

"I'm supposed to be a Poison Ivy Girl, right? That means I'm in this, one hundred percent. You can trust me. *Tell me where we are.*"

"Okay." He shifts in his seat. "You're in a doctor's office, but this place isn't exactly... official."

"How so?"

"Galen treats people on the fringes of society. Everyone here has an injury that would create too many questions if they showed up in the ER. Sometimes I do a little street fighting, and if you have to get patched up, you can't go to a normal hospital because they'll tell the cops. So we come to Galen."

"You do know that people and cats are quite different species, right?"

"Relax, Sunflower. Galen knows what he's doing. He used to treat Eli August's animals before..." Cassius coughs. I think he might've been going to say something else, but changed his mind. "...before Eli hired a proper wild animal vet."

"Okay." I lean my head against Cas' shoulder. He throws a huge arm around me, and I sink into his huge bulk. "Okay."

Cas' lips brush the top of my hair. It's so nice, so reassuring, so *un*-Cas-like. I'm too afraid to move a muscle or ask him what the fuck he's playing at, because I don't want to spoil the moment.

But finally, the strangeness of being in an underground doctor's operating room with my evil stepbrother, waiting to hear news about a kitten, gets to me and I have to say something.

"Is this weird?" I ask him.

"Is what weird?"

"Once, when I was eight, I fell down a flight of stairs at the mall. I was excited about some new toy I wanted and I just wasn't paying attention and my cane... anyway, Dad sat outside my room for *hours* while I was in surgery, and when I woke up he'd filled my hospital room with balloons. I felt so loved, but I remember how trembly his voice was. He was terrified, and I kind of feel that now, like we're parents waiting for our kid."

"Cali would never wait for me outside a hospital room," Cassius says. "She'd tell Galen that whatever was wrong with me was my own stupid fault."

I pat his knee. "I don't think that's true. I think she loves you in her own brutal way."

"Is that so?" His voice tilts with disdain. "You know that my brother is in jail."

"I heard."

"He's in jail because he took the rap for something I did," Cassius says. "I was careless. Gaius would never be so careless. That's why Cali—"

"That's why what?"

Cassius doesn't say anything. I listen to the sounds around us, picking up bits and pieces of conversations between Galen and his patients in the operating room. As well as our kitten, there are at least two human patients – one in the far corner who keeps bellowing. He's been shot in the shoulder. And another with multiple stab wounds who isn't talking at all, but there's a girl and another guy with him and they seem pretty freaked out.

We wait. For hours. For minutes. I'm not sure how long. Every now and then Cas gives me an extra squeeze and murmurs, "He'll be fine. Galen will save him."

And then, finally, the door opens.

"Cassius, Fergie." Galen appears in front of us. We both shoot to our feet. Cassius squeezes my hand.

"Is he okay?" I whisper.

"I think he's going to be fine. It's as I suspected – he's very malnourished and dehydrated, and he's got a nasty case of worms, *and* an infection on top of that. We've cleaned him up and given him a drip and some meds, and I'll give you some more medicine you'll need to put into his food for the next two weeks. I'd like to keep him here for a few more hours, just to be sure, but if he keeps improving, he can go home with you."

I throw my arms around Cas. My coal-heart breaks open with gratitude. "That's the best news."

"It is. He's a real character, and I'm so pleased he's got good humans looking out for him. It's nice to treat a patient who isn't bleeding from multiple bullet wounds," Galen says. He has the loveliest voice. "The little guy is lucky. If you got him to me any later, he probably wouldn't have made it."

"Thank you so much, Galen," I breathe. I didn't realize until that moment just how much it mattered that the kitten pulls through. Cassius squeezes my hand again. "Can we see him?"

"Of course." Galen holds open the door for us. "Just be careful. He's groggy, and he's got a drip, so don't pick him up."

Cassius leads me over to a bed near the stab victim. A little voice whimpers, "Mew?"

"Oh, hey, little dude." I sit on the edge of the bed and lean down, pressing my face to the cotton sheets. A tiny little nose brushes my cheek. Tears well in my eyes. I reach out with one finger and touch his chin, stroke his little ears, and let him lick my eyeball.

He already feels better – his fur isn't as sticky and matted. He feels more solid, something, less like he'll slip through the gaps in my fingers.

"He has both his eyes open now," Cassius whispers, his voice filled with wonder. "They're so *big*."

The kitten rubs himself all over my face, and all my attempts to make him sit down and rest fall on deaf kitten ears. He clambers up on my shoulders again and burrows into my hair. "Mew!" he cries, batting his paws at Cassius from inside my curtain of hair. "Merrrrrw."

"Here." Warm fingers touch my hair, extracting the cat's

claws. "He got stuck. And I don't want him to get his drip tangled."

I'm warm all over as Cas coaxes the kitten back into bed and lets him chew his fingers. This is weird. This guy has been inside me. He's been my biggest nemesis since I arrived in Emerald Beach. He's done countless things to make me miserable. I literally gave him my dirty underwear that smelled like a fart.

And yet this moment feels more intimate than anything else we've done.

"I wish we'd thought to bring him a toy or something," I say as I rescue him from jumping off the edge of the bed. "I think he's going to cause all kinds of chaos to Galen's other patients."

"I think I have something... here." Cas pushes a string into my fingers. "It's my shoelace."

I wave it for the kitten, and he darts all over the bed after it. Cassius laughs. It's not the cruel laugh I've heard from him so many times before, but a genuine actual laugh. Like a normal person.

His laugh breaks off a tiny chunk of the coal that surrounds my heart. It falls away and floats in my bloodstream, doing absolutely nothing to cool the heat in my veins.

Since Coach Franklin forced me into that storage room, I've been trapped in Old Fergie's nightmare, reliving the worst moments of my life on a never-ending loop. I never would have guessed that what drags me back to the present is a tiny kitten and my evil stepbrother, who seems to know exactly what I need.

60

FERGIE

"What are we doing?" I hiss as we crouch in the trees outside the natatorium. I also feel like a cat burglar from a *Simpsons* cartoon.

It's two weeks after Cassius gave me the kitten, which we named Spartacus because he's a real little fighter. Today is my nineteenth birthday. This morning, my dad left me a gift on the kitchen table – a new purse, something expensive and leather with heavy metal clasps – but he'd already left for the clinic. He didn't even hang around to sing happy birthday completely off-key, like every other year.

Dad always went all out for my birthdays. I can't help but think back to last year, when he woke me up at 6AM with a breakfast muffin stuffed with sparklers. I can see fireworks, so when he set it down on my desk, the little sparks danced around my room like fireflies. He'd rearranged all his appointments to free up his morning, and he called the school and told them I was sick. He took me to the zoo, where he'd arranged for me to have a private, behind-the-scenes tour where I fed a baby elephant and held a large snake as it slithered around my body. It was wonderful.

But this year, I got a purse and a father who can't bear to be in the same house as me.

On the way to school, Cassius reached over and squeezed my knee. "We have a birthday surprise for you, Sunflower. Meet us at the car after school. I've put some clothes for you in the back."

I hadn't told him it was my birthday, and I wondered how he knew until I remembered that Torsten had looked up every detail about me. It was on the tip of my tongue to refuse in case my dad had something planned for after school, but I know in my coal-lump heart that it's not true. My birthdays were part of his old life, the life we had before I ruined everything. He hasn't forgiven me, and I can't even blame him.

So I'd squeezed Cas' knee back and told him I'd be there.

When I got to the car and Cassius handed me a bag containing my favorite red bodycon dress and a pair of spiked gladiator heels, I assumed we were heading for a night out at the city's hottest clubs. Instead, we're communing with nature. And I'm freezing. Why didn't Cas think to pack my leather jacket?

"I repeat, what are we doing here?"

"We're waiting for Coach Franklin to finish the boy's swim practice," Victor explains. "It's his very last day here at Stone-hurst Prep."

"Why?" I make a face as my coal-heart pounds against my ribs. Even the mention of that guy's name skeeves me out. "I don't want to go clubbing with *him*."

"We're not going clubbing."

"Then what are we doing?" I pull a twig out of my hair and toss it at Cassius.

"You'll have to wait and see, Duchess." Victor sighs. "And for future reference, this isn't my plan. It's all Cassius' doing. He can have all the credit, or cop all the blame."

"I know my stepsister," Cassius shoots back. "She's going to love this."

I'm curious now. As much as I hate to admit it, Cas is kind of right. He *does* know me – at least, he knows the dark and secret parts of me.

All three of these guys have seen sides of me that I didn't even know existed. When I arrived in Emerald Beach, I didn't know that I craved their unique blend of fucked-up possessiveness, or that I'd get off on pain, or that Torsten and I would find a way to connect through his sensory sensitivities. Cassius has been in my room every night – we play with Spartacus, we trade insults, he teases me to the point where I *almost* consider begging for his cock. But I don't want to give in that easily. I'm enjoying where we are.

"If you want to leave at any time," Torsten says, "just say the word and we'll take you home."

"This sounds ominous."

"She's not going to want to go home," Cas insists.

"Sssh," Victor hisses. "It's time."

I hear wet feet slapping on concrete, shouting, boys jostling each other. The doors of the natatorium swing open, spilling the varsity team onto the athletic fields. I rub my bare shoulders, wishing my birthday outfit had included a coat.

Something heavy and warm falls over my shoulders. I wrap the leather jacket tight around me and breathe in the scent. It's Victor's. Of course it is.

"You're staying here with me," Victor says as the bushes around me rustle and Cas and Torsten stand up. "I'm not making you face him again."

I breathe a sigh of relief as Cassius and Torsten run out of the bushes. "Please tell me that this isn't one of Cassius' games. He's not getting ready to dump a bucket of pig blood on me, right? I know he thinks I'm tough, but I can't handle that tonight."

"It's not a game. I don't know what you did to him, Duchess,"

Victor says. "But Cas wants this for you. I just hope for your sake that he's right, because it's going to bring a world of trouble down on our heads."

I don't have time to ponder that statement because Cassius comes puffing up to us. "Let's go."

Victor takes my hand, and we push through the bushes to a small side parking lot – used mainly by maintenance staff and students and coaches with after-school activities. Torsten and Cassius trail behind us, huffing and puffing. I can tell they're carrying something heavy. Victor pops the trunk, and they stuff whatever it is inside.

"What's that?"

"Wait and see," Cassius cackles gleefully.

We pile into the car. Cassius insists that I slide in up front. I touch the seat, and I find something sitting there for me. It's tied up with a bow, but it feels like... I hold it up and sniff it...

It's a package of raw hamburger meat.

"What's this?"

"So many questions, sis. You'll find out soon enough."

Unease settles in my gut. But I think of little Spartacus at home, and I can't believe that Cas means me harm. Not anymore.

Bang. Bang. bang bang bang.

"Um, Cassius," I ask as Victor pulls out of the parking lot. "What's that banging?"

"Oh, that's Franklin," Cassius replies. "He's probably woken up and discovered the sweaty jockstrap I stuffed in his mouth."

I whirl around. "Wait, what did you just say? What's in the trunk?"

"Coach Franklin."

"Coach Franklin is in the trunk?" My voice rises in pitch. "Why?"

I press the heel of my palm into my chest. My heart races so hard. My head swims. This can't be happening. He can't be in the car with us.

"Shit, Fergie, you look pale." Victor squeezes my knee. "We'll turn around up ahead and take you home."

"She's fine," Cas says.

"She's *not* fine. Look at her, you monster. I told you we shouldn't involve her in this." Victor punches the steering wheel. "Fuck. We shouldn't be doing this."

I know something's going on here that isn't just about me. But I can't focus on digging up the answers because I'm too busy trying not to throw up.

"Do you trust me?" Cas' fingers dig into my shoulder. "Do you trust that I know what you need, little sis?"

Do I trust Cassius? If he'd asked me a month ago, I'd have said *fuck no*. Now, the answer's not so clear.

I can't answer his question, but I *can* focus on what I know to be true. I remember his dick stroking inside me – the cruel, dark things he whispers that make me wetter than I've ever been. I know that he has blood on his hands. I know that he let his brother go to prison for something he did, and that the last girl he shared with Vic killed herself.

I *know* the wild hunger that burns in my veins whenever I'm around him. I know he will never break an oath, and that having a monster on my side gives me a giddy, heady power I've never experienced before.

I know that when I'm with Cas, I'll never be numb.

This is my chance to make the right choice, to walk away from Cassius Dio and his monstrous nature. This is my last chance to choose Old Fergie's safe, unremarkable life.

"Let's keep going," I whisper. "Let's keep going. I want my birthday surprise."

That's that, then. I'm throwing in my lot with Poison Ivy. No turning back now.

Cassius cackles. His hand cups my cheek and he leans forward to flick his tongue over my lips. "I knew you'd agree, sis. Victor, crank the music."

Victor turns up the stereo, and my favorite song by Ghost, 'From the Pinnacle to the Pit,' pounds out the speakers. It feels apt – a song about falling from grace and liking what you find in the depths of hell.

Tonight, I ride with three devils. Tonight, I become one of them.

"How do you like it back there, Roger?" Cassius thumps the back of his seat. Even over the earsplitting volume of the music, I heard Coach Franklin bellow.

I turn to Victor, but he's not saying anything. Torsten's quiet, too. So I don't say anything, either.

Old Fergie would be shit scared right now, but I still enter the supply closet every time I close my eyes to sleep. I taste the chlorine and stale sweat of his dick in my mouth. I'll never be able to wash my soul clean of him.

I don't know what Cassius has planned, but New Fergie is here for it.

We drive and drive, leaving the noise and lights of the city behind us. I wind down the window and let the moonlight kiss my face as I listen to the sweet serenade of Coach Franklin's screams.

We turn down a gravel road. Victor grits his teeth as the car bumps along, intentionally hitting every pothole. We pass through a gate – stone, I think, with a small building or maybe a billboard beside it. Victor slows the car, and I can hear... movement.

Not human, I don't think. But animals out there in the fields. Behind fences. Watching. Waiting.

"What is this place?"

"Welcome to Everlasting Hart Ranch," Victor says as he

parks the car. "It belongs to my dad Eli. His father was building a cattle ranch out here but he had a... change of heart. He gifted the land to Eli, and my dad turned it into a sanctuary for big cats and other animals he rescues from roadside zoos."

"So your dad is the reverse Tiger King?"

"Basically," Victor says with the hint of a smile. "And he has way better hair."

"And why are *we* here?"

"Hush, sis. Don't spoil the surprise. Not everything has to be planned."

Our feet crunch over bare dirt as we pile out of the car. Cassius bounds ahead like an excited puppy. Victor and Torsten appear at my sides. They leave Coach Franklin yelling inside the trunk and lead me up a dirt path, across a creaking wooden porch, and inside a large building.

"This is the old homestead. Some of it's in pretty bad condition, so don't go off wandering by yourself. But Eli's fixed up this wing to use as an office and storage for the food. Up here." Victor and Torsten flank me as we walk up. They lift me over two rotting steps and plant me on the top floor.

Inside, away from Coach Franklin's incessant pounding, I gasp in yoga fire breaths. I'm here and I'm with my three guys, and everything is okay. I hear a door slide open, and the cool breeze bites my skin.

I'm standing on a wide, long balcony. I smell... *something*.

Something that makes my veins pulse with fire.

"Can you feel him?" Cassius asks.

I open my mouth to tell him that I don't understand the question, but then...

I *feel* him.

I don't know what *he* is, but he walks in a slow circle on the ground beneath us, and malice rises from his skin like steam from a hot tub.

He snorts and the air shifts, the world spins a little faster.

"I feel him," I breathe. I don't have to see him to know I'm in the presence of something beautiful and terrifying.

"Fergie, meet Clarence," Victor whispers. He comes up behind me and slides his arms around my middle, pressing his chest into my back. His lips graze my earlobe, and a delicious shiver runs down my spine that has nothing to do with the cool night breeze. "He's an African lion, about two years old. My dad got him from a roadside zoo. Clarence lived in a tiny, filthy cage and was only brought out into the sunlight to perform tricks for crowds of tourists. If he didn't perform as required, he'd be beaten or starved. One day, he had enough and refused to perform. His handler whipped Clarence across his back to force him to jump through a hoop, and Clarence flung himself around. He tore the handler's arm off, and half his face."

As Victor talks, he rocks his body against mine, rubbing his hard cock between my ass cheeks. I can't speak. I'm mesmerized by the creature prowling below me, his presence singing in the night air. Victor's hands slide over my shoulders, down my arms, cupping my cheek and my breast.

"Once they've been mistreated so badly they turn on their owners, you can't rehabilitate them," Victor continues as he trails kisses along my neck and over my collarbone. "Clarence has a taste for human flesh now. Wild big cats are smart enough to be afraid of humans, to stay away for their own safety. But not Clarence. If he was released into the wild, he'd kill anything or anyone that entered his territory."

"I don't blame him," I gasp out through gritted teeth as Victor slides one hand beneath the neckline of my dress to cup my breast, rolling my nipple between his fingers.

"Nor do I," Victor flicks his tongue over my earlobe. "And that's why Clarence will live out his days here, where my dad looks after him. And even though he won't get to be wild again, he has everything a lion needs."

I grip the railing as Vic's fingers work my nipples – first one, then the other – before sliding between my legs and circling my clit nice and slow. Clarence senses something going on. I feel his eyes on me, the danger rolling off him in waves. I lean right over, my head hanging out so I can face the beast.

We understand each other.

"Plenty more where this came from." Victor slides out his hand and pats my pussy like it's a little pet. And normally I hate that shit but tonight, I'm fucking down for anything.

I make this sound in the back of my throat that can only be a purr.

"It is your birthday, after all," Cas says with a huff as he dumps something heavy onto the balcony. "Do you have your present with you?"

"You mean my raw hamburger meat?" I wrinkle my face. "I left it in the car."

"Well, go get it. You don't want to keep Clarence here waiting."

Torsten helps me back downstairs. I trot back to the car and fumble around under the seat until I locate the package of meat. The trunk is silent now. Maybe Coach Franklin has passed out, or perhaps he's realized that it's pointless to fight.

I could open the trunk. I could give him the chance to walk away.

But I'm not that nice.

I return to the balcony and hold out the meat to Cassius, but he pushes my hand back, pressing the smelly package into my hands. Beneath us, Clarence paws the ground. He can smell his treat.

"That's for you, sis."

"Do I throw it over for Clarence?"

"No. I have something else in mind." I hear a splash as Cassius throws a bucket of water onto the lumpy object at his feet. Someone splutters. "Wakey, wakey, Coach Franklin."

Shit. The lump is Coach Franklin. Cas and Torsten must've carried him up here while Victor worked his magic. He's been out cold, so he didn't cry out. But he cries now, coughing and spluttering from the ice water Cassius used to bring him round. "What are you doing?" he growls. "Where have you taken me?"

"Nasty, dirty old men who talk back get punished," Cassius snarls. I hear a *SNAP,* and Coach Franklin howls. Torsten moves beside me and leans his head against my shoulder. He speaks in his low, beautiful voice.

"Cassius broke the fingers on his other hand. Three of them now point upward, a way fingers don't usually point."

I grin. Torsten knows that I want to see everything that's going on. He'll paint me a picture with words so that I can enjoy every moment of what's about to happen.

"Now, Coach, you're going to lie still while I cut off your clothing," Cassius says in this high, singsong voice that's so completely terrifying. "And I wouldn't move an inch if I were you, because this knife is very sharp and I'm awfully clumsy."

The coach whimpers as Cas cuts at his clothing. "Why are you doing this to me?" he cries.

"I think you know why, Coach," Victor says. He sounds so calm, so reasonable. "We made a deal in good faith, even after we found you taking advantage of a student. We deleted your photographs, and yet you decided to hurt our girl, our *queen*."

"You never deleted those videos," he spits.

"We did," Victor says sadly. "We would never break an oath. But you did, and so here we are."

"And now we have your mobile phone," Cas says. "So we'll be able to find out who *did* send the videos. And we'll have access to every other sordid little secret you keep on there. But that's not something you'll have to worry about now."

"You can't do anything to me. I'll tell your parents. I'll get you all kicked out of school. You can kiss those Ivy League acceptances goodbye. Even with your connections, you won't be able to come back from kidnapping a teacher!"

Cassius laughs.

"You're new around here, Coach, so perhaps you don't know who our parents are. But if you can still speak when we're done with you, ask around about our parents. Someone will tell you about the Triumvirate."

Coach Franklin lets out an agonized cry. I don't know what that word is, but it means something to him. "No," he whispers, thrashing around on the ground.

"I told you not to move," Cassius purrs. The guy howls with pain. "Silly old man, now I've gone and cut your nipple off..."

What the fuck? "Cas, you're crazy."

"...oh, and there goes your other one. Such a shame. I'd hate for anything else to happen to you. My, you're bleeding quite a lot."

"Let me go, you perverted fuck!" Coach Franklin screams.

"Sorry, no can do. You hurt my stepsister. Oh, my Sunflower, get over here." Cassius takes my hand and leads me closer, so that my boot slams into Franklin's ribs. I'm standing right over him as he struggles against his bonds. "What do you think about men who take advantage of their students and put their filthy dicks in your mouth uninvited?"

I have *so many* words for what that bastard did, but in this moment, with my monstrous stepbrother by my side, I realize that he doesn't deserve them. I bend over Franklin.

I swing.

My fist connects with his nose. It's not a perfect punch – I do jiujitsu, not karate, and I can't exactly *see* my target. But he grunts and my knuckles bloom with pain, and it feels good. It all feels *so* good.

Cas doubles over with laughter. "It's time to open your present, babe. You're going to spread that meat all over his chest, in his hair. Shove it up his nose, in his eye sockets. Whatever you like. Just make sure he's nice and covered."

As my fingers brush the hamburger meat, it dawns on me what's about to happen. My ears buzz.

This can't be real. It's a dream. No one does this – it's fucked-up on a completely different level. It's fucked-up in the penthouse apartment of the tallest building in the world. It's fucked-up with an infinity pool and a billion-dollar view and a waiter named Jeeves.

"You don't have to do this, Fergie," Victor whispers. "Say the word and I'll drive you home."

"He's right, sis," Cassius says. "You don't have to do this. But you wanted to be part of the club, part of the family. This is what we do for family. We protect our own. This is happening whether you participate or not. Franklin touched what wasn't his. I thought you might like to do it, but if not, that's cool. Victor will take you home."

The real question lingers behind Cas' words. *Are you like me?* he's asking me. *Does a hunger burn inside you that cannot be sated by food and wine and sex? Do you understand, or do you think I'm an irredeemable monster like everyone else?*

I grab the package from Cassius' hands. "Hold him."

Cassius and Torsten hold him down while I dig into the package and pull out a handful of cold, wet meat. I give it a squeeze and it drips through my fingers. My hand trembles as I place the ball of meat onto Coach Franklin's chest. He bucks and thrashes. Bits of meat roll off the sides. I smear it into his skin. It sticks to the fine hairs on his chest.

"Please," he begs me. "Please don't do this. You know I was

only joking around with you in the closet. I would never hurt anyone."

I grab another handful of meat and smear it on his face, pushing it into his mouth the way he pushed himself into mine.

"Fuck you, bitch," he cries, trying to spit out the meat. "You won't get away with this."

I finish spreading the meat all over him and step back. Beneath us, the lion's going crazy from the scent of raw meat and blood in the air. He throws himself at the fence, rattling the structure and making me wonder just how safe we are up here. It's like that scene from *Jurassic Park* where they feed the cow to the velociraptors. I know we're being watched.

Coach Franklin knows what's coming too, because he curses and howls and thrashes about like an idiot. I hear another *SNAP,* and the coach's screams become a whimper as he realizes it's hopeless.

And in that moment when he breaks down completely, when he begs for his lousy life, when he promises us anything we desire, my body remembers being forced to my knees in front of him. I *feel* myself opening the revenge porn site. I *hear* my own moans echoing in my ears, and I know that nothing I do will ever be able to erase this night from my life.

Old Fergie and New Fergie become one.

And she smiles.

Cassius and Victor shove Coach Franklin off the edge of the balcony. He screams as he falls, and his screams intensify when he hits the dirt with a loud *CRUNCH*.

Cassius laughs. I hear someone else laughing, their voice in perfect harmony with his.

It takes me a moment to realize it's me.

Cas' laughter tears at my soul. This is what I've chosen. This is what I deserve.

No. This is the justice I *demand*.

I didn't deserve Coach Franklin locking me in that supply closet. I didn't deserve his pawing hands, the same way I didn't deserve what Dawson did to me. I can't get justice for that, but I can take this moment for all the women this prick would have hurt but now can't.

The moment stretches through time as Clarence pounces on his snack. He growls and tears and slashes, and Coach Franklin screams through all of it. The sounds... I cannot describe how beautiful they are.

"I wish you could see this, sis," Cassius whispers. "I wish you could see the blood spurting from the torn stumps of his arms against the dirt, like red wings. I wish you could see the terror in his eyes."

"I don't have to." I lean my head against his shoulder and listen. The lion's jaw works, and it makes a purring sound as it gnaws at Franklin's flesh, just like Spartacus with his little kitten treats. And I think how good and right and just it is that a man who got off on having power over women will sustain a beautiful creature like Clarence.

Cassius sits down on a bench and pulls me into his lap. His hand grips my arm, and I smell the copper of Coach Franklin's blood on his skin. I'm so fucking turned on. I grind my ass against his crotch, feeling him grow even harder beneath me.

"Careful, sis," he groans. "That's dangerous."

"Oh, yeah? What are you going to do about it?" I smirk as I wiggle even harder.

"Maybe I'll tell your father about what a bad girl you are," he rasps against my ear as his fingers slide under my panties, re-igniting the fire Victor had stoked earlier. He pinches my clit between his fingers, and I gasp at the pain that tears through my body. The pleasure chases it. "Maybe I'll tell him that his slut of a daughter likes to be fucked while she watches a rapist get torn apart by a lion."

I believe that Cassius would do it. He'd march up to my father and say all of that to his face, because Cassius thrives on chaos, and that would certainly bring down a storm of trouble on both our heads.

"Do it, then," I shoot back, because I like poking bears. "He'd never believe you. You're the dangerous thug and I'm the good little girl. I'm his little Fergalicious."

I reach behind and tug on his jeans.

"You don't want to do that, little Sunflower."

"Oh yeah?"

"Yeah. Because I made you a promise. I'm not fucking you until you beg for it. And I don't think you're ready to beg."

He lifts me up like I weigh nothing and holds me in his outstretched arms. My legs scramble in midair. I'm gripped with true terror. I'm suspended in the air above Clarence's enclosure, and if Cas wants to, he can throw me over the side into Clarence's waiting jaws.

"Cas, please," I cry. Raw panic rises in my chest as I try to turn in his grip. "Please let me down."

He throws me into the air. And as I hurtle screaming into the lion's pit, I'm hit by the truth. *Cas hates me. He never wanted me. He tricked me to get me here tonight so he could kill me.*

He betrayed me—

Cas catches me easily and sets me down again, flipped upside down so that I'm kneeling on the end of the bench. I grip it so hard that my knuckles ache, grateful to be back on something solid. As my body trembles through the adrenaline rush and my ass swings in the air, no doubt exactly as he intended, my stepbrother tears off my dress with one hand and tosses it away.

"I'd like to clarify," he says as he kneels behind me. "I won't fuck you with my cock."

A hot tongue plunges inside me. I scream at the suddenness

of it, at the heat and the wetness, at the sheer wanton joy of being *alive*. Below us, Coach Franklin screams too – a bloodcurdling final scream that cuts off abruptly as Clarence finally ends his miserable life.

Cas tricked me. He wanted me to panic. He wanted me to hate him again, just for a moment, because he knows the edge makes this part so much better.

He's not wrong.

Cas digs his fingers into the flesh of my ass, holding me open while his tongue pounds into my hole. My legs tremble as he buries his face in my pussy, pushing his tongue as far inside me as it will go before moving to my clit.

He's not gentle; oh no, my stepbrother doesn't know the meaning of the word. He attacks me with all his monstrous energy, eating me with the wild enthusiasm of Clarence enjoying his meal below us.

It's when Cas sucks my clit into his mouth and bites down on the sensitive bud that I come. My scream cuts through the quiet night. My hips buck as I fight to free my clit from my stepbrother's evil clutches. He holds me with one hand beneath my stomach and one gripping my ass, and continues to pummel my ruined clit, circling and flicking and biting and circling some more, until I'm slammed again with a trembling, howling, *boneshaking* orgasm.

"Fuck." I breathe. "Fuck, fuck."

"Happy birthday, sis." Cas slaps my ass with glee. "Can you handle more?"

"Fuck *yes*."

"Good, because my brothers here would like to give you their birthday presents."

Cas steps away, and I feel different fingers trail down my spine as someone else moves behind me. "You look so beautiful tonight, Duchess," Vic murmurs. His hands explore my body, rolling my nipples, skimming my sides. He's more gentle than Cas, but still possessive.

A pleading whisper escapes my lips. Luckily, Vic knows exactly what I need. He drops his pants and sheaths himself inside me in one long stroke. I'm so wet from Cas' attack that even Vic's enormous cock slides in easy, his piercing rubbing me in the perfect spot.

He doesn't give me time to think or adjust myself to his size. He pounds into me, holding my hips for leverage as he bucks against the bench. He's so forceful that I have to grip the edge to stop myself from flying off.

A litany of curses fall from my lips as he stretches me to my limit. That piercing dances inside me, working all kinds of magic on my lady parts. And just when I think that maybe I have a hope in hell of surviving this onslaught, he reaches around between my legs and plays with my swollen clit.

"Fuck, you feel amazing, Duchess," Vic groans. "I love being inside you."

I want to say so many things back, but speech isn't a thing I can do right now. Not with Victor fucking August buried inside me and his fingers demolishing my clit and that fucking piercing rubbing me in... all... the... right... ways...

Through the haze of pleasure, I'm dimly aware of someone sliding onto the bench in front of me. I move my hand along his leg and reach up to touch Torsten's face. "Hey," I smile at him as Victor buries himself balls deep inside me.

"Hey." He kisses the tip of my nose.

"If you want to, you can take off your pants and lie back on the bench," I puff. "And I'll suck you off. But fair warning, I'm going to come any fucking moment, so I might be a bit messy..."

"That's okay," he says. "I just want to draw you while you come."

I lower my hand to his lap and feel the edges of his sketchbook. My heart thuds against my ribs. He wants to draw me? He never draws anything for himself.

"I'd like that very much," I whisper back.

Torsten's charcoal scrapes across the page, and it feels more wanton and intimate than what Victor's doing between my legs. Feeling Torsten's eyes on me, and knowing he's capturing every flutter of butterflies on my belly and every pulse of fire in my veins, drives me right to the edge.

"Hey, sis, I just counted and Coach Franklin is in at least eighteen pieces," Cas tells me over Victor's shoulder. "Clarence is currently gnawing on his left arm."

My spine curves and my head lolls back as I come apart on Vic's cock. The orgasm blows my brains out of my ears. It shatters my bones and boils my organs. It's not a wave of pleasure so much as a nuclear explosion.

I am Fergie Munroe, and I am a Poison Ivy Girl, and it's fucking *magnificent*.

Happy birthday to me.

WE STAY on the balcony all night, drinking from the flask of fifty-year-old Scotch Cassius brought, and fucking to the sounds of Clarence chewing below. I never get tired of the sound of the lion's teeth sinking into flesh, penetrating Coach Franklin's corpse as he'd tried to penetrate me.

"He was a piece of shit," Victor says as he smokes a cigar, dropping the ash diligently into a tray on the bench beside him. Torsten leans against the railing, still scribbling away on his drawing. Cas is downstairs – he wanted to watch Clarence up close.

"And now he'll never hurt anyone again," I say. "Thank you for my birthday present. That was fun."

Victor lifts his arm, and I settle in his shoulder and take a puff of his cigar.

I've never felt so... wanted. So at peace with who I am. So rooted in a single, perfect moment.

Every day of my life has been a battle against a world that isn't made for me. A world that thinks because I can't see, I don't have a place. I may be a fighter, but I never knew how lonely it is to be the only one on the front lines.

It's every little girl's dream to have three crazy, obsessive men feed her enemies to a lion.

The Poison Ivy Club has given me the best birthday present I could imagine. And in return, I give them all of me. Everything I am.

I have to tell them the truth.

On the drive home from Everlasting Hart, Fergie snuggles in the backseat with Torsten. She rests her head on his shoulder and falls sound asleep. He meets my eyes in the rearview mirror with a look of awe and bewilderment, like he can't quite believe she's real.

I almost can't believe it myself. Everything about tonight was perfect. The way Fergie embraced our form of justice, the way her face shone with righteous triumph as Clarence tore Franklin apart, the way her body and her soul opened for us – a gift that never stops being new and fresh and existing.

She's one of us. She's everything we've ever wanted.

I put on Torsten's playlist, because I know he needs the familiarity of the music after the overstimulation of tonight. He's not the only one. Beside me, Cassius fidgets on the plastic sheet I made him use to cover the leather seats. He's saturated in the coach's blood, and I'm not getting any of that shit on my car. You'd think an entire night of torture and fucking would satiate Cas' appetite, but it's as if being with Fergie only fuels his bloodlust.

As the city lights of Emerald Beach appear on the horizon,

and we start to wind our way through the curving roads of Harrington Hills, the elation gives way to dread.

I've never outright disobeyed my mother like this before.

Relax. You were careful. You got rid of the evidence. There's no way Coach Franklin's disappearance can ever be traced back to you.

But I can't shake the feeling that what we did tonight has set off a chain reaction we can't undo.

My stomach is in knots by the time we pull up at Cali's house. I see lights on in the kitchen and in Seymour and Milo's apartment, but the rest of the house is in darkness. Good. It's better if Cali and John don't know that Fergie was out all night with us. If any shit sticks to us, we'll keep her out of it. After all, she's going to be going off to Harvard soon.

I park on the driveway. Cassius unlocks the front door while Torsten collects a sleeping Fergie from the backseat and carries her up the stairs to her room. Spartacus the kitten leaps off the bed when we enter, scolding us in bold meows for being gone so long.

I can't believe Cassius rescued a *kitten*. Fergie has changed all of us, but him most of all. Seeing him dote on the little guy is completely adorable. Cassius hurries to fill Spartacus' food bowl while I get Fergie in the shower.

For once, she's pliant. She doesn't fight or tease me as I strip off her clothes, lather up her body, and rinse the blood and dust off her. She's covered in bruises from where Cas bit her and I gripped her a little too hard. She peers up at me, her eyes unseeing but hooded with bloodlust.

She's never looked more beautiful than at this moment.

"My Duchess." I touch her face as I towel her off, marveling at the raw power of her. I pat her skin dry, kissing every inch of her. I kneel on the tiles and kiss her feet. "I did this for you. I'll kill any man who hurts you, and that's an oath."

"I know you would. This was the best birthday ever."

She kisses each of us on the lips before she crawls into bed. She's asleep in moments, her long eyelashes fluttering shut.

My eyes droop, and I'm desperate to get home. I don't like leaving Juliet and the rest of my family alone for so long. But Cassius has other plans. He drags us into the library and locks the door.

"Well," he demands as he slaps glasses down on the bar and opens another of his fancy-ass whiskys. Gaius liked to collect Scotch, so of course Cassius has continued the obsession.

"Well, what?"

"Well, hasn't Fergie shown us that she's ready?" He glares at me. "It's time."

I look over at Torsten, who stares down at his hands, his fists opening and closing. I know he wishes he had his sketchbook right now. He's covered in blood and dirt, and the smell must be getting to him, the world closing in as the stress of our secret weighs on his mind. He doesn't want to have this conversation.

But Cassius is too worked up to notice. Cas is right at home, coated in blood, high on the thrill of vengeance. He paces around the room, knocking back his drink, his nervous energy dancing in the space between us.

"Fergie is one of us," Cassius growls. "I want her to know everything. She's earned the right."

Torsten retreats into the darkest corner and makes a flapping motion with his hand – it's something he does when things get too overwhelming for him and he can't sketch. It calms him down. And right now, I kind of want to join him because I am very fucking far from calm.

"We can't do that," I say. "Cas, you know what's happening out there. What our mothers are fighting. And it's closer to us than we think. We know we didn't send those photos to Sierra and Franklin, but *someone* did. We have to protect her from that."

"Have you *met* Fergie? We can't keep her in the dark. If she doesn't get the truth from us, she'll dig it out some other way and land herself in shit in the process."

He has a point.

Cassius grabs my shoulders, shaking me so hard my teeth clash together.

"She *sees* us, brother," he says. "I know you feel it, too. Tonight, we showed her a piece of who we are, and instead of running away, she sank down on my cock. And she makes that noise..." he groans at the memory of it. "I've never felt like this before. I'm not enough for her, and I don't even care. She belongs to all of us. She's our queen and I want her to know it."

It's exactly as I feared. He's fallen hard for Fergie.

He still believes that now that Gaius is behind bars, Cali will choose him to take over the business. And he wants Fergie to join him, to revel in blood and carnage alongside him, alongside all of us.

And I open my mouth to dissuade him, but I can't. Because I've dreamed of it, too. Unlike Cassius, I *will* inherit. When I picture my future as ruler of the August Empire, she's by my side.

I want so badly for him to be right, but the secret Torsten and I are hiding weighs on my heart.

We can't tell him now. It's too soon. We haven't figured out why Fergie and her dad have fake identities. We don't know if it's even connected to the Triumvirate or to whoever's sabotaging the Poison Ivy Club.

But it can't be a coincidence.

I glance over at Torsten, but he's not going to be any help right now. I have to decide. Let Cassius spill our secrets. Let Fergie peek behind the curtain, give her access to everything she needs to destroy us. Or tell him what we found out.

If she's a spy, then she already knows everything.

"Okay," I say. "You're right. After tonight, we can't hide it from her much longer, anyway. We tell her everything."

Cassius' face breaks into a wide, wild grin. Torsten looks to me in surprise. But when Cassius looks over at him for his vote, he nods sullenly.

We're doing this. We're actually doing this.

"Excellent." Cassius rubs his hands together. "I know exactly how to do it, too. We'll make it a big surprise. We know how much she loves our surprises. We'll take her to Saturnalia."

62

FERGIE

I wake. The remnants of a bad dream cling to the edge of my mind. A lion devours a lamb while a bear and a wolf look on, and an eagle flies overhead. And then I *am* the eagle, soaring over the glittering lights of Emerald Beach. Weird, but okay. It probably means I need to fuck fewer hot assholes before bed, and like hell that's going to happen.

I slam my hand into my alarm clock. "It's 12:32AM," the chirpy voice declares.

It's the middle of the night.

And someone's in my room.

I sense them as soon as I'm awake enough to discern their breathing, the silent shuffle of their clothing, the way the air bends around the menacing wall of their presence.

Even after my birthday gift a week ago, even now I know that Franklin is gone (the police are dragging the Acheron for his body following an 'annoymous' tip that he was seen distressed on the bridge one night), my body flips into high alert. My fingers reach for the knife I slid under the pillow.

"Who's there?" I call out. I flex my muscles, preparing to pounce.

"Wakey, wakey, sis." Cassius leans over me.

"Christ on a cracker." I toss the knife in his direction as he cracks up laughing. I don't bother asking how he got into my room. The bastard has been systematically pulling apart every lock I put on the door, so I've finally stopped bothering. Having such a violent monster watching over my bed no longer feels like a violation – it's a comfort. "Why are you here? Tomorrow is a big day for the club. Don't you need your beauty sleep?"

Tomorrow is ED day – the day when colleges across the country announce their early decision and early action results. It's the day that Ivy League dreams are made... or crushed.

It's the day I find out if I got in bed with the right criminals. Will I get into Harvard?

"Oh, and what's so important about tomorrow?" Cas teases.

"You know that it's ED day," I grumble. "And now I'm going to be too wound up about it to go back to sleep, so thanks for that."

"That's tomorrow. Tonight is special too, but for other reasons," Victor says. "We think it's time you learned the truth about who we are."

"I know the truth. You're three annoying bastards who won't let me sleep." I fling my pillow over my head.

"Come on, Duchess. You mean to tell us that after all you've been through, you don't want the answers to all those annoying little questions that we keep avoiding."

Damn. They had me.

"Fine." I roll over and swing my legs out of bed. I fold my arms and flash my best 'don't-fuck-with-me' glare into the space where I think each of them is standing. "Tell me so I can get back to dreaming about being in the hot tub with Benedict Cumberbatch."

"Not here. Not yet." Cassius yanks me up and shoves me toward my closet. "You're getting dressed."

"What? Now?"

"As adorable as you are in those dinosaur pajamas," Victor says. "They aren't going to fly at our destination. Get changed quickly. May I recommend those leather pants you wore the other day?"

I poke my tongue out at him and head into my closet, where I grab the leather pants and a bustier to go with them. My skin sizzles with the heat of their gaze as I pour myself into the pants and lace myself into the bustier, pulling my hair out of its scrunchie so that it spills loose over my shoulders.

I sit down at my dressing table and Torsten does my makeup. He does my hair, too, using the curling iron and a bit of product so that it spills down my back in elegant waves. Every touch of his fingers against my scalp sends the butterflies into a conga line in my stomach.

Where are we going that I need to get dressed up this late at night? Why would they take me to a club to tell me their secrets? You can't talk at a club...

When Torsten's done, I hunt out my trusty Kate Spade purse – the old one that used to belong to my mother. When I check that I've got my cane and keys inside, my fingers brush the edge of my old wallet. The one that came with my mother's purse. The one that contains all the details about Old Fergie's life.

The guys want to tell me the truth about themselves tonight. Maybe it's time I did the same.

I've already told Cas some of it, and it wasn't horrible. It made me feel better, actually.

If they trust me enough with their secrets, then maybe I need to trust them with mine.

Maybe I can finally bury Old Fergie forever.

I shove the wallet deeper inside my purse and snap it shut. *It's decided. I'll tell them tonight, after they've told me their thing. We'll clear the air. No secrets.*

"I'm ready," I announce as I step out of the closet.

These boys suck all the air out of the room. I'm drowning in their scents, and from the way Vic gasps and Torsten makes a strangled noise in his throat, I'm not the only one affected by my entrance.

Cassius grabs my arm and shoves me against the wall, his huge hands pawing all over me, his tongue forcing its way into my mouth.

"Stop. You'll mess up her makeup," Torsten says.

"We could just skip the club," Victor says, leaning against the wall to watch Cas and I make out. "Have a little party right here."

"No," Cassius growls, but his throat sounds tight. He pulls away from me, leaving my body bereft of his touch. "I need this, especially now she's got my blood all hot."

"So we are going to a club. What kind of club is this?" I ask. "Is it one of Livvie's?"

"You'll just have to wait and see," Victor says. "We need to be quiet when we go through the house. We don't want to be spotted. Not yet, anyway."

We slip out of our room and move through the quiet house. Every footstep echoes in the stark, cavernous spaces. A strange pang hits me – a pang of longing for my dad. It's weird, but it's there. We live in this vast, beautiful house and yet, we can't find each other.

We head into the garage. "Are Cali and Dad home? Won't they hear the car start?" I ask.

"That's why we take the Tesla," Cassius grins as he tosses his phone at Victor. Cassius climbs into the passenger seat, and I crawl into the backseat with Torsten, who immediately pulls me into the crook of his arm. I love being with him like this, just feeling the comfort of his body.

"Not too much touching?" I ask him as I rest against him.

"Just enough," he replies in that haunting voice of his.

The car rolls silently out of the garage, and we turn into the street. We drive for a long time. I wind down the window and listen to the city blow past us. I hear the gulls and feel the wind grow colder and know we're crossing the bridge into Tartarus Oaks.

That old sliver of fear returns. These guys could be taking me anywhere. No one knows where I am. I put my hand in my purse, thinking that I'll text Euri and tell her, just in case I don't return. But then I remember that Euri hates me. I remove my hand and place it on Torsten's knee instead.

His body shudders a little, but he doesn't move it. Instead, he curls his fingers in mine. I breathe in. He smells so good. I feel safe with him. Wherever we're going, he's going to keep me safe. I don't miss my phone anymore.

We pass loud bars and people yelling on street corners. Police sirens ring out like an urban lullaby. The buildings become squatter, wider spaced, hollow-sounding – like warehouses rather than homes. The car's wheels crunch over gravel.

Where the fuck are we?

Victor parks the car. "We're here."

I raise an eyebrow. "And where exactly is here?"

"You'll see," he chuckles. "Come on, Duchess. Let us have our fun."

"It's your type of *fun* that I'm worried about," I grumble.

The car door opens. Victor helps me to my feet. He and Cassius flank me, their arms looped in mine. Torsten walks in the rear. I wonder if he brought a sketchbook with him.

As we move toward the venue, I hear voices as other people join us. Something sparks in the air – or maybe that's the knowledge that no matter who's in attendance, I'm surrounded by the three hottest guys here.

Yeah, I can't see the other patrons, but I can *tell*. I hit the honeypot.

The ground slopes away and the crowd presses tighter as we move toward the center of the space. Even though we're still outdoors, I can sense buildings around us, and we have to weave through tables and groups of people. Delicious smells waft on the desert breeze – roasting meats, sweet pastries, and rich spices mixing with the heady scent of sex and danger.

"Please," I tug on Victor's arm. "Describe where we are."

"We're in an abandoned railroad roundhouse," Victor says. "The old locomotive sheds have been converted into the bar, kitchen, and various private rooms. In the center, where the turntable used to be, is an arena. It has a wooden floor covered with sand, and concrete sides with a wire cage over that, and a gangway over the top. All around it are tables and seats for the audience. This place is called Colosseum, and it's the biggest illegal bar in the city."

"And it's run by Torsten's mom," Cassius adds. "You guessed right, sis. And now, I've got to leave you. But first..."

He leans in and kisses me, grabbing my neck and pulling me up to meet him. I love that fierce possession, the way he lays claim to me for everyone at this club to see. His fingers dig into my skin, giving me that pressure I like.

He waits until I melt into him, until my hands begin to explore him, before he pulls away with that cruel, Cassius laugh. "My good luck kiss," he cries. "I'll see you soon. I'm needed backstage."

"What's backstage?" I demand. "Are you in a Magic Mike show?"

Cassius' laugh drowns out all the other noise as he disappears into the crowd.

I guess that's my answer.

Torsten moves beside me. He doesn't say anything, but squeezes my hand. I know better than to ask about his mother and her involvement in this strange club, but I can tell he's on edge here. He doesn't like being in her territory. And he can't enjoy the noise of the crowd or the way people bump and jostle us.

"Follow me," Victor says. "We're this way."

He leads me up a set of narrow metal stairs. Two levels up we emerge onto a metal platform. Below us, the crowd roars, their clamor slightly muted by the distance. I hear voices close by – tables where a few people are seated.

"We have the table right at the front, but first, I want you to meet someone." Victor's hand is warm in mine. He knits our fingers together as he leads us to one of the tables. I hear a woman's tinkling laugh, the clink of champagne glasses, the shuffle of expensive clothing.

"Victor, darling, I'm so happy you made it." The woman who was just laughing stands and throws her arms around him. A possessive stab hits me in the gut. I know my boys weren't monks before they met me, but I don't want my face rubbed in it.

"Mom, this is Fergie," Victor holds out my hand. "Fergie, this is my mother, Claudia August."

I feel silly. Of course he wants me to meet his mother. Claudia takes my hand between both of hers. Her touch is warm. Three rings circle her ring finger. "Hello, Fergie. It's so lovely to meet you. Victor and Juliet have told me so much about you."

"Oh, well it's probably all lies," I smile.

"Nonsense. My son never lies. Come and sit next to me. Tell me how you're enjoying living in Emerald Beach."

"It's interesting. It's different from Massachusetts." I wave my arms to indicate the club. "I've never been anywhere like this before."

"I believe you," she says with a smile in her voice. "You make sure those boys look after you. Things can get a little wild with this crowd, especially at Saturnalia."

"Saturnalia?" I didn't expect a word like that to come from her lips. I vaguely remember Saturnalia from my Classical Studies class. It's one of the Ancient Roman religious festivals, something about honoring the God Saturn, and slaves having the freedom to do and say whatever they liked.

She laughs. "I see you know the word. My ancestors brought some ancient traditions with them when they first came to America. Saturnalia is one of them. You'll learn a lot about these traditions tonight."

We sit down at the table, and a waiter appears to take our drink orders. Victor orders a cocktail for me, and the same drink for his sister, who sits at the other end of the table, talking to a cousin. Eli is there, and Victor's other dad, Noah, who seems nice, if not a little taciturn. His third Dad – his birth dad – is back on tour with his band, which is something I'm dying to hear more about, but before I can ask, the lights dim.

A roar goes up from the crowd. Beside me, Claudia and Eli and Noah rise to their feet. Further down the table, I hear Livvie's diamond rings brush the table as she too rises from her chair. They hurry off somewhere. Weird, but okay.

A voice over a loudspeaker begins with a long string of Latin, including many phrases that the crowd repeats back at increasing volume. Finally, he switches to English. "Welcome to the annual celebration of Saturnalia. This is where we celebrate the bounty brought to us by the union of the Triumvirate, and make our offerings to the gods for another fruitful harvest."

I lean over to Victor. "What's the Triumvirate?"

He presses a finger to my lips. "It's us – our three families. But it's so much more. Listen, and you might begin to understand."

"But you don't want to hear me yammering all night. I'd like to welcome to the stage your three Imperators – the women who keep us in guns, money, drugs, and whores. From the Lucian family, the beautiful but cunning Olivia Lucian."

That's Livvie. Raucous cheers and wolf whistles rise from the crowd below. Beside me, Torsten stiffens.

"Next, straight from the bowels of hell, she's as graceful as an eagle, but she'll peck out your eyes... our very own mistress of death, Cali Dio."

Cali? Cali is here?

What the fuck?

And that announcer guy just called her the motherfucking mistress of death? Is this like a wrestling match or something? I don't have to watch my stepmother get into a pool of jelly in a bikini, do I? Because even though I'm blind, there's only so much a person can take.

I'm so stunned that I almost don't hear the final announcement.

"...and finally, from the ancient, noble house of August, the woman who we credit with ushering in the last twenty years of prosperity... Claudia August."

The applause is loudest of all for Victor's mother. Beside me, Vic leaps to his feet and whistles.

"Thank you, all," Livvie's voice rings clear as she takes the microphone. "We have a full program of entertainment for you tonight. And don't forget the rules of Saturnalia – for tonight, and tonight only, we serve *you*. Not literally, of course, I don't want to break a nail—"

The crowd titters.

"—but we will be serving you with games and wine and all kinds of erotic delights. And if you ask us for a boon and it's in our power to grant it, we'll do it for you."

"Now, drink and be merry," adds Cali. For the first time ever, she sounds almost... happy. "For tomorrow we bathe in blood."

Tomorrow we bathe in blood.

I turn to Victor. I squeeze Torsten's hand.

It all clicks into place. I've had the pieces all along, I couldn't put it together because the truth is so... insane...

...but I *see* now. I see *all* of it.

"Your mothers..." I whisper. "They're the heads of crime families."

"Top marks, Duchess," Victor purrs. "We are the sons of the August, Lucian, and Dio families, otherwise known as the Triumvirate, the rulers of Emerald Beach."

The Triumvirate.
Just the sound of it sends a shudder down my spine.

Their mothers are Crime Lords. Or Crime Ladies. I don't even know the proper vernacular. But my three guys are part of the world of... what? Guns? Drugs? Art theft? Human trafficking? Gambling? Election fixing? Sound the fucktrumpets, what the actual fuckity fuck?

"Tell us what you're thinking right now," Victor says.

What am I thinking? What *am* I thinking? I'm thinking that I'm sitting in the middle of Mafia Coachella and I don't have a feather headdress.

I'm thinking that I have no context for this news, no way to process it because it's so completely out of place with my life experience. Except... is it?

My father purchased fake identities from Cali Dio. I helped Cassius bribe a college admissions officer. I watched a man get *eaten by a lion.*

I became a Poison Ivy Girl, and now I'm *in* this. I'm part of their world.

Fuck.

"I need more," I say. I grab my cocktail and down it in one gulp. "How does this Triumvirate work?"

"Don't get Victor started," Torsten says. "He'll give you a whole history lesson."

"I won't. I promise, Duchess." Victor squeezes my hand while Torsten gets me a refill. "There are three families who've run this city for as long as anyone can remember – the Lucians, the Augusts, and the Dios. Each family is originally responsible for a specific aspect of the city's underworld, and the idea was that the Triumvirate would work together to share information and profits. The Augusts are a shipping family. If you want to move anything in or out of the country – drugs, guns, priceless artworks, people – they can do it. Although the human trafficking thing is only for humanitarian reasons. My mother has standards. The Lucians are the kings and queens of vice. Whatever your darkest and most depraved desires, Livvie Lucian and her family have a way to make your dreams come true."

"And Dio?"

"Dio is the muscle," says Victor. "Your stepmother trains the finest assassins in the world."

"She... *what?*"

"Cali's gym in Tartarus Oaks is a training facility for assassins. She personally has been responsible for some of the most high-profile hits of the last twenty years. Your stepmother is a lethal weapon. A little like you, if my balls remember correctly."

Victor's joke fails to land as the sheer insanity of his news starts to sink in. It's so bonkers, and yet... it completely makes sense. I could never see Cali as a fitness influencer, bouncing all over YouTube with a cute little dog at her side. But training assassins, torturing world leaders, that I could *get.*

"My dad married to a killer for hire." The lump rose in my throat. I'm going to have to tell him. He's going to be heartbroken, if I can even get him to believe me. "And she trained Cas—"

"Yes, he does a little extracurricular work for his mother," Vic says. "We all do. Well, not Torsten anymore, but I'll let him tell you his story if you decide you're still going to talk to us after this. Do you still want to know about the Triumvirate?"

Torsten presses my drink into my fingers. I suck at it like a baby with a pacifier. "Yes. I want to know."

"Okay, so… twenty years ago, our mothers rose to power in a bloody battle for vengeance and dominance. The Triumvirate had become this fractured thing, the families fighting amongst themselves, everyone wanting to be the ones controlling the empire. Our mothers beat out a lot of men who thought that women had no place at the heads of these families. And they decided that instead of fighting each other, they'd get back to how things used to be and work together, with some innovations. The families *share* profits, so there's no incentive to compete. And they changed the structure. It used to be that only men who were blood relatives of the three original families could become the Imperator, but our mothers changed that. Cali's not from the original Dio line – she was adopted by the previous leader, Constantine, and took over after he died. There was a lot of blood spilled over that, but she's more than proven herself."

"And you?" I choke out.

"We're the children of the three most powerful families in this city," Victor says. "My parents raised me and Juliet to inherit the empire, but it's our choice to make. Torsten has no interest, despite his mother's best efforts. And Cassius… our boy wants to be Imperator more than he wants anything in the world, but Cali has always favored Gaius for the job."

"Why?"

"Because Cas is—"

"No, I mean, why did you bring me here tonight?"

"Because you're our girl. You're our Poison Ivy Girl. We

wanted you to know the truth about us. You may have guessed some already. Rumors fly around school all the time, but no one knows the full truth of who we are and what we do. But we wanted you to know because..."

"...because you're the first person who's really seen us," Torsten says, his voice cracking. "The first person who has looked beyond our families and our... proclivities."

You're the first person who's really seen us.

His words stick in my throat. That's exactly the way I feel about them, all three of them. They're the first people who've ever truly seen me for who I am, and they've taken those dark parts of myself that I've kept hidden away and brought them into the light. Thanks to them, I'm no longer afraid of the darkness. I *embrace* it.

I think about my own secret buried in the bottom of my purse. I'd told Cas part of it, and compared to what they've just revealed, it's not really a big deal anymore. But I want them to know *all* the hidden parts of me. I don't want there to be secrets between us, ever again.

"Okay," I say. "Okay."

"You're not screaming," Victor says. "Or running away. You're not wearing a police wire, are you?"

I let out a barking laugh. "No, I'm not wearing a wire. I guess I just... when I think about it, I always knew what you are. I mean, I didn't know about your mothers and their badass Mafia Queen club, but I do know who you are inside, and that's what matters to me."

"So you're still a Poison Ivy Girl?" Vic's voice rises with hope.

"Until the day they bury me."

Torsten's lips brush my forehead, more intimate and precious than a proper kiss. "Thank you," he whispers. "Thank you for seeing me."

"So, where'd Cas really go?" I say. "I thought he'd want to be here to watch my head explode."

"We told you, he's backstage." Vic places a finger under my chin and directs my face toward the arena below. "And it looks like he's coming out next."

The commentator riles up the crowd into a frenzy, talking about some kind of fight. But I can barely focus because Victor and Torsten pick up my chair and move it to another side of the table. I'm facing the arena with the table in front of me. I can hear a few voices nearby, but most of the occupants have moved to the railing for a better view.

The next thing I know, Torsten crawls under the table. Victor arranges me in the chair so I'm nestled between his legs, and his hands roam over my body as Torsten slides his hands up my thighs.

"What are you doing?" I hiss as Torsten tugs the zipper on my leather pants. "We're in a crowd of people. Your *parents* are here. Everyone will see."

"Can't you smell the blood in the air?" Vic sniffs. "This crowd is primed for lust and violence. They're not paying attention to us. And as for our parents, you won't believe some of the shit they've made us watch at these events. They owe us. Now," Victor rubs his fingers over my hardening nipples. "Our duchess, are you going to be a good girl and open your legs for us?"

Victor lifts me while Torsten drags the leather over my thighs. My legs fall open. Torsten drops between them, trailing kisses along my thigh like he's been doing this for years. I want to tangle my fingers in his hair, but I don't want to give him too much stimulation. I don't want this to stop.

"...we welcome to the ring, our reigning champion of carnage, The Bear!"

"Cassius walks into the ring," Victor whispers against my ear as he cups my breast in his hand, squeezing me over my bustier until I moan. "He's naked from the chest up, his ink glistening under the lights. His arena name is The Bear, and there's a tattoo of a growling grizzly in exquisite detail inked across his back. He wears black boxing shorts, gloves with curved bear claw blades in the fingers, and his face is covered with a bear's head mask. He looks like he's eight feet tall. He looks *mean*."

I can *feel* my stepbrother. I taste the danger on his lips. Victor kisses along my neck as Torsten hooks a finger into my scarlet panties (I know they're scarlet because I like the *idea* of red, so I buy lots of red clothing) and pulls them down. *Fuck. I can't believe this is happening.*

Even if I wanted them to stop, I couldn't make them.

I'm a boulder hurtling down a cliff, about to flatten the village below. I'm on this path now. I can't stop. I can't turn around. This is inevitable.

Poison Ivy are in my veins.

They feed my coal-black heart.

"Cassius' opponent is in the ring now," Vic narrates. "If you can imagine this guy, he's even taller than our boy, but he's wiry. He has the Dio mark tattooed on his breast. I heard that he's one of Cali's newest men recruited from her martial arts school. He has no idea what the fuck he's in for."

A whistle blows. The crowd grows insane but I don't hear them. My world has shrunk to the tongue lapping at my clit, to the dark, sensual voice narrating in my ear as his hands wander my body, and down below, to the pull of my stepbrother's malice, threatening to undo me completely.

"They clash together," Victor purrs into my ear as Torsten's tongue moves in slow circles, just the way I taught him. His finger slides inside me, and I'm so wet I'm leaking all over this chair. "Cas has the guy in a headlock. He slams his head into the concrete wall. The guy's tooth just flew out. Cas slams his head again, but the guy manages to roll with the blow and he's up, he's up, but…"

Victor's lips graze my earlobe as he narrates every move of the fight. It's short and bloody and *amazing*. Even though I'm nowhere near the arena, even though I can't see what's happening, I feel every moment with Cassius as though I've crawled inside his skin. My knuckles tingle, like they're the ones pummeling an opponent. My muscles ache from ghostly grappling. It's been so long since I had a proper bout.

I listen to Victor speak each sinful syllable while Torsten weaves his magic on my clit, and down there, in the arena, Cassius tears a man's throat out.

"Cas has him by the neck," Victor whispers. Torsten licks, licks, licks, and I can't take it anymore. The coil of tension inside me unspools. "This is the killing blow…"

Victor's next words are drowned out by the roar of the crowd and the rush of blood to my ears as an orgasm shudders through me. My legs clamp around Torsten's head, and I slide down a little in the chair as I ride the pleasure until it ebbs.

"Cas' opponent is down. He's not getting up," Victor whispers.

"Neither am I," I whisper back. "My legs have turned to Jell-O."

Torsten crawls out from under the table and wraps his arms around me. Victor helps me zip up my pants over my slick skin. The families return to their seats in a jubilant mood. Champagne bottles pop as everyone toasts Cas' win. I hear Livvie telling Claudia that he could come warm her bed anytime. Gross.

"There you are, sis."

I smell him before I sense him – the air grows coppery with blood.

Cas. *He's here.*

I turn around and smack straight into him. His bulk presses against me, sucking the air from the platform. I take a step back, and my ass hits the edge of the table.

"What do you think, sis?" Cas leans in close, covering my body with his. He hasn't showered. He hasn't even put clothes on. His bare chest presses into mine, and I can't help running my fingers over his taut muscles, touching the dried blood. "What do you think of who I am?"

I'm a thirsty bitch, but I don't care.

"I think you should have told me about this sooner," I growl. I fist my hand in his hair, bringing his face close. "I think that you're fucking perfect."

He laughs as he claims my lips, then draws back to graze his bloody knuckles over my cheek. "*You're* the perfect woman, Sunflower. Let's go."

"We haven't eaten yet," Vic protests. "Well, Torsten has—"

I laugh as my cheeks flush with heat.

"I don't care," Cas shoots back. "The only thing I'm hungry for right now is Fergie's pussy."

He picks me up and flings me over his shoulder – a caveman returning to his cave with the spoils of war. Victor and Torsten laugh as they follow us toward the stairs. I hear Claudia call out to us and someone's footsteps coming up the stairs, but Cas bounds down without waiting for them. He's the champion tonight, and the son of a Mafia Queen. Whoever it is will get out of our way—

"Cassius Dio. What the *fuck* are you doing?"

The voice drops into my skull like a lead weight.

Cali.

Cas stops dead in his tracks. "I—" he stutters. Cas, at a loss for words? What is this? "I didn't think you'd come up here. You hate the VIP section—"

"Cassius Brutus Dio," Cali growls. "I see you've brought your stepsister along to Saturnalia, *against my direct orders*—"

"Fergie," the voice cuts in. It's a voice that chills my blood to ice.

"Dad?"

"Dad, what are you *doing* here?"

I try to scramble out of Cas' arms, but he won't let me down. I kick my legs, but that only makes him hold me tighter. Humiliation burns my cheeks. I want Cas, but I never, ever wanted my dad to see me with him.

I don't want to put him through any more pain.

Well, two can play at that, I guess. Because he's *here*. On Cali's arm. Which means he knows who she really is.

Did he just find out tonight? Or has he known all along that he brought us to live in the lair of a killer?

"I'd like to ask you the same question." Dad's using his stern voice, but I'm not a fucking fool. I've caught him in the act, and he's terrified.

"I'm getting to know my stepbrother and his friends. And I guess you're here because you're Cali's date. So you knew that Cali is an assassin. Funny that I only just learned this now."

"Jesus fuck, Cassius," Cali snarls. Her talons wrap around my arm, and she drags me off my stepbrother's back. "You weren't supposed to tell her. Did you do this deliberately to spite me?"

Cas grabs my other arm and yanks me into his chest. "What, no! I—"

"I think we should talk about this at home." Dad grabs my wrist beneath Cali's firm grip. "Fergie and I will go to the car and—"

"I'm not letting Fergie out of my sight," Cas growls.

"Fergie," Dad wheedles. "We should talk about this, *alone*."

"No, Dad. Cas is protecting me, something you obviously have no intention of doing." I'm so fucking angry that I'm shaking. And I'm not even mad because my stepmother is a killer. Weirdly, I'm relieved it's that because it seems so perfect for Cali. I'm mad because Dad and I always told each other everything. But ever since The Incident he's been keeping his whole life secret, and now I find out he's been hiding this, too? "When were you going to tell me, Dad? When I got killed in the crossfire of some gang war? What happened to us being a family? I guess I'm only family to you when I'm a good little girl? But I make one little screw up and suddenly I don't deserve to know that you married a crime boss?"

"I did it all for your own good, Fergalish," Dad protests. "After everything you've been through, I didn't want to give you something else to worry about. I wanted you to be able to start over fresh, to put yourself first for once. I was going to tell you, when the time was right, but Cali and I thought—"

So Cali's behind this... this secrecy. And she's the one keeping Dad away from me at every opportunity. She has no interest in what's good for me. She wants to protect her own interests, whatever the fuck those are.

I don't know why Cali needs my father. I don't know why she had to move us across the country and under her roof to get it. But I know that cruel-hearted bitch has an ulterior motive, and if Dad's too blind to see it, then I have to figure it out.

"You're making a scene," Cali snaps, tightening her fingers around my arm. Her nails dig holes in my skin. "Come and sit down and act like adults—"

"No." I yank her forward and drop, flipping her over my shoulder. She cries as she skids across the VIP platform and crashes into the tables. I hear the shattering of glass and people yelling. I yank Cas' hand. "Go! Get us out of here."

Cas roars like a lion, throws me over his shoulder again, and takes off down the stairs. I hear Victor and Torsten's footsteps behind us. Cas pushes his way through the crowd. People yell at him about the fight, trying to get him to sign shit. Women throw themselves at him, begging for him to take them in a manly fashion. Cas shoves them out of the way, leaving a trail of over-turned tables and crying girls in his wake.

In the car, he throws me into the backseat and climbs along-side me. He cups my face in his hands.

"Tell me what you're thinking right now, sis."

"Right now, I don't want to think," I growl as I grab him around the neck and pull him to me. "I want to *feel*."

My fingers slide through Cas' hair as he punishes my mouth with his tongue. Cas kisses like he does everything else in life, like it's a fight to the death. He sucks, nibbles, and bites at my neck, marking me as his.

He tastes like blood and freedom.

"Drive, you fucker," I yell to Vic as I give myself over to my stepbrother's hunger.

BY THE TIME we pull up at the house, Cas has managed to get my bustier off. Victor parks in the garage, and my stepbrother throws me over his shoulder and runs into the house. My stomach twists to think of someone seeing me like this, but Milo and Seymour will be fast asleep by now, and Dad and Cali are still at Colosseum.

My Dad and his wife, the head of a crime family. Cali the Mafia Queen. Cali the assassin.

It's too much to think about. So I decide that I won't. Dad doesn't think I need to be part of his new life, so I'm not going to let him take over my new life. I plan on enjoying whatever filth Cassius has planned for me.

I expect Cas to carry me to my room or his, but he passes that hallway and moves to the next. He punches a code into the wall, and the doors to his secret library swing open.

We're going to fuck in a *library?* Cool.

"Torsten, music," Cassius snaps as he throws me onto the leather sofa and paws at my breasts. "I want something that'll harmonize with Fergie's screams."

I know the real reason Cas asks for music is because he knows that hearing something familiar, that covering up the sound of fucking with music, helps Torsten to stay present, to be able to be in the moment with us. And he wants Torsten to be there. He wants all four of us to have this moment.

It's so fucking hot, the way they care for each other, the way they always put each other's needs first. They're a real family.

I used to think I had that – me and Dad against the world. But now...

Wait, why am I thinking about Dad now? Fuck, no, that's gross.

A moment later, the soft, evil tones of Nick Cave singing 'Red Right Hand' suffuse through the room. It's perfect for this night – villainous music about angels and devils.

Victor slams the doors behind him. He storms up to the sofa and looms over us. "First, let's get you out of those leather pants."

He grabs me by the hips and spins me around, pushing me so my back is against Cas, who responds immediately by digging his cock into my thigh and growling in my ear. The guy lives up to his arena name. The Bear. Strong and vicious. An apex predator.

I kick my boots off. Victor's wicked mouth holds me in place as he lifts my hips and rolls the pants over my legs. He throws them at the bookshelves before turning back to me and covering my mouth with his again.

"I want to do so many filthy things to you right now, Duchess," he moans against me. "But Cas needs to have his fun. I promise that if he hurts you, I'll kiss away the pain."

"He can't hurt me," I shoot back, loud enough that I know Cas will hear. "I'm made of the same stuff he is."

With a shout, Cas tears me from Victor's arms and flips me onto the sofa. He cups the back of my neck with his hand, pushing my head into the couch as he trails his wicked fingers along my spine and over the curve of my ass, raising a trail of goosebumps. "You watched me fight tonight," he says.

"Yes—"

SMACK. His hand lands on my ass. I yelp. I hadn't expected *that*.

My ass stings where he spanked me – another mark that proves that I'm his.

"You like that I'm covered in blood, don't you?" He towers over me, making me tremble with anticipation.

"Yes," I moan, my voice muffled in the sofa cushions.

SMACK.

I whimper, even as heat surges in my cunt.

"That's for being a filthy girl who craves dirty, forbidden things." My stepbrother's hand slides between my legs, playing with my clit through the fabric of my panties.

"You're so wet. You're soaked," he growls.

SMACK.

I howl as his hand lands between my legs, right on top of my throbbing clit.

"You're soaked because you like what I'm doing to you. You like being my little slut, don't you, Fergie? Tell me that you like it."

"I like it," I moan.

SMACK. Right on my clit again. My whole body arches off the couch, but Cas shoves me down.

"Louder."

"I like it!"

SMACK. Back to my ass now, he decorates the other cheek with his palm print.

"And what do you want me to do to you tonight?"

"I want you to fuck me."

"Do you want all three of us to fuck you? Do you want us to own every one of your holes? Do you want us to worship you like the queen you are and leave you a quivering mess? Do you want me to show you how much pleasure there is to have in pain?"

"Yes. I want it all. I want all three of you inside me."

SMACK.

My ass is on *fire*. I've never been this turned on before.

"Then you know what has to happen, baby sister," Cas coos as he plunges his fingers between my legs, stroking my clit until my legs start to shudder. "You know what you have to do. You have to beg me. Beg me for my cock."

"Please," I whimper. "Please, Cas."

When he first told me that I'd beg for him, I never believed it. His stupid asshole certainty made me determined that I'd never bend to his will. But with his hand between my legs and my ass smarting from his smacks and his gravelly voice commanding me, I cave in a few seconds flat.

I'd be disappointed in myself if I wasn't in the middle of fucking *mind-blowing sex*. You can take away my feminist badge another day, because I have three cocks to conquer.

I can hear the smirk in Cas' voice. "I can't hear you, baby sister..."

"PLEASE fuck me!" I scream. "Please own all of me. Please, I need you inside me again. Please?"

"Well," he simpers. "Since you asked so nicely..."

I yelp as Cassius flips me over. He sheaths himself inside me in one violent stroke. No warning, nothing. One minute my body's crying out to be filled, the next minute I'm impaled on my stepbrother's fucking monstrous cock.

My body jerks against the sofa. I forgot how big he is, how much he stretches me, makes me feel full. He pounds into me, all those weeks of pent-up tension coiling in his muscles as he punishes me for denying us both for so long.

I can do nothing but roll my head to the side and take it. And it's *glorious*.

I can smell Torsten kneeling behind my head, on the end of the sofa. My head bangs against his knees. I reach up and grab his collar, and pull his head down to me.

"No more watching," I growl as I tease his mouth open. I'm being greedy, and I know it. I trust that he'll tell me if it becomes too much, because I have no control any longer. Cas has fucked that right out of me. Torsten's tongue plays with mine, soft and exploring, a contrast to the wicked pace of Cas' thrusts.

"Filthy little slut," Cassius says, but his words are filled with awe. "You really do want it all."

"Yes," I moan into Torsten's mouth. I want everything they can give me.

"You're a bad, filthy girl, Fergie Munroe," Cas says. "And that's just the way we like it."

He slams into me, rubbing his pubic bone against my clit in

just the right spot. My orgasm washes over me, one of those stealth bastards that sneak up without warning. I come to pieces on his dick, chips of my coal-black heart falling away as the pleasure melts and pools and caresses inside me.

Cas wraps his arms around me and lifts me up, still holding me on his dick, which jerks and twitches inside me, desperate for its own release. "Vic, you know what to do."

"What?" I demand, trying to twist around. "What's Vic doing?"

It's hard being a blind girl with three guys. You know what one or two are doing at any one time, but the third is always getting into mischief.

"Never you mind for now. Victor is looking for a very specific book." Cas carries me across the room. His cock twitches impatiently.

Victor curses as he pulls books off the shelf.

"Which one is it again?"

"It's the Marquis de Sade," Cas snaps. Victor makes a sound of triumph as he locates the correct book. My head snaps up at a noise in the ceiling. There's a metallic scraping sound, followed by a *CLICK*. Something heavy drops from a trapdoor above our heads.

I whimper as Cas withdraws from me. He places my feet on the ground and steps back, leaving me bereft of touch. Not for long. Victor wraps his arms around me and directs my hands to feel the thing they unleashed.

I touch a supple leather harness, steel chains and D-rings, leather straps and stirrups with strategically-placed padding. Vic takes my fingers and places them on the pages of the Marquis de Sade's book, and I discover the volume has been hollowed out and filled with some buttons and dials.

"What sorcery is this?"

"It's a swing of fun. My brother installed all sorts of toys in here," Cas says. "We haven't had the chance to use many of them."

"You haven't?"

"We don't let anyone back here," Victor says. "Well, Juliet, but she doesn't count. So we haven't had a girl in here to try this with... until now."

"Okay, so what am I looking at here?"

"It's a sex swing," he says. "It's been specially designed so... more that one person can penetrate whoever's sitting in it, in a variety of different positions. When you're strapped inside it, you won't be able to move. You'll be completely at our mercy. What do you say? Do you want to try it?"

I run my hand along the leather stirrup, which I understand now will hold my legs wide apart. My heart races at the thought. Cas' handprints on my ass sting anew.

This is okay. I'm allowed to desire this. I'm safe with them.

I trust them implicitly. They've proven themselves to me enough times already. And even if I didn't trust them, Coach Franklin's death binds us together. I have dirt on them and they have dirt on me.

And I want it. I *want* to completely let go. All my life I've had to hold on tight to the things I know. Be the good girl. Get the top grades. Be the fucking inspiration porn for people who think having a disability is something Instagrammable.

Coming to Emerald Beach meant casting aside Old Fergie, like a butterfly emerging from her chrysalis. I don't always like the person I've changed into, but I am her and she is me. And she wants in that swing. She wants to feel all of it.

Victor and Torsten help me into the swing. I lie in the leather sling and they strap me inside – there are multiple contact points, all designed to position me exactly where they want me while keeping me as comfortable as possible. Cas stands back like a proud mother hen and makes little clucking noises of approval while they check each strap.

"You have to tell us if it becomes too much or if something hurts in a not-fun way," Vic says. "We're going to use a safe word. Torsten says you have a safe gesture, but you won't be able to use that on yourself. So your word is Harvard. Got it?"

Harvard. I smirk up at Vic. He knows me. "I've got it. I say Harvard and it all stops."

"Yes. You can scream 'no' and 'stop' at the top of your lungs, and we'll keep on fucking until you say Harvard," Cas smirks. "Enjoy yourself, Sunflower."

I yelp as they flip the swing over. Cas yanks on the wires and my body tips backward, so I'm sort of sitting upright with my legs out to the sides. The harness rubs between my breasts – the rope pulling at my skin, giving that edge of pain that I know I adore.

"Torsten's lying on the floor," Victor says. "And I'm going to lower you down on him, okay?"

"Heave ho, Captain."

"You look beautiful, Fergie," Torsten whispers from beneath me. The leather creaks as I'm lowered until I'm hovering over him. I feel his skin as a ghost against my own, even though we're not touching. And then Vic turns the knob a little more, and with Cas lining us up, I ease down onto Torsten's cock.

It's a strange sensation. With my legs out wide and the swing taking my weight, the only parts of mine and Torsten's bodies that actually touch is his dick inside me. The angle of my legs stretches me, and it's uncomfortable, but not unpleasant. Torsten uses his hips to stroke inside me, and I moan as I get used to the feeling of having his cock and nothing else.

The weightlessness makes the sensation of being fucked so

much more intimate. I can't focus on anything except how amazing he feels, how thick and hard inside me. "Torsten..." I moan. "This is incredible."

"I know," he whispers back, his voice crackling with genuine mirth.

That's one.

Victor stands in front of me, trailing the tip of his cock across my face. "Open wide, Duchess," he whispers. He strokes my hair as I open my mouth, and he slides himself inside.

That's two.

He tastes exactly the way I expect Victor August to taste. Like silk. Like an old, expensive whisky – one that should be savored. My tongue curls around his tip. I don't have control of my hands, but Victor works the straps of the harness so that I'm swung forward, impaling my throat on his dick, and as I swing back, I fuck Torsten.

We do this for a bit, and it's so strange and wonderful to be floating, with absolutely no control over what happens to my body. It's freeing to hand my trust over to them and to be rewarded with the pleasure of their dicks inside me.

But I know it's coming. It's been in the back of my mind all evening because there are three of them and one of me and I've got two out of three holes full right now.

"You ever have a guy in your ass before, sis?" Cas rubs the head of his cock down my ass crack, making me squirm.

I try to answer 'no' but I can't speak around Victor's cock, so it comes out like, "mmmmpf."

"Good. Because as your stepbrother, I want to be the first one to claim this virgin hole." I hear the squirt of lube. "This is going to be a lot, sis. And it might hurt, but you have to be a good girl, and not squirm, because that only makes me more excited. Okay?"

"Mmmpf."

Cas slides a lubed finger down the small of my back, teasing my entrance before sliding his finger inside. I cry out at the oddness of the sensation. Vic swings forward and I take him into the back of my throat, and then I swing back and impale myself on Cas' finger and Torsten's dick and it feels *so fucking good*, I'm on the verge of coming right then.

"There's our good girl. See, you like this." Cas works his finger deeper. My body tenses, getting used to it before I relax into the swing. "You like me claiming your ass. But you're going to have to take more than this."

He shoves the swing away. Vic's cock hits the back of my throat. I cough and gag, and Vic tries to grab me but the frame swings back.

And I impale myself on Cas' cock.

I howl. I hadn't expected to take him all at once, but I'm so slick with lube that he slides in easily. No quarter. No mercy.

My stepbrother is inside my ass, his dick rubbing against Torsten's through the thin wall of flesh that separates them.

Sound the fucktrumpets, but it feels *so good*. The harness holds me immobile. I can't move. I can't think. All I have is *feeling*. The feeling of three cocks inside me at once.

It's base. It's primal. It's fucking *fantastic*.

They swing, gently at first, but then they really go for it. I gag around Vic's cock, spit dribbling down my chin as I struggle to take him in. Just when I swing back and I get to catch my breath, I'm impaled onto Torsten and Cas at the same time. I'm so full and stretched and complete.

Fergie the person ceases to exist. I become a vessel for their need, their lust, their *worship*. I come apart for them, and I don't stop there. I lose the ability to discern where one orgasm stops and the next begins. The pleasure flows over me in waves as the swing grants me the freedom to fly.

I've found my family.

Their poison runs in my veins. I'm corrupted. I can never go back to being Old Fergie. And I don't fucking care. If this is what poison tastes like, then I want more.

I want everything these three boys have to give me.

65

CASSIUS

"Cas."

"Fuck off," I answer immediately. I open one eye. I'm surrounded by bookshelves, and someone's dainty little foot is in my face. My temples throb, my bones ache, my neck feels like it's been bent in a direction no neck should ever bend, and my balls feel empty. Last night...

Last night was *perfect*.

"Cas, wake up." Victor shakes my arm. I open the other eye. He looms over me, dark hair flopping over one icicle eye, dressed in designer workout gear. Victor fucking August. How does he find the energy?

"Cas, I have to leave. I've got an early basketball practice. I'll take Torsten back to the hotel on my way, and we'll meet you guys at school."

We peer over at Fergie, nuzzled into a giant stack of pillows, her fiery hair plastered over her naked back, both her feet twisted around my head. No wonder my neck hurts.

"I managed to extract myself without waking her. But do you think she'd want us to say goodbye?" Vic traces the line of her jaw. She stirs a little, murmuring something in her sleep. But she doesn't wake.

"Let her sleep. We gave the little vixen quite the pounding."

My dick hardens at the memory of her big eyes pleading with me, and her tight little ass on that swing. My stepsister. Mine, mine, mine.

Well, mine and Victor's and Torsten's. But I don't mind sharing her with them. Just as long as she knows who she belongs to. Maybe I'll give her a little morning reminder when the other two have gone. There are plenty more toys hidden in this room we can play with.

"Okay. We're out of here." Victor leans in and plants a kiss on Fergie's sleeping forehead. He tries to do the same to me, but I put him in a headlock. He taps out and crawls to the door, where he beckons for Torsten, who is already awake and slumped in his window seat, sketching.

"Don't do anything stupid," Vic says to me. "We'll figure out how to deal with our parents together."

I flash him a maniacal grin. I have no idea what Cali will do to me. I defied her in the open and all but admitted what I was doing with John's darling girl, with my own stepsister.

My mother's wrath will be swift and full of pain, but I'm ready.

Torsten closes his sketchbook and gets to his feet. When he passes the bed, he touches his fingers to his own lips, drawing them over Fergie's cheek. Then, he sticks a Braille label on her forehead. With a final warning look from Victor, the two of them leave.

Fergie and I are alone.

And suddenly I can't bear it – I *need* to talk to her. I shake her shoulder. My dick jabs her thigh. He needs attention. "Wakey, wakey, little sister," I purr in my ear.

"Fuck off," she mumbles, turning over so that she's nestled

into my armpit, her feet tangling with mine instead of trying to break my neck.

I chuckle as I lay there, her body dead weight on top of my arm. I've never lain around like this with another woman. Usually, after a night with me, they're crying and they want to get away. But Fergie took everything I had to give her and demanded more.

The cramp in my arm moves into my shoulder. Fergie's not going to play with my dick, so I decide to go downstairs and get us both some breakfast. Maybe it'd be good to leave her in here, where it's soundproof, in case Cali decides she wants to have it out.

I yank my arm out from beneath Fergie. She whimpers but goes right on sleeping, hugging the sofa cushion to her naked chest. I roll off the sofa and stand over her. She's so sweet like this, so innocent. I run the tip of my dick down her spine, leaving a trail of pre-cum behind.

As I move, the light on the security camera flashes, indicating that it's working. All part of our security measures. I tug on my boxers and pick up my shirt, but I don't put it on. Fergie's claw marks extend down my chest, the cuts stinging where she drew blood. I don't want to cover them up. I want the world to see that my stepsister is an animal, and I'm the feral beast who satiates her.

"I'll be right back with some food, sis," I say as I head out the door.

I whistle to myself – one of Torsten's depressing goth songs. As I walk past Fergie's room, I hear Spartacus meowing and scratching at the door. *Shit.* The little dude is probably wondering where Fergie is. He's used to sleeping curled up in her arms.

I hear voices downstairs. My mother and John. I should go and talk to them before Fergie wakes up. But—

"Meooow!"

"Okay, okay," I grumble. I punch in Fergie's combination for her latest attempt to keep me out of her room (Nick Cave's birth-date. Easy. I cracked that in minutes) and open her bedroom door.

The little guy rockets from the gloom and launches himself at my bare chest. I howl as his needle-claws sink into my bare flesh.

"Cali and I could use these needle claws of yours to torture people," I say as I unhook his death-claws from my flesh and hold Spartacus in the palm of my hand. He immediately curls up into a ball and starts purring.

I drop him on the floor. Fergie's purse is in the middle of the rug where she tossed it in the early hours this morning. The kitten trots over to his food bowls, which have been licked clean.

"Mew," he says, pointedly.

"I don't have any food," I growl. He swipes at my legs, and it's so utterly pitiful, those big emerald eyes that remind me of her.

"Okay, okay." I grab the bowls. I'll take them down to the kitchen. Maybe if Cali knows we're keeping a kitten here, she'll get pissed about that instead of last night.

Doubtful.

Spartacus' neck extends as he sees me carrying his bowl toward the door. He gets that wild look in his eyes and launches himself around the room, whizzing up the curtains, stampeding across the bed, and launching himself at the dresser, where he knocks over a battered Kate Spade purse, and a bunch of cards and things spill out.

"You're a menace, cat."

Grumbling, I bend over to pick up the cards and shove them back in. As I do, I accidentally pop the catch on a small leather wallet, and another stack of cards fall out. As I'm pushing them back inside, I catch the name printed on a student ID.

Fergus Macintosh.

Huh.

Fergie's name is Fergus, and there can't be that many girls with fiery red hair and shattered emerald eyes whose parents named them *Fergus*. This is her card. But her last name is Munroe, not Macintosh. I know Macintosh isn't her mother's maiden name, either. So this is a fake ID?

Why does my stepsister need a fake ID?

I plop my ass on the rug and sift through the rest of the cards. A passport, a state ID, credit and debit cards, a folded copy of a birth certificate. I linger on her student ID. It's from a different school – a place called Witchwood Falls High, which is not the school she told us she attended. It's not the school or the name of the town that showed up in Torsten's research.

But the picture is definitely her.

There are other items in there, too. One of those woven friendship bracelets made of black, red, and gold thread. It's been cut in half, like someone sliced it off a narrow wrist. There's a stack of gold ribbons from the Jiujitsu World Championships, and a photograph of Fergie with a big group of people, sitting around the fire at some fancy-ass ski resort. She's grinning wickedly into the camera.

I dump out the wallet I've seen her use, pull out her Stonehurst ID, her bank cards. All the issue dates are from September, just before she moved to Emerald Beach. There's nothing that dates back before then.

I keep coming back to the name. Fergus Macintosh.

The red mist gathers on the edges of my vision as the rage takes hold.

She's not who she says she is. We let her into our house, into our world.

Who the fuck is my stepsister?

I have to hand it to her, she's an excellent actress. That story she told me about the revenge porn was a perfectly-constructed lie – she probably told my mother, too, and Cali Dio fell for it. She moved them here, probably gave them their new identities, and she can't see that they're connected to all this shit that's going down?

All this time I thought Cali was taking advantage of John and Fergie for a job, but it's the other way around. John's wormed his way into her bed and our life, and we have no idea who the fuck they are.

And I let her get under my skin.

I let her in.

And she fucked me over.

The red mist clouds my vision. This time, I don't force it back. I let it come. I let the rage take over. It will lead me to the path of righteousness.

Fergie Munroe or Macintosh or whoever the fuck she is, she's going to *burn*.

66

FERGIE

I roll over, expecting to feel silk against my skin and the rhythmic purr of Spartacus pressed up against my ribs.

Instead, I slam into hard leather.

I'm not in my bed.

I breathe in deep, taking in the unfamiliar scents. Old books, even older whisky. Leather sofa and fur rug. The faint tang of the three guys mingled on my skin.

It takes me a moment to piece it together, to remember what happened last night and where I fell asleep. I reach down and touch my wrist, wincing as I feel the bruise where the harness from the sex swing dug in.

It's not the only part of me that hurts. My thighs burn and a deep, delicious ache settles in my stomach. The ache of a well-fucked woman.

I sit up, rubbing the sleep from my eyes. "Cas?" I call out. "Vic? Torsten?"

No one's here. The library is empty, their presence lingering like friendly, sexy ghosts.

A Braille note is stuck to my forehead. I peel it off, running my fingers over the bumps. It can only be from Torsten. It reads – 'I had to go back to the hotel. I'll see you at school.'

Okay, fine. Victor probably had practice before school, and he'd drop Torsten back at the hotel. I know he's not supposed to be seen staying here. And Cas...

I don't know where Cas is.

I'd have liked them to be around when I woke up. But actually, I'm happy. It gives me a chance to process what the fuck happened last night.

I learned the truth about my three guys. I now had answers to all those probing questions about why they had the power they had in this town, how they knew all these shady characters and secrets, and why they could feed an abuser to a lion and expect to get away with it.

And that's not even the biggest news.

I slept with three guys. *Three guys. At once.* I had three cocks inside me and it was glorious. And even though I feel like I've been run over by a cock-train, I want it to happen again. As soon as possible. Tonight.

Tonight.

After the early decision results come in.

Win or lose, I'm getting three cocks tonight. And then, I'm going to tell them the truth about who I am. About why I needed their help. About why I want Harvard bad enough to join Poison Ivy.

I've already told Cas some of it, and I was going to tell them all the rest last night, but then... Colosseum, the fight, the library, the swing. It all happened so fast.

I want to tell them. I need to tell them. We shouldn't have any secrets. They may even know, anyway. They are gangsters, after all.

I'll tell them today, after school, after ED results.

I *will.*

I scramble around the floor, locating my clothing from last night. I can't find my underwear, but I assume Cas stole them to add to his collection. I find Cas' shirt on the floor, too, and pull that on over my shoulders. It'll give me a modicum of modesty if I pass Seymour or Milo (or, gods forbid, my dad) on the way back to my room, since I can't be assed pouring myself back into the leather pants.

It takes me a little bit of fumbling to find the door. The last time I was in here, Vic showed me the book you pull to activate a spring that opens the carved doors. I tug on every spine on the bookshelf until I find open sesame. I head back to my room, expecting to hear Cas in the shower. But everything in the house is still and silent.

Except for Spartacus, of course. In my room, the kitten paces around the floor, howling about the lack of service. "I'm sorry, boy." I pick him up and cradle him on my shoulder as I pull out a fresh school uniform. "I've just got to shower, and I'll go and get some food for you."

I push into the bathroom. "Cas, if you're in here, I need to wash your cum out of my hair, and I'm not doing it while you're taking a shit."

No answer. I can smell Cas' shampoo, and the air feels damp and heavy. He showered not long ago. I set Spartacus down on the counter and tiptoe through the bathroom. I push open the door into Cas' room. I poke my head in, and I don't even have to speak to know that no one's there. My stepbrother's presence sucks all the air from a room, and I'm still breathing fine.

He's not here.

He wouldn't go to school with Victor, who had an early training. He must be somewhere in the house, probably in the kitchen bugging Milo to make pancakes.

Or maybe he and Cali are in the basement. Maybe she's punishing him.

Cali and Dad. They know that I know, and they know about Cas and me. I'm guessing by the silent house that they haven't figured out how to deal with us yet. But I can't worry about that now. I'm happy. I haven't been happy in such a long time. I want to hold on to this feeling as long as possible.

I whistle a tune as I take Spartacus' bowls downstairs. "Good morning, Milo. It's a beautiful day, isn't it?"

A container bangs on the kitchen counter. Milo stutters. "G-g-good morning, Miss. Fergie. I didn't expect to see you."

"You didn't?" That's news to me. I never miss Milo's breakfasts. "I don't have some appointment that I've forgotten, do I?"

"N-n-no. I just meant that... I heard you come home late last night. I thought you'd sleep in until at least eleven."

"As much as I'd love a few more hours sleep, I can't skip school today. It's the day when most universities announce their ED results. I have to—" I realize that I've said too much.

"I thought you weren't applying for college?"

"Oh," *shit*. "No, but, um... my friend Euri is. She's going to Princeton. At least, she should be. I want to be there for her when she finds out."

"Well, that's nice of you." Milo slides something across the counter to me. A bowl and a package of cereal.

Cereal? What the fuck?

Not that I'm throwing shade at the chef, but Milo *never* gives us cereal. He's always cooked some amazing international breakfast delight.

"Milo, is something wrong? Where's Cassius?"

"No, no, everything's fine." Milo busies himself with something inside the butler's pantry. He has to yell for me to hear him through the wall. "Cassius had to go out and do a chore for *Her*. Seymour will drive you to school today. I'm sure you'll catch up with your stepbrother later."

A knot of worry twists in my gut. Is this Cali's way of

punishing Cas? Has she sent him on some dangerous job? I don't know what Milo knows about his boss' real profession, so I plaster a smile on my face. "Yeah, I'm sure you're right. Okay, well, I'll see him at school, then."

"Yes, I guess you will." Milo fills the kitten's bowls. As I take them from his hands, he grabs my wrist. "I hope you and your father know what you're doing, Miss Fergie. They have good hearts buried beneath all that rage."

"Milo—"

But he's already vanished, like he's afraid to be caught with me. Weird.

SEYMOUR DROPS ME AT SCHOOL. He tries to make conversation, but I'm too excited to engage. I check my emails ten times on the drive over. The Ivies usually don't post their decisions until later in the day, around 3PM. I don't know how I'm going to survive until then.

Did they do it? Did they keep their promise?

After everything I did, am I going to Harvard?

As I walk into school, I'm hit with this wave of restless energy. 'Hi, Fergie!" people yell at me in this weird, knowing tone. I guess they all know that I'm a Poison Ivy client. They've probably guessed that we had something to do with Coach Franklin's disappearance. Well, I don't care. Now that I understand who Poison Ivy are, I know that my secrets are safe. My boys are untouchable, and so am I.

It's a weird day for everyone. I remember ED day well from my previous school, and it wasn't anywhere near as Ivy-obsessed at Stonehurst Prep. Schools drop their acceptances and rejections at different times. Harvard is usually later in the day, but some people will know already. People whisper in huddled groups. Phones beep.

"That's her," someone whispers as I walk past.

I catch snatches of conversation, listening for word of who got into what schools. But, weirdly, no one seems to be talking about college acceptances. They're all talking about some drama on social media.

"Wow. I mean, I knew they were manwhores, but that is something else."

"And isn't that her stepbrother? That's kind of incesty."

My ears rattle. My mouth tastes like I've bitten into snow.

"But you know they're all like that, those kind of families. It's all arranged marriages and keeping the bloodlines pure."

Don't be silly. They can't be talking about me. And if they are, it's just rumors. No one from Stonehurst was at Colosseum last night.

And even if they were, they wouldn't dare talk.

No one knows a thing about me and the boys.

But I can't help the worms wiggling in my gut. By the time I arrive at my locker, I'm a mess of nerves.

"Hi, Fergie."

It's Juliet. Her voice sounds breathless.

"Juliet, what's wrong?" I ask. "Did you miss out on Princeton?'

"No, Fergie," Juliet snaps. "Nothing's wrong with me. But something is seriously wrong with you. We trusted you. We brought you into our world. You got my brother all gooey in the head, made him forget about that annoying Gemma bitch, and I was starting to like you. I wanted you to be part of our family permanently. Why would you betray us? What are you really here to do?"

"What are you talking about?" I cry. "If this is about Victor, I thought you wanted us to be together. I thought..."

That's when I hear it. My voice, tinny through a tiny phone speaker. "Yes. I want it all. I want all three of you inside me."

It's exactly what I said last night. On that sex swing. And the same words are repeated, over and over, from mobile phones up and down the corridor.

No.

No.

"You made your bed." The nasty smirk in Juliet's voice slices through my gut. "You brought this on yourself. Oh, and I sent a copy to your dad. I thought he might like to know what his precious little girl has been getting up to."

Please, no.

I spin around, but it's everywhere. Their grunts. My screams. The filthy, wonderful things they said as they defiled me in that swing.

They filmed me.

They filmed me and they released it and *every fucking student* at school has seen me getting fucked on a sex swing by the Poison Ivy Club.

I thought I turned my heart to coal so I couldn't feel. I thought I encased myself in ice so I never had to go through this again.

But I've been stupid. I let those three boys whittle away the coal to expose the raw organ beneath. I let them thaw me out with their beautiful smiles.

Cassius.

He's behind this. He's the only one who knows about the sex tape, the only one who knew that this would utterly destroy me.

Cas said that he would break me. He said he'd enjoy it.

He *promised*.

And Poison Ivy never lie.

It's all my fault. I told Cas about Dawson. I gave my stepbrother the weapon he needed to ruin me.

I sag against my locker.

"I wouldn't lean on that," Juliet says. "You'll smudge the paint."

I can't deal with any more shit. "Paint?"

"Yeah. Someone's painted all over your locker again. And the walls. And they've burned ten-foot letters into the school lawn. It's a website address where a certain video can be viewed."

She walks away, laughing.

My legs give out. I slump to the floor. Cruel voices swirl around me. They say the same awful things, make the same misogynistic assumptions, play those horrible moaning sounds over and over and over as the present crashes against my past and the two events become one terrifying, never ending torture.

It was all a trick.

Everything that's happened between me and Cassius and Victor and Torsten, it's all been a ploy to lead to this moment. They took the most vulnerable moment of my life and gave it to the world to ridicule.

They made me trust them. They made me love them, and they... they...

They never wanted me. They wanted power over me. They wanted leverage.

And now they have it. Cas has been playing the game all along, and he brought his two brothers into position to weaken me, to make me believe that we really had something.

Check-fucking-mate.

I can't sit on the ground a moment longer. I can't sit on the ashes of my life. I can't I can't I can't—

I crash through the halls, not caring who I bowl over. The laughter washes over me.

I ran. I ran to the other side of the country, and this shit still follows me.

I'll never get the chance to be better than this mistake. Not not, and—

Dad.

The thought crashes into my skull, sending me reeling into a bank of lockers as fresh laughter drowns me.

By now, Dad's seen this tape.

He knows that all his sacrifices to uproot our lives and start over were for *nothing*. I can't ask him to do it again – not when he's happy here in Emerald Beach. Not when he's made a life for himself with Cali.

What am I going to do?

The question repeats itself, over and over in my swelling, pounding skull. What am I going to do?

And the answer is nothing.

Nothing.

I'm *nothing.*

I'm running again, and I don't even know where I am until I hear the unmistakable sound of a large-format printer. I'm near the *Sentinel* office.

I slam my shoulder into the doorway. It swings open. Someone cries out in surprise. "Fergie? You scared me."

I knew she'd be here. I yank the door shut behind me and slide the lock in place, leaning against it and sucking in a deep breath.

"Fergie, what's wrong?"

Her voice comes from the far corner. She's at her desk, no doubt working on the special college-bound edition of the paper, the one where she announces the ED acceptances for the senior class. She sounds concerned, like she actually gives a fuck about what happens to me. "What are you—"

"Please." I sink to the floor. "I don't deserve your empathy. I just need to hide here for a bit. Pretend I'm not here."

Silence.

Euri drops down in front of me, her hands circle my shoulders. "Fergie, I'm so sorry."

"Did you see it?"

A long silence descends.

"I didn't watch all of it." Her voice is quiet.

And that's why Euri Jones is a better human than I'd ever be. This is her time to say, 'I told you so, Fergie.' But she doesn't. Instead, she crunches something in her hand. "I've got Skittles, if you want some?"

Her arms go around me, and I sink into the warmth of her chest. My whole body crawls with invisible spiders. I slap at my skin, but they don't go away. I'll never, ever feel clean of those three bastards again.

Euri hands me the bag of Skittles and I pour thirty or so into my mouth. My jaw works and I swallow the lump of sugar. I don't taste them.

"Do you want to... I don't know, talk about it?"

"There's nothing to talk about." My words don't sound like they come from my own mouth. My voice is foreign, uncharted territory. "I trusted them. I threw my life away because I wanted to be part of their club. And they betrayed me."

I'm interrupted by a beep from my phone. The alert that I had a new email.

Euri makes a choking noise. I sniff and toss the phone on the floor.

Euri picks it up and puts it in my hand. "Fergie, I saw the notification on your screen. Fergie, it's from Harvard."

"No." I drop it again. "I don't want to know. It's not my spot. Not anymore."

She shoves the phone back at me. "I hate what you did by going to Poison Ivy, but some part of me understands it. I know there's a lot you're not telling me. Read it. We'll deal with whatever happens after."

With shaking fingers, I press the button on my phone that reads my emails aloud.

"Congratulations, Fergus Munroe. We're pleased to inform you that..."

I got in.

I got into Harvard.

Nothing.

This is literally my *dream*, and I'm holding it here in my hands, and I'm completely numb.

It means nothing.

I didn't earn it. I lied to myself, and I lied to all the people in my life who matter. And all because of them.

I drop my phone and wrap my arms around her. "Euri, I'm sorry. I let things get messed up. I forgot the golden rule – chicks before dicks."

"Hey, I can't say I blame you," Euri laughs through her own tears. "From what I saw, you were getting some pretty impressive dick."

"You said you didn't watch it."

"I lied." She laughs again. "I got as far as Cassius' money shot before I couldn't stomach it. That boy is hung like a donkey."

"Too bad it can't make up for his personality." I kick my boots under her desk and stretch out on the carpet. I plan to camp out in here until this horrible day is over.

I know everyone out there is watching me, waiting for me to break. But I'm a different person now. Old Fergie broke down after her ex shared revenge porn. Old Fergie thought about flinging herself off the Witchwood Falls bridge.

New Fergie is eerily calm. She wants only one thing.

Revenge.

"What are you going to do now?" Euri says, as if she's reading my thoughts.

"*We* are going to get even," I growl. "We're bringing down the Poison Ivy Club."

TO BE CONTINUED

Will Fergie and Euri have their revenge? Will the Poison Ivy Club fall? Who is Zack Lionel Sommesnay? Find out in book 2, *Poison Flower* – http://books2read.com/elite2

Victor, Cas, and Torsten think they know everything that goes on in Emerald Beach, but do they? Find out when you sign up to Steffanie Holmes' newsletter and get a bonus scene from *Poison Ivy*, along with a collection of other bonus material from Steffanie's worlds. Sign up here: http://steffanieholmes.com/newsletter

"I was baptized in bloodshed. To the bloodshed, I return."

Discover how the three women of the Triumvirate became who they are in the complete Stonehurst Prep dark contemporary reverse harem series. Start with book 1, *My Stolen Life*: http://books2read.com/mystolenlife

Turn the page for a sizzling excerpt.

FROM THE AUTHOR

Whew! Hello.

How are you doing after that? You okay? Do you need a hug? Or some heart medication?

Things might seem bad for Fergie now, but trust me, our girl doesn't take shit lying down. Sound the fucktrumpets, because she's cooking up a dish of brutal retribution for the Poison Ivy boys. You'll have to read book 2, Poison Flower, to find out what happens next: http://books2read.com/elite2

It's been so much fun to return to Stonehurst Prep with a new leading lady. Fergie is one of my favourite heroines that I've ever written. She's bold and sassy and she acts before she thinks and she's not defined by what she can't see.

Too often in books, blindness is conflated with weakness. As a blind reader myself, I'm always desperate to see more women like me in books, having adventures and doing normal things and getting our happily ever afters. I wrote Fergie for a teenage Steff who desperately needed a heroine and to believe that life gets better.

But Fergie's also not superhuman. Everything she does – the echolocation, her martial arts skills – is a normal part of the lives of many blind people, including me. (I have a brown belt in Gojo Ryu karate and I've done a bit of Jiujitsu, but now I pole dance instead). She's fallible and way too headstrong and stubborn for her own good, as you'll find out in the next book. In short, she's a person, with all the traits and foibles and hopes and dreams that we all experience. I wanted you to see her, because too often, women like her are never seen.

Thanks as always to Meg for the epically helpful editing job, and to CJ Strange and Acacia for the stunning covers. To my crew of Badass Author friends – Bea Paige, Daniela Romero, AK Rose, EM Moore, Selena, Eden O'Neil, Angel Lawson, and Rachel Leigh, who have cheered me on while I've torn my hair out writing this doorstopper of a book.

And to you, the reader, for going on this journey with me, even though it's led to some dark places. Warning: if you thought book 1 was tough, book 2 is going to knock your socks off. Grab Poison Flower here: http://books2read.com/elite2.

If you're curious about Claudia, Cali, and Livvie, and how they became who they are, then you need the complete Stonehurst Prep dark contemporary reverse harem series. Start with book 1, *My Stolen Life*: http://books2read.com/mystolenlife

If you want to keep up with my bookish news and get weekly stories about the real life true crimes and ghost stories that inspire my books, you can join my newsletter at https://www.steffanieholmes.com/newsletter. When you join you'll get a free copy of *Cabinet of Curiosities*, a compendium of bonus and deleted scenes and stories. It includes a fun bonus scene from *Poison Ivy* where you'll learn a little more about the Triumvirate.

I'm so happy you enjoyed Fergie's story! I'd love it if you wanted to leave a review on Amazon or Goodreads. It will help other readers to find their next read.

Thank you, thank you! I love you heaps! Until next time.
Steff

ENJOY THIS EXCERPT FROM MY STOLEN LIFE
PROLOGUE: MACKENZIE

I roll over in bed and slam against a wall.

Huh? Odd.

My bed isn't pushed against a wall. I must've twisted around in my sleep and hit the headboard. I do thrash around a lot, especially when I have bad dreams, and tonights was particularly gruesome. My mind stretches into the silence, searching for the tendrils of my nightmare. *I'm lying in bed and some dark shadow comes and lifts me up, pinning my arms so they hurt. He drags me downstairs to my mother, slumped in her favorite chair. At first, I think she passed out drunk after a night at the club, but then I see the dark pool expanding around her feet, staining the designer rug.*

I see the knife handle sticking out of her neck.

I see her glassy eyes rolled toward the ceiling.

I see the window behind her head, and my own reflection in the glass, my face streaked with blood, my eyes dark voids of pain and hatred.

But it's okay now. It was just a dream. It's—

OW.

I hit the headboard again. I reach down to rub my elbow, and my hand grazes a solid wall of satin. On my other side.

What the hell?

I open my eyes into a darkness that is oppressive and complete, the kind of darkness I'd never see inside my princess bedroom with its flimsy purple curtains letting in the glittering skyline of the city. The kind of darkness that folds in on me, pressing me against the hard, un-bedlike surface I lie on.

Now the panic hits.

I throw out my arms, kick with my legs. I hit walls. Walls all around me, lined with satin, dense with an immense weight pressing from all sides. Walls so close I can't sit up or bend my knees. I scream, and my scream bounces back at me, hollow and weak.

I'm in a coffin. I'm in a motherfucking coffin, and I'm *still alive*.

I scream and scream and scream. The sound fills my head and stabs at my brain. I know all I'm doing is using up my precious oxygen, but I can't make myself stop. In that scream I lose myself, and every memory of who I am dissolves into a puddle of terror.

When I do stop, finally, I gasp and pant, and I taste blood and stale air on my tongue. A cold fear seeps into my bones. Am I dying? My throat crawls with invisible bugs. Is this what it feels like to die?

I hunt around in my pockets, but I'm wearing purple pajamas, and the only thing inside is a bookmark Daddy gave me. I can't see it of course, but I know it has a quote from Julius Caesar on it. *Alea iacta est. The die is cast.*

Like fuck it is.

I think of Daddy, of everything he taught me – memories too dark to be obliterated by fear. Bile rises in my throat. I swallow, choke it back. Daddy always told me our world is forged in blood. I might be only thirteen, but I know who he is, what he's capable of. I've heard the whispers. I've seen the way people hurry to appease him whenever he enters a room. I've had the lessons from Antony in what to do if I find myself alone with one of Daddy's enemies.

Of course, they never taught me what to do if one of those enemies *buries me alive*.

I can't give up.

I claw at the satin on the lid. It tears under my fingers, and I pull out puffs of stuffing to reach the wood beneath. I claw at the surface, digging splinters under my nails. Cramps arc along my arm from the awkward angle. I know it's hopeless; I know I'll never be able to scratch my way through the wood. Even if I can, I *feel* the weight of several feet of dirt above me. I'd be crushed in moments. But I have to try.

I'm my father's daughter, and this is not how I die.

I claw and scratch and tear. I lose track of how much time passes in the tiny space. My ears buzz. My skin weeps with cold sweat.

A noise reaches my ears. A faint shifting. A scuffle. A scrape and thud above my head. Muffled and far away.

Someone piling the dirt in my grave.

Or maybe...

...maybe someone digging it out again.

Fuck, fuck, please.

"Help." My throat is hoarse from screaming. I bang the lid with my fists, not even feeling the splinters piercing my skin. "Help me!"

THUD. Something hits the lid. The coffin groans. My veins burn with fear and hope and terror.

The wood cracks. The lid is flung away. Dirt rains down on me, but I don't care. I suck in lungfuls of fresh, crisp air. A circle of light blinds me. I fling my body up, up into the unknown. Warm arms catch me, hold me close.

"I found you, Claws." Only Antony calls me by that nickname. Of course, it would be my cousin who saves me. Antony drags me over the lip of the grave, *my* grave, and we fall into crackling leaves and damp grass.

I sob into his shoulder. Antony rolls me over, his fingers pressing all over my body, checking if I'm hurt. He rests my back against cold stone. "I have to take care of this," he says. I watch through tear-filled eyes as he pushes the dirt back into the hole – into what was supposed to be my grave – and brushes dead leaves on top. When he's done, it's impossible to tell the ground's been disturbed at all.

I tremble all over. I can't make myself stop shaking. Antony comes back to me and wraps me in his arms. He staggers to his feet, holding me like I'm weightless. He's only just turned eighteen, but already he's built like a tank.

I let out a terrified sob. Antony glances over his shoulder, and there's panic in his eyes. "You've got to be quiet, Claws," he whispers. "They might be nearby. I'm going to get you out of here."

I can't speak. My voice is gone, left in the coffin with my screams. Antony hoists me up and darts into the shadows. He runs with ease, ducking between rows of crumbling gravestones and beneath bent and gnarled trees. Dimly, I recognize this place – the old Emerald Beach cemetery, on the edge of Beaumont Hills overlooking the bay, where the original families of Emerald Beach buried their dead.

Where someone tried to bury me.

Antony bursts from the trees onto a narrow road. His car is parked in the shadows. He opens the passenger door and settles me inside before diving behind the wheel and gunning the engine.

We tear off down the road. Antony rips around the deadly corners like he's on a racetrack. Steep cliffs and crumbling old mansions pass by in a blur.

"My parents..." I gasp out. "Where are my parents?"

"I'm sorry, Claws. I didn't get to them in time. I only found you."

I wait for this to sink in, for the fact I'm now an orphan to hit me in a rush of grief. But I'm numb. My body won't stop shaking, and I left my brain and my heart buried in the silence of that coffin.

"Who?" I ask, and I fancy I catch a hint of my dad's cold savagery in my voice. "Who did this?"

"I don't know yet, but if I had to guess, it was Brutus. I warned your dad that he was making alliances and building up to a challenge. I think he's just made his move."

I try to digest this information. Brutus – who was once my father's trusted friend, who'd eaten dinner at our house and played Chutes and Ladders with me – killed my parents and buried me alive. But it bounces off the edge of my skull and doesn't stick. The life I had before, my old life, it's gone, and as I twist and grasp for memories, all I grab is stale coffin air.

"What now?" I ask.

Antony tosses his phone into my lap. "Look at the headlines."

I read the news app he's got open, but the words and images blur together. "This... this doesn't make any sense..."

"They think you're dead, Claws," Antony says. "That means you have to *stay* dead until we're strong enough to move against him. Until then, you have to be a ghost. But don't worry, I'll protect you. I've got a plan. We'll hide you where they'll never think to look."

Start reading:
http://books2read.com/mystolenlife

MORE FROM THE AUTHOR

From the author of *Poison Ivy* and *Shunned* comes this dark contemporary high school reverse harem romance.

Psst. I have a secret.

Are you ready?

I'm Mackenzie Malloy, and everyone thinks they know who
I am.

Five years ago, I disappeared.

No one has seen me or my family outside the walls of Malloy
Manor since.
But now I'm coming to reclaim my throne:
The Ice Queen of Stonehurst Prep is back.

Standing between me and my everything?
Three things can bring me down:
The sweet guy who wants answers from his former friend.
The rock god who wants to f*ck me.
The king who'll crush me before giving up his crown.

They think they can ruin me, wreck it all, but I won't let them.
I'm not the Mackenzie Eli used to know.
Hot boys and rock gods like Gabriel won't win me over.
And just like Noah, I'll kill to keep my crown.

I'm just a poor little rich girl with the stolen life.
I'm here to tear down three princes,
before they destroy me.

Read now:
http://books2read.com/mystolenlife

OTHER BOOKS BY STEFFANIE HOLMES

Nevermore Bookshop Mysteries

A Dead and Stormy Night

Of Mice and Murder

Pride and Premeditation

How Heathcliff Stole Christmas

Memoirs of a Garroter

Prose and Cons

A Novel Way to Die

Much Ado About Murder

Crime and Publishing

Plot and Bothered

Kings of Miskatonic Prep

Shunned

Initiated

Possessed

Ignited

Stonehurst Prep

My Stolen Life

My Secret Heart

My Broken Crown

My Savage Kingdom

Stonehurst Prep Elite

Poison Ivy

Poison Flower

Poison Kiss

Dark Academia

Pretty Girls Make Graves

Brutal Boys Cry Blood

Manderley Academy

Ghosted

Haunted

Spirited

Briarwood Witches

Earth and Embers

Fire and Fable

Water and Woe

Wind and Whispers

Spirit and Sorrow

Crookshollow Gothic Romance

Art of Cunning (Alex & Ryan)

Art of the Hunt (Alex & Ryan)

Art of Temptation (Alex & Ryan)

The Man in Black (Elinor & Eric)

Watcher (Belinda & Cole)

Reaper (Belinda & Cole)

Wolves of Crookshollow

Want to be informed when the next Steffanie Holmes paranormal romance story goes live? Sign up for the newsletter at www.steffanieholmes.com/newsletter to get the scoop, and score a free collection of bonus scenes and stories to enjoy!

ABOUT THE AUTHOR

Steffanie Holmes is the *USA Today* bestselling author of the paranormal, gothic, dark, and fantastical. Her books feature clever, witty heroines, secret societies, creepy old mansions and alpha males who *always* get what they want.

Legally-blind since birth, Steffanie received the 2017 Attitude Award for Artistic Achievement. She was also a finalist for a 2018 Women of Influence award.

Steff is the creator of *Rage Against the Manuscript* – a resource of free content, books, and courses to help writers tell their story, find their readers, and build a badass writing career.

Steffanie lives in New Zealand with her husband, a horde of cantankerous cats, and their medieval sword collection.

Steffanie Holmes newsletter

Grab a free copy *Cabinet of Curiosities* – a Steffanie Holmes compendium of short stories and bonus scenes, including a bonus scene from *Poison Ivy* – when you sign up for updates with the Steffanie Holmes newsletter.

http://www.steffanieholmes.com/newsletter

Come hang with Steffanie
www.steffanieholmes.com
hello@steffanieholmes.com

Made in United States
Troutdale, OR
03/18/2024

18547063R00336